THE DARK REVEALS ALL SECRETS

Wilde Fae

LADY OF THE NIGHTMARES

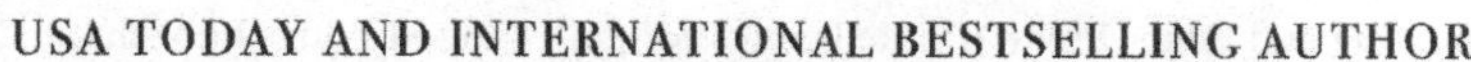

USA TODAY AND INTERNATIONAL BESTSELLING AUTHOR

KATE KING

This book is a work of fiction. All characters, names, places, and incidents, either are the product of the author's imagination or are used fictitiously. Any resemblance to real persons, living or dead, events, or locales, is purely coincidental.

First Cover edition October 2023

Cover design and typography: Flowers and Forensics

Alt Cover design and typography: Story Wrappers

Copy Editing: One Love Editing

Formatting and Edge Design (Printed edges edition): Painted Wings Publishing Services

Unique Character Art: @damianintheden, Rin Mitchell

Published by Wicked Good Romance

For all the girls still in their Prince Zuko era

AUTHORS NOTE

The most common comment I get on social media (after questions about when the next book is coming) is that people need to reread book one to remember what happened.

I get you.

Did I intend my why-choose fairy-corn book to become this complex? No. Do I need a wiki to explain everything? Probably.

The first couple of chapters of this book give a brief recap of the last book, but if you need a more extensive refresher, I have put a detailed encyclopedia at the back of the book, which includes a **summary of book one**, a **glossary of important locations and terms**, and **a character list with descriptions.** That is also where I have moved the **pronunciation guide** and the ***extended* family tree.**

I hope this is helpful for readers who (like me) like to look up the Wikipedia articles on every series they read. There is some background information sprinkled in there that hasn't yet made it into the books, but no major spoilers (beyond book one, which is well and truly spoiled).

That said, I want to make clear that **you do not have to read any of this.** This isn't homework, and your reading experience will not suffer if you don't read my musings. I am not dropping any easter eggs; it's just to help you out, and you can absolutely skip it. Do as you wish!

For those reading on Kindle, you can find it in the table of contents under THE WORLD OF WILDE FAE. In physical books, it begins after the final chapter.

Enjoy!

Kate King

CONTENT WARNING

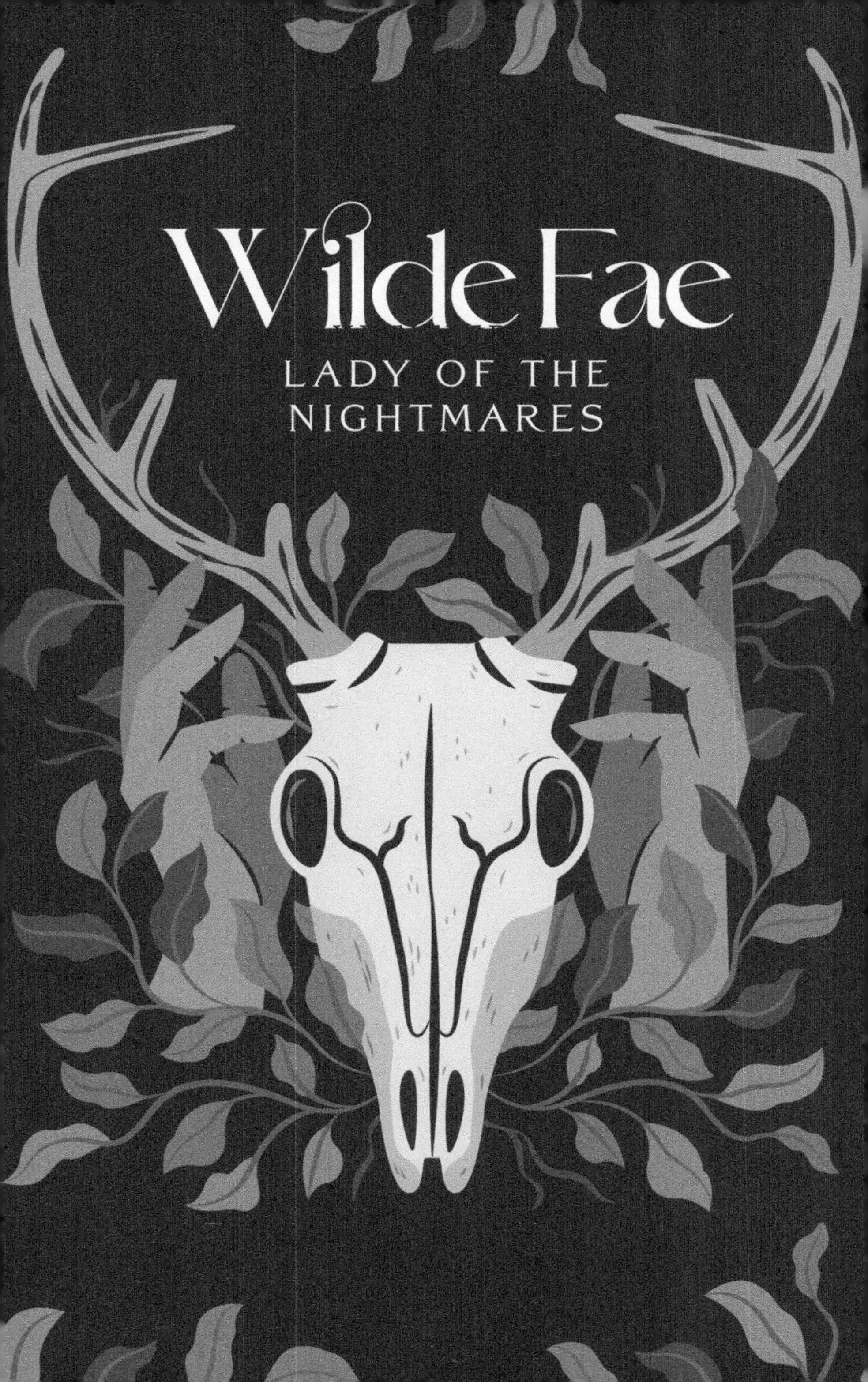
Wilde Fae
LADY OF THE
NIGHTMARES

PROLOGUE

AMBROSE

LAST SAMHAIN (OCTOBER), SIX MONTHS SINCE THE DEATH OF KING PENVALLE

The dungeon was as dark as midnight, but I didn't need my eyes to see.

I kept my face hidden under my hood as the guards led me down the long, rough stone hallway, the bones of rodents crunching underfoot. The stench of death and despair overwhelmed me, and the echo of rattling bars rang in my ears as we passed cell after cell.

No one here was innocent. Nevertheless, their screams put my teeth on edge.

In all the years I lived in the palace, I never once visited the dungeon. It was larger than I expected and more organized than the hole in the earth I'd envisioned as a child. Rectangular chambers lined either side of the corridor, facing inward, with iron bars keeping each captive inside. Sconces on the walls held darkened lamps, the shadows adding to the prisoners' distress and confusion.

The guard on my right, a human, gave a sharp tug on my arm to no avail. I was willing to feign capture, but I refused to let them drag me. The guard on the left, a Fae male, seemed to realize that.

There weren't many Fae guards in the palace, but clearly, my brother feared I'd escape with only humans to confine me. It was a misjudgment on his part. For one thing, this Fae guard posed little threat. For another, I was in no hurry to escape. I wanted—no, needed—to be here. Deep down, I suspected Scion knew that. Just as I suspected that he knew I meant to be caught, if not precisely how it happened.

Outside the dungeon, at this very moment, the city of Everlast was burning, just as I knew it would. Just as I predicted, it must.

Two hours ago, I'd stood in the center of the town square, nearly alone in the chaos. Though it was well past midnight, the square was neither quiet nor deserted. Bright orange flames licked up the sides of houses and shops, catching in the thatched straw of rooftops and colorful cloth of flags hanging overhead. The shouts of my nightmares rang out, mingling with the screams of the villagers as they ran from their houses, clutching whatever belongings they could carry.

I winced as I spotted a human woman carrying a child running down a nearby alley into the night. We weren't here for the humans; we were here because of them.

We came to punish my kind, the High Fae who lived in the city. Those without noble titles but with ten times the strength of those they oppressed. For those who either turned a blind eye to the rot festering in the country of Elsewhere or who reveled in the decay.

We came to attract the attention of my estranged family, who grew too complacent. Who forgot what true misery was. And we came because I'd seen it. Because I knew we would.

A phantom sensation pulled at the nape of my neck, like a thread luring me in another direction. I shook it off.

Riven elbowed me in the ribs. "What was that?"

I glanced over at my friend and grimaced. After all these years on battlefields, he knew me too well and always recognized when I'd had a vision, when the thread of some other future tried to pull me in another direction.

I wanted to say, "Nothing," but it was impossible. Instead, I said, "Nothing we need to concern ourselves with."

Riven stood rigid, shoulders back, as he always did. It was partially the armor breastplate he wore that forced him to stand that way, but he was always intense, regardless. It was one reason we became friends in the first place, if I was honest. *He reminds me of my brother.*

He ran a hand over the tattoos covering his shaved head and looked sideways at me. His green eyes flashed. "What does that mean?"

"It means I already made my choice. There's no time to change it now."

There were many times—this being one of them—that I wished I was born with any magical affinity aside from prophecy. Prophecy was never altogether certain. There were endless branches on the tree of life. Infinite threads on the spiderweb, each with varying likelihood of occurring. Pluck one thread, and the vibration would spawn new webs until the end of time itself.

Riven crossed his arms over his chest and opened his mouth again. No doubt, he intended to argue with me. Before he could, however, something flashed out of the corner of my eye. The shadows between two houses rippled like dark water, and I blinked a few times. I threw a hand up to stop my friend from speaking.

After a moment, the darkness shifted and reformed. A male emerged from the alley and advanced toward us. Beside me, Riven reached for his blade. I closed my eyes for the briefest moment.

In most of my visions, it was my cousin Bael stepping out of the alley, shaking shadows off his hair like snowflakes. Of all outcomes for this meeting, that was the most likely and least violent.

"Interesting choice of monocle," he would say, glancing at Riven. "Not the choice I'd make, but to each their own preference."

"And what choice would you make, cousin?" I'd ask.

"I dunno. I'm merely saying that if I could never be left alone, I might use that to my advantage."

I'd roll my eyes. "It might shock you to know that I don't enjoy the company of tavern whores as much as you do, cousin."

Of course, Bael didn't yet understand the value of good friends over good sex—not yet, at least. He was still too young, and no one had yet given him any reason to change.

The corner of Bael's lip would turn up in a smirk, completely unashamed. "Fair enough."

But none of that mattered.

Evidently, I'd miscalculated because it was not Bael who stepped out of the shadows and fixed me with a withering silver stare. "Hello, brother."

"HOW DOES IT FEEL TO KNOW YOU'LL DIE DOWN HERE?" THE HUMAN guard sneered at me, shaking me from my reverie.

I jerked, blinking several times, and assessed him as he pushed me into a cell and slammed the door.

I typically liked humans and fought for their rights in Elsewhere, but this man was unmistakably the exception to the rule. His ruddy face and cruel, beady eyes spoke of one with a small amount of authority in a lightweight arena. Sadly for him, his future was as bleak as his appearance.

"I could ask you the same," I said lightly.

"What's that 'posed to mean?" he spat.

I opened my mouth to answer and closed it again as another prickle of awareness tugged at the back of my neck. Not a vision, but certainly a presence. I looked to the side, as if there were someone in my cell with me…but that was absurd.

The guard looked at me with a mean smile, probably thinking I was already going mad. I ignored him. It wasn't that…not yet, anyway. It was something else.

The guards walked away down the corridor, the echoes of their footsteps and voices growing quieter with every breath. "I'm not sure it's really him," the human said, his voice carrying back to me. "Does anyone even know what the Dullahan looks like without his mask?"

"It's him, you fucking idiot," the Fae guard replied under his breath. "I'd get my affairs in order if I were you."

"What're you on about?"

"I've worked in this palace for nearly two centuries, more than long enough to remember when the prince left and changed his name. Believe me, that's him."

They moved away, their voices fading, and with them, so did my only means to *see*. I now stood, frozen in the dark, as blind as any mortal for the first time that I could remember.

I sank onto the ground, prepared to fall into silent meditation for the coming weeks.

As a prophet, I could not see myself and therefore always traveled with a companion, but the other prisoners were too mad and too far away to be suitable subjects to see through. I'd known that I would be mostly blind for these weeks until my brother came to find me.

Leaning my head back against the filthy stone wall, I closed my eyes and tried to even out my breathing.

The gentle sound of breathing and the faint rhythm of a heartbeat on the other side of the stone sent a shock wave through me. Sucking in a breath, a faintly familiar scent reached me through every other foul smell clouding the air.

My eyes widened, my heartbeat speeding up.

It was impossible, and yet, there she was.

The source of my weakness. The source of that faint hum of awareness. The source of everything, right here, in the dark.

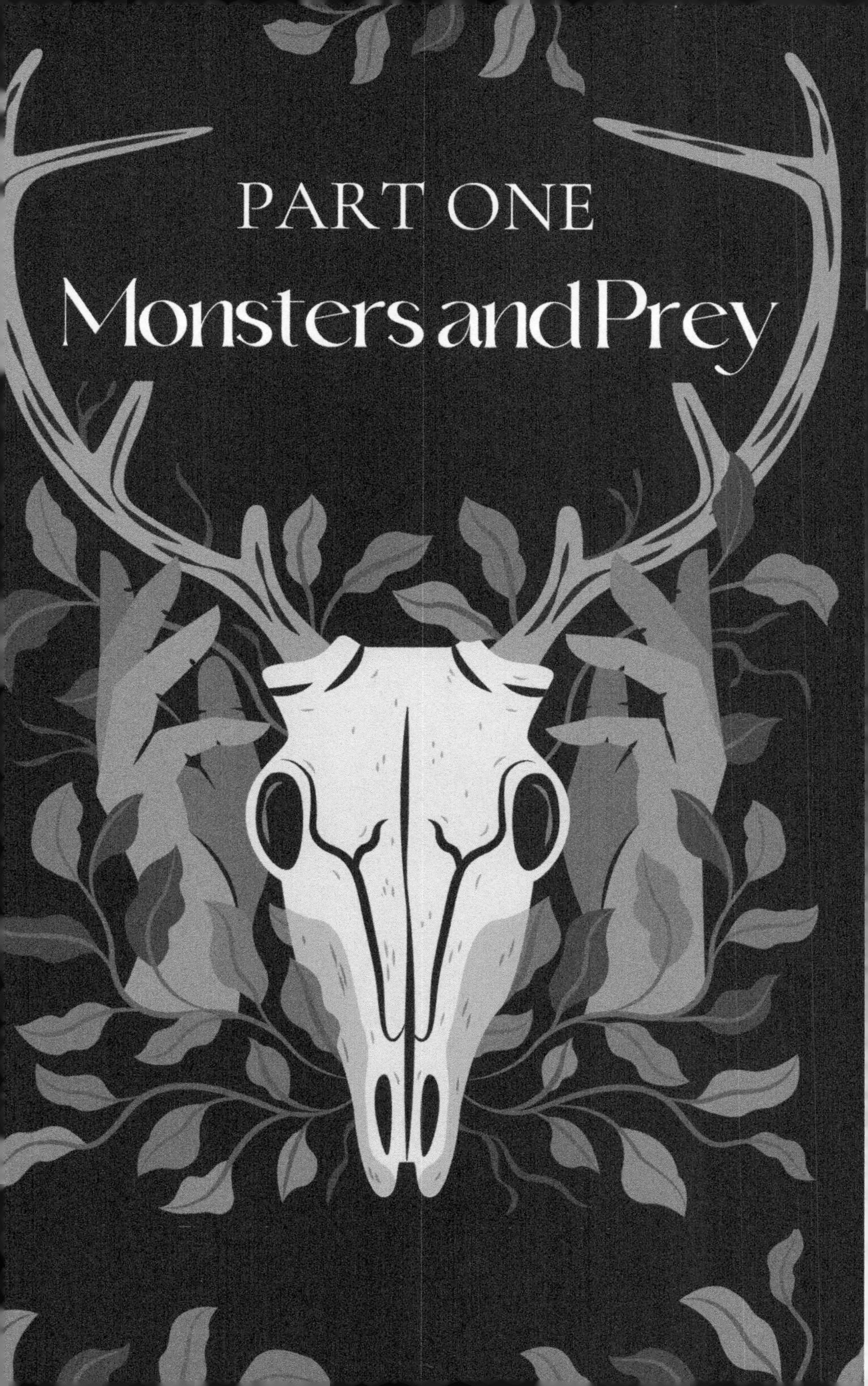
PART ONE
Monsters and Prey

1
SCION
THE OBSIDIAN PALACE, EVERLAST CITY, PRESENT

She wasn't even fucking here, and Lonnie Skyeborne's loathsome presence was ruining my life.

Like a virus, she'd seeped into every aspect of this castle, waging silent war on everything she touched: the monarchy, my family, my tower; she'd even tainted this damn room.

In another life, I might have held council meetings in this room, but not now. Now, I sat, nearly catatonic, staring down at the gleaming black steps that led to the obsidian throne. It was the throne that had once belonged to my grandmother and should now belong to me; the throne that, like so much else, remained just out of reach; the throne that Lonnie Skyborne ruined with her mere existence.

By the Source, if this was how my legacy was to end, I only hoped history did me the kindness of forgetting my name altogether.

"How is she?" Gwydion's voice rang hollowly through the echo-filled room.

My head lurched up so quickly that the bones in my neck cracked. "What's that supposed to mean?"

"How's Lonnie doing?" Gwydion repeated at twice the volume. "What else would I mean? If we can't be there to watch, we may as well get updates."

I growled low in my throat, unable to find the words to express my frustration. Now, she was ruining my cousins, too, and every infernal conversation.

Gwydion, tall, curly-haired, and muscular, rested on a bench against the far-right wall, absentmindedly oiling the silver blade of his sword. His brother, Bael, paced up and down the long, cavernous room, exhibiting every bit of agitation that I felt. Their sister, Aine, lay on the floor to my left, staring up at the ceiling, so still she could have been sleeping.

"Does it fucking matter how she's doing?" I snapped.

Gwydion chuckled, ignoring my challenging glare. "Yes, actually, it does matter. Unless you want to start over with a new queen."

"Or king," Aine muttered, her eyes still closed.

"It's irrelevant," I barked. "That's not going to happen. She's fine."

She'd better be fine, after all the threats I'd made to keep her so.

Bael made a derisive noise in the back of his throat as he paced by me at top speed. "You sound quite certain."

I ignored him—anything I said would only start another argument. In any case, I was certain that Lonnie would survive the hunts for two reasons, neither of which I was happy about.

First, unbeknownst to my family, I'd sent my pet raven, Quill, to watch her. He was circling the quarry now, and should something happen, I would know. Second, it was only days ago that I'd murdered a group of bandits who'd snuck onto our grounds to attack her. I'd spared one, only to make sure he spread word far and wide that the queen was not to be touched. I wasn't yet sure what I wanted to do with her, but until I decided, no one hurt Lonnie Skyborne. She belonged to us, and if anyone was going to kill her, it was damn well going to be me.

But I couldn't say any of that.

Bael had spent the better part of the evening with his eyes rolled into the back of his head, ignoring all of us as he watched Lonnie's progress in the hunt. Clearly, if anything went wrong with the little human queen, he'd leave for Inbetwixt in an instant.

As long as I'd known him, Bael had never cared so much about anything. She was fucking ruining him.

"So?" Gwydion asked, jerking me from my musing. "How is she?"

Bael dragged both hands through his reddish-blond hair and paced faster, nearly breaking into a jog. "The same. She's nearly at the top of the hill on the south side of the quarry. She had the good sense to bring a lantern this time, and there are some Underfae with her."

"That's strange," Gwydion said.

"What is?" I asked too quickly.

"Humans can't see the Underfae. Why would they follow Lonnie if she doesn't even know they're with her?"

Admittedly, that *was* strange. Just another thing to add to the ever-growing list of Lonnie Skyeborne's suspicious behavior. There was far too much about that woman that wasn't right.

It was more than her unusual smell and the way her skin tasted like magic; it was *everything*. How my power had no effect on her, and she'd survived a year in a dungeon literally built to drive mortals insane within days. How she seemed to waver between almost unbelievable naivete and a brashness that should have gotten her killed years ago. How she'd clearly brought my cousin over to her side in only a few short weeks. *Everything*.

"How far is she from the boundary?" Aine asked.

"Not you too," I muttered. "Can we speak of nothing but the Slúagh?"

"I don't know," Bael answered his sister as if I hadn't spoken. "Perhaps a mile?"

I made the mistake of looking over at Bael, and my stomach lurched as I watched his right eye roll backward, spinning in his skull as if he were looking for something just out of reach. "I fucking hate it when you do that."

The walls around us seemed to sigh, and every shadow shuddered. Bael blinked, his eyes returning to their usual yellow as he fixed me with a mutinous glare. "Why? Jealous?"

"Hardly," I scoffed. "Revolted, perhaps."

I'd never be jealous of such blatantly Unseelie magic. Not when it was what kept my cousin out of the running for the throne.

As if reading my mind, Bael rolled his eyes again, showing me the whites. "I think perhaps you don't like reminders of darkness in what's left of your gleaming court."

What the fuck? That wasn't it at all, and he knew it.

He'd been like this all day—sulking, agitated, easily startled—and it was driving me to the point of homicidal ideation. "If you are so intent on leaving, don't let me stop you."

"It was your idea to stay in the first place," he snapped. "Getting cold feet?"

"No," I retorted. "I'm simply beginning to regret asking you to join us."

Uncharacteristically, Bael didn't snap back with any sort of insult. He barely seemed to be listening. "I said I wouldn't go unless I was called for."

"Careful, Bael," Aine said lightly. "You are dangerously close to making Scion sound like the reasonable one in this family by comparison, and I daresay if we stoop that low, we may never recover."

"Fuck off." I glared at her before shifting my attention back to Bael. "Why the hell would you say that?"

"The Source only knows," he groaned, fading slightly at the edges. "I'm going down to my chamber. I cannot stand this anymore."

I sighed heavily, watching as he disappeared into nothingness. I'd wanted Bael here in the event of an attack and assumed it was only because I'd asked that he wasn't already by Lonnie's side. Aine and Gwydion were far from useless, but neither would be half as helpful as he would. Still, with half his attention focused on the hunt and his mood more erratic even than my worst days, I'd almost rather see my cousin off myself.

"How will we know what's happening now?" Gwydion griped.

I stood, agitated. "If all we're going to do is watch from here, we may as well have gone hunting after all."

"I don't know why we didn't."

Of course he doesn't. Far be it from me to expect anyone to give a shit about this country or pay half a mind to anything going on outside their own ass.

"*Because,*" I said, struggling to hold in my frustration, "we were attacked last night. Rebels infiltrated the castle without anyone having any gods-damned idea how they got in."

And also, because it was a highly convenient excuse to explain away my ambivalence toward hunting Lonnie at all, but I couldn't very well tell him that. A half-truth was better than no truth at all, I supposed.

"I know," Gwydion said. "I'm not daft."

I grunted in mild disagreement. It was either that, or he was doing an exceptionally good job of pretending to have no fucking idea of what was going on. I wasn't sure which was worse. "Then you should understand the problem. There have been rebels in the village for weeks, growing in numbers every day. Now, they get into the castle the night before we will all be out of the city. It would be the perfect time to seize the capital."

"Or that's what they want you to think," Aine suggested. "Maybe they're attacking Inbetwixt instead."

I shook my head. "I thought of that, but the risk is still too great to ignore."

"What about Lonnie?" Gwydion asked.

"What about her?" I ground out.

"You seem to have had quite a change of heart, Sci. Wasn't it only yesterday you were trying to kill Lonnie yourself?"

Sooner even than that.

"It's more important to guard the capital," I replied, all too aware that I hadn't really answered his question. With any luck, he really *was* daft and wouldn't notice.

I hadn't yet told anyone about my visit to the dungeons, the advice I'd received from Ambrose, or the bargain I'd made to get it. Even now, I was already beginning to regret the decision, and my rebel brother had only been free for a matter of hours.

"There's more than one way to become king," Ambrose had told me. *"You could simply marry the queen."*

I ran both hands through my hair.

I'd had barely a few hours to consider it—less than a day before I'd had to decide whether to kill her, and I had to admit, the excuse of an impending attack could not have come at a better time. Now, at least, I had another two and a half weeks before we traveled to Nevermore in which to decide if I would take my brother's advice.

I LEFT AINE AND GWYDION AND MADE MY WAY DOWNSTAIRS.

Bael's room was once located in one of the towers alongside the rest of us, but he'd moved down alongside the kitchens at some point over the last decade while I'd been away. I supposed it was easier to hide the cage and avoid the visitors I knew he despised. Out of respect for my cousin and a desire to avoid further infighting, I walked down the many flights of stairs rather than shadow walking directly into his room. It was absurdly rude to do so, anyway, but Bael reveled in rudeness except when it came to what he considered to be his territory. Trespassers did so at their own risk.

Finally coming to a halt in front of the plain wooden door set into the stone wall of the basement corridor, I knocked three times.

There was a long silence where I could picture my cousin, golden-haired and almost cherubic-looking, rolling from his bed within the enormous bronze cage to open the door. Sure enough, the door cracked open, and one yellow eye peeked out. "Whatever it is, Sci, it can wait."

I wanted to ask if he was alright, but what came out instead was "What the fuck is wrong with you?"

Ah, well. He should know he'd been a prick.

Bael let out a harsh laugh. "Should I read into that? Or just assume this is your usual aggression showing?"

"You're the one acting like a damned lunatic," I growled. "If we are attacked, at this rate, you'll be no help."

His lip curled. "This wouldn't have anything to do with last night, would it?"

I tensed. Last night—which part? Did he know already what I'd done?

No. Impossible. So, he could only be referring to the hours before I'd gone to visit my brother. The revel.

Unbidden, an image of her rose to my mind. Of her mouth, falling open in ecstasy, her syrup-colored eyes finding mine over Bael's shoulder. I blinked, trying to banish the image, only for it to be replaced by her wild red hair covering her bare skin in that torn dress. *Fuck.*

I swiped an angry hand across my face, as if I could wipe the image away. "I don't give a fuck what you do with her."

His eyes widened, seeming slightly surprised. Him and me both, if I was honest. I hadn't realized I didn't care what he did with her until I said it…so if I wasn't jealous of Bael, what was bothering me?

A question to be considered later. Much later. Perhaps never.

Seeming mollified, at the very least, Bael opened his door slightly wider. "I take it you want to come in?"

"Well, given that I no longer have a bedchamber thanks to you, yes." My tone softened ever so slightly. "But if you would prefer not..."

He moved out of the way so I could step over the threshold. "It's fine."

The moment I entered, the scent of honey and magic hit me, so strong it was almost overpowering. "You let her in here?"

He narrowed catlike eyes on me. "Is that what you want to talk about?"

I paused. Yes and no.

I strode across the room to step within his enormous cage, which took up two-thirds of the chamber, housing all the furniture. I remembered when it was first built and the ones that had proceeded it that had not been strong enough. Taking a seat on a chair in the corner, which I noted had a claw mark on the seat, I said, "What else should I want to talk about?"

Bael leaned against the cage bars, kicking one foot over the other casually. "Since when do we keep secrets from each other?"

I barked a laugh. "You're one to talk."

We were at an impasse. He had to know his behavior was erratic, abnormal, concerning at best. Even if we were not close, it would have been my responsibility to ask about it as head of the family...granted, I had not a fucking inch of ground to stand on regarding erratic behavior, and I knew that. Any other time, I would have told Bael immediately what Ambrose had said, but as he pointed out, things had been strangely tense as of late.

"True enough." He nodded. "I'll tell you whatever you like, but you go first."

"Why?"

"Because of the two of us, I am far less likely to kill the messenger."

"I wouldn't attack you," I snapped. "We don't fight."

In fact, we made a conscious effort never to do so. It had been that way for many years. Bael was the youngest of our generation—save for Elfwyn and Lysander—but he and I were not so far apart in age. We had more or less been raised together, and it had become clear from an early age that no good could come from our testing who was the stronger fighter, either physically or magically. We might spar, but we never really tried to learn who would win in true combat. I did not want to know, as knowing would mean either death or the death of my only close friend.

Bael grinned, looking something like himself for the first time all day. "And I would like to keep it that way, so you first, and then I swear on my name, I will tell you whatever you want to know."

I rolled my eyes. "It's hardly a good oath when I was present for your birth, Baelfry."

In any case, I was not sure it would matter if we invoked a name oath. Name oaths only mattered to those of weaker power.

"Fine, then," he said, pushing off the bars of the cage and moving to sit on the end of his unmade bed. "I swear on Celia's immortal soul. On the crown. On the heart of your infernal bird when I eventually catch it. Whatever you want."

"Use her true name," I said, looking him straight in the eye.

"I don't know it." His smile slipped. "And even if I did, I wouldn't tell you. I'm not about to hand you a way to hurt her."

I scowled, noting that he'd known exactly who I meant without my having to clarify. "Should you not be on my side over hers?"

"I don't see why they need to be different sides. I told you from the beginning I thought we needed her." His smile turned rueful. "You still owe me fucking money, by the way."

I pulled back, surprised into changing the subject. "What?"

"Gold—I know you're good for it, yet my pockets remain light."

"I have no gods-damned idea what you're raving about."

"I bet you last year that Lonnie wasn't human."

I scoffed. I only had the vaguest recollection of that. His exact wording had been lost to the past year and entirely overshadowed by more vivid things, like the taste of her skin and the constant reminder of some wine-drunk thing I'd apparently blurted out about my boots that had evidently burrowed into her mind, now coming back up at every available opportunity. "I remember you betting me she had magic and then using entirely unclear means to prove your point…proving nothing, I might add."

"Well, I can prove it for certain, now," he said, eyes flicking toward the door as if afraid we might be overheard. "But again, you go first."

I shook my head. "Why is that so important to you?"

"I merely want to be sure you're not going to rush off and kill her the moment I tell you."

"If I were, would I have kept us all back from the hunts?"

He merely stared at me, waiting, clearly unwilling to say another word before I explained my piece. I sighed, leaning back in my chair and staring up at the stone ceiling through the bars of the copper cage. I had to admit, it was not as horrible in here as I'd expected. Almost…comforting. How strange.

"I visited Ambrose this morning," I said without looking at Bael. "To ask him about the note she left."

There were only two names to voice in that sentence, and I'd struggled to say both of them.

First, my brother, who'd begun to use another name once he left our family thirty-odd years ago. Most called him *the Dullahan*, no longer Prince Ambrose Everlast, but I always struggled to distinguish between the two—both names feeling like a lie and ripping like fire through my throat.

Second, this time, the "she" I avoided speaking of aloud was not Lonnie Skyeborne but our grandmother Celia. We'd always spoken of her thus, as if she were some all-knowing, omnipotent presence in the room listening even after death. I wondered if my brother would ever reach such a status, as he had inherited her powers, or if his betrayal had regulated him to a nameless, cursed state, more threat than anything else.

"And I take it that came at a price?" Bael asked.

He had no fucking idea.

Even now, I already regretted it. Was already sure I'd done the wrong thing in letting my brother walk free in exchange for his vague, infuriating advice. Now, I'd merely have to track him down again—it was like a cat playing with a rat, letting it escape only to chase it again. Only this rat led an army and always knew the cat was coming before it took a single step.

"What did my traitorous cousin have to say?" Bael asked.

I gritted my teeth. "That there is more than one way to become king."

He stiffened slightly, yellow eyes finding mine. He did not look angry, as I'd feared, but wary perhaps. "Meaning?"

I didn't know what to say, and it had little to do with how Bael might answer. It was the mere idea that sent my mind into a state of ruination.

My thoughts flickered through a brutal tableau, choking the life out of her or wrapping my fingers around her throat while she screamed with pleasure. Chaining her in the dungeon or to my headboard. Her blood pouring over my hands, my tongue. Sinking into her and — I shook my head, trying to banish that thought before it was allowed to grow roots.

The sound of Bael's boots hitting the floor jogged me back to alertness. I looked up, concerned. "What's wrong?"

His face was stricken as his eyes rolled into his head, spinning faster, clearly searching for something just out of reach. "We'll continue this later," he said too fast. "I must go."

"What happened?" I asked, even as he faded around the edges.

"Lonnie needs help."

How the fuck did he know? For once, he hadn't been watching her. Not for the last five minutes, at least. Anyway, she should be fine. I'd made it absolutely fucking clear she was ours. "Who the fuck would attack her?"

"It doesn't matter. I need to go," he said sharply.

I was shocked to realize my own heart had sped up, something akin to anger, anxiety, moving too close to the surface. "Bael! We're not done. This is important."

"I think she's my mate," he said, his voice trailing off as he disappeared into shadow. "So nothing else could be more important than keeping her safe."

I stared, dumbstruck, for so long that by the time I found the words to reply, Bael was long gone. Probably deep in the forest of Inbetwixt by now, with no way to hear the string of confused, hateful words I wanted to spew at him.

I should've been surprised, but I wasn't. Perhaps I'd known… suspected. Perhaps it was simply that nothing had gone right as of late, and why should this be different? If I was honest with myself, a large part of me found this confirmation gratifying—if only because it explained so much. By the Source, he'd fed her his fucking blood to heal her. I should've known.

The worst part about this revelation was that it changed nothing.

The Everlast family always rejected our true mates—we couldn't risk a moment of true happiness destroying the entire family, but we didn't just let them go…we were far too selfish for that. They died by our own hand, or we kept them close, married into the family through siblings or cousins.

I ran a hand through my hair, the full picture becoming clear. Finally, *finally*, the prophecies made sense.

Lonnie Skyeborne might be my cousin's mate, but her life was mine. Either I would kill her or marry her to keep her close.

And either way, I was already certain she'd find a way to ruin me too.

Fuck, if I didn't hate her for it.

2

LONNIE

THE DEPLETED QUARRY, INBETWIXT, PRESENT

A deafening roar rumbled through the forest, shaking the trees and striking fear into my heart. The sound wrapped around me like grabbing claws, filling me with a primal urge to retreat or curl into a ball on the ground. *"You're food,"* it seemed to say. *"Run or be eaten alive."*

I straightened my shoulders, my feet remaining rooted to the spot as a piercing scream followed the roar, like my own fear had found a voice in someone else half a mile away.

An odd sort of relief filled me. As fucked-up as it was to consider, I was almost grateful for that scream. Now, that monster would hopefully be satisfied, and whoever filled its belly was one less enemy to worry about.

One less person between me and victory.

When I was a child, I believed there was nothing more important in life than winning.

When I was a child, I was a fool.

The most important thing in life is not winning; it's surviving. The best feeling in the world is taking a breath when you didn't think you would get another, and there are no rules in matters of life and death. Ironically, my early love of winning prepared me well for surviving now, as the only way to survive in the court of Elsewhere is to *win.*

It was the second event of the Wilde Hunts, and I stood alone in the dark forest of Inbetwixt. The quarry was depleted of obsidian long ago and had not been mined in over one hundred years, leaving a huge crater in the earth that, over time, filled with rainwater to form a seemingly bottomless lake. The surrounding area, once barren and rocky, was now dense with new foliage. Young trees and brush obscured the old paths to the worksites, and leftover tools lay scattered and rusted on the ground.

I squeezed my hand tight around the dagger clutched in my fist, my knuckles turning white, and raised my lantern in the other hand. An overgrown path snaked its way up the slope of the man-made mountain ahead of me, nearly invisible under fallen leaves and dislodged stones.

Shifting my lantern to the opposite hand, I hauled myself up and over a rounded boulder, ignoring the blisters on my palms. The ground sloped down sharply on my left side and slunk back up on my right. I picked my way forward toward what I hoped was the top of the quarry.

As I walked, the soft echo of a raven's cry drew my ear from the surrounding silence. I'd hiked for so long alone that any single noise rose the hair on the back of my neck, and the rustling of the wind always sounded like footsteps.

My feet slipped, and I stumbled again and again on loose pebbles, but finally, the ground seemed to even off. The trees thinned, and my lantern shone on the sudden drop at the edge of the quarry, reflecting off the glassy surface of the water below, and dizziness overwhelmed me at the mere sight of it.

"I'm not sure if I should be pleased or horrified," I muttered to myself.

In the bushes to my left, a few stray Underfae tittered an incomprehensible response, as I'd been speaking for their unseen ears alone. Ignoring them, I squinted out across the dark quarry to the shadows on the opposite side.

There were two ways to win the Wilde Hunts: First, you could cross the boundary established at the beginning of the trial. Second, you could still be alive in the morning. Since I was human and most hunters were immortal, it made the most sense for me to win by crossing the boundary before I died of injury or exhaustion. I could only assume that the boundary was on the other side of the water, otherwise, the quarry would be an odd choice for a hunt.

I peered over the ledge, frowning. Would I survive a fall into the water below? Would it be safer to walk around?

Off in the distance, a sharp laugh cut through the night, and I froze, every thought fleeing from my mind. *Fuck.*

Turning slowly on the spot, I scanned the darkness behind me. My skin prickled with fear, and my breath caught in my throat as three dark figures melted out of the trees, moving toward me far too fast to be human. *Hello, again.*

"Hello, Slúagh," the nearest male said in a gravelly voice.

Relief and fear hit me in equal measure. I didn't recognize the voice, and now that I looked closer, these males weren't quite as tall nor as muscular as the ones I'd initially expected. Still, encountering anyone on the hunting grounds was bad for your health.

My grip tightened around my knife. "Don't even think about coming any closer."

The three Fae males laughed, high and cold, the sound seeming to echo off the trees and fill the entire clearing.

The male to the left, who was slightly shorter than the first, stepped forward into the light and leered at me. "Oh, she's a pretty one. Do you think she'll cry before she dies?"

The first male—the leader, I guessed—looked sharply at his companion. "Eyes off the Slúagh, Thelonious. We're not here for her, just the crown."

I swallowed thickly. Normally, I might be offended by their use of the word "Slúagh," a rude name for humans, but not now. Not when I was solely focused on surviving the next ten minutes. It was almost impossible for a human to defeat a fairy in any type of combat, and I'd never been all that good at fighting, anyway, but I wasn't about to simply lie down and let them kill me; I'd come here to win.

"You want to be king?" I asked, trying to instill a note of derision into my voice. It came out sounding a bit like Lady Aine, one of the Everlast princesses. I supposed there were worse comparisons. "Let me advise you against it. The Everlasts don't appreciate losing their crown. You'll only end up in the dungeon until your own hunting season, and if you somehow survive that, they'll either kill you or attempt to use you as a chess piece in their games. It's hardly a fate I would endorse."

"You look alive enough to me, Slúagh," the third male jeered at me. "Like a well-kept pet."

"Something like that," I muttered.

"Where are the Everlasts now if they care so much?" the leader called. "Shouldn't they have finished you off by now?"

I paused, pondering that. Undoubtedly, the male had meant to taunt me, but in truth, it was a fair question.

The house of Everlast had held the throne of Elsewhere for the last seven thousand years. That was, until a year ago, when a band of rebels attacked the kingdom, and my twin sister tried to murder King Penvalle and was instead cut down right in front of me. I hadn't even known she was working with the rebels, and in the chaos, I lost all sense and murdered the king while covered in Rosey's blood. According to the laws of Elsewhere, that made me the queen—assuming I could defend the crown in the Wilde Hunts.

Over the last year, the Everlast family had been obsessed with taking back their throne—some more than others.

Prince Scion, the heir apparent to the obsidian throne before my unexpected takeover, was particularly intent on taking back his power by any means necessary. He wasn't allowed to kill me outside the hunts, but that hadn't stopped him from making threats or imprisoning me beneath the castle. I'd entered this arena tonight, fully expecting Scion to attack me and wondering—though I was loathe to admit it—if my bargain with Prince Bael to protect me would still stand.

The last I'd seen of the youngest prince had been this morning in his bedchamber. Flames had danced in the prince's hand, mocking me. The proof of my lies lay bare between us.

I gazed into their flickering, blue-white depths, and for the briefest moment, I could swear I beheld my own reflection projected back at me. Wide-eyed and caught, at last, in a lie I couldn't wriggle my way out of. Snared in a fairy-trap of round-about words and slow, methodical trickery. I'd always heeded my mother's warnings and never intentionally given in to the simmering heat that seemed to lay beneath my skin, ready to erupt at any moment. Never spoken my secrets out loud. Never given in to temptation, and yet, none of that mattered now.

"Why don't you tell me, mate," he'd said. *"What are you lying about?"*

It wasn't the question that stunned me so much as the wording. *Mate.* He'd called me "mate," mere moments after proclaiming that I was not, could not be, human. Seconds after announcing that he'd been using his blood to bind me to him.

My heart pounded too hard against my chest, and my breath rattled—uneven and conspicuous as a wave of fear swept through me. "Put that out," I'd hissed, eyes darting to the flames. "Now."

The prince's saffron eyes locked onto me as I edged away from him, backing toward the door. "Why? What are you afraid of, little monster?"

That was the question, wasn't it.

I should've been afraid of him, standing before me holding fire in his palm, the shadow of a cage looming behind him, his too-sharp teeth giving his inhumanly beautiful face a predatory edge.

But no, the terror was for me.

Of me.

And of what I knew might happen if, after all these years, I voiced the one secret I'd sworn never to speak aloud. "Just put it out!"

I moved faster backward out of the room before finally turning and sprinting for the corridor, away from the questions, from him, from the flames now burned into the backs of my eyelids. I could see the irony in it—I was literally running toward death and toward the hunts that, until this morning, I would have called the most frightening thing in my life. Now, I would rather be hunted every day than answer a single truthful question.

"I'll wait for you to call for me," he yelled after me, his voice echoing off the stone.

A chill ran down my spine, and I knew his predatory gaze would stay on me until I was out of sight.

Something Bael said to me on the day we met floated back to me, as if on a phantom wind. *"I think it will be fun to watch you try and escape me, only to be caught in the end."*

3

LONNIE

THE DEPLETED QUARRY, INBETWIXT

I shook myself, refocusing on the threat in front of me rather than the one who, for all I knew, still stood in the cage where I'd left him. "I think you should worry less about what the Everlasts think of me and more about what they'll do to you if you try and take the crown," I said with as much confidence as I could muster. "Your life expectancy will go up quite a bit if you walk away right now."

I needed to take my own advice and stop worrying about where the royals were. It was for the best if the Everlasts kept their distance—the longer they stayed away, the better off I would be.

The nearest male sneered, his eyes fixing on my heavy, obsidian crown. "Or, I could kill you and sell that trinket back to the highest bidder."

Fair enough. Fuck, he wasn't a total idiot.

I clenched my teeth together and slowly surveyed each male in turn. Each held a crossbow, all aimed at me and ready to fire in an instant. It felt like I was playing chess without enough pieces—and I was the queen.

"That's not how it works," I blurted out. "You can't give the crown away. It's magically bound to you."

Lie.

If that were true, I'd already be long dead. The whole reason I was still standing was Prince Bael had bargained with me to hand over the crown to him after the final hunt in Aftermath in exchange for his protection. *Some help that was, now.*

"Who says?" one of the hunters jeered.

Dammit, I don't know. Who would he care about? Or rather, who would he believe? "The priestesses at the Source."

Another lie.

I had no idea if anyone still communed with the gods, now that the area surrounding the Source was a barren, war-torn wasteland, but I was betting that these Fae didn't know either.

Sure enough, the three men stood stock-still as soon as the words left my mouth. Fear of the gods ran deep, and I supposed they forgot that humans could still tell untruths since they themselves were incapable of lying.

One of the men nudged their leader. "Maybe the Slúagh bitch is right. I don't want to meet the royal executioner today."

"Shut up," the leader barked, his voice like gravel scraping against glass. He took a step toward me, his face breaking into a grin. "Don't kill her, but take the crown. I'm willing to take my chances with a few priestesses."

My stomach dropped with a sharp sense of dread. Well, I supposed I'd done my best, but now it was time to fight or flee.

I dragged my feet backward, feeling blindly for the edge of the cliff. The ground beneath me sloped down into a deep ravine and curled around a cavernous overhang framing paradise several hundred feet below. The water that had made me dizzy seemed infinitely better than taking my chances against three Fae males. My boot grazed the jagged edge of a flat stone, and I clenched my jaw in preparation for the gravity-defying feat. It was a gamble, but staying put was an even riskier option.

The nearest fairy lunged for me just as I threw myself backward into midair. *Please, please, Source, let there be no rocks at the bottom.*

For one wild moment, I seemed to hang, suspended in midair, before I was plummeting so fast into darkness I had no chance to think. Fear and adrenaline coursed through my veins, and tears streamed from my eyes. My stomach tickled, pulling tight, and far above, the distant shouts of the Fae grew faint, lost in the wind.

Then, all too fast, pain splintered my body, and I submerged into freezing darkness. Then, there was only *pain.* Bone-crunching, mind-numbing *pain.*

For a moment, it seemed as if every bone in my body was breaking. As if all my muscles had stretched and torn, and the rocks I'd feared had indeed become my final resting place. Then, water closed over me, and I bobbed up again, my head breaking the surface.

I gasped for air that felt like it was tearing my throat, and I whimpered, my lungs screaming with the effort of every breath.

Alive—I'm alive. If I could have laughed, I would have, but every movement felt like murder.

I floated in the water, unable to move, for what felt like a very long time, and finally, slowly, *slowly,* the agony started to subside. The burning sensation turned into a dull ache that dissipated with every breath.

I inhaled deeply and raised my arm for one stroke, propelling myself toward the shore. A second stroke, then another. It certainly wasn't the worst pain I'd endured in the last year—it wasn't even the worst pain I'd endured while living in Elsewhere. No, that honor might belong to the long months I'd sat hungry and cold in the dungeon beneath the castle, courtesy of Prince Scion himself. There was a reason they called him the "Royal Executioner" and the "Prince of Pain," and it wasn't only because of his magic.

I fixed my gaze on a point on the shore and swam slowly on, pushing my way through the frigid waters, considering my options.

Distantly, I knew that as soon as I got out of the water, I'd need to find a way to dry off, or the cold would kill me faster than anything else. During the first hunt, the cold and the rain had been a far greater obstacle than any of the Fae, something that Prince Bael hadn't thought of when trying to protect me.

My chest constricted slightly at the thought of the prince, and I immediately shook myself, sucking in a sharp breath. That was not something I needed to think about right now. Possibly not something I needed to think about *ever*. Clearly, he was not thinking about me.

I supposed the word "mate" didn't mean all that much to him, or he would be here right now protecting me, regardless of our argument.

The shore grew closer, and I swam faster. Great mounds of seaweed or some sort of reeds floated on the surface of the water ahead, and I winced, realizing I'd be not only freezing but filthy when I finally emerged from the water.

I was so focused on the task at hand that I almost didn't notice when my foot touched something slimy just beneath the surface. Then, my fingers brushed the same slippery surface, and I recoiled in shock, my heart leaping into my throat. Fear shot up my spine before I whipped around again. *Nothing there.*

I squeezed my eyes shut. It was probably just a fish, and I needed to calm down and focus on getting to the edge of this lake before I could worry about the strange things that lurked beneath its surface. But it wasn't easy—the icy-cold water had sapped away most of my strength by now, and the few remaining strokes seemed never-ending.

Opening my eyes again, I blinked several times. *What...*

My vision blurred as every muscle in my body tensed with fear as I realized what lay ahead of me—not seaweed or reeds, but something far more sinister. My stomach churned, and my eyes widened at the sight of the decaying corpse, facedown in the murky quarry.

I opened my mouth in a silent scream, and I splashed, flailing as far away from the motionless bodies as physically possible. My hands brushed into other bodies, hair, floating limbs. My stomach roiled, and I retched, panic rising in my chest. My heart raced, and my legs pumped beneath me, propelling me forward at breakneck speed while my mind begged me to go faster.

Something splashed in the water behind me, and my heartbeat swelled in my ears.

Most monsters didn't hunt this way—leaving meat, uneaten and abandoned. Most creatures killed for food and would consume entire bodies before moving on to their next target. This looked like the battlefield after some war, which could only mean two things: either this monster was sentient and an intentional obstacle in the hunts, picking off players one by one, or it was playing with its food. I was betting on the latter.

A louder splash crashed behind me, and I didn't bother to stifle my scream as I struggled toward the shore. With sudden relief, my feet hit mud, my toes kicking into the bottom of the man-made lake rather than into dark, fathomless water. I struggled to stand, water pouring from my clothing and hair as I scrambled out onto the bank. *Thank the Source.*

The pebbles crunched beneath my feet as I took a few steps away from the lake, even as a thunderous sound rose behind me, shaking the ground and making the trees wave overhead.

I turned slowly on the spot, dread pooling in my stomach.

An enormous blue-black snake rose out of the water. At least twelve feet tall and still half-obscured, it towered over me, poised to strike.

I screamed loudly enough to shake the entire forest and stumbled backward into the underbrush.

Panic clamped me in its jaws as the snake looked down at me with intense, menacing eyes. Its tongue flicked out of its mouth, tasting the air between us, and its scales shimmered like diamonds in the moonlight as it swayed this way and that, as if dancing to some unheard music.

Oh no. Oh no, no, no. "Bael, where the hell are you?"

Before I could think anything other than, "Run!" the monster's immense jaws unfurled, flashing rows of jagged, yellow teeth that glinted in the twilight.

My sore muscles came to life, and I dodged quickly to the side as it lunged, letting out a hiss that smelled of decay. Pulling my dagger from my belt, I turned and sprinted into the darkness, giving little care to where I was going. Branches and thorns clawed at my skin as I blindly pressed forward, but I paid no attention to the stinging sensation that followed in my wake. My only focus was the sound of scales on leaves growing closer and closer by the second.

I stumbled as I fled, my back hitting the ground with a force that knocked the breath from my lungs. Spots filled my vision, like sparks flying free of a bonfire into the darkness.

My dagger shook in my trembling fingers, and an icy chill of dread crawled up my spine, and the blue-white flames that had danced in Prince Bael's hand filled my mind.

I'd never done it—not really. Not since I was too young to recall if it was real or a half-remembered dream.

I'd wondered, certainly.

I'd guessed and agonized over what-ifs and maybes, but I'd never intentionally called on those flames as Bael had. The only time I'd even thought about it, it hadn't worked.

My mother had always warned me never to draw attention to myself. Never, ever to use the power, or terrible things would happen, beyond my wildest comprehension.

But perhaps it didn't matter anymore. Perhaps, if Bael had used them already…if I was to die, anyway…

The scent of decay filled my nose again, and I felt the oppressive presence of death breathing down my neck.

4
LONNIE

THE DEPLETED QUARRY, INBETWIXT

Two enormous orange, split-pupil eyes stared down at me, swaying this way and that, as the giant snake loomed. Its body was covered entirely in blue-black scales that flashed in the moonlight as it danced, more radiant on one side than the other. It had a small ring of yellow around the base of its head, like a collar, several shades lighter than the orange of its eyes.

It opened its mouth and hissed, showing me two terrifying fangs and a reddish-brown tongue, larger than my arm, that darted in and out of the flat, triangular head, as if tasting the air. Like it was savoring my scent before it sunk its teeth into my flesh, injecting venom to paralyze and poison.

It need not bother. I was already paralyzed, I realized, sitting unmoving without the snake having to do anything at all. Caught in its swaying gaze, mesmerized by its stalling, waiting to attack.

As if coming back into my body, I jolted. My breath heaved in my chest, heat and adrenaline pounding in my veins nearly as fast and erratic as my racing thoughts.

I wished I had more time to consider—to think—but I squeezed my eyes shut and dug down inside myself for that place where heat always simmered until it began to crawl up my skin. The air fizzled with electricity, and I gritted my teeth, aiming my burning hands toward the oncoming serpent.

I felt tiny pinpricks erupt on the tips of my fingers for the briefest moment—not as strong as what Bael had done, but certainly not nothing. The feeling was like a spark to my memory—a long-distant muscle, unused and nearly forgotten, buried, so often ignored it was as if I'd severed the limb altogether.

The snake bent its head, coming to loom in front of me, mere inches from my face.

I felt its breath, and my eyes snapped open. It opened its mouth wide, showing rows of tiny teeth behind its two large fangs, a gaping throat that could swallow me whole, eyes that were the size of my head. "Ssstop!"

Ice seemed to pour into my veins. I let out a startled shriek and scrambled back, the heat in my fingers dying with my rising shock. I gasped, unable to move as the snake's putrid breath filled my nostrils. My heart pounded wildly, and I could feel the sweat trickling down my back.

But the snake was not finished.

"Ssstop, you fool," the snake hissed. "You will only call the Wilde things that live in this forest and far beyond."

A new wave of terror washed over me, stealing my breath, twisting my innards. Worse than before, worse than the fear of being torn apart, this was the fear of the unknown. Of the things unseen in the dark. I tried to call back the fire, and it stuttered like a wet match.

"Wh-what..." I could not find the words to express myself. *What are you? Who are you? How much will it hurt when you eat me?* I was paralyzed, every muscle in my body tense and frozen.

The snake let out a small sound, like a rattle, that I thought might have been a terrible laugh. "I have never enjoyed the fleshhh of a queen," it said in a grotesque rattling hiss that I felt more than heard. "I wonder, will you taste different from other humansss?"

I hoped I tasted like ash and burned like fire on the way down.

"Wh-why not just eat me, then?" I asked, my mind stuttering as I struggled to force out every word.

"Becaussse," it said, dragging the word out far too long. "I would rather live to enjoy my ssslumber once I have finishhhed my meal."

"I don't understand."

It twisted its enormous neck, curling, a bit like how a human might cock their head. "Don't you? Curiousss. You cannot use your magic, human queen, lesssst you doom usss all."

It dragged out every word into horrible long hisses that made it hard to focus on what it was saying, but as the seconds ticked by and it did not strike, my mind slowly began to work again. Slowly.

Putting aside the impossibility of conversing with a snake, the high probability that I'd simply slipped on a rock and hit my head, or perhaps never come up from beneath the water of the quarry and was hallucinating as I ran out of air, the words it spoke were not unfamiliar; my mother had made it perfectly clear to me my whole life that I was never to use my...peculiarity.

Before she died, my mother had three cardinal rules:

1.Never make a bargain with a fairy.

2.Never enter the Waywoods on hunting day.

3.Never give the High Fae a reason to notice you.

She also had other rules, tacked on later, as my sister and I aged, "always lie" being the most prominent of these. Every rule, however, came back to the same purpose. Never reveal your secrets. Never use the magic, or terrible things might happen—not only to me but to the entire continent.

My mind raced with this as the tip of the snake's tail coiled around my feet. The muscles of the serpent's scales shifted and pulsed, its long, slithering body gleaming in the moonlight, and I could feel the heat rising in my chest again, the ice clearing as my terror turned back to anger, my frozen body beginning to thaw. Strangely, the old rules were like an anchor, a mantra, and the all-consuming terror dissipated.

Never make a bargain. Never enter the woods…too late.

My eyes were locked on the spot where the tail created slight swirls around my feet, almost bewitching me in a trance-like state. Hypnotic. I shook my head. "I have no magic."

"Liar," it rattled, abrupt and deafeningly loud. "Liesss. You know if you use the magic that wasss given to you, it will only call the othersss like you. You mussst have been warned."

"How do you know of this?" I asked.

"The forest whispersss. Your very exissstence interests usss. The queen who is bothhh human and not. Who was born as the Source erupted and hid for years in plain sssight in the kitchens of the black castle."

I went stiff at the hissing sound of its words, but this time, not from fear. "What do you mean, I am human and not?"

My pulse quickened as it seemed to take too long to reply. Bael had said much the same thing—not human. Could that be true? I'd never known who my father was, and now, I'd never wished more that I'd pushed my mother harder for answers when she was alive.

The snake released a menacing hiss. "Do not think I will answer your questions simply because you ask them. I am not an oracle to be held at your disposal."

"But do you know?" I tried, almost desperate. "If you know about me, then do you know more—"

It snapped its great jaws, so close to my face that I jumped back just in time to avoid losing my head. Terror shot through me again, and I clamped my mouth shut.

"You foolish, insolent child. You could be a sssymbol of hope for the revolution or a beloved pet living in luxury at the dark castle. But now it seems your fate is to be nothing more than an insubstantial morsel—quickly gulped down and discarded without thought."

I tore my eyes away from the shimmering scales, forcing myself to meet its too-large eyes as, again, I pulled the heat from deep within my chest.

This time, there was no hesitation. No spark, no shaking in my fingers as the tiniest orange flame appeared in my palm.

"Extingguishhh that!" it hissed. "Ssstop!"

"If you intend to eat me anyway, why should it matter to me what happens or what is called? I will be dead."

I held my breath, and this time, I was quite sure it was thinking. It was hard to tell when the creature had no nose, no humanoid mouth, yet its expression appeared contemplative. "True enough."

I let my shoulders slump, uncaring if it could see my relief.

"A bargain, then," I said quickly, not liking how fast the words sprung to my lips. My mother would be horrified. "I will not use the magic if you let me go."

I could not have held that flame longer than another second, anyway. Unlike Bael, who I imagined must have years of practice with all sorts of magic, I was grateful to have simply made a single light. Now, I felt as if I could crawl into bed and sleep for eternity.

The snake waved its head back and forth, and it took me a moment to realize it was shaking, as if to say "no." It opened its wide mouth again, hissing its reply. "But I am hungry, ssstarving. Ravenousss."

I glanced back and thought of the other bodies in the water, not wanting to point out that it could have easily eaten any one of them. "Fine. I'll…bring you other meat."

I did not have to specify when or what meat I would bring it. It could be twenty years from now and a single rabbit. Even thinking that worried me…that was far too Fae-like. In fact, if not for the fact that I could still lie fluently, I might be on the verge of nervous collapse.

I did not want to be anything like *them*. Did not want to think like them. It was no hardship to swear against powers I'd never wished for.

"Not jussst any meat," the snake replied. "Royal blood?"

Shit.

I still had some time to decide what to do—maybe there was a way I could capture Prince Scion? It would surely be better for the country if he were fed to a snake. "Fine."

"Ssswear it," the snake demanded. "Ssswear on your name."

I quickly surveyed the area, my body stiff. I hadn't uttered my name for years, let alone twice in a matter of weeks. It felt so foreign that had I not spoken it aloud to Gwydion only recently, I might have had to consider for a moment to remember. Instead, my hands only balled into fists, and my stomach tightened as I anticipated regretting this decision.

"Elowyn," I said bitterly. "I, Elowyn of Nightshade, swear to return to you with an offering of royal blood."

Though it may not be for a century, I added in my head. If I couldn't lure Scion here, I'd come myself when I was old enough to be on my deathbed.

"Ssso it is done."

The snake swayed its large head as if nodding, then turned abruptly, its gigantic tongue darting out to taste the air. Without another word to me, it darted, quick as a whip, back into the trees, looping in the direction of the water.

I barely had time to catch my breath, slow my beating heart, before I heard footsteps firm and fast, breaking branches behind me. *No, no, no.*

This was what I got, I supposed, for thinking this hunt too simple. For wondering after the Everlasts. For finding the initial hours easy. Now, I'd die not by snake but by some stray hunter or, more likely, Prince Scion, just after swearing not to use my one weapon.

"Come back," I yelled after the snake. "This is undoubtedly your offering come to present himself!"

But the snake was gone, and I was alone again.

Every muscle in my body screamed at me to run, but I'd done so much running already, and it had never helped. I was done running from monsters.

Instead, I squared my shoulders and glared, intent on looking death in the eye when it came for me.

And, indeed, it had.

"Hello, little monster."

5
LONNIE

THE DEPLETED QUARRY, INBETWIXT

Every muscle in my body went tight, and my skin seemed to hum with awareness as I tilted my chin up and stared into the all-too-familiar face of Prince Bael. The shadows between the trees seemed to shift around him as he approached, brushing tendrils of smoke off the lapels of his maroon coat.

I swallowed thickly, my adrenaline still racing, fingers still burning.

I would far prefer to see Bael than Scion, if caught alone in the dark forest, but at the moment, neither was welcome. I instinctively reached for the knife in my belt. He might have sworn to protect me, but it was hunting night, and everyone was my enemy. "What are you doing here?"

His lip curled in a smile, flashing too-sharp teeth, and he inched ever so slightly closer, like a cat stalking its prey. "I believe the correct response when one saves your life is 'thank you.'"

My eyes flitted between the prince and the spot where the snake had disappeared, my brow furrowing in confusion. "You did not save my life," I snapped, pushing to my feet. My muscles screamed in agony, but I refused to let it show on my face. "I was doing just fine on my own."

Bael's red-golden curls bounced with mirth. His yellow, catlike eyes glinted playfully, and he took measured steps toward me. "Oh? And what were you going to do?"

I practically shook with anger. He believed he'd scared it off. Believed he was the one who had saved me, having lifted not a finger, as if I was so helpless. Granted, he had some evidence with which to support that assumption, but still…my indignance burned hot like anger as his eyes darted to my balled-up fists. I shoved them behind my back, a strange sense of shame washing over me.

I couldn't say what I'd promised or even mention the magic. I doubted he had any idea of the implications, of what I was risking. "Never mind. I'll ask one more time: what are you doing here?"

"You called for me," he said far too calmly.

I recoiled. "I did not."

He smirked. "Do I need to keep a tally of your lies?"

"What are you…" I trailed off and felt my face contort as horror washed over me. I *had* called for him. Though not with any real intent behind the words. *Oh, by Aisling*. "I-I was not calling for you. I had a single thought."

His smirk was infuriating. "Glad to see you've realized you need me after all."

I huffed an exasperated sound. That was hardly fair.

It had only been a day or so since we'd seen each other—less than a day, really, as it was not yet morning—but it felt so much longer. I thought Bael might chase after me when I stormed out of his room this morning, but he hadn't. To my knowledge, he hadn't even traveled with the caravan from the capital to Inbetwixt. Not that I wanted him to.

"How did you hear me?" I asked mulishly. "I haven't seen you all day."

"I was watching," he said as though it were obvious.

I glanced behind me reflexively, as if some hiding place might reveal itself. "From where? Where have you been?"

He huffed an annoyed breath. "Scion believes the capital is going to be attacked, and for once, his paranoia is likely more along the lines of intuition. The entire family stayed behind to protect the city."

I cocked an eyebrow, moving to step around him. "I see."

"He's convinced that since the rebels were able to get into your tower last night, Dullahan will use the opportunity of us all being in Inbetwixt to seize the castle."

I sucked in a startled breath. It was the first time I'd heard Bael refer to Dullahan—the rebel leader whom my sister had invoked in her final breath, and were I not so suspicious of his motivation for being here, I might have questioned him more about it.

I might also have mentioned that Prince Scion was likely wrong; I didn't know what the rebels were planning, but I had a note signed "Ambrose Dullahan" currently burning a hole in my pocket that suggested he may see me in Inbetwixt. I didn't know if I would actually see the rebel, but I doubted he was still in Everlast City.

I *might* have mentioned that, but I didn't.

"Well, don't let me hold you back from guard duty," I said, distrust heavy in my tone. "I need to go."

He moved to the left, blocking my path. "Wait," he said. "There could be any number of other creatures between here and the boundary. That was a Beithir serpent—you're lucky to be alive."

"Well, then I don't want to keep its friends waiting any longer." My tone dripped with sarcasm. "I'm sure they're quite hungry."

Bael darted in front of me again, like we were doing an odd sort of dance. "Lonnie."

I set my jaw, my nails cutting into the skin of my palms. "Move."

He *did* move. So quickly, in fact, that I didn't see him until it was far too late.

Bael lunged forward, pressing my back against the nearest tree, caging me in with both arms. "Don't be foolish."

Electricity shot up my spine, and my breath hitched. My mind immediately ran to last night, when we'd stood in this exact position, only far, *far* closer. My stomach turned over, and my pulse thrummed with mingled fear and anticipation. "The only foolish thing I've done is not run the moment I saw you."

"Don't be so stubborn, then. You don't have to cross the finish line on your own," he said sharply. "And as for running…you know I'll always catch you, little monster."

I shuddered. There were a thousand ways to interpret that and even more things to say in response, but I simply had no energy to spar with him. "Let me go."

His intense, golden gaze trained on me as if ready to strike. "No, I don't think I will. You might not want my help, but you're going to get it, and anyway, I think you still owe me an explanation."

Anger mixed with hurt rose in my throat. He had absolutely no right to judge me. None. Not when he was hardly forthcoming with his secrets. "I owe you nothing."

"Nothing?" he asked, a mocking lilt to his voice.

"Nothing more than what we bargained for. Not an explanation. Not my honesty or my loyalty, just the crown and to win these *damn hunts*. Which you are currently keeping me from, by the way."

"Not even an end to our earlier conversation?"

I winced slightly at that, but I recovered. "No," I snapped. "You have a lot of nerve to demand I share all my secrets with you while flaunting your own like nothing is amiss."

"What does that mean?" he growled.

I let out a humorless laugh. "I don't claim to be an expert, but I do not believe most Fae princes sleep in cages, *my lord*."

I'd had quite a lot of time to consider this argument while traveling to Inbetwixt. So much time, in fact, that it had almost entirely distracted me from my fear of the hunt. I was not precisely certain I believed Bael's assertion that we were mates—I wasn't certain I disbelieved it either. I was certain, however, that he would get absolutely nothing from me until I got equal treatment in return.

"That's a different situation," he growled.

"Of course it is." My tone dripped with sarcasm. "How foolish of me. It's always different when it applies to you."

I went to push against his chest, both determined to pass by him and knowing it was futile.

Sure enough, Bael caught my wrists in one hand and held them above my head like shackles, holding me in place. His eyes raked over my body, and I became all too aware that I was still soaking wet from my leap into the water, every part of my clothing sticking to me everywhere that mattered. Mingled embarrassment and something else, something hotter, joined the anger already taking root in my belly and combined into a whirlwind of confused emotions.

He exhaled sharply through his nose. "It's different because knowing would put you in danger. I can't do that anymore."

I twisted my legs, trying to kick him while he held me suspended by my wrists. "But you have had no problem letting me almost get murdered repeatedly. That's logical."

He barked a laugh that sounded a bit more like a snarl, his grip tightening on my wrists. "Oh, you're wrong there, little monster. I absolutely do have a fucking problem with that. I'm here, aren't I? Do you even realize how many people I've killed to keep you alive or how many times I've had to go against my family?"

"Is that supposed to make me happy?"

"It's merely a fact. Even now, Scion is likely livid that I've left midconversation to come save you from yet another near death."

"Well, we wouldn't want that. Aisling only knows we can't upset the precious Prince of Ravens," I spat. "And stop looking at me like that!"

"Like what?" he said, dark humor coating his tone. His eyes flashed hotter as he intentionally focused his gaze on my throat. "How am I looking at you?"

I stopped squirming and looked down, not wanting to reply any more than I wanted to answer any of his other questions.

It wasn't love, exactly, that I beheld in Bael's face but *need*. Desperation. He was looking at me like I was all that was wrong with his life and somehow everything he'd ever wanted, and it scared me more than anything else in this forest ever could.

"Just let me go," I said quietly.

To my surprise, he laughed. "That is never going to happen, little monster. I could never leave you, even if I wanted to. Not really."

I stiffened slightly and glanced around, as if someone might hear us, but there was no one there. "You don't…that's not certain, and even if there is a bond, it won't ever be sealed. You told me that yourself."

Finally letting go of my wrists, Bael leaned in even closer as my arms fell limply by my sides. "You are my mate. I should have realized the moment I saw you, but I have been absolutely certain for some weeks now. You can be angry as long as you like, but understand that the only reason I am entertaining this tantrum is because you were raised by humans. If you had any idea about mate-bonds, you'd realize there's no chance I will ever be able to let you go. You made sure of that on the day we met."

My mouth fell open in surprise. "What does that mean? How did I make sure of anything?"

"Instinct," he replied.

Then, before I could ask any more questions, he stepped forward in one swift movement, closing the remaining inches between us, and captured my lips with his.

My breath fled from my lungs, and I gasped against his mouth. In an instant, all rational thought left my head as my body suddenly became painfully aware of every inch of him pressed against me.

Everything around us seemed to evaporate—the water of the quarry lapping in the distance, the sounds of the forest, and the rustling of leaves all turned silent. Tingles erupted all across my skin, and my heart thundered wildly in my chest as if trying to keep up with the pure force that seemed to pass through us whenever we touched like this. Violent. Destructive. Inevitable.

His hands roamed slowly down my body until they rested on the small of my back, pulling me closer toward him as if he wanted to consume me entirely. Moving lower, he gripped the backs of my thighs, lifting me easily into the air. Instinctually, I curled my legs around his waist, but I need not have worried about falling.

Long fingers trailed up my thighs and dug into my hips, shifting me closer. We were still mostly clothed, but my entire body was on fire, and seemingly any second that could change, tipping everything over the edge of reason.

I bit down hard on his bottom lip and froze as the metallic taste of blood filled my mouth. The familiarity of that taste, laced with power and magic, had reality washing over me, hard and fast, as if I'd once more plunged from the top of the cliff into the freezing water of the quarry.

Bael groaned and nipped gently at my lip in return but didn't break the skin. Instead, he pulled his head back suddenly, and the smug smirk was back on his face. "You bit me."

I blinked dazedly. "What?"

"When we met, you bit me," he said. "I believe I told you I wanted to see if you would do it again, but you didn't, and I thought perhaps it was a coincidence."

But then it happened again, I finished for him.

I hastily reached up and wiped the blood off my mouth with the back of my hand, but the metallic taste would not so easily be ignored. It should revolt me—I'd always wondered why it didn't. "I don't understand."

"It's an instinct. Humans don't mark their partners, little monster. Not like that." He reached out with his free hand and dragged his thumb over my bottom lip. "You will simply have to come to terms with the fact that you've always been mine."

My mind spun, and I tried desperately to focus, but it was almost impossible when we were so close we could share the same air. "What if I don't want that? Maybe I don't want you."

I heard the pathetic note of desperation and false protest in my voice, and he must have, too, because he laughed.

"We both know that's not true. You want me. Don't even bother lying—everything about you is giving it away. I can hear your heartbeat. I can see your eyes dilating." He grazed his bloody thumb over my hardened nipple through the thin fabric of my tunic as if to prove his point. "I can even smell you."

I let out an involuntary moan. Heat pooled in my core, and the air seemed to flicker, crackling around us. I shook my head, trying to ignore the primal, animalistic feeling that churned inside me at those words. I wanted—needed—more and at the same time needed him to put me down so I could run as far as I could in the opposite direction.

I squirmed, sliding from his grasp at last, but of course, he would not let me get far. It was only moments—seconds, really—before Bael was hauling me back. My back pressed against his chest, and I sucked in a breath, feeling his cock hard and thick against my ass.

Seeming to sense the need building inside me, Bael reached down with his free hand and cupped me between the legs over my trousers. I gasped as the heel of his hand ground into me, making the heat rise higher and higher around me and sending sparks of pleasure shooting up my spine.

"This is madness," I whimpered

"Why?"

"Because you told me we couldn't do this. If it's true that I can, er, kill you..."

Heat crept up my neck. Not that I should be embarrassed, given what we'd done last night, but somehow, the morbidity of it made me squirm.

Bael froze, as if just remembering that tiny problem, himself. "True," he admitted. "My entire family are cursed. We can't bond with our true mates, but that won't last forever. I'll have you eventually."

His fingers trailed over the waistband of my trousers, and even as he spoke, his long fingers eased the end of my belt through the closure. A small whimper I barely recognized escaped parted lips as he grazed the points of his teeth lightly over my skin. He nipped against where my pulse pounded in my throat, and I pressed my back firmer against his chest.

"What do you mean it won't last forever?" I asked breathlessly, trying desperately to focus.

Bael ground his hips harder against my ass, causing both of us to groan with mingled pleasure and frustration. His fingers trailed down, dipping into the front of my trousers, and he buried his nose against my throat.

"It means—" he said, tracing delicate circles slowly over my center, seeming to punctuate his words. "—that I'm going to lift the curse. It means, little monster, that this changes everything."

My stomach dipped, somewhere between excitement and fear. He'd made the Everlast's curse sound like a lifelong sentence. Something insurmountable that couldn't ever be lifted. Perhaps that was why this had not yet fully sunk in for me—what would it mean to be Bael's mate, the mate of any fairy, if the bond could be completed? And what would happen if it never was?

More importantly for me—us—how did it work that he was using my magic? I needed to warn him to stop before something terrible happened…but to do that, I'd have to explain what I knew, and that would mean trusting him. Admitting this could be real.

"Open your legs wider for me, little monster."

Fuck. My eyes fell closed, and I sighed. How could I remember warnings and rules when he said things like that?

I moved to spread my legs for him, to help ease the trousers down over my ass. The air nipped at my skin, freezing the moisture from where my still-wet clothing had stuck to my now bare skin. I shivered. All I'd really managed to do was trap myself, half-naked, with my calves bound by the fabric gathered just above my boots. Somehow, though, I couldn't bring myself to care anymore.

That was, until I looked up, straight ahead, and my eyes met nothing but dark woods…but for how long? This was hardly a good time to lose concentration. At any moment, another fairy or some terrible creature might happen upon us. "What if someone sees?"

"Don't tell me you're suddenly shy. I thought you enjoyed being watched."

My stomach seemed to fall away, and I gasped. I hadn't realized he'd known about that, but he could only be talking about the other night when I'd come apart in his arms, spurred on by Scion's attention. "How?"

He chuckled darkly against my hair. "It's alright, little monster. I don't mind sharing."

An embarrassing heat washed over me again as I was reminded of my dream. He couldn't mean like that, though. Of all the impossible things, I would say that felt more unlikely than my ever becoming queen in the first place.

Bael resumed his stroking, then plunged a finger inside of me, and a ripple of pleasure fluttered through me. I moaned and ground harder against him, smiling slightly when he twitched against my ass.

I reached back and ran my hand over his length, holding in a groan when it grew impossibly thicker beneath my touch.

Bael moved his free hand to my hair, scraping long, too-sharp nails against my scalp, and yanked my head back. "Stop, little monster, before you make me forget why I care to keep breathing."

I became boneless, letting my head fall back against his chest, my knees falling as wide as I could make them without tripping over my own trousers.

He made a sound of approval as his thumb found my clit, stroking over me in small, gentle circles that had sparks shooting to every part of my body. "I love how wet you are for me."

Small ripples of pleasure and comfort fluttered through me from the top of my head all the way down to the base of my spine, and I keened in his arms.

And then, just as my breath began to lose rhythm, he pressed two fingers inside me, curling against my inner walls. Bael ground the heel of his hand gently against my clit, still stroking inside me. He pushed my hair off my neck so he could run his tongue over my skin, as if tasting the sweat that had beaded there. "Do you want more, little monster?"

I shuddered, realizing I recognized the words. A coincidence, surely, but a good one. "Yes," I breathed.

He slid his fingers out slowly and then shoved them back in again, as if savoring the movement before picking up the pace.

My breath caught, and goosebumps erupted on my skin, and I knew I was about to be done for, yet Bael didn't let up, pumping harder into me so fast that his palm slapped against my clit with each punishing thrust.

I squirmed, the pressure almost too much, somewhere between pain and ecstasy, and choked as the sting of his hand drove me closer to an edge I wasn't familiar with.

I whimpered, my heart pounding so hard against my ribs it must have been audible outside to any nearby Fae, and I couldn't bring myself to care.

"Now, little monster," he demanded. "Come for me."

I couldn't have denied the order if I'd wanted to. Heat washed over me, and my inner walls clenched so tight I squeezed my eyes shut as every muscle in my body tightened painfully. I tried to press my thighs together, but Bael held them apart, and I shook, a cry falling from my mouth that was nothing like any sound I'd made before.

Stars broke behind my eyes, and I slumped back, panting against him.

Bael waited a beat until my breathing slowed slightly before turning me slowly around to face him. Our eyes met, and I had nothing left to say. Perhaps he was right, but there were so many confused emotions swirling inside of me I wasn't even sure myself.

I dragged the back of my hand over my mouth, and fleetingly, I became aware of pain and moisture coming from my lips. With a start, I realized I'd bit down on my own bottom lip. A shiver of fear and awareness traveled through me. *Instinct.* Was that what would take over if we were ever together for real?

6
LONNIE
THE DEPLETED QUARRY, INBETWIXT

The morning light dawned over Inbetwixt, and with it came the end of the second hunt.

During my last hunt—my only official one to date—I'd survived by crossing the finish line before anyone managed to hunt me down, taking the crown and the throne it represented by blood and force.

This time, my win was far less dramatic.

Once Bael arrived, I encountered no further trouble, causing me to wonder if his escorting me would make all hunts nothing more than a simple stroll in the woods. That almost seemed too easy, yet there had to be some reason that the Everlasts held on to their crown for so long, and it could not be simply that there were so many of them.

"Do not get used to it," I said out loud as the haunting sound of the hunting horn rang over the quarry, echoing far too loudly, as if it were right beside me and flowing through me at the same time.

Bael, walking beside me, was not listening. "Did you say something?"

"Er, no. Nothing." I looked over at him and did a double take, jolting in alarm. "What are you doing?"

His yellow eyes were invisible, only the whites showing as they rolled up into the back of his head as if he were having a fit. Oddly, though, he was having no difficulty walking in a straight line beside me. He blinked, and his eyes returned to normal.

"I thought I saw Scion's horrible, great bird lurking in a tree back there." He jabbed a thumb over his shoulder. "But now I can't find it."

"Were you looking at the trees just now?"

He nodded. "If you ever got around to practicing what you could do with your abilities, little monster, you may realize there are secondary applications that may not seem obvious at first."

"What do you mean?" I asked, curious in spite of myself.

"Magic is like any other skill. You may be born with a natural affinity, but you still must hone the skill over many years to be worth a damn at using it.

Was he saying that offhand, or was it meant to be instructional? I shook my head, refusing to indulge the trail of questions and self-loathing that would arise if I let myself wander too far down the path of "what if."

"And what's *your* natural affinity?" I asked, hoping to distract him into changing the subject.

I recalled a comment that Aine had made once about her brother's magic and how I likely did not know what his abilities were. That, coupled with the cage, pulled at my curiosity.

Bael looked from me to the smoke rising from a campfire some twenty feet ahead of us. We'd almost reached the camp where the group from the capital had set up. He gave me a sheepish smile. "You will think this is too convenient, but I'd rather not discuss it near others. I'll show you when we have more privacy."

I narrowed my eyes. "I'll hold you to that."

"See that you do."

Perhaps it was due to the prince at my side as I walked unaided back into the camp on the edge of the quarry, but there was far less fanfare than I'd expected. No snide glances. No whispered comments. Yet, that was not to say that no one noticed us.

All eyes turned to me and Bael as we strode back into the camp. Colorful tents, reminiscent of those that had filled the clearing on the edge of the Waywoods last year, stood erect in a haphazard circle, campfires and tables overflowing with food set between them. Servants and guards milled around, some attending to lesser nobles, some seeming to try to look busy or already packing up their horses to leave.

We made a beeline for the golden tent at the back, where Enid had unpacked my things the previous afternoon. No one said a word to us, but there was the occasional bow or lowering of the eyes. *Strange. Just…impossibly strange.*

"Where is everyone?" I asked.

Bael let his arms hang loosely by his sides, as casual as anything. "What do you mean?"

I worried my bottom lip, thinking of the mob that had formed outside the castle last month. "I suppose I expected a crowd like at the first hunt."

"Inbetwixt has never been the most elaborate of hunting grounds," Bael replied. "Likely, it's due to their culture. In other provinces, grudges will be held off for years before they play out in the hunts. In Inbetwixt, violence is a more common practice, so the hunts are less sensational. I don't believe a hunting season has ever ended in Inbetwixt, much to their chagrin, I'm sure."

I furrowed my eyebrows. "You say that as though you've seen a hunt before, but that's impossible. The last one would have been…what? Hundreds of years before you were born?"

Fae might be immortal, appearing young and beautiful far longer than humans did, but they still showed signs of aging in their own way: lighter hair, wiser eyes, more scars from battles long ago. Even if Bael hadn't told me that he was only in his mid-thirties in human years, I still would have guessed he was young from demeanor alone.

He grinned. "Ah, but I've seen enough of them to feel as if I've been there, little monster, but that is also an explanation for later —when we are not in the open."

A raven cried in the distance as we walked further into the camp, making the ominous feeling all the more obvious. People seemed to go stiff, and all conversations ended as we passed.

"I still think something feels off. I only saw one group of hunters, and you were not picking them off this time, as last time, correct?"

He shook his head. "No."

"That's odd then, and does it seem…tense to you?"

Bael glanced around, as if only just realizing anyone else was present. "I could only guess. I have hardly spoken to everyone here."

I struggled not to roll my eyes. The Everlast family as a whole had a nasty habit of forgetting to give me even the most basic information, then berating me for ignorance. Bael was perhaps the least guilty of this, but that was not a glowing endorsement. "I'll take it. Your 'guess' would be better than the silence I am usually graced with."

"I suspect many thought you would die last night, and yet here you are, uninjured."

"Well, none of you came to hunt me," I said uncomfortably.

"Yes," Bael agreed, his lip curling in a feline smile. "And what does that say to the people? They're trying to decide if their impression of you was incorrect and if they've made any missteps so far if you turn out to be a larger threat than they anticipated."

I remembered Prince Scion's taunting after the first hunt—that if none of the real competitors were present, I could hardly call myself the winner. In this case, I almost agreed with him. I bit the inside of my cheek and shook myself—that was an absurd line of thinking, ungrateful at best and suicidal at worst. I'd always thought curiosity would kill me. Now, complacency seemed the greater threat.

I shook my head, and a few strands of filthy hair fell into my face. I gestured down at myself, still covered in drying mud and scratches from the quarry. "This is hardly the picture of a threat."

He looked me up and down. "I don't think you see yourself very clearly, little monster. To me, it simply looks like you survived."

I felt a heat crawl up the back of my neck and shrunk under the weight of his compliment.

"And if you want information," he added seemingly as an afterthought, "might I suggest you start asking better questions."

PART ONE

Bael held the flap of my tent open, and I ducked under his arm and stepped inside, only to jump at the sound of a small gasp.

Beside the bed on the far side of the tent, a girl with mouse-brown hair in a long braid whirled to face me. Enid dropped the gown she'd been folding and reached down, as if to pull an invisible weapon from her pocket. "Y-you're back."

"Don't sound so disappointed." I raised my eyebrows at her, glancing at her twitching hand by her side. "And you're unprepared. If you want to fight, get yourself a knife or something."

She flushed and looked from me to Bael. "I wouldn't."

I pressed my lips together, not entirely sure I believed that, but it wasn't the most pressing thing at the moment.

The tent was small but extremely well furnished, given that we'd only used it for travel. A small bed took up most of the space, and a table with a washbasin and a plate of fruit sat beside it to the right. At the foot of the bed, there was a large traveling trunk, on which sat a silver mirror and a hairbrush.

I crossed to the trunk and, tossing the mirror and brush on the bed, began rifling through it for something dry to wear. What I really wanted was a bath, but that was still likely out of reach until we returned to the obsidian palace. The best I could do was to be dry and perhaps get a few hours of sleep before we set off again.

"Did you watch?" I asked Enid absently as I shoved a mountain of fine garments aside, searching for something simple.

When Enid didn't answer, I pulled my head out of the trunk and looked up at her. She wasn't watching me but rather had fearful, narrowed eyes fixed on Bael. For his part, the grinning golden-haired prince seemed to be pretending he couldn't see her, feigning interest in the embroidery on my bedspread.

"Enid?" I asked lightly.

She jumped. "Oh, right. What did you say?"

I frowned. I could sympathize with her dilemma. If I stood where Enid was, I'd be thinking about all the many ways my tongue might be cut out later for misstepping.

"Could you leave us for a few minutes?"

To my surprise, Bael shook his head. "Apologies, little monster."

I wrinkled my nose when he gave no explanation and did not continue.

Making wide eyes, I gestured down at myself. "But I need to dress."

He scoffed. "And what? Are you trying to preserve your modesty? Don't be absurd—that is long since forsaken."

I choked and threw Enid a nervous look. He was right, of course, but embarrassment still washed over me. "I wouldn't say that, exactly."

"What would you say?" He gave me a mischievous grin, and I could swear his eyes flicked to the servant behind me. "Be explicit, and I will fill in anything you forget. Or, we could simply talk of the fact that I saw all you have to offer on your first night in—"

"Alright!" I screeched, throwing my hands up in defeat. "Just stay out of the way, then."

He laughed, seeming to take humor in my discomfort, and went to lie on the bed, throwing one arm over his eyes as if he were sleeping. My stomach turned over at the realization that if he never intended to leave, there would be nowhere else for me to sleep but in the foot of space beside him. *One problem at a time.*

With a shake of my head, I turned back to Enid. Heat crept up my neck when I found her as I'd expected: her mouth hanging open slightly, her expression just shy of accusatory. To be fair, she'd been in the room last night when Bael had quite literally dragged me to his bedchamber by my hair, so this could not have been a total shock.

I gestured down at my ruined clothes. "Could you help me?"

She nodded curtly and nudged me out of the way of the trunk, taking over searching with far more efficiency than I'd shown. "I suppose I should congratulate you on your win."

"You would be the first. It's not as though I have legions of admirers."

The edges of Enid's cheekbones turned slightly pink, and she sniffed disapprovingly. "You certainly seem to have enough."

I pressed my lips together and tossed my head toward Bael. "One, maybe."

Enid and I had a tempestuous relationship. We had not been friends when we were both servants, mostly because she was afraid of what my proximity to the Fae might do. Enid cared little for anyone else but herself and detested thrill-seekers and those who might put her in danger. It was easy to see why I might be a problem. Still, now she viewed me as her safest option, and I was fine with that.

"I brought the books as you wished," Enid said as she finally straightened, a plum-silk nightgown in hand. "They are in the bottom of the trunk."

I cast Bael a nervous glance before forcing a benign smile onto my face. "Thank you."

Enid nodded. "Of course."

"Did you watch?" I asked again, hoping to change the subject. "The hunt, I mean."

She shook her head. "They are not all that well suited for spectators. I wonder if that's to encourage participation."

I knew this, of course, when it came to the hunt in the capital. Still, villagers lined the edge of the woods anyway, as something of a holiday, regardless of the practicality. "No, I don't think so," I said, more to myself than her. "It's simply not designed to be a festival."

Not that I could tell Enid, but Bael had explained the true purpose of the hunts to me during the same conversation when he revealed his family curse.

The Everlasts had been cursed by their ancestors to never be able to experience happiness until their crown was returned to a worthy wearer. They'd designed the hunts not with governing in mind but as a way to find someone to lift their curse. Whoever could take the crown, then defend it would, in theory, be worthy of it. This, I could only assume, was why none of them wanted me to have it. Whether through death or bargain, they'd all been adamant that I return the crown since the moment I touched it. It seemed that none of them, even Bael, thought I could ever be worthy.

That begged the question, though: if not them and not me, then who? Bael's desire to lift the curse was worth nothing without a plan; he had suggested himself that I ask better questions. Perhaps I would start there.

As soon as she'd helped me to dress in some soft, plum-silk sleeping clothes and brushed out my matted hair, Enid made a quick escape. She claimed to want me to "rest" before we traveled again, but I wasn't sure what sort of rest she was expecting, as Bael didn't look willing to give me a single moment to myself. Perhaps she didn't care as long as it meant she could leave the tent.

"Were you planning on moving?" I asked, anyway, placing my hands on my hips.

Bael shifted his arm so one yellow eye became visible. "Perhaps eventually. It depends what motivation you provide, little monster."

I sighed. "I don't feel like playing one of your riddle games. I have barely slept in two nights."

The corner of his mouth twitched, and I knew he was remembering *why* I had not slept the night before the hunts. To my surprise, however, he did not bring it up. "What was the servant referring to?"

I stiffened. I'd thought he was listening—it would have been impossible not to. "What do you mean?"

Bael looked down his nose at me. "Feigned ignorance doesn't suit you."

I looked down. I thought that might have been a compliment, but it was hard to tell. "If you are going to tell me again about how I owe you my secrets, you would be better off waiting until I've slept and am in a better mood."

Bael cocked his head at me, considering. "I was not going to say that," he replied, leaning back against the pillows. "Owe me nothing, if that's what you want. Keep all your secrets, but perhaps consider that you owe it to yourself to share the burden."

I jerked as if struck. He couldn't realize it, but he'd inadvertently said something I'd already been wondering—something I was afraid to voice, even to myself.

My entire life, I'd been taught to never draw attention to myself, to always lie and never get close to anyone. My mother spent years instilling her lessons, and even as time went on and I stopped following every single rule, I never forgot that I was always supposed to lie about who I was.

Yet now, when I was completely and utterly alone, I was realizing every day that maybe my mother had been wrong. After all, both she and my sister had kept secrets, and they'd taken those secrets to early graves.

"So, what?" I said caustically. "I'm just supposed to trust you?"

Bael turned only his head and raised an eyebrow at me. "Why not me?"

I opened my mouth and then closed it again. For some reason, none of my typical responses—"because you're Fae," "because you're a prince," or simply, "because I hate you"—felt quite right on my tongue. I didn't want to think too hard about why that was and, more so, why I cared.

Fortunately, Bael filled the silence, seeming not to notice my internal struggle. "If you don't trust me for me, or because I quite literally cannot hurt you, then perhaps consider that whatever you are concerned about, I might be better equipped than most to help you."

That, at least, was true. Only an Everlast would have the resources to find anyone in Elsewhere or seek the answers to any question. I bit my lip, walking slowly to the trunk to buy myself time.

Bending low, I undid the latch yet again and opened the heavy wooden lid with a creak.

Sure enough, on the floor of the trunk, beneath a mountain of embroidered trousers and silk riding jackets, sat a stack of worn and faded books with no titles printed on the covers. My lips tipped up with a smile. Once again, something had gone right—after so long with not a single moment of joy, not one tiny success, several in a row was almost overwhelming. *I really should not get used to this.*

I grabbed the first journal off the top of the stack and closed the trunk with a snap, holding it tight to my chest as I breathed in deeply through my nose and crossed the tent to stand beside the bed. Bael looked up at me through his lashes.

"What's your magical affinity?" I asked. "You said you would show me when we were alone."

He tensed slightly but did not seem surprised, and I thought he must understand the question for what it was: a bargain. Only once he answered my question would I answer his.

Bael sat up. "Are you asking better questions now, little monster?"

"I don't know what you consider to be 'better,' but I have many questions, and you won't get anything from me for free anymore."

His face split into a wicked grin. "How very Fae of you."

My stomach turned over. I wasn't sure I liked that comparison, or the undeniable truth of it, but I wasn't about to back down. "Stop stalling."

He glanced around the tent, his eyes finally landing on the plate of fruit on my bedside table I'd left nearly untouched. "Give me that."

His smile faltered, the grin no longer reaching his eyes as he plucked a slice of orange off the plate with two fingers. He held it out in front of me, just inches in front of my face, and I had to lean back so as not to go cross-eyed.

I watched, transfixed, as the orange seemed to shimmer in his palm, then crumbled, turning to dust before my eyes, just like he'd done with the apple so many months ago.

I realized I was holding my breath. "Illusion?"

He shook his head. "Time."

7
BAEL
THE WILDES, INBETWIXT

The monster in my head was hungry,

The scent of honey and magic overwhelmed the tent, welcoming and comforting in a way that no other scent was. Except, perhaps, the scent of death. Both were soothing to the creature, driving him further dormant.

Dormant, sleeping, but never completely gone.

"Are you alright, little monster?" I inquired, forcing my voice into a light, neutral tone that felt so unnatural I could have growled instead.

The monster was a constant presence and keeping it at bay a daily battle. It rose when I was too tired or drained. On nights when the dead were loudest, and my other abilities made it too hard to ignore.

Lonnie looked up at me, her motions brisk and unnatural. "Yes," she answered rigidly.

Like fucking hell she is.

Lonnie's entire body seemed to quiver with nerves as she leaned toward me to inspect the dust in my hand. One curl of her unruly red hair had already sprung free from its braid, and it was an effort not to reach out and correct it for her. My jaw tensed, and I looked up at the ceiling, trying not to think about how easy it would be to reach out and grab her, have her flat on this bed before she'd even caught her breath.

Perhaps I'm the one who isn't alright, then.

My little monster put her fingers out lightly and touched the dust in my palm as if it were poison. "You…killed it?" she breathed, sounding uncertain. "Even though it wasn't alive?"

I let out a small breath. If she was still asking absurd questions, at least she wasn't thinking of all the ways I might murder her. Not that I could or would harm her—not now—but she didn't seem to understand that.

"You could think of it that way. If anything is left unattended long enough, it would rot or crumble and eventually return to the earth. I have an affinity for time—for speeding it along in small amounts and for communicating with those who once walked where we now stand."

"Can you do that to living creatures? Speed them along?"

I nodded. "Does that scare you?"

She swallowed thickly, and I watched, fascinated, as the muscles in her throat worked.

"It should," she said finally.

The monster in the back of my mind purred.

Lonnie feared Fae, at least in the abstract. The irony of that floored me, but it didn't make it any less true. I'd never before cared if anyone was afraid of me—I welcomed it, in fact, as a simple fact of life—yet I didn't want her to be afraid. The fact that she wasn't was proof she wasn't ignoring all her instincts. Some part of her knew we were connected.

"I thought your magic was all hereditary?" she asked suddenly.

I was glad she could not hear my heartbeat speed up at her question. "It is."

"But no one else has this power."

I paused. It was my own fault for telling her to ask better questions—admittedly, that was quite a good one. "My mother is a seer like Queen Celia, which is a more passive form of time manipulation, and my father—" I broke off awkwardly. "Might be a story for another time."

She sat up straighter, clearly sensing my tension. "Why?"

Because I'm enjoying you not being afraid of me, and that truth would likely send you sprinting for the trees.

I ran a hand over the back of my neck. She'd likely find out soon enough, anyway. If I was certain beyond any doubt that she had accepted what I knew to be true—that we were mates—I might have told her now. But not yet.

Discovering her and yet not being able to claim her was making it harder to maintain the façade of calm that had become my personality over many years of repetition. The beast was too close to the surface, making me quicker to anger, agitated, erratic.

I'd managed to keep her away last month, but now that she'd seen the cage—now that I couldn't stay away from her—I doubted the monster would allow such a long separation.

I'd long suspected that I might have better control over my two halves if I wasn't forced to keep one contained, letting it out only when it became too hard to ignore—usually once a month. But, of course, I'd never been able to test that theory. Unseelie abilities couldn't be allowed to simply flourish in the High Fae court.

It wasn't exactly a secret that I had a different father than my brother and sister—you only had to look at us twice to start asking questions, after all—yet the identity of my father had always been closely guarded, and for good reason. If anyone looked too deeply into how my existence came to be, unions like my mother and Auberon, Gwydion and Thalia, or Penvalle and Mairead would suddenly make less sense.

Secrets were only kept if no one asked questions.

"Because that is a more valuable secret, little monster, and if you are looking to bargain, then I will not lay down all I have on the first round."

She narrowed her gaze, and I could practically see the wall of suspicion falling over her eyes. *Two steps forward, a hundred back.*

It was likely for the best—better for both of us if she kept some distance—but it was torture to consider.

Everything about this was fucking torture.

It had been growing worse for weeks, but I hadn't fully recognized it for what it was. Perhaps because of the unusual way in which I'd discovered our bond. Casual sex wasn't unusual in the court, and most Fae who found their mate did so that way. I'd never heard of it happening this way, where the blood was exchanged first.

For a normal bond, the frenzy would be immediate and then die down once fulfilled, but I only felt more unstable by the hour.

I could already feel myself rationalizing alternatives—ways to keep her if I could not find the person meant to break the curse. Perhaps if we never shared blood again, it could work. I might be able to have her without dooming myself and everyone I loved. My teeth ached at the very idea—not a good sign.

The monster in my mind might crave her, hunger for her surrender, but every other part of me knew to stay away. I was already too deeply invested in this woman, far more than I ever should have been, and if I allowed her any closer, I feared that the walls of self-control I'd built between myself and the creature sharing my mind would crumble altogether.

"Your turn," I managed to say, my voice coming out more like a snarl than I'd intended.

Lonnie looked at me strangely, and I wished I could see myself through her eyes. Had something changed? *Perhaps I'm already too far gone. Not thinking clearly.*

She scowled but let out a long breath. "Fine, but I do not have quite so clear an answer as you seem to believe I must."

I raised a surprised eyebrow. I honestly was not expecting her to hold up her end of the small bargain. Humans, unlike Fae, did not take their word seriously. That aside, I was half-convinced she believed her own lies, likely the product of so many years ignoring or denying magic that it had gone almost dormant. Detangling her misbelief from the truth would be more difficult than simply discovering for myself what she was capable of.

She sat on the edge of the bed, legs hanging over the side, and looked down at the book in her hands. It was filthy, shabby around the edges, with loose pages sticking out of the top and nothing on the cover, yet she held it like a priceless treasure.

"Before my sister died," she said without looking at me, "she'd kept these journals. She wrote in them every day since we learned to write, and I've never read them."

I raised an eyebrow at that, tempted to question her assertion.

Never? Never once had she looked? That seemed like something a sibling might do. I would know, having two myself. Before I could ask, however, she continued:

"For the last month, I'd been looking for them. I keep wondering if I'll find something about what caused her death. We were—" She paused. "—very different when she was alive. I had no idea she was part of the rebellion, and I keep wondering what would have happened if I'd read her journal just once. If she'd be alive now."

My stomach clenched with something like guilt. I didn't handle emotional upheaval well but wished I could have, for her sake. Sorrow was a grayscale emotion I had never mastered, somewhere in the shadows between pleasure and rage. I would have gone to fucking war to protect her, but I didn't know how to talk to her about her grief.

"Your servant has seen them?" I asked stiffly, knowing it was hardly the right response.

She shook her head. "I had to leave them in the garden the other night. Enid found them for me."

I waited, expecting her to offer more, but she merely stared down at the book. Perhaps she wished to read them alone? Should I allow that?

It felt…different to consider anyone's feelings over the most practical course of action, and I couldn't say I liked it. I'd never worried about anyone's feelings before now, but I held my breath, waiting to see if she shoved me away.

"If I keep putting this off, I'll lose my nerve altogether," she said finally, letting out a short breath.

I nodded, still not sure I was following what she wanted to do. Indeed, I kept becoming distracted by the pulse in her throat and the way the silk of her nightgown clung around the curves of her body. Entirely inappropriate given the circumstances, but the monster didn't care for secrets or politics, only for claiming his mate.

Lonnie moved up the bed until she was sitting against the headboard, her small shoulder just brushing mine, and placed the book against her raised knees. Flipping the cover open, she held it flat and began to read.

I waited stiffly for a moment, unsure if I was invited to join her and even more unsure if I cared. Finally, I leaned closer to peer over her shoulder. I sucked in a breath, her honey scent overwhelming me, and balled my hands in my lap. My heart pounded in my rib cage like a war drum.

Focus.

For fuck's sake, we were supposed to be reading the words of a dead woman, and all I could think about was sinking my cock into her all-too-alive sister beside me.

Perhaps Lonnie did have a reason to be afraid after all.

I shifted against the headboard, letting the sharp wooden ridges dig uncomfortably into my back, and dug my nails so hard into my palms I was sure I'd drawn blood. Then, finally, when the pain had cleared the fog in my brain slightly, I began to read…

8
ROSEY

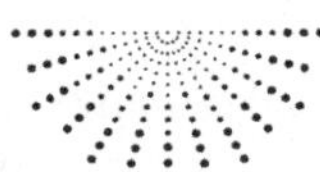

WRITTEN WINTER, SIX MONTHS BEFORE THE DEATH OF KING PENVALLE

NINE DAYS TO YULE:

I found myself on a ship headed for Nevermore. An icy fog coated the deck, so thick I was nearly blind to the waves crashing over the sides of the ship. The salt air stung my nose and throat, and each breath became like shards of ice stabbing through my chest. The wind howled in my ears, and I tried to run for cover, yet my boots felt like lead weights as they slipped continuously over the wet deck. Another sailor approached, shaking my shoulders. "They're boarding!" he screamed in my face. "We'll fucking lose everything."

I had no answers for him. I knew we'd lose far more than cargo and wished I'd argued harder against this trip.

Even now, writing this, I feel quite certain that whatever that ship is carrying, both the cargo and the sailors will sink before the new year.

YULE:

The dream of the valley haunted me again last night. I can only assume this is nothing more than a memory, as I only ever find myself looking on from what I think must be my own eyes. I don't recall ever seeing him in the old house, but little else makes sense—I only wish I could be certain. The image of myself at that age is vague and hazy around the edges. I could just as easily be watching myself as Lonnie; it feels like we were sharing a single face.

FOUR DAYS UNTIL THE COMING OF DANU (NEW YEAR):

Last night, I know I was close to finding him again.

The dream was the most vivid in weeks. I was sitting in a tavern in Inbetwixt. The table was sticky, and the air was thick with smoke, and the crowd pulsed around me like a living, breathing thing. I could barely hear the woman next to me over the din, but it didn't matter. She wasn't the one I was waiting for.

"Oi," someone yelled in my ear. "You the one here about the ships?"

I turned to face the other man and felt my face twist in a sneer. "Keep your voice down, you fucking soft-handed fool."

The other male looked affronted. "I won't stay where I'm going to be insulted by some Slúagh-born savage from Wanderlust."

I gritted my teeth and bit back another retort. I might have hit him, but Ambrose needed this kid alive. At least for now.

TWO DAYS AFTER THE COMING OF DANU (NEW YEAR):

Nothing clear this week. Not sleeping well. Went to visit Ciara in the village for a calming draft and heard a storm sunk several merchant ships from Inbetwixt.

9
LONNIE

THE WILDES, INBETWIXT

I stared down at my sister's journal in confusion…or, perhaps, disbelief. My hand shook slightly, and I was almost afraid to turn the page.

Disappointment washed over me, and I held my breath, trying not to give in to the wave of grief that threatened to follow.

The first entry itself was entirely nonsensical and sounded nothing like Rosey at all. It was a dream, I supposed, that she was describing. Nothing else made sense.

Bael exhaled sharply beside me, and I shuddered, the feel of his breath just grazing my skin. "Your sister was a seer?" he asked in a tone that was more statement than question.

"No!" I said too fast, even as my stomach sank as he essentially confirmed what I'd been thinking. "I mean, not that I was aware of. She never said anything about it or exhibited a single sign."

He raised an eyebrow. "Aside from the journals, of course."

"What do you mean?"

"My grandmother kept books like this, as does my mother. I have some. Fuck, half our palace library is this sort of random musing—most seers get a barrage of information that they have to keep track of to find patterns."

"Like the boat?"

He nodded. "I'm damn curious to know if the boat comes up again. Sometimes, something as small as that could lead to a thread that predicts the outcome of a great war. Sometimes, it's just the weather. It's hard to say without knowing how powerful your sister was."

I gaped at him. "I...I have no idea."

He cocked his head to the side and bit the inside of his cheek. "Nor have I, but from that one page alone, I'd say she was above average."

"Even if she was a seer, this doesn't seem to be connected to how she died," I said, frustration creeping into my voice. "And if all the books are like this, I'll never know what she had to do with Dullahan."

Bael looked up at me sharply. "With Dullahan?"

"She'd joined the rebels," I told him. "That's the name of their leader, I suppose."

He laughed hollowly. "I know who he is, little monster."

My heartbeat sped up. I supposed that wasn't so surprising. I'd heard him mention the name earlier this evening, and it would have been more surprising if he wasn't aware of who his enemy was. After all, the rebellion had been going on for some years now, gaining strength in the North and pushing south, gaining strength and support from the non-noble classes in every province they targeted.

I gnawed on my lip, then slammed the book shut and placed it hurriedly on the nightstand beside me. "I don't want to talk about it anymore. I'm too tired. I—I need to go to bed."

It was a lie, and I was sure we were both well aware of it and one I felt somewhat guilty for. I simply could not continue this conversation—this line of thinking—right now. To go from no information about my sister, from sharing nothing at all, to possibly sharing everything? I could not. It was too much. Too overwhelming to take in one sitting.

I would peruse the rest later in private, and perhaps then I would tell him what I'd found.

For once, Bael didn't push me, for which I was infinitely grateful. Instead, his gaze darted down the bed and back up, lingering over my body. "Then, by all means."

I froze. I'd slept in far worse situations than beside a prince in a plush feather bed, yet suddenly, this seemed far more alarming than sitting beside each other to read or even another night on a dungeon floor or in the filthy servants' quarters.

The foot of space I'd expected to use as my own felt impossibly small in practice, and my heartbeat thrummed in alarm. As long as we did not touch each other, it wasn't all that difficult to remember all the reasons why I would be far better off staying away from Bael. However, even I couldn't ignore that when we got too close, it was nearly impossible to think straight.

"I don't feel like arguing with you about this." I gestured to the bed, a quaver of uncertainty in my voice. "I haven't slept in nearly two days."

I hoped he would assume that meant I was too tired to engage in any sort of sparring. Verbal or otherwise. In truth, I should have been tired. By all accounts, I should have been exhausted, but instead, my mind and body hummed with adrenaline and awareness.

He smirked. "Nor have I, if you recall."

Heat flared on my cheeks. I certainly did recall—the memory of that party in the field would likely be burned into my mind for the rest of my life.

My pulse quickened at the mere thought of all those bodies, wild and writhing. Of Bael's teeth against my skin and silver eyes meeting mine while we both came apart.

Without warning, Bael's hand shot out and closed around my upper thigh, tugging me closer. "Careful, little monster."

"With what?" I gasped, trying to steady myself before I fell on top of him.

"Controlling myself is hard enough when I'm with you, without your scent driving me fucking insane."

My eyes widened, mortification heating my cheeks. "S-sorry. Like I said, I'm tired."

He tightened his grip on my leg and gritted his teeth. "Well, think of something else."

He may as well have asked me to stop breathing. The moment he demanded I not think of sex, any other more important thing fled my brain, and suddenly, that was all I could imagine.

My mind flew, unbidden, to a tableau of the dreams I'd had over the last month.

Every time, I'd woken, gasping for breath with need pounding in my core, sweaty from the all-too-real memory of hot breath at my throat and fingers digging into my skin.

Oh no. No, no, no, no.

He could smell my arousal—this could not be happening. I squeezed my eyes shut and pressed my thighs together, willing myself to think of anything else. Anything but the whisper of Bael's voice behind me—*"Do you want more, little monster?"*—while Scion knelt at my feet, promising my pleasurable destruction.

"Fuck," Bael hissed, sounding angrier than I'd often heard him. "What are you trying to do to me?"

I jumped and sat up, my breathing uneven. "I should go. Or you should. This can't work."

He made no move to shy away from me, and I knew I shouldn't have been surprised. Like most Fae, Bael wasn't all that straightforward when it came to expressing his feelings, but he'd been downright direct about how difficult it was to be around me, which likely meant it was ten times worse than I'd thought. I needed to be the voice of reason for both of us.

I tried to pull away, tugging at his fingers still curled almost entirely around my upper thigh. "I want you to let go."

Instead, he reached around with his other arm and wrapped it around my waist, pulling me into his lap. "At least try and sound convincing," he purred. "We both know you're a better liar than that."

I shivered. We were almost nose to nose, and I could feel every breath, every quiver of movement, every inch of how hard he was against me. Worse, he was right—so right, it was almost painful. After the party in the field and what had happened mere hours ago in the woods, I should have been satisfied, but I was far from it. I had to imagine it was far, far worse for him. At least I'd had some relief. "Fine, maybe I don't want that, but this is still becoming more dangerous by the hour. You know you can't touch me like this."

He leaned his head forward a quarter of an inch to whisper in my ear. "I can't fuck you and mark you and share your blood because that would be a completed bond…but any one of those things individually?" He paused, and the tension nearly lit me ablaze. "Who knows? I have to believe there's some way around it."

My heartbeat sped up, pounding against my ribs. He could not possibly be serious. "You won't risk it."

"Wouldn't I?" The hand on my leg moved even higher, and I gasped when the inside of his thumb grazed the bare flesh of my thigh, mere inches from my core.

I let out an involuntary moan. He was barely touching me, but it was the anticipation that had wetness pooling between my thighs and my nipples hardening to tight buds in quivering need of his fingers finally brushing against them. I shifted on his lap and, in doing so, only brought his hand closer to my center. Our eyes met as his long fingers brushed against me. Awareness sparked in his eyes, and I beheld the moment he realized I wore nothing beneath the nightgown. His gaze flashed golden, and a predator stared back at me, hungry and wanting.

"It's not in my nature to be this restrained," he growled, yanking me harder against his chest. "What if I told you I don't care anymore? What if all I want is you?"

By Aisling, I should be terrified, but instead, a shiver of excitement traveled down my spine. "I know that you wouldn't risk your own life. Or your family's lives."

"You have no idea what I would do."

No, he was wrong. I knew exactly what he might do, and I had the uneasy feeling that if we let this continue much longer, we would find ourselves intimately familiar with the parameters of his family curse, and while I could not say that I would be heartbroken to lose most of them…that was not true of all.

"This is dangerous," I said distractedly, my voice trailing off a bit at the end. "You'll die."

I trembled slightly as I pushed up on my knees and reached down to pull the nightgown over my head. I was, indeed, wearing nothing beneath it, and I watched as his eyes dilated, then trailed over me in an appreciative way that made me feel as if he were running warm hands all down my body rather than just looking.

"You are not making a very good case for my family's lives, little monster," he said with a harsh laugh. "Or mine, for that matter. I might die to touch you, but at least I would die happily."

Heat burned up my chest and neck, blooming over my face. No one had ever said anything like that about me, ever, and it was hard to imagine he could be serious, if only for the fact that he couldn't be lying.

I took a deep breath, and somehow feeling more vulnerable even than I had in the woods, I said, "Just hold me?"

He looked slightly taken aback but immediately tugged his shirt off and then opened his arms for me to lie against his chest.

I sighed, relaxing as soon as I hit that almost too-warm skin. This was what I'd wanted. What was more terrifying by far to want than sex was comfort.

Which, I supposed, was hardly surprising. For me, who'd grown up in the Fae court where sex was abundant but comfort was negligible. Even I, who'd been treated as a pariah most of my life, was never short of offers for a night, a week, perhaps a few months in the case of those like Caliban. My face might have afforded me that, but I could not remember the last time anyone held me like this. Perhaps when I was a child or maybe the occasional hug from my sister.

"Say something," I said as Bael tugged the blanket up around me.

"I was just thinking that I'm a larger monster than I thought for not realizing you would be exhausted." He shook his head. "I truly cannot think straight lately. It's…alarming."

I yawned. "Is that an effect of the mating?"

He stiffened. "You said it?"

I tilted my head to look up at him. "What?"

"You have not been mentioning the bond."

It was my turn to stiffen. He was right, of course, and I still was not sure I wanted to acknowledge it. Still wasn't sure it was something I could accept. "Tell me about how it works," I said as I tried to swallow another yawn.

I closed my eyes and felt him pick up a lock of my hair, twisting it between his fingers. Mating bonds are sealed through sex and sharing blood on both sides," he explained. "You could do that with anyone, I suppose, and share their power. It would create a bond, but it wouldn't be a fated bond. That's taboo, though, even among married couples."

"Why?" I asked, eyes still closed.

"Because fated mates have comparable power levels. An unequal bond almost always results in the death of one partner. Like, you remember the story of Aisling?"

"Mmmhmm."

I was not sure I ever wanted to hear about Aisling again. I'd gone my whole life knowing only the barest amount about history, but since moving into the royal area of the palace, I'd had more lectures on history and politics than I ever would have imagined were possible…and I suspected we were barely scratching the surface.

"Aisling had three mates because she was the most powerful queen of her age," Bael continued. "She was powerful enough to sustain the power of three other Fae kings, but I suspect they were not fated mates, merely a political match, or else they wouldn't have died. I presume that they drained themselves to save her."

His words were starting to blur together into a dream tableau, where I felt as if I could see what he was saying. The queen. Her mates. The attack of the Unseelie…

"But there were four of them," I mumbled. "Were her mates not also bonded to each other?"

I felt him shrug. "I don't know, little monster. This was, of course, seven thousand years ago. However, I have always suspected that they were not. If all four were bonded to each other by blood, then that's unlikely to have happened, but they were probably only bonded to her. You have to remember that she mated with the individual kings of three separate nations to bring them all together, so I can imagine that perhaps they were not a perfectly aligned family unit."

I thought I asked another question. I felt myself slipping away into sleep.

Smoke filled the air, blinding me, choking me, as I ran.

My feet pounded a familiar, violent rhythm against the stone floor of the corridor that I knew led to the kitchens. Screams followed me. Screams and crying, the sounds of crumbling stone and metal against metal. The air was hot and oppressive, and I coughed, feeling as if my lungs were scorched from the inside out.

Ahead, shadows moved—people running, half-obscured by the smoke. There was light behind them. The door, I guessed, and yet I didn't run toward it.

Turning a sharp corner, I thundered down another hall, even as my head swam. The nausea still churning in my stomach threatened to send me to the ground, but I willed myself to remain on my feet. Just a bit further. Only a few more steps.

I—we—would not die here.

I ran, faster, faster, reaching a familiar door and shoving it open. Darkness engulfed me. Shadows. Spinning. Falling.

I slammed too hard into something solid, arms coming around to catch me. I looked up and recoiled—the face of the stranger, unusual. Unclear.

Hidden, as if by a mask.

10
LONNIE
THE ROAD TO EVERLAST CITY

In the morning, I barely remembered my dreams as we packed up the camp and departed for the capital. In short order, the procession of fairy horses walked in a perfectly straight line carrying all the lovely High Fae through the Waywoods—a perfectly straight line that was marred only by me.

Fae horses did not like human riders. It was a universal truth that had managed to derail many journeys before now and would hold true today. My horse bucked and kicked, veering off the path more times than I could count, stopping the party over and over as it tried to dislodge me from my saddle.

"At least we know you're partially human," Bael drawled, riding up beside me on his own enormous chestnut horse. "Would you care for assistance?"

I clung to the horse's neck for dear life, peering at her through its mane as I swung back and forth like a leaf in the wind. "No, I'm fine. It is the beast that is having the difficulty, not me."

Upside down, I watched Bael's lip twitch as if trying not to laugh. "How did you make it all the way to the quarry in the first place? I am shocked you didn't die on the way."

A gasp escaped my lips as my horse turned in a circle, jumping and bucking wildly. "You would know if you had been there."

"I assure you, I am regretting missing the show."

"And I am regretting not simply making my escape while all your backs were turned," I grunted through gritted teeth.

Despite my protest, Bael reached out one gloved hand and grabbed my reins.

The horse calmed immediately, and I rolled my eyes, even as I struggled to catch my breath. It seemed as if nothing was ever easy in Elsewhere, especially for humans, and I was loath to admit it, but I was grateful for the momentary reprieve.

"If you must know, I rode in a carriage on the way," I sniffed. "Also a mistake, apparently. I thought you were all in the other carriages. If I'd known I was alone with only the servants, I would have taken the opportunity to run."

Bael smirked at me. "Haven't I warned you enough never to run, little monster? One might start to think you like being chased."

Inbetwixt was the closest neighbor to the capital, so even accounting for my difficulty with the horse, the trip back from the hunting grounds only took half a day's ride. Of course, Bael could have carried us much faster through the shadows, but I didn't like traveling that way on the few occasions I'd done so, and he'd made no objections to my refusal.

"Taking you with me at that distance would use far more energy than I feel like wasting," he'd said. "It would be more efficient to teach you to shadow walk on your own."

I recoiled, almost laughing at the thought. "I could never!"

He'd merely pressed his lips together as if withholding comment. Rather than replying verbally, he held out a hand, wiggling his fingers at me.

"Put that out!"

Just as they had before, dancing blue and white flames appeared in his palm. He was holding it there as we rode, like balancing an egg on the end of a spoon in some sort of children's game. "Why?" he asked, grinning over at me. "Scared?"

"No," I lied, glancing around as if the enormous serpent with the ominous warning, or perhaps something worse, might spring from the bushes. "I'm…I can't think when you might set us ablaze at any moment."

He cocked his head to the side. "Now *that*"—he put too much emphasis on the word, as if it were supposed to mean something to me— "would be impossible. I couldn't hurt you even if I wanted to. Mates can't use magic against each other."

I ignored that. No matter how many times he said the word "mate," it was not going to sound any less foreign to me. Every time he said it, my stomach did an odd lurch—not unpleasant, exactly, but certainly uncomfortable. Like I was falling down stairs.

"Prince Scion's magic doesn't affect me either," I pointed out. "And he'd love nothing more than to see me dead, so that's hardly evidence of anything."

Bael seemed to consider that for a moment before brushing it off as if the words had never been said. "Hmmm. Well, if you're not going to practice using your abilities, someone should."

"I don't care to practice."

"You might be able to shadow walk. It's not overly difficult, you know."

"I don't care," I practically yelled. "Just put it out!"

I didn't want to shadow walk any more than I wanted to discuss the fire or what might or might not happen if he continued to play with it. Anyway, shadow walking would only bring us back to the capital faster, and I was in no great hurry to see the obsidian palace again.

Returning to the palace would also mean returning to my daily torment of politics, taunts, and threats. I didn't for one moment believe that it was by chance I'd avoided Prince Scion two hunts in a row and could only assume he was planning some new torture to spring on me at an unsuspecting moment. Bael might act as a shield, but he couldn't be with me every waking hour, especially as I knew he disappeared for at least several days every month.

"You will have to give up on this denial eventually, little monster."

I did not reply as I glanced at the golden-haired prince, taking in his sharp profile as he rode beside me, guiding my reins. He leaned forward in his saddle, and his muscles made the fine silk of his jacket pull slightly, reminding me that while he may dress like a court-fly, that was far from the reality. What secret would he like in exchange for the answer to the riddle of his monthly disappearance?

I chewed on that question as we continued to ride in the direction of the village on the edge of the city of Everlast. The capital was, of course, named for the royal family and was broken up into two distinct districts: the free human village, often called Cheapside, and the upper city, which was home to High Fae of non-noble descent who did not live at the court itself.

"As soon as we return, I need to find Scion," Bael told me.

I opened my mouth, then closed it again, biting my tongue. I wasn't precisely sure if he was asking for my input or my company or simply stating a fact. "Why?"

"He was near certain before I left that something would occur during the hunt. It's nothing you need to worry about, little monster."

Nothing I need to worry about. Of course not, because I didn't actually *do* anything. I sighed, my smile fading. "I suppose I will return to my room, then..."

I trailed off, leaving the question open-ended, my stomach sinking further. This was only serving to remind me of all the problems that had not seemed so apparent in the tent last night but in the light of day felt glaringly obvious, and it took every bit of my energy to hold his gaze.

It wasn't that I wanted to join him in whatever discussion he intended to have with Scion. Indeed, I felt my heart quicken in trepidation at the mere thought of the Prince of Ravens. Scion always provoked a dark thunderstorm of emotions in me—fear, loathing, and an unsettling pull that I could never explain, even to myself.

No, it was more that Bael had reminded me of how aimless my existence was within this palace. How I had no purpose, no daily tasks, but to be moved about by those around me as a pawn rather than a player in my own right.

In short, Bael could call me "mate" all he wished, but in truth, there was more than one curse that hung over us. As long as the hunting season loomed and we stayed in the castle, where I was treated as little more than a well-dressed prisoner, nothing would ever be real between us.

I turned to Bael again, thinking to perhaps voice this concern, but was distracted by the tension in his brow. "What is it?"

He shook his head ever so slightly. "I thought I heard someth—"

It was the only warning we had before chaos descended upon us.

A tremendous rumble sounded behind us, like the stampede of hundreds of tiny feet. Then, everything began to lurch and tumble over, the ground shaking.

Ahead, the procession stopped suddenly, and I blinked in confusion as one of the large carts wobbled as if shaken by invisible arms. Shouts and screams rang out as it tipped over, spilling baskets of food and what looked to be part of my bed frame out onto the road.

I squinted, horror and realization dawning. Looking wildly around at all the trees that might fall, the horses that would undoubtedly cause a stampede, terror shot through me. I knew that sound—that feeling—but had not encountered it in many years. Certainly not since moving to the capital.

Before I'd had a moment to fully process what was happening, the ground shifted and shook underfoot, and the trees trembled like their roots were twisting beneath the ground, struggling to emerge of their own accord. Loose dirt and bark rained down overhead, spraying painfully into my eyes and stinging my skin. Some men hung on to their animals while others abandoned them, stumbling as they tried to flee.

The horse beneath me bucked upward and sent me flying out of my saddle. A scream broke free from my throat, and I braced for impact.

Bael lunged forward and grabbed me before I could hit the ground. Plucking me out of the air and onto his horse, he pulled me against his chest protectively, shielding me from view with his body.

"Tremors," I gasped, struggling to catch my breath. "I've never seen anything like this in this area."

I hadn't seen anything like this in years. Not since…

Bael cursed fluidly. "We need to go now."

I wholeheartedly agreed. Tremors—when the ground shook, like thunder incarnate—weren't an uncommon occurrence while living in the valley near the Source. We had to get out of the way of the trees, except…

"What about them?" I yelled back, looking around wildly at the fleeing courtiers. *We can't just leave them.*

Many were already out of sight, and those who could travel through the shadows had clearly done so at the first sign of trouble. But others were still here, struggling to pull themselves free of the fallen carriages or tripping, unable to run as the ground shuddered underfoot.

I knew they would not give me a second thought in my position, that most of them would see me dead in an instant, but there was at least one face I needed to make sure made it home. "I need to find Enid."

"And I need to get you out of here," Bael replied, already turning his horse around.

"No!"

He either wasn't listening or pretended not to be as he dug his heels into the flank of his horse. "Hold on to me. I don't want to take you through the shadows, but I will if I have to."

I didn't care why he would want to avoid that; I only cared that he was leaving my friend behind. "Stop right now! They'll die."

He craned his neck around to look at me, and the savage look in his eyes stopped my breath. "Let them," he said coldly, finally turning his horse around. "And let their bodies block the path between you and anyone who means you harm."

11

LONNIE

THE ROAD TO EVERLAST CITY

With a quick urging from Bael's heels, we took off into the forest, racing away from the scene as fast as we could possibly go.

As we rode, it felt as if the tremors followed us, trees falling and rocks shifting in our wake. Bael controlled the reins with one hand and held his other out to the side, palm up. I watched, astonished, as trees so tall they had to be hundreds of years old crumbled in our wake.

"What are you doing?" I hissed.

"Leaving something else to feed on."

I didn't have the courage to ask what he meant.

We'd been galloping for what seemed like hours, the rhythmic pounding of hooves against dry earth our only companion. Then, between two towering pines, I saw it—a soft wisp of smoke curling up into the crisp morning air. Hope swelled in my chest, and my heart raced in time to the horses' thundering hooves.

And then I smelled it.

The scent of sulfur and ash greeted me, burning the inside of my nose, turning my throat dry, and coating my tongue with rotten char. It was a familiar acrid scent but one that I had not encountered in many years or thought I would ever have to again, like inhaling the iron-smoke from a matchstick. It transported me back to a time when I'd not been able to run. When there had been no prince to protect me, and I'd been far too young to protect myself.

I looked back over my shoulder, and a scream died in my throat.

The ground quaked and rumbled, shaking my feet. A deep fissure tore through the ground, widening with each passing second. The crack was filled with a swirling mist that seemed to come from some unknown abyss below. Then, all at once, things began to pour out of the crevasse. Dark, shadowed, noncorporeal *things*.

Like smoke taking shape, nightmares coming to life, the creatures descended on the trail of destruction Bael had left behind us, thundering after us like a ghostly hunting party. Here and there, it seemed as if I could make out a face among the shadows, twisted, ugly, monstrous faces, all screaming with rage or pain.

I felt Bael's heart quicken under my palms, and he seemed to stop breathing. "Don't look."

I closed my eyes, even knowing it wouldn't matter if I looked or not. Merely knowing would keep me awake at night for months to come.

"How?" I asked in a strangled whisper. "How are they here?"

"I don't know, little monster. I've never known the afflicted to leave Aftermath."

His confirmation of the word—afflicted—was a stone dropping into my stomach.

The afflicted were a terror that I hadn't known since moving to the capital, a nightmare that made all other monsters seem benign by comparison. If I feared the High Fae, it was nothing compared to the terror I harbored at the thought of even one afflicted rider.

Somewhere in the back of my mind, a horrible idea lurked: Was this my fault—our fault? Was this the doom that I'd been warned of? The Wilde things, called by the magic I was never, ever supposed to reveal?

Bael leaned lower on the horse, seeming to try to force it off its feet and into the air. "Hold on to me."

I clung to Bael's back, feeling the powerful muscles beneath me tense as I heard the screeching, unnatural sounds of our pursuers rapidly closing in.

The horse whinnied and reared up, its hooves pawing wildly at the air. I gasped in panic as I tumbled backward, and time seemed to slow as I caught a glimpse of Bael twisting around in an effort to break my fall. Then, with a bone-jarring thud, we crashed to the earth at the same time, both of us enveloped in a cloud of dust and dirt.

The impact sent a jolt of pain through my body, coursing from my toes to the tips of my fingers, but I had no time to nurse my wounds.

Bael was already up, pulling me to my feet. He clasped my hand tightly in his and all but dragged my limp body along after him as we ran.

"Take us through the shadows," I gasped.

Mere hours ago, I would hardly have believed I'd ever beg to travel as the Fae did, in that twisting way through the darkness that left me nauseous and disoriented. Now, however, I would rather travel across the continent than be caught by one of the stocking shadows behind us.

Bael didn't answer, only tugging me along faster, and I chanced a glance up at him.

His jaw was tight with determination, yellow eyes practically glowing, and for the briefest moment, I was reminded why I'd had so much cause to be afraid of him. There was something in the prince's face that spoke of a darker energy than he usually portrayed, like whatever lurked behind his eyes was banging on the bars of its cage and snarling to be let out.

"When you get to the palace," he continued as if he wasn't listening to me, "tell Scion that they're here."

My heart stuttered. "You tell him yourself."

Abruptly, Bael stopped running, jerking me to a halt. Everything shook around us, and the roar in my ears was almost unbearable, yet he stood firm and pulled me around to face him. "I won't be able to."

"What?"

He bent his head slightly to look directly into my eyes. His hand found the back of my neck, and he dragged me in, pressing his lips against mine as if trying to force every ounce of courage into me before we parted. I closed my eyes and concentrated on the feel of his lips, hoping to commit the sensation to memory.

It felt like a goodbye and tasted like an apology.

One of his long incisors pricked my lip, and I'd only just had a moment to register that I was bleeding when, without warning, the air seemed to thicken and come alive, thrumming with electricity.

My stomach lurched as I felt myself ripped away from reality. The darkness swallowed me, my footing unsteady in the void of nothingness.

Then, all at once, it was as if I'd awoken to find myself crushed under the weight of a thousand bricks. Light pierced through my closed eyelids, and shock rocked my body as I fell headfirst into something hard and unyielding.

I jerked as a pair of callused hands came up to grip my arms, steadying me. "What the fuck?" a familiar voice barked, harsh and violent. "What's wrong?"

The smell of freshly cut pine trees and a smoky fireplace surrounded me, and I nearly collapsed into the unnatural heat of that aroma.

I opened my eyes and felt my pulse quicken as his sparking silver gaze locked onto me like moonlight on the darkest night. I blinked blurry eyes, my exhausted mind unable to reconcile the angry outcry with that panicked gaze.

"Lonnie?" Scion's voice was far away. "What is it? Did rebels attack?"

Not rebels, no. Far, far worse than that.

While I might not trust Scion, might not care for him on the best of days and hated him on every other, he had to know—Bael wanted him to know, and I couldn't even comprehend why he might not be able to deliver the news himself.

Distantly, I heard the chaotic sounds of screaming mingled with what I thought must be the roar of a great beast, yet I couldn't focus. Couldn't find the will to turn around.

I forced my mouth to open. "*Afflicted.* The afflicted are coming."

And it's my fault.

12

SCION

THE OBSIDIAN PALACE, THE CITY OF EVERLAST

"Get out."

The healer jumped as if I'd struck him and scrambled away from where Lonnie lay asleep on my bed, as immobile as she'd been for the last day or so. He wrung his hands in the fabric of his midnight-blue tailcoat, quaking as he took slow steps backward toward the door. "But, Lord—"

"I said get the fuck out!"

The male didn't need to be told again. He abandoned his bag and instruments and sprinted out of the tower, the door banging shut behind him with an echoing clang.

I let out an aggravated sigh. I had not killed by mistake for many years, but I'd just come dangerously close. Shadows were already leaking out of my fingers, filling the room with an unnatural darkness despite the light streaming through the large window.

I couldn't quite explain where the surge of rage had come from —the healer hadn't been doing anything more than touching her

—but all too fast, my entire body was trembling, throwing all my thoughts into disarray.

It had been the same when Gwydion tried to help, and I had no fucking idea why.

Heaving a sigh, I took a seat in the chair beside the bed and stared down at the delicate face of the sleeping woman, conflict warring in my mind.

I can't kill her right now, anyway, I reminded myself. *There's still time to decide what to do.*

The door creaked open again behind me, and I stiffened, twisting in my chair, ready to murder whichever servant or guard had been fucking stupid enough to interrupt my brooding. However, my anger drained at the sight of the female in the doorway. "I'm not in the mood, Aine."

"I take it things are going well?" my cousin asked, a hint of dark amusement in her voice.

I glowered at her. "What gave you that impression?"

"Even if I hadn't seen that healer go sprinting out of here, I would have been able to hear you shouting from practically anywhere in the castle."

"Leave if it bothers you," I snapped.

She made no move to retreat, instead coming further into the room. She came and stood beside the bed and looked down at Lonnie. "She really hasn't moved?"

"No. Gwydion doesn't know what's wrong with her, and neither did that last healer."

I didn't mention the fact that the moment either of them had tried to so much as examine the woman, I'd spun into a panic that I couldn't have explained if my life depended on it. I didn't want anyone touching her, but the Source only knew why.

Aine didn't look at me. "It's only been a day, Sci."

I ground my teeth. Where she said "only" as if it were nothing, I viewed the last day as the longest of my immortal existence. "Every moment matters if there are afflicted in the capital. I sent for a second healer."

"Has it occurred to you that she's simply sleeping? Humans do tire easily."

"This isn't sleep. It's closer to death."

She hummed. "Have you tried speaking to Bael?"

"Yes," I grunted, my voice sounding bitter to my own ears. "Pointless, as always. You?"

She chuckled softly, sparing me a sympathetic look. "Yes. I believe our mother even tried to speak with him, if you can believe that. I saw her go downstairs earlier with all her ladies in tow."

I blinked, surprised. "Don't tell me that the threat of the afflicted was enough to force Raewyn to actually *do* something?"

Aine sniffed. "Someone should call a bard to record the momentous occasion."

"I'll have the legend etched in stone," I replied dryly. "But in all truth, did he speak to her?"

She looked over her shoulder and rolled her eyes. "No, of course not. You know how difficult he is. Like conversing with a particularly angry wall."

I snorted a laugh for her benefit, but the disappointment that stabbed at me was potent if unreasonable. Bael had never been any help to us in that form before; there was no reason to think that would change now.

I got to my feet and crossed to the other side of the bed, looking down at Lonnie from another angle. Quill hopped off the windowsill and fluttered over to land on the foot of her bed, looking up at me. It was likely a testament to how serious the situation was that Aine didn't threaten my bird, whom she hated more than the King of Underneath himself.

"Ah, well," I said. "I don't know if we could have expected much else from Raewyn."

"Quite," Aine agreed. "In fact, I believe the experience was enough to send her fleeing the capital altogether. That's actually what I came to tell you: my parents have absconded to Overcast for a holiday, with no clear indication of returning."

I rolled my eyes. Not that Raewyn mattered much, but Auberon was somewhat helpful when he felt like it. *Somewhat.* "They didn't happen to do me any favors and bring the children with them, did they?"

"Of course not," Aine sighed.

Perfect.

The longer I spent with my family, the more I was reminded why I'd elected to spend nearly my entire life surrounded by rebels and afflicted rather than cloistered in a luxury castle. Most would view the battlefields as the more odious option, but one hour in the obsidian would disabuse any such fallacy.

"Have you considered visiting the dungeon?" Aine asked, evidently following her own train of thought.

I stiffened, choosing my words carefully. "I would if I could."

I watched Aine's shoulders tense as if my one clumsy answer alone had shifted her entire mood. She let out a harsh laugh.

"Now I understand why you haven't been gloating that you were right about the attack: you've already fucked this up, haven't you?"

"I wouldn't gloat anyway. There's nothing amusing about this."

She narrowed her eyes. "Don't deflect."

I had no good answer for her, but still, I gave her a quick explanation of my bargain with Ambrose and how I'd agreed to release him in exchange for information about our grandmother's final prophecy.

"Grandmother isn't here to ask further questions," I muttered. "Ambrose has always been the next best thing."

"Is he?" She gave me an almost pitying look. "You can't tell me you've forgotten everything he's done."

"Never," I growled. "But I had no choice."

Aine, along with Bael, had seen the note from Grandmother Celia some time ago. The note, written by the queen before her death, had prophesied that I would be the last Everlast King. That could only mean an end to our curse in my lifetime—if only I could work out how to do it.

"Fool." Aine looked down at Lonnie before pacing circles around my tower as if she'd already worn the path many times before and knew the steps by heart. "You need to kill the human. It's as simple as that."

I wasn't so sure she was wrong. In any case, Ambrose hadn't said I must marry the queen, only that I *could*.

I could have said that, but instead, I said, "Do you really think Bael will allow that?"

"Bael isn't here, in case you hadn't noticed. Anyway, what are you implying?"

I didn't need to imply anything, but it wasn't my secret to share with her about the mating bond. Still, perhaps I could still run a theory past her...something that had been working its way through the back of my mind. "He told me that he healed her by bleeding."

Aine's eyes bugged out of her head, and she made a sound that might have been a curse or a sign of incredulity. "When?"

"Before the first hunt," I said dully.

"And since?"

I ran my fingers through my hair. We'd fought about it when he first told me and again after the hunt. I'd demanded he stay away from her, and by all accounts, he had, right up until she was attacked...it was hard to say when he would have realized that the bond existed. Clearly, it wasn't sealed, but if she wouldn't wake...

"I don't know." A sickness churning in my stomach. "Surely even he wouldn't be fool enough to do that twice?"

Aine's eyes widened in horror, and the uncertainty in her expression was all the answer I needed.

"How long has she been like this?"

I moved my gaze from where the latest healer ran her long, grayish-blue fingers over Lonnie's sleeping cheeks and glared mutinously at her. "A day."

My jaw ached from how hard I'd been clenching it over the course of that day, and perhaps in the days prior, and I shifted on my feet, moving my weight back and forth with nervous energy. On my shoulder, my raven, Quill, tittered in discomfort.

The healer stood on her toes and leaned further over the bed, moving her needlelike fingers down Lonnie's slender throat as if feeling for a pulse. I swallowed thickly, my gaze locking on where her throat bobbed.

"More specifically?" the healer asked.

I narrowed my eyes. "One sun cycle? How would you like me to fucking tell you that it was a day?"

She turned to me with wide, pupilless eyes and seemed to be assessing. Judging. "Apologies, my lord. It is my mistake. I'm not accustomed to the High Fae court."

I nodded, not precisely appeased. "You're Underfae."

This woman was the third healer in twenty-four hours. When I'd asked for another healer, I'd expected a human. Another breed of Fae had not been what I'd been expecting; however, as she was the first healer whom I'd not wanted to murder simply for touching Lonnie, I'd decided not to ask questions.

Until now, that was.

The woman blinked slowly. "Wrong, my lord. I am half Unseelie. Does it bother you?"

"No," I said flatly. "It does not bother me. I want to know what's wrong with her, and if you can fix it, I don't care what you are."

The healer looked surprised, her too-large eyes blinking strangely at me. She had a second eyelid beneath the first, like a clear membrane. "That's an uncommon position for a Seelie prince. Does that mean that the rumors are true, then?"

I smiled at her, and it wasn't nice. "If by the rumors, you mean that I will kill those who threaten my family, then yes, healer. Those have been proven time and time again to be true."

The Unseelie woman tensed and nodded as if to say she understood. She turned back to Lonnie. She reached up and fingered one strand of her long, red hair gently as though to push it back from her face. Then, without warning, she tugged the strand out and shoved it in her mouth.

I jerked, alarmed, and lunged forward with an almost unconscious move to stop her. "Don't touch her."

"I'm tasting her magic, lord," the healer replied calmly. "It's there but depleted. She's resting."

I narrowed my eyes. "What the fuck does that mean? When will she wake?"

It was a poorly phrased question, and I couldn't bring myself to care. I knew what that meant—or I would if it happened to one of us. But Lonnie didn't have magic like we did.

The healer licked her fingers one by one, as if savoring the taste of a particularly decadent dessert, then jumped down from the trunk she'd been using as a step stool. "I can't say. Perhaps another day?"

"What if she doesn't," I growled.

"If not in a day or so, then I would search for an alternative. I cannot claim to know everything, but there is no one better in this city, I swear by the Source. I might suggest consulting a seer."

If the irony wasn't so idyllic, I would think it impossible.

The sound of the door banging shut echoed through the room, and I was too exhausted to care if it meant the healer had finally left or someone else had arrived.

I jerked in sudden pain as Quill's sharp talons scraped down my arm, digging deep into my flesh. For half a second, I welcomed the pain—grounding—before I blinked to alertness.

"What the fuck." I tried to shake him off. "Get off."

He let out a mournful sound and leapt into the air, tearing at my skin as he went.

I hissed, glaring down at the shallow cut, then up at the raven now perched on the end of the bed.

My eyes shifted from the open wounds on my arm to the slumbering figure on the bed, and my heartbeat sped up, a plan beginning to take shape in my mind.

A chill ran through me as I thought of the barely formed notion, mixed with an odd sensation of interest. Was this what it had been like for Bael? Or was the decision easier for him? Simpler.

Lonnie rustled in her sleep and swallowed, her throat bobbing. I imagined sinking my teeth into that creamy skin. Feeling her pulse pound against my mouth while she shuddered beneath me, her mouth open like—

I shook my head, shocked at the direction of my own thoughts. That could not…would not happen. That was the entire point of this. Nothing I did was for or about me, and that's how I would justify this latest villainy.

Staring at my arm, I sighed with displeasure to see it had healed over. Clenching my teeth, I steeled myself and inhaled deeply, wishing against all hope that not looking would make the act less wrong. Any less fucking depraved.

Even though I had my doubts about this woman, I wished I had the chance to at least ask her permission. At least warn her that her emotions would be tampered with in the upcoming days or even weeks. Then again, I presumed she would prefer that to death.

Better still, if she turned out to have information about the afflicted, then it would be worth it.

I'd do anything to protect the kingdom, no matter who it sacrificed—whose life it ruined—me, her, Bael, it didn't matter.

It wasn't as if I was bonding her to me…maybe she didn't even have to know.

I glanced at her once more, still asleep and unmoving. Then, before I could think twice about it, I bit down hard on my own arm and brought the bleeding wound to her mouth.

13
LONNIE

THE OBSIDIAN PALACE, THE CITY OF EVERLAST

I stepped out of the shadows into a crumbling chamber and froze as someone cleared their throat. "Your heart is beating rather quickly."

My gaze traveled up, and my breath caught. An unfamiliar Fae male lounged before me, treating a faded, threadbare armchair as if it were a throne. His face was obscured, but somehow, I could tell by his tone and posture that he was smirking at me.

"Did you steal that?"

I almost laughed at myself. "Who are you?" would have been a better question. He seemed surprised as well.

"What?" he said in a tone that was so arrogant—so familiar—that it only added to my confusion.

"That's the mask the herald wears to open the hunts. Did you steal it?"

The fairy ran his fingers over the too-familiar stag skull mask. "How do you know I didn't kill him?"

"Did you?"

"No."

My eyes traveled from the fairy to the room behind him, and my confusion deepened. Where was this? Had I not just been…nowhere. It didn't matter.

Thick cobwebs clung to every nook and cranny while sunlight filtered in through a pile of broken stones where a doorway used to be. Hints of gray sky peeked through the open ceiling, and shards of light burst through the cracks in the walls while gusts of wind whipped around me like a wild symphony.

What might have once been stately furniture had been reduced to splintered fragments. Dead leaves scattered across the cracked marble floor, mixed in with dirt and shattered glass. Some walls still boasted faded blue and gray tapestries, while others had begun to crumble away, showing a magnificent view of the mountain range in the distance.

I licked my lips, tasting sweat and a hint of wine. "Who are you?"

The fairy sat up, his self-satisfied grin widening. "Do you often threaten strangers?"

I considered that. Maybe? I wasn't sure. "What's your name?"

He cocked his head to the side, giving the odd impression of the fathomless eyes in the skull shifting to watch me. "I've told you before, Elowyn, don't ask questions of the Fae."

I HAD NO NOTION OF HOW LONG I SLEPT.

Consciousness eluded me, and I drifted in and out, hovering somewhere between sleeping and waking, wrapped in warmth and the scent of woods and roses surrounding me.

When finally awareness dawned, I was swathed in a cocoon of warmth and luxurious sheets. I shifted slightly, feeling my mattress softly move with me to cradle my body. My eyes opened slowly, still full of sleep, and I blinked up at the soft, bluish light of my surroundings with confusion. My heartbeat sounded softly in my ears, and a metallic taste coated my tongue.

How?

I was in the tower—the obsidian tower room that I had not seen since before the second hunt. It looked the same as I'd left it—or rather, the same as it had before it was destroyed by rebels. The black masculine furniture, the ornate carvings and silver accents, the huge windows and towering ceilings.

Everything must have been repaired. Either that or I was trapped in some elaborate dream. *It would not be the first time.*

I blinked several times, the sleep clearing and reality setting in. How did I get here? I couldn't remember anything except… I jolted, alarmed, and sat up.

Wincing as my muscles pulled with a strain I wasn't aware was there until that moment, I ran my hand through my hair and pressed it against my forehead as I looked around. There was a pile of clothing on the bedside table—the clothing I'd been wearing when we left Inbetwixt, complete with my belt and dagger placed on top. Hurriedly, I looked down at myself to find I was wearing an unfamiliar nightgown. *Fuck.* Fuck!

"Hello, rebel. Nice of you to rejoin the living."

My breath caught, and my gaze darted toward the sound before hardening on the black-haired, silver-eyed Fae male lounging in the ornate armchair to the right of my bed.

Somehow, that image felt all too familiar.

"What happened?" I jerked, sitting up straighter, and bared my teeth. "What's going on?"

Prince Scion lowered the ancient leather-bound book he'd evidently been reading and leaned forward, cocking his head at me. "How are you feeling?"

I gaped at him, unable to find words. *How am I feeling?*

Prince Scion usually dressed as if he were about to walk into a diplomatic reception, but today, he sat at the foot of my bed in his full set of armor. I assumed it had to be his because the breastplate fit his body as if the metal was poured molten onto his skin and allowed to harden around him. It was black and mirrored, as if it were made of obsidian rather than iron, and marred only by his house crest carved into the right shoulder. He moved slightly, and nothing creaked or rattled as it would with regular armor, again giving the impression that it was a second skin. I'd seen soldiers in the city and around the palace, but I'd never seen it look like *that*. Indeed, I'd never seen Scion look more comfortable than he did right now.

He was taller and sharper in appearance than Bael, with finely carved features, pale skin, and hair like the obsidian wall behind him. Where Bael was beautiful in a way that was undeniable to anyone with eyes, Scion made you think of sex just by looking at him. You knew instinctively that it would hurt, but something about his scorching silver eyes made it difficult to care.

I had to remember to care because Prince Scion didn't just want to hurt me; since the moment we'd met, the heir apparent to Elsewhere had made it perfectly clear that he intended for me to die and would take great pleasure in being the one to do it. We spoke infrequently and always in the form of insults or threats veiled by dangerous flirtation, but if he was here, it couldn't be for any good reason.

"What am I doing here?" I asked, trying to keep my voice even, even as my gaze darted to the knife on the bedside table.

"You were attacked returning from Inbetwixt."

My entire body tensed, and a hysterical laugh bubbled up in my chest. Was that concern on his face? *Impossible.* Prince Scion, the former heir of Elsewhere, the war general and feared executioner, the male who had locked me in a dungeon for a year, could not be sitting vigil by my bedside. "Yes, I know that," I said slowly. "But why am I *here*? How long has it been? Is everyone alright?"

He didn't answer me directly. "Take a moment to collect yourself."

"Where's Bael?" I tried instead.

"Unavailable."

My heart started to beat faster with alarm. "I want to see him."

"You can't. He's fine. He's..." He seemed to struggle for words and changed tactics. "He's having a bad week."

Oh. I still didn't know precisely what that meant, but at least it sounded like something I'd heard them say before. I relaxed very slightly at the knowledge that he wasn't dead in Inbetwixt. Still, that didn't change my current situation. *If I could just reach the knife...*

Scion stood with a grace that didn't match the image before me, and again, I was surprised when the armor made no sound. He came to stand in front of me, and I was forced to look up so as to see him clearly, somehow feeling even smaller than I usually did when in the presence of any of the Fae males who so often invaded my personal space. "Are you hungry or..."

If the situation wasn't so alarming, I would have rolled my eyes at the vaguely confused expression covering his too-handsome face. Bael had also done this when we first interacted—exhibiting a strange ignorance of human biology, as if it wasn't the same as theirs. It seemed as if they were taught we ate and slept differently or something equally absurd. As it was, I couldn't have eaten a thing if I'd wanted to—it was the furthest thing from my mind.

"I'm not hungry," I muttered.

"Fine," he replied, moving slightly closer. "Can you get up? I need—"

He never finished his sentence, and I never learned what he might have needed, as in that moment, he reached out his hand. Perhaps to help me up, perhaps to snap my neck, I had no idea, but I reacted immediately and without thought.

Throwing my arm out blindly, I closed my fingers around the handle of the knife on my bedside table and whipped it around to try and strike at any bit of flesh I could reach.

Evidently, Scion hadn't expected that because he didn't react quickly enough.

He moved out of the way just in time to avoid the blade but fell sideways, landing ungracefully on one elbow on the end of the bed. "By the fucking Source!"

I pounced, ignoring the faint throbbing in my skull, and clambered after him in a tangle of ebony sheets. The blade flashed through the air between us, and I rolled, landing on his chest, my knees braced on the mattress, thighs holding tight to either side of his body.

Heaving for breath, I spit my hair out of my mouth and pressed the blade against his throat. "I want to know what the fuck is going on."

Prince Scion blinked up at me, wide-eyed. His gaze darted to the blade and back up to my face. "What are you going to do with that, rebel?"

A tiny spark of triumph lit inside me, and I smiled, enjoying *him* being at *my* mercy for once. The powerful Prince of Ravens, the queen's executioner, flat on his back because of a human. "Want me to show you?"

"Please do." He smirked. "I doubt you know how to use it."

I pressed the blade in harder until a tiny line of red formed on his neck. "Really? Did you forget that if I wasn't willing to kill royals, I wouldn't be here?"

A dark heat flared in his eyes, turning silver to pewter. "Careful, rebel," he drawled, moving his hands slowly up to grip my thighs. "We wouldn't want you to get in over your head, would we?"

His long fingers held me in place, and I stiffened. Goosebumps erupted on my skin, and I was suddenly all too aware of the hard muscles of his body pressing against the inside of my thighs, of my own heartbeat pounding in my ears, and my rough breathing matching the tempo of his. I could feel the unnatural heat emanating from him. That heat that all the Fae seemed to emit at all times, like their blood boiled while mine merely flowed.

"Let go of me," I hissed.

Scion only tightened his grip on my legs and shifted me lower so I was straddling his waist. "Make me. You're the one with the knife."

I pushed the blade in further, then sucked in a startled breath as he pressed my hips down, and I felt exactly how little my display had frightened him. Worse, he was *toying* with me.

Heat and shocking need erupted in my core, warring with the hatred I harbored for this confusing, devilish prince. My heart-beat pounded in my ears, deafening, but the longer he held me there, the more I could feel that pulse thrumming lower…elsewhere.

My entire body trembled, humiliating heat pooling in my core as my heartbeat went out of control. “You’re not worth it.”

My breathing uneven, my body aching, I started to let my hand drop—but he wasn’t done with me yet.

With an ease that proved he’d merely been pretending to be caught—most likely waiting to see what I would do—Scion rolled, flipping our positions, bracing his arms on either side of my head.

I landed with a sharp exhale on my back. The mattress, which had seemed so soft and luxurious before, now felt cold and hard against my tingling skin. Goosebumps rose up my bare arms and traveled over my neck, and my chest heaved as Scion loomed over me. The knife slipped from my grip and clattered uselessly to the floor.

I shoved at his chest, and whether he meant to or not, he dragged his body against mine, pressing me harder into the mattress. I shuddered.

“I’m curious,” he said with a slight edge of menace to his tone. “Do you ever stop to think through the consequences of your actions?”

“Not when I wake up to find you looming over me.”

He smiled slightly, saying nothing for a beat, and reached out, gently running one hand over the column of my neck. I shivered involuntarily at the touch, and he smiled slightly. Then, without warning, his fingers closed around my throat.

I choked, gasping for air, as his silver rings cut into my skin. He leaned down even closer and brought his lips close to my ear. “Never try that again, or there will be fucking consequences.”

He let go and leapt off the bed, taking several steps back toward the middle of the room. I coughed, gasping for breath as involuntary tears welled in my eyes. "Your threats don't frighten me anymore," I coughed. "I've already seen the worst of what you have to offer and survived."

To my surprise, he grinned. "No, rebel. Believe me, I can be far, far worse."

I swallowed thickly, holding my tongue for once. Although, as he stepped further back, all I could think was *So can I.*

14
LONNIE

THE OBSIDIAN PALACE, THE CITY OF EVERLAST

Scion left the room, allowing me a moment to myself to dress and bathe, but not before announcing that he'd return shortly to discuss the attack.

Part of me wondered if I'd overreacted—if that's all he'd meant to discuss all along—while another part felt somewhat vindicated for finally getting the upper hand. Granted, now that I'd played that hand and lost, I'd never be able to catch him by surprise again.

That was alright. I'd simply have to wait until I could feed him to my new snake friend.

I swallowed thickly, that thought jerking me back to reality with an unpleasant lurch. Was it truly possible that the attack was my fault? Could my failure to warn Bael have caused such a disaster? Or was I spinning too far into panic and ignoring more rational possibilities?

The attack had changed any other plans and shifted all priorities —at least for me. I could only hope the Everlasts viewed the threat as seriously as I did, but one thing was certain beyond any doubt: I needed to find Bael.

After a quick bath that was more utilitarian than relaxing, I flung open the wardrobe and selected the first dress I touched.

The gown was made from a lovely mulberry silk, but to my dismay, it turned out to be one of the more difficult ones to put on without the help of a servant. As I stood in front of the vanity mirror, struggling to do up the back, I thought wistfully of Enid. As far as I could tell, she'd been running in the opposite direction from the afflicted after the attack, and I hoped desperately that she'd escaped.

A knock sounded on my door, and I stiffened. I'd grown to dread those knocks, as no one I wanted to see ever bothered, and the list of those I would welcome was depressingly short. "Who is it?"

"Thalia," came a soft voice from the other side of the door.

I froze. Lady Thalia, who was objectively one of the loveliest Fae I'd ever seen, male or female, was Lord Gwydion's fiancée, as well as a cousin of the Everlasts, though how closely they were all related, I'd never really known. She'd always been relatively kind to me, though I couldn't say I exactly trusted her.

I went to the door, anyway, and opened it a crack so as not to expose her to my half-dressed body. "Hello."

She looked down at me, her expression bemused. "What are you doing?"

I held my intricate gown to my bare chest and opened the door slightly wider. "I have never put something this complex on by myself."

She looked like she wanted to laugh, which was unusual for her. Tall, blonde, and willowy, Thalia had haunted gray eyes that often appeared as if she'd recently been crying. It was something I'd wondered about before but had no business asking about.

"Would you like help?" she asked.

I paused, then nodded, letting her inside, where she immediately made her way over to the vanity. I followed, holding all the mulberry straps up with immense difficulty.

"What is this?" Thalia asked, picking at the end of one of the straps.

"I don't know," I bemoaned. "I could choose another, but they are all like that. Anything I chose for myself was in the trunk in Inbetwixt. No one told me how long we'd be staying."

As I spoke, I realized for the first time what else had been in the trunk in Inbetwixt. Rosey's journals, which I'd so painstakingly brought with me to the hunting grounds, were now likely destroyed or else lying on the ground in the forest, somewhere, never to be seen again.

My stomach twisted in a knot, and a lump pushed at the back of my throat, despair threatening to overwhelm me. I'd only read one page, feeling that it was too much to keep going, and now I would never see any of the journals ever again.

"Turn around. Let me see what I can do," Thalia said.

"What?" I shook my head—I'd momentarily forgotten what we were discussing. "Oh, of course."

I moved to stand in front of the mirror, trying to force the misery from my mind while she moved each strap into place in a pattern I never would have been able to work out on my own.

"What are you doing here?" I asked, simply looking for a distraction.

"In truth, I simply wanted to be in the room ahead of the others."

I narrowed my eyes at her in the mirror. "The others?"

She nodded. "Now that you're awake, I imagine everyone will descend like the pack of vultures that they are."

I snorted a bitter laugh. "Are you not speaking of your own family?"

"Of course, which is how I know I am correct. I'd prepare yourself for the onslaught, lest you find yourself picked apart to the bone."

I nodded, appreciating the warning. "I'm not sure there's much left for them to pick at. This whole family has already pecked away at fears I didn't even know I had."

As soon as the words left my mouth, I regretted them. Thalia wasn't a friend; she was an Everlast, and it was important that I keep that in mind. Much like I needed to keep in mind that Bael, too, was first and foremost a prince, and Scion was a prince always and a friend only if it benefitted him.

Yet even as my thoughts turned dark, Thalia surprised me by saying, "They do that, but I find that the best defense is information. Like, being here ahead of the others means they will not be able to force me out of the conversation."

I raised an eyebrow. "I would think you would be privy to all conversations as Gwydion's betrothed."

She shook her head. "No, but that doesn't mean I can't demand to be included, and so can you."

Interesting. This sounded like another way to say what Bael had told me: ask better questions. Though, Thalia seemed to be implying that I not so much ask as force my way in.

"Lady Aine seems well-informed," I hedged, wondering how far Thalia would let me push before she shut down again. Granted, I supposed I was doing her a favor by letting her stay in the room, if that was what she truly wanted.

"It has little to do with being female, if that's what you're implying," Thalia said briskly, "and everything to do with being too far removed from the direct bloodline. Aine is a princess, though she would prefer otherwise, and more importantly, she is close confidants with Scion."

"I didn't know that."

"Well, now you do." She pulled another strap tight. "Begin hoarding information like treasure."

We fell silent again while she worked. I noticed that unlike the dress I'd chosen—which was far too formal for daytime, though I was not about to ask to switch it now—Thalia wore the least ornate outfit I'd ever seen her in. A simple blue-and-white linen dress, cut similarly to something Iola might have worn.

I was about to ask her how Iola was faring when she said, "You look quite healthy for someone who was just attacked by the afflicted."

I shook my head. "Does everyone know?"

"Well, you did crash into the dining room in the middle of breakfast. It was…hard to miss."

"We did?" My eyes widened, heat staining my cheeks. "I don't really recall much of that."

"Of the attack? Or just the traveling?"

The only thing I remembered was spinning through the air with Bael and then falling into strong, comforting arms—though I wasn't about to say that.

"The traveling," I replied and shivered as she moved a strap into place and her nail scraped over my spine. "It was disorienting. We rode for quite some time first. I don't understand why Bael wouldn't have shadow walked immediately."

"Conserving energy," Thalia said. "I wasn't there, of course, but I can only assume that's what it was. Moving through the shadows at such a distance is difficult, nearly impossible for most. Bringing a second body along would add to that. None of us have infinite energy, not even Bael, so if he'd already been using a lot of magic, he was probably trying to get you both closer to the castle before traveling. Good thing, too, since you both passed out when you got here. I've never seen Bael collapse from anything, least of all shadow walking."

I sucked in a breath. "Is he alright?"

She paused. If she said he was having a "bad night," I thought I might scream.

"Yes," she said after a moment, seeming to choose her words carefully. "Bluntly, I suspect if you want to see him, all you would have to do is cooperate with Scion, and he'll give you anything you want."

I startled. "What makes you say that?"

"You have been asleep for just over a day, and you have not seen how the castle has been turned upside down. There were *three* healers."

"So?"

She tied some kind of knot with the still-hanging straps near my shoulder. "I just think it's interesting that anyone who would claim to want you dead would put out a moratorium on anyone harming you, then allow Unseelie healers into the high court palace."

"What moratorium?"

She smiled slightly. "You didn't hear? No one is supposed to harm you. It's put quite a damper on the hunting season."

My stomach lurched, and I suddenly remembered how everyone had looked at me in Inbetwixt. I knew something was strange. Even the Fae that approached me in the woods had said they weren't there for me, only the crown…

"But that's illegal," I spluttered.

"Yes." She smiled. "It certainly is, but I do not think he cares."

"Why the fuck would he do that?" I demanded.

She laughed, presumably at my use of foul language, but only shrugged. "You would have to ask him."

I was certainly not going to ask. If Scion wanted to make the hunts into a stroll through the woods, that was his prerogative; it wouldn't make him king. I would still give the crown to Bael in just over a month, and then…what.

Would I still leave?

Thalia and I fell silent again, and I watched her in the mirror, now untangling the mess I'd made of my hair and rebraiding it to fall smoothly over the open back of the gown. My thoughts raced, unclear and as impossible to unravel without assistance as the straps of the dress. "May I ask you something?"

"You may, but I may choose not to answer," she replied.

It was such a typical Fae response that I couldn't help but roll my eyes. "You are Gwydion's mate, correct? But how can he marry you, then?"

"Should I take that to mean that someone has been telling you stories?" She paused her braiding and met my eyes in the mirror, cocking her head. "Bael, perhaps?"

I flushed slightly and nodded. "I only wondered…I just…"

In truth, I'd wanted to know if there was some way around their curse, but the way she was looking at me gave me the impression that no matter what her answer was, I would not like it.

"I am not," she said simply, returning to her braid. "His mate, that is."

I thought back, trying to remember if anyone had ever actually told me she was or if I'd just assumed. I couldn't recall. "Then why…"

"You're awfully bold to ask for secrets without offering any in return, you know."

"I didn't get the impression that you would care much for my secrets."

"True," she sighed, sounding impossibly bored. "It's been a long while since I told this story to anyone, and I doubt we have time to get into every detail."

I didn't care—any details would be more than enough for me, and perhaps my face told her so because she sighed again and obliged me as she resumed brushing my hair.

"I believe I told you before that I was sent to the court to marry Scion, but that's not the whole of it," she began. "In truth, I was sent in order to keep me away from my mate."

My eyes widened. "But why?"

"My mother and Queen Celia shared the same grandparents, which makes me, and the entire governing family of Overcast, for that matter, too closely related to the house to be ignored. If Bael told you of the curse, he will have told you that any one of us could destroy all the others, and that was their fear when I discovered my mate at our Solstice celebration two years ago."

I gaped at her reflection, but she didn't look up to meet my gaze. I couldn't tell, but I suspected that she was crying again. Every time I'd seen Thalia since coming here, she'd looked as if she'd just recently been crying, and I supposed this explained why.

"So, what did they do to him?" I asked, not sure I wanted to know the answer.

She shook her head. "Nothing. I have never revealed the name of who it was, but my mother knew immediately that something was wrong. She'd already been planning for several years to use mine and my brother's marriages to gain favor for Overcast. We're the smallest province and rely entirely on the Everlast army to protect us from Aftermath, so we need the families to remain connected. The moment she realized that she might have leverage with which to send me directly to the capital, she sent a message heavily implying that unless I was taken away, my bonding would destroy us all."

She'd finished braiding, her hands still in my hair, but neither of us moved.

"I'm sorry," I said flatly, not knowing what else to say.

She pursed her lips. "Are you really? That's a very human thing to say, you know. To express sorrow for someone else's sadness."

"Do you not feel sorry when others are hurting, then?" I asked.

She thought about it. "I suppose, but I would not say so. "To give someone else knowledge that you have affected them gives them power over you."

That sounded like a miserable way to live and was yet another reason why I wanted never to dip too far into thinking like the Fae. "I am sorry, though, that this happened to you."

"Thank you," she replied stiffly.

"But how did you switch from Scion to Gwydion?" I asked, hoping to move on from the awkward silence that fell around us.

To my relief, she laughed. "I asked to. Believe me, his royal moodiness was perfectly happy to oblige."

I sucked in a startled breath. "But why?"

I couldn't imagine why anyone would choose that. I might prefer Gwydion slightly, if only because he was nicer and had never threatened or imprisoned me, but if I were her...well, there was no contest. I flushed slightly at the realization that despite everything, my preference was entirely clear and possibly hinted at some unresolved masochistic tendencies.

"Scion's greatest love is this country. He needs to marry a queen, and I have no taste for power or politics." She glanced from me to where the obsidian crown lay on the bedside table, unmoved from where it had been when I awoke. "I do not envy the position you are in, and I will feel no differently should you survive and find yourself queen in earnest."

I had to swallow a laugh. That seemed too far out of the realm of possibility. I'd never even let myself consider it. I was still planning to follow the bargain I'd made with Bael and give him the crown before returning to the valley where I'd grown up.

Though now, I wondered if that plan would have changed as well. When Bael had said our bond changed everything, did he mean the bargain as well?

I wondered what Thalia would say about Bael—who did she think he needed to marry? Would she have picked him over his brother? Was that an option available to her? What about Bael over Scion?

I flushed warmer. Why I was thinking this at all, I had no idea. I could only blame the fact that Thalia had put it in my head.

It was foolish of me to waste my thoughts this way. Impossibly stupid.

"I'm finished," Thalia said.

I wasn't sure if she meant with fixing my appearance or her story, but regardless, I spun to face her. "Thank you. I will have to get something else to wear before tomorrow. I can't do this again."

Her eyes widened. "Are you certain? I'm not sure I've ever seen you look better."

I scoffed, thinking of how I'd looked when we left Inbetwixt and my recent neglect of food, sleep, and anything better than the most basic hygiene. "You must be joking."

She shook her head. "Truly. It's fortunate that your scars are healing so they don't distract the eye."

"What?" I jolted in surprise and turned to look in the vanity mirror and gaped.

She was correct. I could admit that I did look better—healthier—even after the last time Bael had healed me. Even more than that, I'd had many scars, both from my time as a servant and, more recently, from when I'd nearly died, impaled on my own crown. I gaped at my own smooth flesh. Some scars were nearly gone, while others were far lighter than they should have been, looking years old rather than months. "How is that possible?"

"You would have to tell me," she said shrewdly. "Perhaps the next time we share secrets."

15
LONNIE
THE OBSIDIAN PALACE, THE CITY OF EVERLAST

Only a short time later, Thalia's prediction came true, and an entire war council worth of hungry vultures descended on my bedchamber.

Prince Scion paced angrily around the tower, a veritable cloud of incandescent rage. Shadows seemed to erupt in his wake as he walked, materializing and fizzling as quickly as they'd come. The shadows fell over Gwydion and Aine, who were seated on the silver braided rug, but seemed to avoid Thalia, who leaned against the wall with her arms crossed over her chest.

"Well?" Scion demanded finally. "What the fuck happened?"

I sighed, annoyed with his erratic behavior, and shifted where I sat on the bed. "Starting when?"

He paused his pacing, seeming to consider that question. "I don't know. Whatever you deem important."

That gave me more leeway than he should have, and I might have abused it had the topic not been so dire.

I explained the beginning of the attack in Inbetwixt with as much detail as I could recall, and they all stared at me with rapt attention. I squirmed, uncomfortable with their scrutiny. It seemed impossible that not only were they listening to me, but no one had yet interrupted, threatened me, or asked me to leave. Like they'd all forgotten to hate me in the face of more pressing issues.

"I don't understand," Aine said finally. "The earth tremor was first?"

"It's always first," Scion replied. "The afflicted carry so much Wilde magic it disturbs everything around them. Tremors, storms, enormous waves. We're lucky it wasn't worse."

I nodded in agreement. I hadn't been old enough to fully understand the impact of the disaster in Aftermath when I lived in the North, and certainly not when it first occurred, but I could recall the tremors and the smell of death and flames.

"Who sent them?" Gwydion asked.

I froze, feeling as if I were caught. Could I—should I—say I feared it was me? No, of course not. If there was ever a time to heed my mother and lie, it was in this moment. "I don't know."

"How many were there?" Scion demanded, still pacing.

"I don't know. Dozens, perhaps?

"What do you know?" he snapped.

I gritted my teeth. "I know you have afflicted moving into the south, *my lord*. What the fuck are you planning to do about it?"

He glared at me. "I don't know, *my queen*. Isn't that your decision now?"

His temper was more tempestuous than a summer storm, and I had no idea what to make of it.

When he'd left my room after our—admittedly intense—row, things had seemed to be heading in a calmer direction. However, when he'd returned some thirty minutes later, he took one look at me, still sitting at the vanity with Thalia, and scowled, his mood immediately turning blacker than the shadows now literally leaking from his fingers. The only good thing about his return was he'd brought his enormous raven, Quill, who now sat perched on my knee, preening as I stroked his feathery head. Most of the court seemed to despise the bird, but I'd always liked him. Far better than I liked his master, that was for damn sure.

"Personally," Aine said lightly, reclining backward on the rug, "I would like nothing to do with the decision-making, but I do suggest that we not leave it exclusively up to either the *human* or the *fool* who lost Ambrose mere hours before the afflicted appeared."

My ears pricked up at that. They'd lost Ambrose? As in, Ambrose *Dullahan*. If they'd ever caught him in the first place, it was news to me.

"Fuck yourself," Scion growled. "I wouldn't have told you if I knew you were going to go on about it for the rest of our damned immortal lives."

"Just as you deserve, frankly," she quipped, examining her long, painted fingernails. "I don't know why we're arguing about this when we all know exactly how the afflicted got here—"

My heart stopped.

"—obviously, Ambrose summoned them," Aine snapped.

My heart beat again.

"Be quiet, both of you," Thalia said, pushing off the wall. "This is exactly why you are having these problems. You are relying too heavily on physical strength from a few individuals while ignoring every other aspect of your government and allowing yourself to be weakened from within by petty infighting."

Everyone turned to look at her. Scion stopped pacing. I gaped, my jaw going slack, and even Aine sat up straight. Thalia never said anything so direct to anyone—at least not that I'd heard. Every time I'd seen her since I'd gotten here, she was weepy and quiet, never showing any magic or playing politics like the rest of the family. I balled my fist in the skirt of the dress she'd helped me with. Perhaps I'd misjudged her?

"Excuse me?" Scion said, but for once, his tone was not entirely full of judgment or derision.

"You heard me, cousin," she snapped. "It is abundantly clear that half this family is mad, and the other half has relied on prophecy for far too long."

"Careful," Scion growled. "You are only here because this is as much your family as ours."

"I am free to speak on it, then. What you need is a general. Someone to lead your armies, someone with tactical experience, *something*. You need political advisors, not just Mordant. You need ambassadors and a court that isn't made up of exclusively those who fear you. In Overcast, where we have less magic, we rely on other things. There is power, but it's not the only reason to have a position."

"Overcast doesn't fight wars," Scion said darkly. "You rely on our army for aid. It's different when lives are at stake rather than dinner parties."

"Which is why you need a general," she said, growing frustrated.

"We would have both a seer and a general if Ambrose hadn't fucked off," Gwydion said, speaking for the first time.

"Shut up," Scion barked.

"Well, it's true," Gwydion retorted. "She's not wrong, Sci. We all know you'll be king, but you're shit at leading the army. Ambrose would have done that."

"Spoken by a room full of people who weren't actually *in* the army," Scion said. His voice had grown into sort of a quiet rage that was almost more disturbing than when he yelled. "I'll remind you that I'm the only one here who's been to Aftermath and killed an afflicted."

"No you're not," I blurted out. All eyes turned to me, and I shrunk back, having no idea why I would say that. "You're not the only one, I mean…"

Gwydion raised an eyebrow at me. "You've killed an afflicted? Yesterday?"

"No," I scrambled, knowing it sounded panicked. Fuck, I was usually far better at lying. "I mean. I lived in Aftermath, so. Never mind." That caused more raised eyebrows. Only Scion seemed unsurprised. I cast around for something to say to get them off this topic. "When you mention 'Ambrose,' do you mean Ambrose Dullahan?"

Breathing in the room seemed to stop, and I realized I'd said precisely the wrong thing.

Scion took a step toward me, his lip curling in a snarl. "And how would you know that, rebel?"

His expression was entirely too threatening for someone who had supposedly not wanted me hurt in the hunts. Thalia must have been mistaken, or else I'd said something so bad that it had overshadowed anything else.

I stiffened, running quickly through my options. Had any of them actually used that name in front of me…or was it only on the note? Could I blame this on Bael, perhaps?

Lying is the best way to protect yourself against the Fae...that's what I'd always believed, except it kept failing me over and over in practice. At least this time, I had nothing to lose by telling the truth.

"Wait!" I said as he took another menacing step forward. "I'll show you."

16
LONNIE

THE OBSIDIAN PALACE, THE CITY OF EVERLAST

I look forward to meeting you under the cover of darkness in Inbetwixt

Your friend,

Ambrose Dullahan

"He fucking signed it," Scion said for perhaps the third time, waving the note in Aine's face. "The prick signed it like a goddamned love note."

Lady Aine swirled the bloodred wine in the bottom of her second conjured glass and nodded at him. "I know."

I'd moved to sit in the armchair in the corner and now nursed my own glass of wine—normal, non-Fae wine—and watched incredulously, still marveling at my own good fortune that the note was not only still in the pocket of the trousers that were folded on the nightstand but that they'd all recognized the handwriting and believed me that I did not know Ambrose Dullahan.

Of course, I hadn't explained everything. I didn't tell them about Rosey's journals or everything Bael and I had discussed in bits and pieces over the last weeks. I didn't mention the red-haired man in the tavern who'd led me to the journals when I'd gone looking for information on the rebellion myself. I certainly didn't tell them about the encounter with the snake or my fear that perhaps it was me—or Bael, for that matter—who had somehow summoned the Wilde magic that called the afflicted. I only told them about the note that was left in my room when it was ransacked and that I had yet to meet Dullahan in person.

Gwydion sidled up beside me, nursing his own glass, and grinned. "Well played, my queen."

"Don't call me that."

"No? Would you prefer I use your name?"

I looked up at him sharply, knowing exactly what he meant.

I'd been doing my best to sit quietly and watch. Following Thalia's advice—and Bael's, too, I supposed—and treating information like treasure. Now that I was looking for it, I could guess that Gwydion was employing that strategy as well.

Gwydion knew my true name and was the only one in the castle who did. Until yesterday, he may have been the only one left alive who knew it. He'd coerced it out of me after my friend Iola was poisoned in exchange for saving her, though now, I wondered if he might have saved her anyway since she was one of Thalia's ladies.

Perhaps I would feed Gwydion to the snake instead.

"What do you want?" I snapped.

"Nothing. I merely appreciate a well-thought-out plan. Anyone who really was a rebel wouldn't be fucking stupid enough to say that name to Scion in his own castle, much less within arm's reach. Congratulations, I believe you just cleared your name."

"That was hardly a plan," I said vehemently. "And I don't know anything about Dullahan, except that he leads the rebels, so if any of you would care to fill me in, I would greatly appreciate it."

Gwydion's smile told me clearly that he didn't believe me, but it seemed that the others did. Scion certainly did because, yet again, his mood had shifted, and he was being pleasant again. Or as pleasant as he was capable of being. He was not actively trying to murder me, and his smirk had gone from condescending to dangerously flirtatious.

I could swear if this family didn't kill me outright, I would die from emotional whiplash.

Clearly listening to us, Scion glanced up, still clutching the note in his fist. "There is no simple way to answer that question, rebel."

Did he realize what he said—if he no longer believed me to be a rebel, then why say it? I supposed it did not matter. "Fine, what is the simplest explanation?"

He chewed on that as if choosing his words carefully. Asking a fairy to give a short answer was paramount to asking the sun to rise in the west. "Most families have at least one black sheep," he said finally. "We have many."

"If there are many black sheep, at what point is the white sheep the odd one out?" I asked.

Aine laughed, catching my eye across the room. "Perhaps it would be better explained as a wolf among the flock."

"So, you're related?"

Scion leaned against the nearest post of the four-poster bed, petting Quill, who perched on the baseboard beside him. He fixed me with a long look and finally nodded gravely. "Ambrose is my brother, but we have never known each other well."

I blinked at him, feeling suddenly a bit numb,

That wasn't the right reaction. I should be swearing, shouting, fainting, *something*, but I didn't so much as gasp. I wondered if perhaps my ability to feel surprise had been somewhat damaged by every other impossible thing I'd been told lately. In a way, the leader of the rebellion being a part of the Everlast family was poetic.

If I was upset by anything, it was that Bael hadn't told me himself when we'd read Rosey's journals. Had that not been the ideal opportunity to bring it up? He'd clearly known.

"How did this happen?" I asked.

"No scathing remark, rebel?" Scion asked. "I've come to anticipate your ill-mannered observations."

"I'm sure I'll think of one if you'll only give me a moment to consider."

"Ambrose is the oldest of our generation, but in layman's terms, he's Gwydion's age," Aine said before Scion could snipe back at me. "It's common in immortal families for children to have friends of their own age group, even among siblings, cousins, or aunts and uncles. So, while we are siblings"—she pointed to herself and Gwydion—"*we* were raised together." She pointed to herself and Scion.

"How old are you, then?" I asked Gwydion, if only to get a full understanding.

I had to crane my neck to look back at him, and he did me the courtesy of stepping around my armchair to face me as the others did. For a moment, I had the oddest sense of sitting on a throne while they all stood before me, giving their report. I shook my head—*it's the wine*.

"Two hundred and thirty or so," Gwydion said thoughtfully. "We don't keep careful track after maturity. Only the centuries start to matter."

My eyebrows rose. "So what happened?"

No one had to clarify what I meant.

"I don't know for certain," Scion said slowly. "In fact, no one does. At some point, when I was barely older than Elfwyn is now, he simply left. Several years after that, he reappeared in Nightshade."

I tried to do the math in my head and struggled to make the timeline fit. "He reappeared in Aftermath, you mean."

"No, in Nightshade. He left before the fall."

"Even so, that's not that long ago…not even for humans. Why does no one remember him?"

They all laughed, but it was again Aine who answered. "They do. But Grandmother wouldn't allow anyone to speak of the traitor for some time, and with each passing year, word of mouth gets warped further. At some point, I'm sure, he will be written out of history altogether. It wouldn't be the first time."

I frowned, considering that. "Is that why he would change his name? To avoid the association?"

"Perhaps," Scion said, "but I do not think so. Hiding one's name is hardly uncommon, *Lonnie*." His tone dripped with derision, and I flushed.

"He was hiding his name to avoid bewitchment, then?" I furrowed my brow. "I always assumed you all had secret names that you chose not to share."

"None of us is using a false name." Scion looked around at his family, and his gaze lingered on Thalia for a moment, a question in his eyes. I took that to mean he didn't know her well enough to be sure.

"No," she said softly.

He continued as if uninterrupted. "We have several middle names and titles, mostly for the sake of ceremony, but the risk of a name-binding to any of us is far smaller than it would be to you..." He paused and gritted his teeth as if pained by his next words. "Probably."

Aine whipped her head around to look at Scion so fast that her wine sloshed in her glass. Based on her extreme reaction, I expected her to say something, but she remained stonily silent.

I narrowed my gaze, still focused on Scion. "But a true name gives you power over anything."

"No, it doesn't," Aine said slowly, a small smile spread across her face as I turned to her instead. She laughed, high and delighted. "It's only logical that it would only be possible to hold power over something weaker than yourself."

I stared blankly at them all, flabbergasted. "How can that be right? Everyone knows to hide their names from the Fae, or you'll use them to bewitch us into bargains."

"Yes," Scion said, as if explaining why the sun rises and sets to a very small child. "*We* will use them against *you*, but do you think that when we pray to Aisling, we are invoking her false name? What about other gods?"

I blinked. "I...I don't know."

"I do. No god or high queen, for that matter, would use a false name. Queen Aisling had three mates, so we know from that alone that she was far more powerful than anyone else of her time."

"So, true names make no difference to you?"

"That's not what I said," Aine replied. "I said that you can only control someone weaker than you, and name-oaths are only dangerous to the weak."

I bit my lip, thinking. This was staggering information and something that my mother couldn't possibly have known, or she wouldn't have been so fearful every day of her life. Or perhaps she still would have. I supposed it might not have mattered much to her. "Would that not be true for your brother too, though?" I asked. "Dulla—er, Ambrose? Or was he less powerful than you?"

Scion crossed his arms. "Ambrose is far from weak, but there are few Fae who can do as we do and simply flout common convention. I have wondered if he was attempting to downplay his own power by adopting an obviously false name, as if he were trying to hide his own."

Interesting. It was possible, I supposed. "Is it obviously fake?"

Scion smirked. "I take it you do not speak the old language."

"No." I took a sip of wine. "I never found I needed to know any word other than Slúagh."

Gwydion laughed, as if I'd been joking. Aine smacked him, while Thalia looked uncomfortable, and Scion just held my gaze, refusing to look away. "'Dullahan' means 'Nightmare.' There used to be creatures known as the Dullahan. They were phantom horsemen who rode at night across worlds, leaving carnage in their wake as the afflicted do now. They are one of the Unseelie monsters who haunt the realm of Underneath, banished from the rest of Elsewhere by Queen Aisling and her mates."

I shuddered, unable to tear my gaze away from his. "Why Dullahan, though? Why that monster specifically?"

"Scion," Aine said, warning in her tone. "She doesn't need to know all this."

He ignored her, barreling on as if now that the floodgates were opened, he could not stop. "The Unseelie court is ruled by might as we are, rather than by a particular hereditary line."

I scoffed. "Elsewhere certainly has a hereditary royal family."

"No, we don't," he said sharply. "That's not how it works and was never meant to be. Our courts are ruled by the right of power; it's simply that there has never been a stronger force in courts above the wall."

I didn't feel like arguing that with him. He was not currently making a very good case for himself, given that technically he'd lost the throne to me but had made no move to leave. The entire Everlast family—save for Bael—was simply carrying on as if nothing had happened and things would eventually return to as they had been before. "Fine. And in Underneath, is it the same?"

"No. They have power struggles often among creatures of all races, not just Fae. There have been dragon kings and banshee queens, and I believe there was a leshy ruler a few centuries ago. At one time, their leadership shifted at least twice a year."

"At one time?"

"There has been only one king for several decades now, as no one has been able to unseat him, but that's not the point I was trying to make." He glanced at his cousins as if trying to communicate something to them without words.

Aine picked up the story. "The original king who built this palace was not High Fae," she said carefully. "He was rumored to be a Dullahan."

Oh. It dawned on me that they didn't know I'd heard the legend of their curse or of the Unseelie King. They wouldn't know I'd heard about their ancestor and Queen Aisling already, and I had a feeling that perhaps I should not reveal the fact that Bael had told me.

"Do you think that's true?" I asked.

Scion shook his head. "Most likely not. I'm not sure how any High Fae could breed with something that is almost entirely smoke, but the rumor is enough to be frightening to some."

I sighed, collapsing back into my chair and rubbing my temples. I wasn't sure which I preferred—this, where I was allowed to sit in the room among them, or the silence and torment I'd experienced before. It seemed as if the choice should be obvious, but the overwhelming pressure of all this information made me long, in some ways, to go back.

And that was without even considering everything...*else.*

"May we revisit the issue at hand," Thalia said tersely. She was the only one who had not moved much from her original position in the room, still hovering quite close to the wall, but now she moved away from it and began to pace. "This history is all well and good, but Aine is right; Ambrose was the only one with the ability and motivation to bring any of the afflicted this far south."

I was not sure I understood what motivation they were referring to, but I would far rather believe that Ambrose Dullahan had summoned these creatures than that somehow *I'd* done it. Still, something didn't sit right. "I did not think it was the goal of the rebellion to destroy the continent, merely to liberate it."

Everyone glared at me, but for once, I didn't back down. What were they going to do?

No one had ever come through on a threat to whip me or cut off a limb, and they were not allowed to kill me between hunts. Moreover, if Thalia was to be believed, Scion's inscrutable mood had yet again shifted. Now, perhaps he didn't want me dead, anyway. Scion could try to imprison me again, but Bael would find me soon enough.

It was all quite liberating, actually, and I nearly laughed.

There was nothing they could do to me.

"You don't know what the fuck you're talking about," Scion growled.

I merely smiled. It was hard to rise to his bait now, with my new armor of temporary protection surrounding me. "At least you know where he's going next," I said offhand.

"What do you mean?" Scion asked.

"He said he would see me in Inbetwixt, and he didn't…does that not mean that he still will?"

Scion gave me a long, searching look that felt as if I were being examined from the inside out. My heart sped up, and I stiffened under his gaze, realizing that perhaps I'd made a mistake.

Had they not just said that Ambrose was a seer? Or had Bael told me that? *Where did I hear that before?*

Scion clenched his jaw and narrowed his eyes, then released a sigh of resignation. He tore his eyes from mine and looked from Aine to Thalia, curiously ignoring Gwydion altogether. "It seems the only option is that she must return to Inbetwixt."

The finality of his words echoed through the room, and I startled.

"Wait!" I rushed to say. "That's not what I meant."

Aine ignored me. "Agreed. Perhaps we should send guards?"

"No," Scion replied. "I'll go."

"What did you just say?" I gasped, my voice trembling. My hands balled up into fists. "You must be out of your mind if you think I am going anywhere with you."

He gave me a long, imperious look, and when he spoke, his tone dripped with sarcasm. "But we seemed to be getting along so much better."

I barked a humorless laugh. "I already did my part to assist you. I am in no way obligated to travel the continent with you, my lord."

"You are hardly my ideal travel companion either." His expression was more annoyed than angry. "But you just said yourself that Ambrose intends to see you in Inbetwixt, so obviously, you will have to be there."

Foolish. Stupid. Impossible… This was why I should never enjoy anything. Never have a single moment of reprieve. The very second I believed they could do nothing more to me was when they started plotting. As if my thought alone was a jinx. A curse.

"But…" I cast around wildly for some excuse as to why I could not travel with him. "What about the next hunt?"

Aine took a sip of wine and shrugged. "The hunting season will matter little if the country is destroyed in the meantime."

I had to press my lips together, afraid the next sound out of my mouth would be a sob or perhaps a scream. How sad that I would prefer to attend the event where I would be hunted down like prey rather than put myself at Scion's mercy for even one moment. How much sadder that I almost wanted to suggest that perhaps Ambrose Dullahan was not going to destroy the country at all—perhaps it was my fault, and I certainly had no intention of doing it again.

But I was not so distraught as to say anything quite *that* stupid. Not yet.

I shot up from my chair, causing it to squeak and rock back against the plush carpet. "No. I will not submit to this."

Everything stilled in the room, mingled anger and confusion splashed across every face. The royals exchanged glances, seemingly unsure what to do. I assumed they weren't used to being defied and were debating whether it was better to use torture or bribery to bring me around to their way of thinking.

Perhaps my armor had a kink—regardless, I had no intention of staying around long enough for them to reach a conclusion.

LIKE MOST OF MY DECISIONS IN RECENT WEEKS, THE CHOICE TO RUN was neither effective nor did it endear me to the Everlasts. Still, the effort made me feel as if I still had some semblance of control over my life—small as it was.

The corridor outside my room had a door to a spiral staircase on one side and a long hall flanked by dozens of closed doors and flickering sconces on the other. I took the stairs, quickly descending the steps two at a time, my heart pounding wildly in my chest.

Scion's thundering footsteps behind me echoed all through the stairwell, only drowned out by his voice. "Where the fuck do you think you're going?"

Good question.

It wasn't until that exact moment that I realized I was heading for Bael's room.

I no longer cared for the excuse that he was unavailable to speak. I didn't care that I likely wouldn't make it all the way downstairs or that I wasn't even sure if the prince would be in his chamber. I didn't care that he'd wanted to hide his secret from me when we last discussed it. All that mattered was finding him, as truly, I had nowhere else to go.

"Are you ignoring me for sport?" Scion growled, moving closer with every step.

"No," I replied, gaze fixed on my feet, thundering down the stone stairs. "I simply assumed you would continue speaking no matter what I said. You do like the sound of your own voice."

He barked a harsh laugh. "And yet, the moment you open your mouth, I curse the evolution of language itself."

I snuck a backward glance at him, only to find that he was staring intently at me, and my look did not go unnoticed. Caught in his murderous gaze, I stumbled over my skirt and threw out an arm to catch myself, flailing as my stomach leapt into my throat. In the blink of an eye, Scion was there, catching me around the waist before I could break my neck.

However, it was no act of mercy.

I gasped when instead of placing me back on my feet, he continued to hold me, just far enough off the floor that I'd lost all control. "Missing your pathetic little knife now, rebel?"

I reached for him, trying to claw at any free bit of skin I could reach, kicking wildly. "Put me down, you arrogant prick."

The prince snorted derisively. His fingers fanned out across my stomach in a move that felt as much like a threat as an embrace. "I believe I've been quite lenient thus far today, but you have finally managed to run out my patience."

I shivered, and I wasn't sure if it was fear or excitement that sped my heart. I let out a shaking breath. "Likewise."

He leaned in, his own breath caressing my ear. "Allow me to remind you who holds the power here."

17
LONNIE
THE OBSIDIAN PALACE, THE CITY OF EVERLAST

For the second time in so many days, I spun through the darkness, wild and disoriented.

This time, when I felt the world start to fall away, I had some idea of what was to come, though I was not sure that improved the experience. Which was better? To jump from a cliff or be pushed?

The only real thing to me for the brief moments of darkness was my churning stomach and Prince Scion's large arm holding my waist before my feet slammed into hard ground, first one and then the other. It was as if I'd taken a running start and leapt too far off a slight ledge or missed a step walking up stairs.

I wavered, wobbled, and tipped forward as the world seemed to crumble beneath me. My stomach lurched, positive it was left behind, and when I opened my eyes, my head swum. Scion let me go, and my knees crashed into soft earth.

"Breathe, rebel," came Scion's voice from somewhere to my right.

I opened my mouth to snap at him. No doubt his next words would be something biting, anyway—some mocking about how I was too weak and human to travel like he could. "I—"

Nothing else emerged. Nothing verbal, at least.

My stomach churned in protest, and my skin turned clammy, my throat tightening and nausea making the earth spin. My back arched, and I promptly vomited what little was in my stomach onto the ground before me. Water and bile climbed up my throat, and I coughed, doubling over for what felt like a very long time.

"Give it a moment. I imagine it's a strange feeling if you're not accustomed to traveling this way."

I wiped my mouth with the back of my hand and craned my neck to glare daggers at the prince. "Are you mocking me?"

Scion leaned against a tree, watching me with only mild interest. "No."

He had better not be, as this was his damned fault, the miserable bastard. Coughing one final time, I finally focused on where he'd taken us. My eyes widened again, this time from shock.

We stood in the forest surrounded by dense, swampy wetland with moss and vines hanging from the overhung trees. Now that I was paying attention, I could hear the distant sounds of insects and birds and see the faint hint of a weak, setting sun peaking the branches overhead. "Where are we?"

"Inbetwixt." He shoved away from the tree with the heel of his boot and gave me a condescending look. "More specifically, this is Cutthroat. It's the northern district of the city. The gate is just up there."

Ice filled my veins, and my mouth went impossibly dry as I stared at him in incredulous disbelief. "You…you—" I spluttered and broke off, unable to think of something bad enough to call him. There were no words to express my horror. "You…fucking *Fae*."

"Is that supposed to be insulting?" He stared down at me, an eyebrow raised. "Keep trying, rebel. I'm sure one of these days, you'll learn to string two words together effectively."

"Fuck you."

"Congratulations." He smirked. "*Two words.*"

I could have screamed in frustration, but instead, I spun around, turning my back on him as I lowered my voice to almost a whisper. "Take us back this instant."

"You know I won't do that," he replied. "Not until we've found Ambrose."

"But—" I broke off as a buzzing filled my head, and a numbness seemed to wash over me.

Scion was many things—some I'd be embarrassed to voice aloud —but he'd never given me any reason to believe he was weak-willed. In fact, he might have been the only person I'd ever met who was more stubborn than I was. There was no point in arguing. This was completely and utterly *pointless.* "Do not speak to me."

I marched in the opposite direction from where he stood, paying no attention to where I was going. My mind raced. What was I to do now?

I couldn't very well go running back to the capital when I had no sense of direction, and in any case, who would even know where I was? Where would I go? Maybe if I could escape him in the city, I could get a message to Bael, but then what? Maybe…*maybe*…

Scion strode after me, walking at a normal, leisurely pace as I practically jogged through the underbrush, holding my too-long gown over my knees, to get away from him.

"Let us speak frankly," he said, tone unbothered.

"Let us never speak again," I snapped.

"Oh, but if only that were an option."

My head had begun to pound. My skin was flushing too hot, and I was quite sure that now it had little to do with traveling. I scowled and heaved in breath after breath, trying and failing to calm the rage coursing through my veins. Anger tended to lead me down dangerous paths…paths that resulted in my becoming the queen in the first place or spending a year in the dungeon. Paths that often nearly revealed secrets that could destroy everything I'd sacrificed so much to keep hidden. Paths that might or might not have summoned a horde of afflicted from Aftermath to the capital.

I needed to calm down, yet this male was testing my resolve. "Stop following me."

"Isn't it ironic how much more peaceful both of our lives might have been had you felt that way before now?" Behind me, Scion let out an exasperated sigh. "You are wandering deeper into the woods."

"Good!"

"I can chase you all night if I have to," he warned. "But it would be better for you if I don't."

"And why is that?" I snapped, annoyed that he'd managed to make me reply at all.

"Because you are already driving me to the point of near total insanity, and you do not want that, rebel. Trust me."

I could have laughed. *I* was driving *him* insane? "I don't know what you expected, my lord," I drawled, hatred dripping from my tone. "Most women don't appreciate being kidnapped. I suppose I should think myself lucky I am not yet caged."

His silence was telling.

"Think carefully, rebel," he said after a moment. "There can be animosity between us or agreement, but the only person who stands to gain anything is you."

I stopped walking, my entire body practically vibrating with anger as I spun to stare defiantly at him. He was making it impossible to calm down, and now, much to my dismay, sparks of heat had begun to travel down my arms, almost like spreading flames.

I could not, would not, let them erupt. Not only because I feared my bargain with the snake creature in the woods or because I was not sure of what might happen—was not sure if perhaps my mother's warnings had meant more than I'd realized, and it was my fault that the afflicted attacked. No, it was more stubbornness than anything. Scion didn't deserve my rage. He wasn't allowed to win.

"I don't understand you, my lord," I said too quickly, leaving on the honorific out of habit. "Why would you want to spend any time with me, anyway? Let alone travel with me."

There was deep irony in the fact that mere hours ago, I would have loved nothing more than to set off in search of Dullahan. I'd spent weeks looking for him myself. If only I'd realized I could have asked Bael about his cousin…but there was no fixing that now. Even for a chance to speak with Dullahan, I would never willingly spend time this close to Scion, especially alone.

"It isn't about you," the prince said bitterly. "The afflicted are too dangerous to be allowed to roam free for any reason. Thousands of people will die."

Regardless of my anger, I was loath to admit that we agreed on that much. The threat of the afflicted was real, yet so was the threat of the male in front of me, and only one of those two had made it clear that they wished to personally see me dead.

If I was perfectly, entirely, without a doubt certain that it was me who summoned the afflicted, perhaps I would have said so, but was that the only option? Was it not possible that Ambrose Dullahan had something to do with it as well?

Was that denial? I wasn't sure.

"Fine, if it's so important, then let Bael take me to Inbetwixt."

"We're already here."

"Semantics," I replied, wondering if I truly sounded like Lady Aine or if it was only my fear of behaving like the Fae rising again.

Scion ran both hands through his inky hair, his silver rings glinting in the low light of the setting sun through the trees. "If it were possible to wait, I might agree to that, but Bael will not be free to speak with you, let alone travel, for several days at the very least."

"Why?" I demanded, propping my hands on my hips.

He cocked his head at me. "If I tell you, will you cooperate?"

I sucked in a startled breath. He'd reached for the offer so readily that I had to wonder if it hadn't been something he'd already been thinking of…in which case, he likely didn't care much about the information, or else, thought I would eventually find out, regardless.

Or, perhaps, I was overthinking it.

I paused, biting my lip. I couldn't imagine any way that a bargain with Prince Scion would benefit me, but then I thought back on Thalia's words: *"Cooperate with Scion, and I suspect he would give you anything."*

Was this what she meant?

"No," I said after a moment. "I'd be a fool to agree to that, as Bael will tell me himself. Anyway, I don't trust you."

"A pity." He scowled. "I would far prefer to make a bargain with you, but if you won't agree, then I won't feel a shred of guilt in forcing your hand."

"Of course not. You never do when you cut down innocent people to meet your own ends."

"You are far from fucking innocent, Kingslayer," he hissed. "And there is nothing more important than preventing what is happening in Aftermath from moving south. I thought you, of all people, would understand that."

"I would understand that?" A note of hysteria crept into my tone. "Me? The person you have been accusing of being a part of this absurd rebellion for over a year? By the Source, why would *I* understand that?"

His eyes narrowed, apparently not liking being mocked the way he constantly mocked me. "You lived in Aftermath, did you not?"

That was the second time he'd either referenced or seemed unsurprised that I'd lived in Aftermath before coming to the capital. I narrowed my eyes. "So?"

"Do not pretend you don't understand the threat of the afflicted." He took a small step closer until there were barely inches between us. "And as for the rebellion, you proved to me earlier that I have been...mistaken. No one who truly worked for the rebellion would have returned to the castle as you did. We would be the last souls on the continent you would ask for help."

He didn't look particularly happy about having been mistaken, but his expression was the least of my concerns. If that was Prince Scion's idea of an apology, he could shove it up his ass.

"So does that mean you're sorry for imprisoning me? Does that mean you admit that you're wrong? I never thought I'd see the day."

He paused, holding his breath. "I had every reason to think you were guilty."

For some reason, those words sounded like a cell door closing. "So you're not sorry, then?"

His expression darkened, and he bared his teeth, looking more dangerous than I'd ever seen him, even when he was threatening to kill me. "I will never apologize for protecting the kingdom by any means necessary. If I'd been right, it would have been worth it, and I'd do it again. If you can't understand that, it's further proof that you're unworthy of the crown."

"Fine," I sneered. "As long as you understand why I will always find you unworthy of redemption."

His eyes shuttered, yet he moved infinitesimally closer until I could feel his breath on my face. "I know."

Distracted by our argument, by his all-too-consuming presence, I realized slightly too late that the shadows of the forest were growing slightly darker around us, shifting, churning, dancing, like arms creeping between the trees and over the ground. I hadn't noticed—hadn't realized it was anything more than the slight rustle of the leaves or the movement of the wind until it seemed as if night had fallen early.

A shadow crept up from somewhere near my feet, twisting around my forearm like a slithering vine. I let out a sound of alarm and tried to pull back, but it only gripped me tighter like a rope, pulling taut, imprisoning me where I stood.

The prince's silver eyes met mine as I stared up at him in horror, his shadows continuing to whirl around us like a twisted, translucent cage. He smiled, looking entirely too beautiful and too horrible at once. Like the first bloom of deadly nightshade.

"Fortunately, I have never needed your forgiveness, only your surrender."

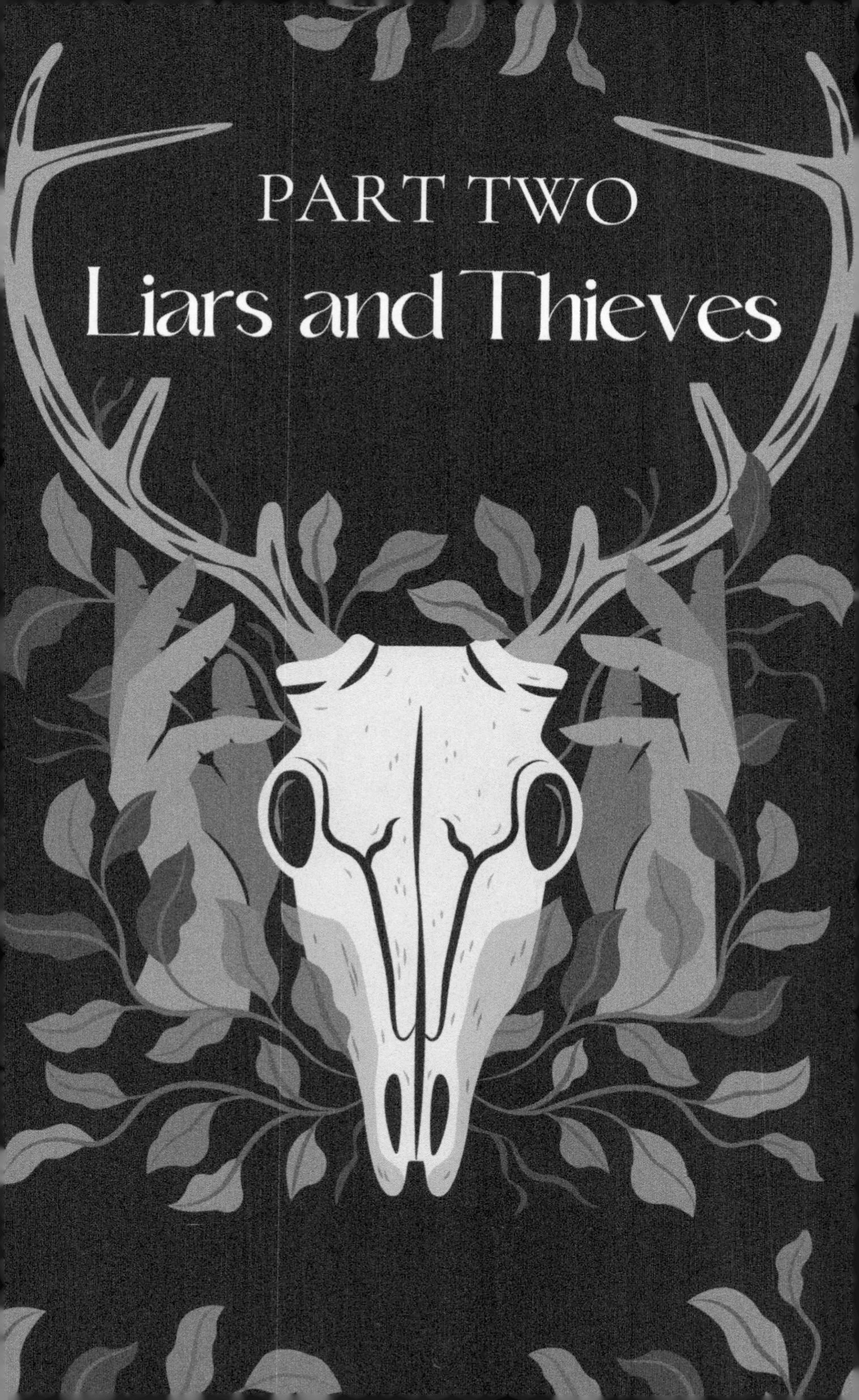
PART TWO
Liars and Thieves

18
LONNIE
THE CUTTHROAT DISTRICT, INBETWIXT

Shouts of drunken laughter, catcalls, the clang of metal, and distant music reached my ears as Scion and I trudged out of the trees and up a short hill toward a high, wooden wall. The fortification was broken only by the roofs and spires of buildings peeking over the top and a large iron gate in the center. Two lightly armed guards stood at the gate, and they made no move to stop us as we strode inside.

"By Aisling," I breathed.

I'd expected something like Cheapside, the human village on the outskirts of the capital city, but Inbetwixt was far larger than I'd envisioned. The houses that lined the street were easily as large as those in the Fae district of Everlast, and there were nearly twice as many people walking past, even though it was nearing sundown.

"Inbetwixt has the largest city on the continent, even eclipsing the size of the capital," Scion said, answering my unspoken question. "What little you saw of the province already was only the Wildes—little more than no-man's-land. This is the northern district of the actual city. The road we entered on would ultimately lead to Overcast."

I glanced up at the prince beside me with narrowed eyes and debated if I should respond at all. I gave a small tug on the shadows that wrapped around my arm, only to feel it pull back as if it were alive. I scowled.

Scion's shadowy rope twisted around my arm like a vine and seemed to end nowhere, vanishing at the end into thin air. Yet, whenever I tried to pull at it, there it was, solid and visible again, like he could feel my tugging and was only ignoring his end out of convenience. The prince was not literally dragging me, but it was a near thing, and I was very aware that if he wanted to force me to walk faster or in any direction he pleased, it was more than possible.

Motivated by the rapidly setting sun and my rumbling stomach, I'd finally reached the conclusion that I could just as easily hate Scion in the city as in the forest. My desire to prove uncooperative did not extend as far as freezing to death or starving myself, or worse, letting him physically drag me through the street, in protest of his refusal to return to the capital, nor did I want to be eaten by one of the many monsters that lurked within the Waywoods. I already had my hands more than full with the silver-eyed monster beside me.

"If the city is so large, then why is it not the capital?" I muttered, my tone mutinous.

"Tradition," he replied just as stiffly. "And their leadership is often in flux. Inbetwixt has four gates and four corresponding districts that all operate somewhat independently of each other. Cutthroat, the northern district, is overrun by the guilds."

"The who?"

Scion stepped out of the way of a man passing on horseback and was separated from me for a moment before he could answer. I took the opportunity to see if I could escape, only to find that the rope on my arm was just as sturdy as ever, whether he was standing beside me or not. *Fucking fairy magic.*

"The guilds," he repeated, falling back into step with me. "Assassins, mercenaries, the followers of Phillipa Blacktongue—"

"Who?" I asked again, interrupting him.

"Whores," he replied flatly, glancing down at me as if to gauge my reaction. "There's the thieves in the house of Doublecross and several more groups that I could not readily name."

I almost forgot to be hateful as my curiosity took over. "Are the guilds the reason you haven't conquered this city?" I asked as we turned a corner onto another street, equally as crowded as the first.

Not that I thought they should do so; it simply seemed like the kind of thing the Everlasts *would* do. They ruled by right of power, after all, and what was power if not controlling the largest city?

"No, we simply don't want to. The land isn't worth the headache that would come from managing it."

"Why?"

"I'm sure you'll see for yourself shortly, rebel."

I HAD NO IDEA WHERE WE WERE GOING AS WE WOVE OUR WAY DOWN the crowded city street, and I refused to ask. I was too angry about the situation overall. About the shadowy rope digging into my arm, the gown that was getting ruined every time I stepped on the hem, the fact I wasn't even allowed to see Bael before we left. I might not be in a cell, but I felt just as imprisoned as I had before and entirely stupid for ever thinking I had a leg up on Prince Scion.

He'd said he wanted to remind me who held the power. The message was received and my hatred entirely renewed.

The longer we walked, the thicker the crowd seemed to become, and the more eyes followed us. Scion seemed to notice as well because his shoulders tensed. "I suggest you stay close, rebel. Cutthroat is dangerous, even as far as Fae cities go."

"You say that like I have a choice," I muttered.

Regardless, I hadn't planned to wander away from Prince Scion —not yet, at least.

More and more eyes turned to look at us, and I looked down, watching the street to avoid all the prying eyes. I barely paid attention to where we were going until Scion finally came to a halt. The shadow-rope pulled me tight against him. "Ooph."

He looked down at me with an expression similar to assessing a dead animal in the road as I righted myself again and smoothed my dress.

"We've arrived," he said, sounding just as bored as he had in the forest.

I ground my teeth. The least he could do was argue with me—I had nowhere to vent my frustration, and I feared what might happen if my anger were allowed to bubble over. "Where would that be, my lord?"

His brow ticked up in something like annoyance. "The home of the Lord of Inbetwixt. I cannot say we are exactly friendly, but he should, at least, give me use of my own soldiers to find my brother."

I shook my head. Whatever he wanted, I supposed. I hardly cared, and I didn't get a say, anyway. I was merely hoping for a bed and something to eat.

We'd stopped in front of a large, white stone building, somewhere between a palace and a town house. It was well-kept, three stories, with a garden to the left and what appeared to be a rooftop veranda. Still, if not for the red and gold banners hanging from the upper windows and the fact that it was slightly larger than the surrounding homes, I wouldn't have ever known that this was the house of the most important male in the province.

Most of the houses in Inbetwixt seemed to be made of sturdier stone than the ones in Everlast, and the city as a whole felt a bit more solid. With the exception, I supposed, of the obsidian palace. The jewel of the capital, the palace was impossible to compare to the home of the Lord of Inbetwixt. There was no contest in size or stature. The palace was perhaps six, maybe even twelve times larger, and I was sure when we ventured inside, the decor would be nothing as compared to what I'd stolen from the Everlasts.

Scion ascended a short flight of white stone steps toward a door with a single footman standing outside. I followed, unable to do anything else with the rope around my arm.

"Do you really intend to meet with the Lord and Lady like this?" I hissed.

"Like what? It is not my fault you dressed inappropriately."

I glanced down at my too-ornate mulberry gown and made an angry noise in the back of my throat. "Perhaps if you had not kidnapped me, I might have chosen something else."

"I do not have the energy for this, rebel." He looked down his nose at me. "What is your concern?"

"You plan to drag me in front of other nobles like a dog on a rope? Do you not realize that will reflect worse on you than me? I had not realized you wanted all to know what a tyrannical monster you really are, *my lord*."

His lip curled, looking almost flattered. "Yet again, you fail to understand our culture. I'm not sure anyone would bat an eye."

"Take it off," I demanded.

"You know I'm not going to do that. I hardly trust that you won't go sprinting off into the crowd."

"Where am I supposed to go while we're inside?" I asked sourly. "At least take it off while we speak to the lord and lady."

It was a small concession but one that suddenly mattered to me. I didn't know or care about these nobles, but I did care that Scion seemed to think he was able to parade me around like he owned me in front of others he deemed to be of his station. He was wrong to say I didn't understand anything about Fae culture; I understood enough to realize that was likely the larger issue than the rope itself—the perception of control.

His smile grew wider. "Say 'please.'"

I closed my eyes. I could think of a whole host of other things I would rather say, none of them involving the word "please." Then again, I might like to slit his throat, please. Please, dance on his immortal grave. Please, beg my snake friend to chew *very* slowly.

"If you are hoping to make me beg, we will be standing here a very long time."

"On the contrary, I don't care either way what you do." He gave a sharp tug on my rope, forcing me to step forward. "We will be going inside either way."

Infuriating, odious, vile bastard!

I gave him a sickly sweet smile that I hoped conveyed every bit of my hatred and swallowed several times, trying to force the word from my suddenly dry throat. "*Please*."

He smirked at me, looking far too triumphant for my taste. "That's a good girl, rebel," he purred as the shadows unfurled from my arm. "Now, come."

My stomach flipped over, and I stared after him for a few seconds before following. *Shit*.

I should have known better. The Fae—the Everlasts, especially—were predators, and their beauty and sexual appeal was only one more way that they trapped their prey. Prince Scion was a master who wielded compliments and sexuality like all his other weapons—with deadly precision. Everything was intentional, calculated, two steps ahead of me. There was no innuendo he didn't mean, and it was all a choreographed dance to put me off guard.

I would just have to try harder, be on my guard at all times, or I was sure the shadows would be the least of what I needed to be afraid of.

19
LONNIE
THE CUTTHROAT DISTRICT, INBETWIXT

"No," the Lord of Inbetwixt said, his voice shaking slightly.

I blinked up at the lord in surprise a split second before Scion's enraged voice echoed off the ornate wallpaper. "What the fuck do you mean, 'No'?"

Everyone in the room, aside from Scion, tensed. This was not going well.

As soon as Scion and I had entered the home of Lord Bard and Lady Acacia of Inbetwixt, we'd been ushered into a small parlor. Small, I supposed, was relative.

Before I'd spent any time in the upper floors of the obsidian palace, I would have found the room to be enormous—it was nearly as large as the entire kitchen where I'd spent most of my formative years, with a seating area on one end and a spindle-legged piano on the other.

Either the lord and lady were expecting us, or they simply always spent their afternoons entertaining because they were already dressed to receive guests and seated as if in a painting, both on the same velvet-wrapped settee.

Lord Bard was thin and sharp-looking, with thick black hair and close-set dark eyes. His wife was waifish, almost frail, with a face that had probably once been round and a permanently saccharine smile. Two other Fae, who could only be their son and daughter, stood off to either side of the couple, looking like they would rather be anywhere else.

As soon as the butler led me and Scion inside, I suddenly remembered that I'd met not only the eldest daughter of Lord Bard and Lady Acacia before, but Melina of Inbetwixt had been rude to the point of threatening. Now, the brunette in the tangerine-orange gown stared meekly at the floor while her parents struggled to negotiate with Scion over the use of the Inbetwixt army.

"We mean, Prince Scion, that we cannot spare the soldiers." Lady Acacia gave an awkward chuckle. "If only we'd had more notice, then perhaps…"

"I don't need to give you fucking notice. It's my damn army you're borrowing."

Scion shook with rage, and I could see the shadows moving around his hands. In the corner, a guard winced slightly, and Scion made his hands into tight fists, digging his nails into his palms. I wondered distantly what Thalia would have to say about that observation—was it worth hoarding if I had no idea what it meant?

"Yes," said Lady Acacia. "But it's only that they're occupied, my lord."

"Doing what?"

The lord and lady stiffened. A silent communication seemed to pass between them—her widening eyes, his thinning lips. Lord

Bard turned back to Scion. "You must realize that the guilds have been growing in power. The rebellion might be your largest concern, but here, we have more pressing issues."

Scion's face remained unmoved. "I will give you pressing issues if I'm not permitted to take my soldiers."

I watched as the nobles exchanged uneasy glances, their brows furrowed. There was a silent understanding between them that no matter how much they wanted to, they could not surrender their military forces.

"Where are the soldiers?" I asked abruptly.

"Most are on the eastern gate," Lady Acacia replied, her small voice shaking.

I stared at her, feeling the tension in my eyes mirrored in hers. I had no idea what was relevant about that, but it seemed to mean something to her. Granted, I could barely keep track of the winding streets and alleys, let alone remember who was fighting whom for control of this city. "Is that relevant?"

Scion still looked annoyed, but for once, I did not think it was at me. He answered, "They control that gate. It's the closest to the seaport."

I narrowed my eyes. Should they not control all the gates as the rulers of Inbetwixt?

"Exactly," Lady Acacia continued before I could ask for clarification. "An entire fleet was recently attacked and sunk by the thieves' guild around the new year. We have not yet been able to recover, and what ships have been repaired or replaced are in greater danger than ever."

I startled, my heartbeat picking up. *I found myself on a ship bound for Nevermore…*

"We can't spare any soldiers," Lord Bard continued, "and if you take those we have already, then the trade route to Nevermore will undoubtedly fail entirely."

Another sailor approached, shaking my shoulders. "They're boarding!" he screamed in my face. "We'll fucking lose everything."

Was it a coincidence? It couldn't be.

"Perhaps if you actually did something about the damn thieves, we could spare the soldiers," the son said from the corner of the room.

I looked up, taking him in for the first time. His tone was sullen, bitter, a bit like Prince Lysander. He was built like his father, with his mother's lighter hair, and his attire matched that of the rest of his family—a flashy coral waistcoat paired with a pale blue pair of trousers. When we locked eyes, I saw a mix of curiosity and revulsion in his stare.

Scion made no reply, ignoring the younger male's comment. His silence was heavier than usual, and I saw a hint of something in his expression before he masked it with another emotion: apathy.

Finally, he said, "None of this is worth discussing, as in the end, I will still need to take the soldiers. Your inability to protect your gates is your problem and perhaps a sign that we should consider new leadership."

Lady Acacia sucked in a sharp breath, her eyes wide with shock. As if a jolt of electricity had shot through the room, Melina snapped her head up from where she had been focused on the floor, staring at her mother in alarm.

She turned narrowed eyes on me, but when she spoke, she was addressing Scion. "I might point out they are not your soldiers, lord. They're hers."

There was a long, heavy pause while every eye in the room turned to me. I froze, not having expected to be needed in this conversation.

No one, least of all me, knew how to handle the political nightmare that had been thrust upon the country. Perhaps if the Everlast family had been more willing to work with me, if their advisors had been helpful rather than dangerous, things might have been different. As it was, things were incredibly tenuous for both me and the country.

"Oh…" I said awkwardly. "I am not here in that capacity. Believe me, I would far prefer not to be here at all."

But the lord and lady had pounced on the realization of who I was—apparently, they had not put two and two together before now, or perhaps they had simply not cared enough to consider why Scion would be dragging a human around with him on his diplomatic errands.

Or maybe it wasn't so odd. Maybe he often spoke of politics surrounded by pets and concubines. I'd certainly beheld stranger things in the courts and seen Scion himself with human women on at least two occasions. Unbidden, heat rose to the back of my neck at the thought, and I willed it away.

"Yes," the lord said, new life in his voice. "Is it not true that the Slúagh now commands the army?"

I almost laughed. He'd said that with so much confidence it was like he saw absolutely no problem with his words.

"Lonnie," Scion said dangerously. "Tell the lord that the soldiers belong to me. That you don't understand nor care about the army and would never presume to…correct?"

Scion turned wooden beside me as I bit the inside of my cheek. The urge to spite him—to give Inbetwixt the soldiers just because he did not want that—was almost too strong to ignore.

Of course, the lord and lady were likely no better—they might have even been worse; I'd had no time to know—but they were not currently holding me hostage in a strange city.

"The thieves are the ones preventing you from sparing the soldiers, correct?" I asked. "Then what if we were to help be rid of the thieves?"

Eyes widened at me. Even the son who'd suggested it looked surprised. When I glanced at Scion, however, he was not surprised but furious. A prickle of fear traveled down my spine, and I ignored it.

"Er, yes," Lord Bard said quickly. "That would be agreeable."

"Fine," I replied flatly. "Then I don't see why we can't all come to some quicker resolution than sitting here and arguing."

I did not care about the thieves or the soldiers overly much. I might like to find Ambrose Dullahan, but not precisely for the same reasons as Scion, and not enough to spend infinite time with him.

I would never see Rosey's journals again—I'd accepted that, albeit bitterly—but the one thing that stood out to me was her dream about this ship sinking and a message that was meant to be delivered. If, by some chance, it was the same ship…it was a slim chance, but better than nothing, that the group who'd sunk it would know what the message was.

If I could not read Rosey's words, could not speak to Dullahan directly without giving up too much of myself in exchange, perhaps I could ask the thieves about my sister.

If, indeed, the dream was real.

Just as easily, this could prove to be nothing—unrelated—I'd almost prefer that. But either way, I had to know.

Scion barely looked at me as we stepped back outside onto the city street. I was not sure I'd ever seen him so angry without shouting or shooting shadows from his fingers, and indeed, the silence was almost more alarming as we set off again—toward what, I was afraid to ask. He didn't even remember to put the rope back on my arm. Not that I was going to remind him.

The streets had grown, if possible, busier in the time we'd been in the home of the lord and lady, and I found myself shivering as more and more eyes followed us. Strangers shouted unintelligible things, and on occasion, some brave fairy would try to approach. Despite the animosity between us, I found myself pushing closer into Scion's side and berating myself for it.

My worst enemy had turned himself into my safest harbor, and I could not have hated him more for it if I tried.

"This is worse than I imagined," Scion hissed as some brave Fae took a jolting step toward us as if he intended to reach for me.

Oh, is he speaking to me now, then? I did not know why I cared. I hardly wanted to speak to him either.

I danced out of the way and kept moving. "What is?"

Prince Scion turned to look back and shook his head. "It crossed my mind that bringing you out in public would cause a commotion." He paused and shouldered a Fae male out of the way, his expression growing darker as he did so. "...but I did not think it would be this obvious."

I coughed, sucking in air too sharply in my surprise. "I assumed they were staring at *you*."

It was impossible to deny that whether they realized they were staring at the Prince of Ravens or not, anyone looking at Scion would be taken aback. He was a head taller than most anyone else on the street and startlingly good-looking, even by Fae standards. His presence alone was like dangerous, violent waves of shadow, and when he looked at you, it was impossible to decide whether to run toward him or as far away as your legs could carry you.

"No." The prince spoke low and pointedly. "They're not looking at me."

I gaped at him. It had not even occurred to me that I could be the cause of the commotion, but of course, it should have.

My entire life, the Fae had been drawn to me like moths to a flame. As a servant, it had been hell and made it impossible for me to make friends, as everyone viewed me as dangerous to be near. Now that he mentioned it, however, I realized something I hadn't noticed before: in the last month or so, the curse had not been nearly so debilitating. "I didn't think—"

"We should not discuss this here," Scion growled, reaching down to touch the back of my elbow and steer me to turn to our right down a less crowded alleyway. "Go this way. I would prefer to avoid a fight in the next fifty yards."

I followed his lead, supposing it was better than being dragged or allowing some strange fairy to accost me in the street. Scion, at least, was the evil I knew, which could only be better than some unknown threat.

We crossed the street and came to a halt in front of the shabby, pinewood front door of a two-story stone building. Scion let out something like a growl mixed with a sigh of relief and leaned against the wall to the left of the door. "Thank the fucking Source."

I glanced around the street, hoping to glean for myself more about where we were. There was faint noise coming from the building, and a sign hanging off the roof above the only window on the first floor read "The Crossroads."

"Where are we?"

Scion sneered down at me. "You don't know? I thought this was your mission to run now."

I drew myself up, annoyed. "Is there something you wanted to say? You weren't exactly getting anywhere back there—excuse me for coming up with another solution."

He looked at me, more disgusted than angry. "Is that what you think you accomplished? No, rebel, you've hardly come up with a solution. What you've done in addition to destroying the monarchy and ruining my family is gone and nearly started a fucking civil crisis because you do not understand how the country is run and never will!"

I reeled back as if he'd slapped me. "What are you talking about?"

"I can't discuss this with you right now."

Scion pushed off the wall and stepped in front of me to open the door and, huffing an angry breath through his nose, gestured for me to walk ahead of him. Then he stopped and stood in the doorway, frozen for a moment, his too-intense gaze fixed on me. I stared back, perplexed, and finally took a step forward to walk ahead of him.

"No, never mind," he muttered, stepping into the warmth of the tavern and motioning for me to follow. "Get behind me."

"Struggling with manners versus station, my lord?" I breathed. "Are you truly that concerned with letting the human filth walk in front of you?"

"No," he snapped back. "I was trying to decide how best to protect the human filth, given that she goes out of her way to taunt death at every opportunity."

"I see no one here more likely to murder me than you."

He sighed. "You are certainly testing my resolve, I will give you that much."

20
LONNIE
THE CUTTHROAT DISTRICT, INBETWIXT

I peeked out from behind Scion's armored back as we walked inside and saw that the room beyond was nothing more than a tavern, unremarkable as compared to any other I'd seen. The few patrons grew quiet as we crossed the room to the bar. All conversation stopped, and a lonely flute player in the corner gave up his tinkling tune and stared slack-jawed and terrified.

This time, I was positive it wasn't me they were staring at, but Scion barely seemed to notice as he reached for the nearest empty stool and sat down. Begrudgingly, I took a seat beside him.

At least this tavern was bound to have food, I told myself. *You're doing this for your dinner. Wonderful, warm stew. Tasty, flakey biscuits…*

"What are you smiling about?" Scion asked.

"I am imagining your death."

"And when you imagine it, are you still there tormenting me? Or am I finally at peace?"

"Could you achieve peace if you hadn't killed me first?" I snapped back. "Has that not been your singular purpose for quite some time?"

"I told you. I'm not going to hurt you."

I had to think for a moment to recall when exactly he'd said that. In my room—his room—I supposed, though I had not taken it all that seriously. I was more inclined to believe Thalia's rumor that he'd tried to prevent my death in the second hunt for some inscrutable reason, if only because there was more clear evidence. Still, I couldn't understand why the sudden change of heart.

"Tell me again, then," I said. "I'm not sure I believed you."

He looked me directly in the eye, and it was a struggle not to look away. As if I'd been sucked into a pool of silver, haunting, hypnotic. "I'm not going to hurt you." He sat perfectly still for a moment, and then his face contorted, as if in pain, and he added, "Right now."

I tore my eyes away.

"Ha!" I should not have been pleased to hear he wanted to murder me, but it was simply the fact that my world made sense again. "Because you need me, but how long will that last?"

He ground his teeth. "We will never be able to do a single thing if you constantly question my every motive."

"Then say what you mean, my lord. You evidently cannot say that you will not hurt me."

He smirked, and his gaze turned heated. "What if you liked to be hurt?"

Heat rose to my cheeks. "I know what you're doing. You cannot constantly distract me with sex."

"Evidently, I can, rebel. Why stop when it works so well?"

I swallowed thickly. *Bastard.* "Answer the question."

"It's too broad of a statement." He scowled, looking annoyed with himself. "I should have said I have no intention of killing you."

"Do you?"

"Not currently, but I may reassess if you don't shut the fuck up."

I raised an eyebrow. That was not all that comforting, as it meant he could still kill me tomorrow, but I left it. I had no intention of going around in circles all night long and still getting nowhere. "So what are we doing here?"

"I am drinking." He looked sideways at me, even as he raised a hand and waved for a bartender. "You can do whatever the hell you like. I hardly care as long as you do not attempt to leave before we are able to locate Cross."

"Who?"

"Cross. The founder of the thieves' guild." He raised a brow at me. "The male that you all but forced us to pay a visit to. He owns this tavern."

"I didn't—"

"It's fine, rebel." He waved me off. "Don't misunderstand, what you did was still absurdly foolish, but I will throw you a proverbial lifeline this one time."

I was not sure I liked the sound of that. "I take it you know this 'Cross'?"

"Of course. The guilds can only exist with our blessing."

Ah, there it was. The real reason for all his anger.

He might say "our blessing," as in all the Everlasts, but I presumed that truly meant "his" blessing. He was unwilling to help the Lord and Lady of Inbetwixt because he had some dealing with these guilds, perhaps with this "Cross," and now I'd ruined it for him—or, at least, made it harder.

Thalia would be proud of me for hoarding my information, and Scion, it seemed, was a wealth of accidental secrets. Perhaps he thought he was beyond reproach—so powerful that he did not have to be too careful with what he said. Perhaps he simply didn't care. Whatever the case, I was going to pay better attention to what he let slip from now on.

"So if you know Cross, then how will we get the soldiers of Inbetwixt to help?" I asked. "Which one will you betray?"

"How indeed?" he snapped. "It's almost as if I was attempting to avoid this very situation, and some hapless fool bumbled directly into it."

My cheeks burned. This time, I could see what he was getting at, yet I refused to admit it. "Perhaps if you hadn't dragged me along in the first place or had told me what we were trying to accomplish—"

"It is no matter," Scion said. "Fortunately for you, rebel, I have already planned for this possibility."

"You…what?" I stopped before I could blurt out something stupid.

"The Lord of Inbetwixt has always been difficult. You asked earlier why we do not wish to overtake Inbetwixt or use the city as a capital, as it is larger and better positioned for trading." He looked sideways at me, seeming to almost be hiding a smile. "The high court family has been losing territory in their own city for years and now control only the eastern gate, which suits us fine. That means they still have control over the docks and the waterways, but we don't have to worry about them trying to provoke any kind of uprising."

"I don't understand."

"As you saw, they live in the Northern district, but they are surrounded by territory that they cannot control. The situation is…tenuous."

"I empathize," I grumbled.

"I can imagine," he said lightly. "I have long known he might deny the use of my soldiers for any reason, but it is far better for him to know we are in the city than not. Now, we are unlikely to be bothered while meeting with Cross. You might even say Cross is the reason why we are here."

I stiffened, preparing for yet another revelation I was sure to hate. "I thought Dullahan was the reason we're here."

"Yes, but I don't want to simply sit and wait for him to appear." His tone was slightly resentful. "Who knows how long that might take, and I assume you hadn't planned to stay in the city indefinitely?"

"No!" I said too fast. "I—I can't."

"It's not as though you have much else to do," he pointed out.

"I want to return to Bael."

I'd reconciled the fact that we may have to stay the night but assumed there would be some inn or perhaps the home of another noble where I might lock myself in a room and ignore Scion as much as possible. Now, however, I realized how impossibly short-sighted that had been.

Of course, it might take more than a single night to track down Dullahan. It could take weeks or even months…but Scion was right—weeks wasn't an option.

"There is no chance that Bael even realizes you have left," Scion said, sounding almost bitter for no reason I could understand. "If he did, I'm sure he would be here."

"How long will that last?" I asked, sounding almost hysterical now.

He looked at me seriously, and I was sure he was going to withhold the information from me again as some form of torture, but oddly, he didn't. "The shortest I've seen is two days. It could be a week."

"A week!" The next hunt in Nevermore was in just over two weeks. If we stayed here for a week and then returned only to leave again…what if they didn't want to travel with me again? "Two days. I want to go back in two days."

Scion looked over at me with faint interest. "I would also prefer that this be a short excursion, but Ambrose has a way of turning up only when he chooses and never when you'd like him to."

"I don't care. I want to go back in two days."

He licked his lips. "I'll consider it after we talk to Cross."

I frowned, not liking to leave the issue open. "Who is this Cross? How do you know him?"

"An old friend of mine from the army. He may have been a soldier once, but no longer, and now he has the best information network in the city. If my brother is here, Cross will find him."

Oh, so he didn't just know Cross—he *knew* him. *Wonderful.* It was so lovely to be not only moved around on the prince's chess board but flung off it altogether. Like the game had changed without me ever being warned.

I glared at him. "If this worked out exactly as you planned, then why yell at me?"

"It was not exactly as I planned," he replied. "Merely one of the possibilities. I would have far preferred you kept your mouth shut. As for the rest, you should understand that by behaving like a selfish, spiteful fool, you may very well end up burning our castle to the ground."

"I don't know how you can say that without withering from the hypocrisy of it."

He smiled. "Spite me in your own time, rebel, but do not try to use the kingdom against me. I will destroy you to save it."

That felt more like prophecy than threat, and the words rumbled through me, chilling me to the bone.

Before I could reply, the bartender appeared in front of us—or rather, in front of me. "Hello, darling."

I looked up, slightly alarmed, and my mouth fell open.

I'd spent so much time around the Everlasts as of late I was growing somewhat used to the beauty of the Fae. I certainly couldn't say I was immune to it. Bael absolutely had an easier time than he should have to convince me to not argue with him, and there was something quite strange about how easy it was to get stuck in Scion's unusual eyes, but I didn't fall to the ground elf-struck and sobbing in their presence. I'd never done so, though I knew that could happen to humans…rarely, but it did happen.

This bartender, deep in a strange, nearly empty tavern in the heart of Inbetwixt, made me believe in the stories of mortal women falling to pieces at the mere sight of Fae males. He wore all black, except for a red armband high on his left bicep, and in parts, he was probably no more good-looking than any of the princes—chiseled features, straight nose, dark hair—but there was an unusual, glittering glow to his skin that I couldn't stop staring at. I wanted to touch it. *Now.*

"Kaius," Scion said sharply.

Oh gods. I hadn't even realized I'd reached out before strong fingers gripped my hand, and I jerked, nearly toppling off my stool.

It took me a long moment to realize he wasn't speaking to me—that the word he'd uttered was a name and not, in fact, some mysterious language I didn't understand.

What the fuck is happening?

"Sci," the bartender replied in the same too-sensual purr he'd used with me. "I didn't know we were expecting you."

"You weren't," Scion replied without inflection. "I thought Cross might be here."

My eyes widened as the male bent down to pull two glasses from beneath the bar. He placed them in front of us and looked up at me, winking. I flushed, noticing he had horns poking out of the top of his head between his dark waves, a bit like a baby goat.

"Kaius!" Scion barked.

"Right," Kaius said smoothly. "Haven't seen Cross yet, but the night is young. He still might make an appearance."

I shifted in my chair, struggling to find a comfortable position as my pulse pounded too low in my core, and I desperately wanted to press my thighs together. The bartender chuckled low in his throat, and again, I had the strangest urge to reach out and touch him. His skin sparkled like glittering gems, enticing and mesmerizing. There was a light that seemed to play around him that I couldn't explain…I wanted it. Wanted it inside me, and—

Scion moved his hand from my fingers to my thigh, physically holding me down. The bite of his nails into my skin was grounding, and I blinked a few times, turning toward him. My head swam.

Scion's nostrils flared, and he cleared his throat. "We'll wait, then."

"Please do, as long as you're both staying." The bartender laughed.

I felt more than heard Scion growl. "Careful."

I wasn't sure to whom he was speaking, and perhaps the bartender wasn't either because he leaned closer to me, meeting my eyes with his enormous blue ones. "Hungry?"

Was that a question or a declaration of intent?

Scion slammed a hand flat on the bar between us. "She's not your concern. Don't fucking touch her."

The male's eyes flashed a paler shade of blue, and he took a deep breath through his nose before he took a step back, his mouth falling into a comical pout. "Yes, I can see that. Interesting smell. Like…dogs marking territory."

Scion growled low in his throat. "That's enough. We'll take two of whatever's fresh while we wait and—" He glanced at me. "—tell the cook to warm up something to eat, but no fruit."

The unnerving bartender's smile faltered, his eyes narrowing, before he nodded and turned away.

"I'm fine," I muttered. "I don't need anything to eat."

"Don't be absurd," the prince said without looking at me. "You haven't eaten since you woke up."

Oh, I was well aware of that, but my appetite had suddenly fled, and now I wasn't sure I wanted to eat anything offered in a strange Fae tavern by a sparkling male who looked more like he wanted to eat me than feed me.

I shook my head, trying again to clear it. It became easier as seconds ticked by with the bartender not standing in front of me, better still the further away he walked. "You know him?"

"In a sense." Scion ground his teeth and glanced down at his hand on my leg. I looked down as well, having only just realized it was still there. "Will you be alright?"

I wasn't sure. "What happened?"

He removed his hand, running his fingers through his hair. "Kaius is an incubus. They have abilities that are the exact opposite of a mating bond. They feed on lust, not love. They seek out power, not to share in it, but only to take it and leave you drained."

That probably should have been more alarming to me than it was, but I could hardly focus through the remnants of the fog in my mind. "Really?" I craned my neck for a better look. "He looks like High Fae."

Scion laughed harshly. "No, he doesn't. He's quite adept at glamour, which apparently you are susceptible to. It's strange—I thought you could see through glamour."

I frowned. I didn't have to ask why he thought that—I'd been able to see through his glamour when we first met, and for the most part, his powers didn't work on me. "I have never claimed to be immune to all magic."

"Yes." He frowned. "But that is less easily explained."

Sidestepping the issue, I focused on my folded hands on the bar. "If this is your friend's bar, I take it he's a thief?"

Scion nodded. "This tavern is something of a waystation. I'm sure someone is already on their way to let Cross know we're here."

"Fascinating." I bit my lip, feeling a bit embarrassed now that the sparkling haze was wearing off.

"Do not concern yourself over Kaius, rebel. I will not let him eat you." Humor flickered in his gaze, and a smug male smile crept across his face. Then, without warning, he reached over and ran his thumb over my bottom lip, pulling it free of my teeth. "I have no intention of sharing my meal."

I choked, even as heat crept up my neck. "I despise you."

He merely smirked, as if to say that hardly mattered.

I knew what he was doing, flirting with me as a way to both remind me who was in control and distract me from more pressing issues. To be fair, I'd played into the game myself, but not today. "Do not speak to me unless you have to. I want nothing to do with you."

He didn't reply, which I took to mean he understood, but I did not like the way the smile had not left his face.

21
LONNIE
THE CUTTHROAT DISTRICT, INBETWIXT

The scent of the roast stew proved too hard to resist, and I wolfed the entirety of it down despite my initial hesitation. If I died from poisoning, at least my final meal would have been well spent.

When the stew was gone, and so, too, was most of Scion's ale, we sat in uncomfortable silence, staring at the unmoving door.

"If I was allowed to speak to you, I might ask what you wanted to do if Cross doesn't appear this evening," Scion said without looking at me.

I stiffened, knowing all too well that he was making fun of me. The Waywoods were starting to look better and better the longer I sat here.

"I might suggest," Scion drawled, gaze fixed on the wall, "that we could go look for him, though I don't know how safe that would be for you. Since I can't hear your opinion, I cannot suggest that we—"

"Oh, stop it," I blurted out.

He said nothing, and I heaved a sigh. This was what I got for acting as if he were a normal human man and not a fairy. I'd had only one relationship with a human man, and it had hardly been more than sex, but I felt confident that Caliban would have laughed in my face or stormed out in anger if I'd told him to remain silent. Scion was taking it extremely seriously and would not break until I gave in first.

Biting the inside of my cheek until I tasted blood, I let out a garbled sound of aggravation. "Would you please speak normally? I am growing concerned for your health."

A smile spread across his face that did nothing to dissuade my fears. "I might, but only if you do. I refuse to spend days wasting energy fighting with you."

"You are the one who constantly insults me."

He looked like he had something to say about that but managed to reply with only, "I shall do my best to refrain."

"Why bother? I'm already here, and should I become too difficult, I'm sure you could conjure a shadow gag to go with your rope."

His eyes darkened slightly. "You should not give me ideas, rebel, or I will think your protest is as much a lie as most everything else that comes out of your mouth."

I opened my mouth to reply but was interrupted once again as Kaius appeared before us. He held Scion's latest drink in his right hand but did not hand it over, instead waiting to catch his attention. His presence felt wrong somehow—intrusive. He was of this world where the noises of the tavern still bustled around us, but I felt as though we were sitting apart from everything else. They were all here in Inbetwixt, but we were on a field in Aftermath, the acrid scent of the afflicted choking every breath.

I shook my head and looked up, glaring daggers. "Yes?"

Oddly, this time, I was not nearly as entranced by his sparkle and was unsure if it was the effect of the conversation Scion and I had been having or that the incubus was not attempting to charm me.

"Some advice?" He looked at me with mild amusement. "You should watch your tone. Some Fae might think you aggressive and not find it nearly as adorable as I do."

"Perhaps," I said blandly. "Or perhaps my tone is exactly as it is meant to be. Is it my fault if those around me are too stupid to hear a clear warning?"

Scion chuckled softly before turning toward him, his knee brushing mine again as he moved. "What is it?"

"I merely came to tell you that Father will not be coming upstairs this evening but wants me to tell you that the den is open if you wish to go down. He hopes you won't be too offended."

Scion cocked his head. "He did not fucking say that."

"No." Kaius agreed. "He said that he doesn't believe you're fucking here, and if you are, then there's bound to be an assassin lurking nearby, and he's too damn old to deal with such things. He wants you to go down and prove you're not only here but living before he considers stepping a single toe outside. Then he swore several more times and used a name I can't pronounce."

Scion snorted. "That sounds more like it."

"Quite," Kaius agreed. "But I thought you would prefer the condensed version."

Scion stood from his stool and offered me his hand as he walked away, notably taking the drink with him. I watched him go for a moment before shaking my head and taking the prince's hand somewhat grudgingly. "What was that about?"

"You heard him," Scion said. "Cross invites us down to the den."

I shook my head—although I did have questions about that, but it wasn't what I'd meant. "No, I meant…well, he lied. He made up a different version of what your friend said."

Scion didn't answer immediately, instead directing me to walk behind the bar and down a hallway toward a long flight of stairs descending into what I could only assume was a cellar.

The stairs were smooth, polished stone, unlike the rough wooden floor of the tavern, and the air grew slightly colder as we climbed down into the dim light of the floor below.

"Incubi—and succubi, for that matter, which are more common, are more Unseelie than Seelie. If Kaius can lie, that would be why."

At the base of the stairs, there was indeed a small cellar, filled almost entirely with barrels of mead. At the back, a rounded door stood hidden by the shadows of a stack of empty crates. Scion walked straight toward the door and yanked it open without any preamble, as if he'd been here many times before.

My eyes widened as I beheld the long, twisting tunnel only just visible under his arm. "I don't suppose you're going to tell me where we're going, are you?"

He looked down at me. "I would have thought that was obvious, rebel. This leads to the thieves' guild."

"If you know that, why didn't we simply go straight here in the first place?"

He looked appalled and heaved a sigh as he ushered me into the tunnel. "One king does not simply burst in on another in his own kingdom."

The door slammed behind us, and we started down the tunnel. My body tensed for a moment at the memory of being confined.

I took a deep breath in and out, trying to force my brain and body into alignment. I was not trapped; I was simply inside. Inside in a small, dark space. With Scion.

To my relief, it was a very short tunnel, and already I could see the exit. All too quickly, we stopped in front of a rounded front door engraved with patterns of leaves and vines. I held my breath as Scion slowly stretched out his hand and knocked, my mind racing with possibilities. Voices and footsteps sounded in the room beyond, and my entire body tensed. If everyone inside was like Kaius, I wasn't sure I'd survive the hour.

With a bang that shook the very stone around us, the door flew open. I blinked, startled by the sudden light flooding the tunnel, and looked up at the man framed in the doorway. Behind him, I could see the better part of a large, warmly lit warehouse room and a few curious faces peeking in at us.

Scion, unruffled, stepped forward to say something, but I beat him to it.

"It's you!" I blurted out before anyone could speak. "I remember you."

22

SCION

THE CUTTHROAT DISTRICT, INBETWIXT

"Sorry?" Cross asked, eyes widening on Lonnie.

She took a step forward, and I instinctively threw an arm out to catch her. She huffed out a breath as I trapped her around the middle and held her back from doing something idiotic that I would no doubt have to intervene in. "Calm down, rebel."

She laughed harshly. "If you should be calling anyone that, it's him. He's the one who works for Dullahan."

Cross looked back at us, and his mouth twitched behind his mustache, and then he tipped his head back and guffawed. "Me? You've got a screw loose, lass. Suppose that's to be expected, though, if you're runnin' with him."

I shook my head and met my friend's pale green gaze over the top of Lonnie's head. "Hello to you as well."

"Evening, mate," he replied. "Have to say, I didn't believe it when Kaius said you were here, and with a human no less." He stroked his beard. "Perhaps I should apologize."

Cross was nearly as tall as I was, with tanned skin and broad shoulders. His hair was a bright copper, several shades lighter than Lonnie's flaming red, and curled slightly around his ears, hiding the small pointed tips. He wore a full beard, unlike most High Fae, which gave him a less refined look and disguised his appearance somewhat so he could more easily blend in among any crowd—human, Fae, or otherwise.

Lonnie glanced between us, anger and confusion warring in her eyes. "I remember him," she insisted. "I met him at an inn in Everlast. He's a rebel."

"In the true sense of the word? Maybe, but not how you mean it," Cross answered as if she'd been speaking to him. "Now, are you coming in or not? One shouldn't linger on doorsteps. It's bad luck."

It was my turn to roll my eyes. "We're coming," I grumbled. "One moment."

He gave me a salute and walked backward away from us back into the guild den. "Godspeed, mate."

Lonnie's eyebrows pulled low over tantalizing honey-brown eyes. "I'm not wrong," she hissed. "Or crazy. It was only a few days ago. I'm sure I've met him before."

Well, that was a fucking twist of events.

"He's not a rebel," I told her. "Of that, I'm completely certain."

That was about the only thing I was certain of, though. There was always the possibility she was wrong or lying about seeing Cross before, but for some reason, I didn't think so, which begged the question: what was he doing in the capital, and why wouldn't he tell me? *A question to be answered once we get inside.*

"But—" Lonnie began again.

I heaved a sigh. She was so fucking stubborn it was going to kill her one day.

I wanted to tell her to simply trust me, but that would only result in a new wave of arguing. I couldn't believe I'd ever thought she was unintelligent. She was uninformed, certainly, but far from mindless. Our verbal sparring matches always stoked the unfulfilled tension between us and left me painfully and inexplicably hard, almost as aroused by fighting her as I would be fucking her.

No, This cannot keep fucking happening. I should not be thinking about her like that. Lonnie belonged to Bael, regardless of if he'd ever be able to claim her. All she was meant to be for me was a means to an end. An instrument. Just another tool to be used in my lifelong pursuit of protecting the kingdom.

Unwilling to engage in yet another roundabout verbal battle that would only test the limits of my splintering self-control, I reached for her again.

"What the fuck are you doing?" she yelled.

Ignoring the question, which would soon be self-explanatory, I swung her up into my arms and over my shoulder. I might have used ropes again, but she'd destroyed that image for me. Now, I would never be able to do it without picturing her bound and gagged, naked in my bed. "Every conversation cannot be a fight, rebel."

It was a plea as much as a statement, but I doubted she heard it as such as she kicked wildly, attempting to free herself from my hold. "You cannot keep doing this!"

Oh, but I could. More importantly, I *would,* now that I'd realized it was far more efficient than trying to persuade her. She already despised me anyway, so it hardly mattered what I did.

I shifted her slightly on my shoulder and clamped one arm down over her flailing legs as I marched determinedly after Cross.

The thieves' den was long and rectangular, like an underground warehouse repurposed as a meeting space. The ceiling was covered in gleaming copper metal, while the walls were stone and set with wisp lamps every foot or so. The light reflected off the ceiling, giving the whole room a warm glow.

There was a bar set on one end of a wide, rectangular room, nearly identical to the one upstairs, if not slightly better kept. To the left of the bar, crates and barrels were stacked against the wall beside the door where we'd entered. To the right of us, a few small tables and chairs were set up, mostly empty but for a couple of men and one woman playing cards. The sound of fighting echoed off the walls, stemming from the opposite end of the room from the bar, where two people were rolling around in the middle of a roped-off square set up beside a row of weapons racks.

I reached Cross, standing beside the bar, and to his credit, the male said nothing of the screaming woman in my arms, only grinned as he glanced over his shoulder at me. "So what do you think of the new operation?"

"Fine," I replied grimly. "Nothing will compare to the old barracks, though."

Cross laughed. "You'll grow to like this just as much, I promise. Want a drink?"

Lonnie had found a gap in my armor and was now stabbing sharp fingernails into the back of my right arm, but I did my best to ignore her. "This isn't a social call. I have something important I need to discuss with you."

That, and I'd just had several drinks already, spurred on by my irrational irritation.

"You never come for a social call. Have the ale, Sci, pretend to be a friend, for once. We just brought in a crate of fawn-made ale from Nevermore. It's good shit, I tell ya."

"Don't tell me that," I complained. "We tax Nevermore, so you're really stealing from me."

"No, I'm stealing from her." Cross nodded toward Lonnie—what little he could see of her with her ass in the air, legs still trying to kick me in the face. "Anyway, if you ask me, taxes are the real theft."

"I—*fuck*!" I exclaimed, surprised as pain shot through my arm. "You bit me."

"Put me down, you ass," Lonnie snarled.

"Alright, never mind," I grumbled to Cross. "Give me the fucking drink."

"That's a good man." Cross chuckled, directing me toward a bar that was nearly identical to that of the one upstairs, if slightly better kept. I deposited Lonnie in the chair nearest the end and sat down to her left, the wall to my back. I leaned back on my stool and rubbed the back of my arm, amazed she'd been able to sink her teeth in so far from that angle.

"What is wrong with you?" Lonnie hissed, practically spitting with anger.

So much. "At the moment? You."

I could have sworn that feeding her my blood was supposed to make her more amenable, not less. Perhaps I needn't have concerned myself over it since she seemed completely healthy and angrier than ever.

"I don't think I've ever seen a woman so unhappy to be here," Cross said jovially.

He walked around the bar and pulled three bottles out from underneath, sliding one to me and the other to Lonnie. She ignored the bottle, and I only just caught it before it crashed to the floor.

Lonnie scowled. "I met you. I know I did."

"Stubborn, are we? Perhaps you did, but I am not who you seem to think I am. I have no more time for wars."

"Too busy?" she sneered.

He crossed his arms. "Quite. Do you like my place of business? I should hope so. Many noble-Fae lost a lot of coin to pay for it."

"It's…fine," she said grudgingly.

"This is just the main hold. Back there—" He pointed toward the opposite end of the room, where the two rolling blurs were still sparring. "—is the entrance to the barracks. Many of my children are asleep currently, as they typically work odd hours."

"Your children?" she asked, a note of disbelief in her tone.

"Everyone in the guild is my family." He grinned. "You're suspicious by nature. That's a good quality in a thief if you ever want to make a change."

I cleared my throat. That was not going to happen. "She steals quite enough as it is. No candlestick is safe in the obsidian palace."

Cross tipped his chair back and roared with laughter. "A human queen who steals from the palace? What god did you piss off in a past life to get cursed with this, Sci?"

"Excellent fucking question."

"Nothing he doesn't deserve ten times over," Lonnie muttered.

Cross looked delighted. "I like you, even if you have spit on my hospitality by not taking that drink."

"I know better than to drink anything handed to me by a stranger, and I know nothing about you except that you're a liar."

That was fucking rich coming from her.

"You know more than most," he told her. "Do you know how hard it is to get into this room?"

She shook her head. "From what I can tell, it has all the exclusivity of a sewer. Difficult to reach, but not necessarily because anyone would want to venture inside."

Cross glanced at me and leaned his elbows on the table, his smile now impossibly wide. "See? I knew I liked her."

As long as he didn't like her too much. That was all I needed—whatever strange power she had to ruin everything seeping into my friend as well.

It wasn't lost on me that while Lonnie seemed not to trust Cross, she was still far less reserved around him in a few short minutes than she'd ever been around my family. Perhaps she thought he was human, like her?

I scowled. If they talked too long, the next thing I knew, he'd be helping her escape the city.

"How does a thief become friends with a prince?" Lonnie asked.

"Aw, you're lucky I like that story, lass," Cross said.

"*No.*" I narrowed my eyes in a warning. "No more fucking stories."

He seemed unfazed by the implied threat and plowed on as if I hadn't spoken. "I met this prick when he was dumped into my military unit, as green as they come with no training and not a shred of common sense."

This was why I hadn't wanted to come directly to Cross in the first place, although he was undoubtedly the better option than the Lord and Lady of Inbetwixt. Well, this and the fact that it was just the sort of diplomatic bullshit that would cause another hundred-year feud if anyone realized I was here and I hadn't notified the ruling family of my presence.

That was most of the reason I hadn't brought Quill—without him, I could typically go somewhat unnoticed, but as soon as he appeared with me, strangers would begin to put two and two together. I supposed now I could call for the bird. A small consolation.

I hadn't wanted to go directly to Cross because he knew me too well. I didn't want him to meet her. Didn't want him to tell war stories or see any of our interactions, especially after I'd fed her blood. I didn't need anyone swaying my decision. Bael was certain to do that enough already when he recovered from his issue, and a third opinion in the mix would only make things worse than they already were.

Lonnie choked on a laugh. "Excuse me?"

"Yup! I was furious because the prince here couldn't see an inch in front of him with his head shoved so far up his own ass."

"You would be wise to stop now."

"Oh, have a laugh once in a while, you overemotional milk-drinker." He grinned.

I ground my teeth bitterly and shot him a look that promised violence.

Lonnie, noticing nothing, looked absolutely fucking delighted. "So what happened?"

"He came to realize the error of his misjudgment," I snapped.

"He nearly got me killed," Cross spoke over me.

"I will complete the task if you don't shut your mouth," I barked. "We have more important things to discuss."

Cross scoffed, clearly exasperated. "Ten minutes won't make a lick of difference."

Cross turned to Lonnie, leaning back in his chair and interlacing his fingers behind his head. Her eyes sparkled with anticipation, waiting for a story.

Running my hands through my hair, I pressed my lips together, resigned.

Not for many years had Cross feared me as others did. Not since we'd served together, and especially not since he was the king of thieves, powerful in his own way. Usually, I liked that about our friendship, but today, I'd never resented it more, and there was very little I could do about it at the moment…not without scaring Lonnie.

I'd have to wait.

"I joined the military while we were in peacetime to make some money to send back to my family," Cross began. "This was before I realized there were other ways to support myself, you understand, and it was a good job for someone like me."

"Someone like what?" she asked.

He raised his hair to show her his ears, and I watched her eyes widen. It confirmed what I'd suspected—she thought he was human. But then, she believed she was human too, and the longer I spent with her, the more I wondered if that, too, was incorrect.

"But why someone like you?" she asked. "If you're Fae…"

The corners of his mouth turned up, and the dimple in his cheek deepened. I stifled a groan. Like everyone else, Cross's eyes sparkled as he gazed at her, completely enamored by her mere existence.

Every muscle in my body was tense, and I had to clench my fists to stop them from lashing out. I sucked in a slow breath, resisting the urge to kick the legs out from under my friend's chair and drag her away from him.

"I don't have any magic," he replied simply. "But during peacetime, the army wasn't bad. Lots of guard work, essentially, until a few years after I joined up, Aftermath fell, and then everything got far less fun. There was still money, o'course, but suddenly, we were expected to fight."

My thoughts turned mutinous. *Expected to fight in the army? What a shock…*

Here was further proof of the cost of ruling—something I'd always known to be a steep price. It wasn't only the prisoners who'd become afflicted who'd died, but the young soldiers as well.

"And you were in the same unit?" Lonnie prompted.

"In a sense," I ground out.

Cross laughed, some of the haunted look vanishing from his eyes. "Prince Belvedere was in charge o'all of us, see? And he would go around to all the units to check up on things. Then, after a while, he started bringing around his kid, showing him off like he was some god among us."

Again, Lonnie's eyes shot to mine. "How old were you?"

I shrugged as if it didn't matter. "To begin with? Perhaps eleven."

She looked appalled by that, but the context that both she and Cross were missing was that Ambrose had only abandoned the family a year or so before. He was older, and though I likely would have ended up the heir anyway based on power, Grandmother Celia was adamant that we appear strong in the eyes of the people—as if I'd been meant to be on the frontlines all along. "Move this along, Cross. I'd like to do more than reminisce tonight. We have actual plans to make."

Cross seemed unbothered. "Fine, fine. So, a few more years pass, and the princeling here was brought to my unit and told he could run it. See, we'd just lost our commander, and he got handed the title by birthright rather than actual ability, except then we actually went into Aftermath, and yer man here realized he was fucked."

My anger sparked. "Anyone would have realized they were fucked."

"Actually, no," Cross said thoughtfully. "Not everyone would have. See, lass, we all realized that this was supposed to be a test for the princeling. Either we'd win, or we'd all be slaughtered, but either way, Prince Belvedere was going to spread the story far and wide as proof of his son's heroics."

Lonnie's jaw dropped, and her eyes widened in disbelief. When she spoke, her words were laced with revulsion. "Are you telling me your father was willing to let you die?"

If only it were so simple.

I shook my head, my teeth gritted so tight I thought they might crack. "No. I can shadow walk even when injured."

She blinked, confused. "Is that uncommon?"

Cross snorted. "Yes. Not all Fae can do it at all, what with the way that magic has been dwindling over the years. Most can't go long distances, and fewer still can take others with them or do it under duress. Yer man here is an exception."

"Not the only exception," I mumbled.

Bael might have nearly drained himself the other day, but that was only further proof of how difficult it really was to travel that far with another person, especially while under attack.

Lonnie's brow was furrowed and lips pursed in concentration. She seemed lost in thought, and I couldn't help but wonder if our minds had wandered to the same place.

"See," Cross continued, "if things went wrong, the prince here could have just walked out and left us all to die, but instead, we never went in at all. We retreated before we even got there, and daddy was not pleased about the optics of that. It didn't have the war-hero look that the crown was going for."

"But you all survived," Lonnie said, incredulous.

I barked a harsh laugh. "My father didn't care that I'd saved thirty men; the ripple effect killed multiple other units in the end."

"So what happened?"

I sighed, resigned. "I realized I was in an impossible situation. I don't work well in a unit because my magic can't determine who is an enemy and who is a friend in a combat situation. Anyone near me in a battle would die no matter what side they were on. So, I started going in alone."

Lonnie looked up at me sharply. "Excuse me?"

"A lot of us who appreciated what happened stayed and kept traveling around with him."

"But you weren't fighting?"

"No. We stopped being frontline soldiers and became other things. Friends, healers, spies…thieves. We set up information networks in every city we visited."

…*and became the guilds,* I finished for him in my head. Or, at least, bolstered existing organizations.

"Alright," Lonnie said, a little uncertain. "But I still don't understand. You two have been friends for years, but I know I met you at the pub. You remember me, right? You told me to look at the moondust trees."

I shifted beside her. "What trees?"

"Ah." Cross grinned again. "'Don't hide in the moon dust tree at noon.' You know the saying?"

"You do remember," Lonnie hissed at the same time as I said, "No."

Cross stroked the pale red stubble on his chin. "I used to know a woman many years ago who used that expression. The moondust trees grow new leaves every night, which wither in the sun and turn to dust. If one was to hide in the tree at noon, they would be easily seen, as there are no leaves."

"You told Lonnie not to draw attention to herself?"

"Correct." Cross looked at her. "You were asking loud questions in public places. It was arguably quite good advice."

She narrowed her eyes. "So you didn't intend for me to find anything at the tree?"

He seemed genuinely confused now. "Did you?"

They stared at each other in confusion, but for once, the answer seemed glaringly obvious to me. "This sounds like exactly the kind of convoluted fucking treasure hunt of coincidences Ambrose would set up."

Where Grandmother Celia had always been too vague with her gifts, leaving us all to fucking drown in a whirlpool of her own conjuring, Ambrose was the opposite plucking strings to pull people and events together, sometimes years in advance. Half the time, I wasn't sure whom I resented more.

"Ambrose?" Cross's eyebrows rose, and his attention left me entirely. "What does he have to do with this?"

"Everything, I expect." I pushed my hair roughly out of my eyes, unable to hide my agitation any longer. "Now, if we're all done wasting time, can we get to why we are here?"

"Fine," Cross said. "One might think after so many years you'd want to do a quick hello and catch up, but whatever you like."

I scowled as I poured out the entire story of the last few days in a rush, and when I was finished, Cross looked at me with an expression near enough to pity. "Sci, we've been down this road how many times?"

"I know," I growled.

I know, I know, I know far better than anyone else.

Cross was still speaking. "Ambrose is impossible to find unless he wants to be found, even with all my resources. I can't outmaneuver a seer—he is always ten steps ahead, one to the side, and somehow comes out behind me."

"I'm well fucking aware," I snapped. "But I suspect this time, he wants to be caught again."

We both looked at Lonnie, and I grimaced. I hated the idea that my brother had found some way to get a note to her, that she'd become a piece in one of his never-ending chess games, but there was nothing to be done for it. She would have been involved anyway, I supposed, for more reasons than I could readily count.

"I'll speak to my children about it," Cross said evenly.

"Why?" Lonnie asked.

"Because they all work overnight and report back any changes in the city to me in the morning. If Dullahan is here, we'll know in a few hours."

I nodded. This was what I'd expected when I decided to visit Cross. I'd helped him to set up the guild, after all, and the system worked well. Granted, I didn't think my brother would be in the city, but if I knew him, there would be some outpost stationed somewhere, watching for our arrival.

"You should get some sleep while we wait," Cross said. "You look like you need it."

"I'm fine," I grunted.

"You might be, but she's not." He nodded at Lonnie.

I wanted to argue, but she was indeed looking a bit gray, her shoulders slumping despite her best efforts to hide it. I supposed it had already been near nightfall when we arrived in the city, and that was several hours ago now. The only problem was the den itself.

I cast a glance over at the group still playing cards at the table and frowned. The pair in the sparring ring had long since left, but I could hear sounds of life coming from the barracks, and this place would be crawling with thieves later when all Cross's children returned.

"No—" I began.

"You're welcome to stay up in the main house," Cross offered, seeming to predict my concern. "It's empty for the moment."

"Fine."

"You go on ahead," I told Lonnie roughly. "I want to speak with Cross about something else."

She stood from the table, waving me off. "As you like."

"I'll have one of my children bring you to your room," Cross said, clapping his hands together. "And come get you in a few hours when everyone returns. Then, we'll devise a plan."

23
LONNIE
THE CUTTHROAT DISTRICT, INBETWIXT

My body felt like it weighed a ton, and my eyelids kept wanting to close of their own accord as I trudged out of the den.

I wasn't sure at what point in the evening I'd grown so tired. Perhaps while Scion was recounting the story of his brother, which I'd already heard earlier in the day, or when he and Cross started making plans for finding the male. Their voices had started to drown into a dull hum of low, melodic tones, almost hypnotic in the way they tried to coax me to sleep. By the time Cross offered that we stay the night, I was nowhere near arguing.

"We'll go up to the main house," the Fae woman in front of me said far too cheerfully. "It's much more pleasant than the barracks, and you won't get woken up in the middle of the night when someone returns from work."

The woman was almost pixie-like in appearance, though still with that same ethereal beauty of all the High Fae. Her skin was dark, and her hair almost blue-black in the low light of the stair-well. I'd noticed her when we arrived, standing with the males playing cards. When Cross called for her, she had bounded up to us with almost indecent enthusiasm, introducing herself as "Siobhan."

"The barracks?" I asked, stifling a yawn,

"Where the rest of us sleep," Siobhan replied easily. "There are so many tunnels and stairwells down here you could easily get lost, but the barracks is that way." She jabbed a thumb back the way we'd come. "And the tavern where you came in is somewhere over there—" She pointed into the wall. "—next door to Father's house."

"You view Cross as your father, then?"

"Why wouldn't I?"

Interesting. The guild fascinated me, and I desperately wanted to know more about it, but I was struggling to stay awake. "How long have you been here?"

"In the family? Years."

That was vague, but I was too exhausted to properly interrogate her. Except, perhaps… "Did your, er, family perhaps have anything to do with some ships sinking recently?"

She glanced back over her shoulder at me. "Why?"

Should I lie? "The Lord and Lady of Inbetwixt mentioned it today," I said bluntly, yawning. "It just sounded interesting."

Siobhan opened the door at the top of the landing to reveal another long hallway. This one, however, reminded me less of an underground tunnel and more of one of the palace corridors. Soft carpets covered the polished wooden floor, and expensive-looking paintings hung on the walls, illuminated by the glow of mounted wisp lanterns.

She laughed. "Interesting is a word for it, but you'd have to ask father about that sort of thing. No one else will tell you anything, yes, no, up, down, or otherwise."

"Got it."

At the end of the hall was a lavishly decorated sitting room, unlike any home I'd seen in the capital. The walls were covered with fine silk tapestries and paintings, and golden candelabras lit every corner. Everywhere I looked, there was luxury nearly as grand as the obsidian palace.

Up another flight of stairs, I barely paid attention to where we were going until we came to a halt outside another closed door.

Siobhan pushed the door open and gestured for me to enter. "I'm sure you'll both be comfortable."

The room was smaller than the tower room I'd occupied as of late but still three times the size of the room I'd shared with Rosey down in the servants' quarters. Heavy velvet curtains draped over the windows, and a thick braided rug covered the wooden floor. In the corner sat an antique chest, and beside it, an old trunk bursting with books and glittering knickknacks—beads, coins, feathers from exotic birds—no doubt stolen, I supposed. Against the far wall, a large bed was the focal point of the room, covered in a plush red blanket and a mountain of feather pillows. I almost moaned at how inviting it looked.

"Thank you," I mumbled, already itching to launch myself into the pillows.

Later, I realized I should have asked her to clarify what she meant by "both."

The sound of the door opening shook me awake.

My heart pounded against my ribs, and I sat up, disoriented. I ran one hand nervously over the sweat-dampened skin of my neck and peered into the darkened room.

Pale moonlight cast a long beam across the floor, and it was only by its glow that I could make out the dark figure prowling toward me out of the shadows.

My mouth fell open in a gasp, and for a split second, I was quite sure I was dreaming. I kicked off my quilt and scrambled up, letting out a startled scream loud enough to wake the entire city. "By the fucking Source!"

Scion sauntered toward me through the shadows, coming into sharper relief the closer he came. His moonbeam gaze drank in every inch of me, a confident smirk plastered across his too-handsome face. "The Source may very well be able to hear you, darling, if you keep screaming like that."

"I—"

My mouth went dry, and worse, my eyes betrayed me, gliding down his bare upper body and finding nothing but corded muscles, as if he'd been carved from stone to stand on some pedestal rather than born of life itself. His onyx-colored hair was dripping wet, as if he'd just bathed in the time that I'd been asleep, and he wore nothing but fitted black trousers, his armor nowhere to be found.

My hand twitched ever so slightly as if wanting to reach out and touch him—if only to ensure this wasn't some latest trick of my subconscious. Some new illusion. A fairy trap.

"Have you gone mad?" I choked, shaking my head to clear it. "What would possess you to simply barge in here?"

He smiled. "You didn't answer the door."

I made a noise in my throat that was nowhere near speech—an entirely unattractive gurgle of shock.

I'd had many vivid dreams since moving to the obsidian tower, most of a nature that I wouldn't dare speak aloud. This had to be a dream, yet… I sunk my teeth deliberately into my lip, and a sharp sting of pain jolted through me, grounding me in the present. "Why the fuck would I answer the door? This is my room."

The prince reached the edge of the bed and thrust out a hand, tangling his fingers in my hair. He dragged me up to kneeling, rough and hurried, until I was nearly eye level with him. His eyebrow ticked up. "Is it not my room as well?"

My eyes widened, even as tiny sparks seemed to flit down my neck, where his fingers pressed into my skin. I glanced down at my own pale flesh, barely concealed by the thin fabric of my underthings, heat rising to my face, my chest, my entire body, then to his outstretched arm. His body seemed to glow slightly in the moonlight.

He was acting very strange, indeed.

"You shouldn't be in here," I said, slightly dazed.

"Shhhh," he whispered.

What were we discussing? And more importantly, why was he touching me?

I tilted my head up, and our eyes connected. He flicked his gaze down to my mouth for the briefest second, as if weighing his options, before he pressed his lips against mine.

It wasn't a shock, and still I gasped as his tongue traced over my lips, tasting me, owning me with his attention alone. I opened my mouth wide, hungry, starving, and moaned when he plunged his tongue into my mouth.

Scion lifted me with one arm and pressed a thigh between my legs, forcing my hips to grind down until heat pounded in my core. I couldn't recall what I'd been concerned about a moment before as his fingers tightened in my hair, sending sharp tingles over my body from the crown of my head all the way down my back.

Pushing me back roughly, he climbed over me on the bed. My knees fell open, and I tilted my head, another soft moan of surrender escaping my lips.

I felt his warm fingers trace up my sides, and I shuddered in anticipation, desire rattling through me. Brutal. Unyielding. My pulse thrummed too quickly as he moved his mouth to the curve of my neck, down to my breast, tugging thin fabric aside to wrap his lips around one nipple. "Do you like that, darling?"

I wrinkled my nose, something dissonant pricking at the back of my mind, like an insect, humming, nipping, stinging.

"Say that again?" I breathed.

"Darling."

He moved to the other breast, tongue swirling, and sparks of pleasure that trailed down my body to my core dragged another ragged gasp from my throat.

I opened my eyes, blinking, and stared down at where the moon hit his skin, shimmering, glowing. I reached out, pressing a hand to his face, and felt a slight buzz beneath my fingertips. Then, he shimmered around the edges, and I pulled back, watching as some of the hazy fog dissipated from around us. "Wait, what did you call me?"

24
SCION
THE CUTTHROAT DISTRICT, INBETWIXT

I watched with narrowed eyes as one of Cross's daughters led her up a flight of stairs to the main house. The moment they disappeared, I stood as well, my chair screeching against the floor. "What the fuck were you doing in the capital?"

"Hello to you too." Cross leaned back in his chair. "It's good to see you, mate."

I ground my teeth, not feeling all that friendly anymore. It was good to see him before he decided to be a prick and drudge up ancient history for her amusement, like he had any reason to have to please her. "Answer the damned question, Cross."

He looked at me like I'd sprouted a second head. "I had business in the capital. Is that alright with you, Your Highness?"

"Not if it involves her, it isn't."

"She involved herself," he scoffed. "And why the fuck do you care, anyway? Am I mistaken, or is that not the woman who killed ol' Penvalle?"

"Among other things." I nodded shortly, not particularly liking the reminder. "She was attacked recently. Know anything about that?"

He stood and crossed in front of me, making his way to the bar he'd been eying for the better part of the last hour. Reaching out of sight, he pulled out a bottle and knocked it on the edge of the wood to remove the cap before taking a swig. "Yeah, actually, I did hear about that. The whole damned continent heard about it. That's what you wanted, though, right?"

I tried not to smile at that. Yes, actually, that *was* what I'd wanted. Glad to know the surviving thug was doing his job well, running messages all over Elsewhere for me. Perhaps I'd track him down again since it seemed he was better at getting shit done than two-thirds of the people who worked for me currently.

"The tavern upstairs is practically empty," I said, my anger not entirely abated. "Kaius said you were worried about assassins, and I heard you're giving more trouble to the lord and lady than usual."

"So?"

"*And* I noticed the district has expanded. Are you taking on different contracts?"

Tiny tendrils of shadow began to leak, unbidden, out of my fingertips, and I brushed them angrily away before they could spread. I looked up to find Cross watching me curiously.

He laughed. "You're paranoid as ever, Scion. Not that I owe you an explanation, but I was in the capital to collect a new recruit. I didn't know anything about your girl, only spoke to her because she'd been served elf-mead, and she reminded me a bit of a woman I used to know. Didn't want anything to happen to her. That's it."

"That's it?" I sneered.

"Yeah." He took another sip. "*That's it.* But I think the question we should be asking is, what the fuck am I witnessing right now?"

I stiffened, every muscle in my body going taut. "What do you mean?"

"You're not fucking her, that much is obvious, but you sound possessed, mate."

I heard him as if the words were spoken from very far away, and it took a moment for the meaning to penetrate.

By the gods-damned cursed fucking Source.

That woman was like an infection. Even hating her became an obsession. Now, she was ruining me just like everyone else, and it was happening far faster than I'd expected, without me even realizing it was happening.

"I'm—" I tried to say "fine" and found I couldn't. I coughed instead, blurting out, "Managing."

He didn't look convinced, and I couldn't say I blamed him. I was hardly even managing, not now when all I could fucking think about was taking her. Punishing her. Giving her lying little mouth something to—

By Aisling, it was a terminal fucking condition.

The only positive thing about this whole situation thus far was that she was rapidly making my decision for me. I could see no world where Ambrose's theory bore fruit—Lonnie would rather die than marry me, and fortunately for her, she would get to make that very choice.

Something pulled tight in my chest, and I bit back a growl. *Fuck this.*

It was the blood. That had to be it—it was simply affecting me more than her because I knew about it. That had to be it.

Sharing blood was absurdly taboo, except among bonded mates, and even then, it would be odd to do it as I had, simply to heal. I never would have thought of it had Bael not done it first. Part of me wondered if it wasn't some dormant Unseelie perversion finally breaking free in him after all these years that had given him the idea in the first place. Who the fuck knew what they got up to in Underneath.

I was half-ready to kill my cousin for all the trouble his little experiment had caused so far, and another part of me almost wanted to thank him, eagerly anticipating the day he finally shook off his darker tendencies and was able to discuss it with me.

Maybe he would have a suggestion for the next time, and…

I shook myself violently. "She almost died yesterday," I said flatly, trying to get my heart rate under control. "I had to heal her. That's likely all this is."

Cross frowned. "I don't know why that would make a difference. Even Kaius said you seemed jealous."

"You're gossiping with Kaius now?"

"Not gossiping, observing. We might be friends, but I still like to know when a threat has entered my city and is acting out of character."

I scoffed, smiling slightly for the first time. "It's hardly out of character. I just fucking hate Kaius, you know that."

My dislike of the incubus had little to do with Lonnie—though that wasn't helping—I simply didn't like his kind in general. The glamour was alarming, and all female succubi were dominant by nature. Something I'd never be interested in for any reason.

"He's useful," Cross said dismissively. "Phillipa Blacktongue knows he's one of mine but lets him into her place anyway for some reason. I've been keeping an eye on it."

I waved Cross off. I didn't really care about guild dealings or what Cross was doing with Phillipa—the mistress of the pleasure guild. Now, if he was working with assassins, I might have wanted to know *that*, but anything else was too trivial to bother with.

"That isn't what I wasn't to talk to you about," I said roughly.

He gave me a mocking "You don't say?"

My scowl deepened to the point I was half-concerned my face might stick that way. "I spoke to the lord and lady earlier."

Cross grinned. "And how are they faring these days? It must be nice to have so little to do, what with how they have hardly any responsibilities left."

"They claim you sunk their fleet."

He shrugged. "Had to, mate. I got wind there was Gancanagh's Dust being smuggled on those ships."

I raised an eyebrow. That opened a whole host of questions and perhaps answered some as well. "Not yours, I presume."

Cross looked a bit wounded. "Of course not. You know I wouldn't, and if it was, why would I sink my own product?"

I nodded. "You're correct. My apologies."

Gancanagh's Dust was the worst drug known to our continent. A single dose caused insatiable lust, obsession, and euphoria, but if used too often or over a long period of time, it would lead to madness, uncontrolled rage, and violent hallucinations.

"I don't want that shit in my city," Cross muttered, looking more serious than he had all evening.

"Your city?"

He waved me off. "You know what I mean."

I did. He meant he viewed Inbetwixt as his—or as good as. Perhaps this should have concerned me more, but I'd always known Cross was ambitious, and I'd rather him managing things than the current lord and lady. "Who was moving the dust, then?"

"Don't know yet, but I'll find out. It's being handled. Kaius is working on it, actually."

I nodded curtly. As long as it didn't take away from finding Ambrose, then that was fine—good, even.

"Fine." Turning on my heel, I marched toward the stairs. "If that's all, I'll see you in the morning."

"Sci," Cross yelled after me.

"What?"

"Make sure she stays in her room. If she goes wandering around, you know I can't guarantee her safety."

My lip curled. "I wouldn't worry about Lonnie so much as your children. If anyone so much as touches her, it will be the end of the guild before it's the end of her."

"I know," Cross said. "That's what I'm afraid of. Just keep her in her damn room, and there won't be any problems."

"Noted."

Halfway across the room, I gave up walking and vanished into the shadows, reappearing instantly in the upper hallway of Cross's home. My feet thundered against the carpeted floor as I passed room after room, following little more than instinct and the faint trace of a honey-sweet scent. Lonnie was sure to try and run the moment I told her I was planning to stay in the room with her, and I was already running through ways to convince her. Thus far, I could think of nothing more likely to work than tying her to the headboard.

For the sake of the fucking Source, perhaps I should simply give all this up now and send her back to the castle.

Trying to force the outcome of prophecies clearly hadn't succeeded so far, and holding Lonnie here until Ambrose saw her in the city was starting to feel flimsier the more I thought about it. That may have been the blood influence again—or perhaps merely me, this time. I'd never claimed to be entirely free of corruption.

A crash sounded from somewhere down the hall, and I froze, ice filling my veins.

My pulse sped up, and I lurched forward, moving so quickly toward the door the hallway blurred. There was a second loud thud, followed by her voice echoing through the hallway. "Don't fucking touch me, *darling*."

What the fuck?

A haze of black spots lingered on the edges of my vision, a haze of rage clouding everything. Who would have the audacity to lay their hands on her?

Reaching her door, I crashed through, distantly grateful it was already hanging open. Lonnie knelt atop the bedding, her hair a wild tangle, her back bared, and her long legs curled around a Fae male. Her weight pinned him beneath her, his throat compressed between her bent knee and the mattress. The cause of the commotion was instantly evident as she bashed an old book into his skull with a similar force to how I'd once seen her wield a crown.

My anger burned brighter than ever, consuming me and leaving no room for anything else. I could hardly see as I lurched forward, fingers numb with rising magic. Darkness rose near my feet, mingling with the black tunnel obscuring my vision. I raised a hand to strike, then stopped, my mind reeling. I stared in disbelief.

It was my own bloody face that stared back at me from the bed, pupils blown wide. A wave of nausea and confusion rolled through me as Lonnie lifted her eyes to meet mine, holding the book tightly in her trembling hands.

Her chest rose and fell quickly as she struggled to take deep breaths. Her lips parted, and I watched the calculation going on in her face—not shock, exactly, but confirmation.

Her shoulders slumped in exhaustion. "I hate fairies."

25
LONNIE
THE CUTTHROAT DISTRICT, INBETWIXT

"It has been taken care of," Scion's smooth voice echoed through the dark room a split second before he appeared in the center of the carpet.

Even if I'd been worried that it was not truly him this time, I would have known from his scowl alone. This version of Scion—the real one—was the same in the sum of his parts yet so impossibly different it was hard to believe I'd been fooled for even a moment.

He still wore his armor and clearly had not yet had a chance to bathe as his hair had dust in it, and there was a smattering of blood across the side of his face. He had none of the carefree energy of the false version of himself and, indeed, looked like he had not smiled in more years than I'd been alive.

"What did you do to him?" I asked from where I now sat, wrapped in a quilt in the center of the bed.

"Nothing that was not deserved," Scion replied unhelpfully. "Kaius was warned not to touch you, and he elected to ignore that warning. You do not need to worry about him returning."

I wasn't worried. Scion's help wasn't exactly unappreciated, but for once, I hadn't needed it. If I had not already realized that the creature in my room was not the Prince of Ravens, I would have known by how easily I'd overpowered him.

"I didn't realize glamour extended to turning into others."

Scion nodded. "The face you saw earlier was not his true one either, though I could not say who it belonged to. Incubi are monstrous like all the Unseelie, though they hide it better than most."

I frowned. I wanted to wonder aloud why the incubus would have chosen to impersonate Prince Scion, but the answer seemed embarrassingly obvious: *Because I fell for it.*

I sighed and pulled the blanket I'd pulled from the bed more tightly around myself. I was not cold nor as traumatized as I thought I likely should have been by the situation. No, the blanket was more to preserve what was left of my modesty. Not that it mattered much—the real Scion had gotten an eyeful, I knew, when he burst in to help.

"His mistake, of course, was impersonating me," Scion said with no inflection as he strode across the room to sit on the edge of the rumpled bed.

I glanced up sharply, my eyes darting between his for a moment. Then, relief flooded me.

He didn't know. Didn't realize anything had gone on beyond what he'd walked in on. He was assuming I'd known immediately and attacked. I might have laughed with the relief of it.

"Of course," I lied. "I would rather die than let you touch me."

He reached the edge of the bed, and his silver eyes raked over me, scorching me from the inside out. "Then you'd best move over."

"I…" I blinked up at him in confusion. "Excuse me?"

"Not that I'd object, but if you do not want to share a pillow, you will need to move over."

I swallowed audibly and resisted the urge to reach up and slap myself across the face. Surely, *surely,* this could not be happening. *Again.* "Absolutely not."

"You've been sleeping quite soundly in my bed for the better part of two months. Another night won't kill you."

I wasn't so sure about that.

"That's hardly the same, and you know it." I scowled. "You must be out of your mind to think I would let you sleep in here, especially after what just happened."

"It is precisely because of what just happened that I'm going to be sleeping in here. You are clearly unsafe."

I pulled the blanket tighter around myself until only my head was visible. "I thought you said you took care of it. Gods, *I* even took care of it."

His eyes darted to the bloodstained book on the trunk beneath the window, and he bared his teeth in something like a feral smile. "That may be so, but who knows what else is lurking in this cursed fucking house. This whole place is crawling with thieves."

"Why should you care?" I bit out, forcing my mind to stay in the moment. "You're friends with Cross."

His gaze flicked to the door, and for a moment, his self-assured smile flickered. It was as if the mask of bravado slipped, and I caught a glimpse of genuine worry, if only for a moment.

"You're impossibly naive for someone who spends every other sentence lamenting the dangers of the world you grew up in."

He shook his head. "Yes. I am friends with Cross, but were he not my friend, he might be seeking out the assassins' guild right now to see what price is on your head, or perhaps the mercenaries, if he chose to play them against each other." He gave me a pointed look. "There are a dozen thieves downstairs and a dozen more scattered around the city. They are all trained by Cross, and I am not their friend."

I gaped at him but recovered quickly. Loosening the blanket enough that I could walk, I slid off the bed and made to push past him. "Nothing out there could possibly be more dangerous than you. I'll take my chances with the thieves."

Scion blocked me, using his height and imposing stature to try and intimidate. "You're right, rebel. I am by far the most dangerous thing in this city, which is why you're going to stay right here where I can protect you."

"I don't need or want your protection."

He raised an eyebrow. "No? Tell me, have you ever managed to survive an encounter with even one fairy without help?"

I gestured to the bloody book again, my eyes widening. "What do you call that?"

"That wasn't really a High Fae. It's not the same."

I rolled my eyes. He was splitting hairs now. "Short of tying me to the damn headboard, you are never going to win this argument."

His mouth turned into a flat line, his nostrils flaring, and his gaze darted down to my still nearly bare, blanket-wrapped body for the briefest second. "You really need to stop saying shit like that, rebel."

Fair enough. I wasn't sure why I kept taunting him. The words might have been bitter, but even to my own ear, they were starting to sound a lot like a challenge…and I wasn't sure it was one I desired to honor.

Just like that, all the fight drained out of me.

I was tired—so, so, tired—and fighting with him was becoming harder and harder to justify. Like fighting for the sake of it rather than because I actually believed the words coming out of my mouth.

"Fine," I said on a breath. "What did Cross say?"

He cocked his head at me, seeming surprised by the change of subject. "In regard to what?"

"You said after you talked to Cross, you'd think about when I could go back to the castle."

His eyes widened slightly. "Bael will find you the moment he's aware you're gone. You must understand that, yes? Any other scenario is nearly physically impossible."

"I don't care. I want to go back." I bit my lip, thinking yet again of what Thalia said. "I'll cooperate…in the meantime, I mean. I'll stop arguing with you, but I want to go back in two days."

He ran his hand through his hair, clearly frustrated. "Two days is hardly long enough. We don't know if Cross and his children will have found anything."

Perhaps not, but I knew I would not be able to tolerate any longer than that here with him without an end in sight, especially if he was going to insist on sleeping in my bed. I was not sure if I wanted to murder him or…vent my frustration in other ways, but the encounter with the incubus had been illuminating in that I liked every aspect of it, perhaps a bit too much.

Glamour or not, I liked Prince Scion kissing me, touching me, and then I liked smashing his head in just as much.

What that said about me, I did not even want to think.

"Two days," I said on a breath. "That's my bargain."

He gave me a long, piercing look I felt everywhere, and finally, he nodded. "I would ask you to seal it, but I have no name you don't already know, and I hardly need yours."

"Bael always sealed our bargains with a kiss," I blurted out.

By Aisling. Why? Why would I say that?

Scion's lip curled in a suggestive smile, and he laughed—a darkly male chuckle. "He was taking advantage of your ignorance, then. That does nothing."

Humiliation stained my cheeks. I wanted to say I knew that and appear less foolish but struggled, as feigning ignorance wouldn't let me save face now.

I scowled, scooting back on the bed at last to give him room.

"Fine, just…stay over there. Don't touch me."

The prince snorted a derisive laugh that I interpreted to mean it was absurd to think he would ever want to touch me for any reason before lying down stiffly on the opposite side, several inches of space between us.

My face flushed. *Right. Of course not.* Perhaps that was a foolish thing to say. And yet, I had the oddest urge to defend myself.

To point out that I'd seen him with human women before, so it was not such a strange assumption.

To say that I could see the way he looked at me on occasion and that his flirting might be calculated but still did not go unnoticed.

That I'd felt clearly how I affected him when he'd held my hips against him in the tower.

That he was the one who had dragged me here and then insisted on climbing, half-naked, into my bed.

But I didn't say that.

I said nothing, and instead, I lay flat on my back, unmoving, staring up at the ceiling.

I tried not to breathe too loudly, all too aware that he could probably hear my heart beating and was more aware of every tiny movement I made even more so than I was. He didn't move either, and it was only from the intense heat radiating from his skin that I knew he had not turned to stone.

26
LONNIE
THE CUTTHROAT DISTRICT, INBETWIXT

My vision swam, disconcerting and unfocused. I'd been here before—this time, I was sure of it. Yet, the room seemed different. The walls were dark, the air thick with smoke. In the distance, a battle raged, steel on steel echoing through twisting halls.

I stared at the herald in the skull mask. "What do you want?"

The stranger rose from his threadbare throne and took a step closer, and his appearance swam into sharper relief. He was tall—at least as tall as Prince Scion—and wearing a black hooded cloak over a similarly dark tunic.

"Merely to offer you a bargain."

Whatever else felt unclear, I was certain of this much: "I would rather die than make another bargain. The ones I have already are chafing enough as it is."

He laughed, and the sound seemed to wrap around me. Most of the laughter of the High Fae felt eerie and dissonant somehow, but not his.

"What is so amusing?"

He smiled again, but this time, it was a bit brittle. "Come find me, and I shall tell you."

I AWOKE THE NEXT MORNING TO SUNLIGHT STREAMING THROUGH THE still-open curtains and the sound of hushed voices at the door.

It took me a long moment to remember the events of the previous evening—where I was and the reason for the adrenaline buzzing through my veins. A slight embarrassment washed over me, yet in truth, I was not surprised. This was precisely the sort of dream I'd been plagued by for weeks, and given the events of last night…well, it wasn't precisely a shock.

I peered into the corner of the room, now flooded with weak sunlight, just to completely dispel myself of the notion that anyone could have been standing there, watching me—watching *us*.

The face of the stranger swam in my mind, growing more clouded with each second I moved away from the dream. I wasn't sure I recognized him—in fact, I was almost certain I had not, yet the feeling of his presence there lingered longer than the dream itself.

It was nearly impossible to name…like power or electricity.

If I had never read Rosey's journals, I would never have given this more than a passing thought—a minor humiliation—but now…

My entire body still felt far too hot, a burning flush I couldn't expel. I worried my lip. Gods, if my subconscious had begun to view Scion with something other than loathing after only a few sad stories, I couldn't trust myself with *anything*.

Opening my eyes slowly, I glimpsed the object of my ire himself. Scion's smooth, muscled back and disheveled hair were halfway obscured by the doorframe as he spoke to whoever stood in the hallway. Cross, I supposed, or perhaps one of his children came to deliver a message.

Rolling over, I found the space in the bed next to me still warm. Part of me was already embarrassed by giving in and allowing Scion to stay.

I could have tried harder to argue with him.

I could have left, damned the consequences.

And I could have fought the impulse to inch closer to the impossibly comforting warmth of his body sleeping beside me in the hours I'd lain awake listening to his breathing long after I'd finally given in.

But I didn't.

Refusing to indulge in my own self-loathing, I instead focused on whatever was being said in the hall. Straining my ears, I could still only make out every third word or so. The tone, however, was urgent. Angry. I stiffened. Had something happened?

"Get dressed," Scion said abruptly, slamming the door.

I peeked over my shoulder. "If I'd been sleeping, that would have been a terrible way to wake me up."

"I knew you were awake." He rolled his eyes as he strode over to the chair in the corner where his armor was neatly stacked. "I can hear the difference in your breathing."

I shook my head slightly, having been momentarily distracted by all the hard planes of muscle before me. "I suppose I should just call myself lucky that I am still breathing at all, trapped in here with you all night."

He gave me a long, searching look, his mouth slightly ajar, and I could almost feel the tension that hung in the air, but he only said, "Dress quickly. I'll wait for you in the hall."

I wasn't sure why I felt slightly guilty as the door slammed behind him.

I TOOK FAR LONGER THAN I WOULD HAVE LIKED TO REDRESS MYSELF in the same clothing as yesterday.

Finally, I managed to tie the straps of my dress into something resembling a corset, tight enough that it hardly mattered that I could not manage to find the sleeves. I sighed. The dress now covered about as much as my blanket had last night, and yet I was now about to walk into a room filled with strangers. If we were going to stay for two more days, I would need some additional clothing. Even as a servant, I hadn't been forced to wear the same filthy clothing for days on end. No, that sort of thing was only for days spent in dungeon cells, and if I was not meant to be a prisoner, I deserved to at least bathe and wear fresh undergarments.

Resolving to tell Scion this as soon as I readied myself, I made my way to the bathing room and looked in the small mirror. I winced. My hair—wild on the best of days—had reached a size three times larger than my head.

It was times like these that I was reminded how much I missed my sister, as she would have teased me relentlessly before taming the nest. I had no extraordinary skill with braiding but managed something simple that at least kept the curls at bay, then darted out into the hall.

Scion leaned against the wall outside the door, waiting with his arms crossed and one ankle thrown over the other. He looked up at me through his long, dark eyelashes. "Ready?"

"Yes," I mumbled. "You know, if we're going to be staying long, I'll need something else to wear."

I expected him to argue or at least ask questions, but he only gave a curt nod. "I'd rather see you out of that dress, anyway."

I glanced down at the mulberry gown. I would give him that it was now dirty, and I'd tied the straps far worse than Thalia had done, but I'd thought it looked nice yesterday. That was, before it was ruined by being practically dragged through the street. "Forgive me if I do not take your advice on clothing, my lord. If I did, I'd find myself dressed for mourning every day of my life."

He looked down at his all-black attire and scowled. "You and Bael both with your…colors. This is practical."

I grinned. "Practically morbid."

He cocked his head at me. "Was that a joke or an insult? I can never tell with you."

My lips tipped down, turning back into a flat line. I wasn't sure, and pointing it out had ruined the moment. Anyway, he was far worse when it came to insults than I was.

I was saved from having to respond as an enormous blue-black raven swooped out of the still-open door behind me and landed hard on my shoulder. I winced, ducking, when his talons dug into the bare skin of my shoulder. "Ow!"

Quill dug his talons harder into my skin and cocked his head at me, blinking slowly. He opened his wide, black beak and let out a croak of greeting. *"Hello, you."*

"Yes, yes, hello," I said to the bird, still somewhat annoyed as my shoulder smarted with pain. "Let go of me."

Scion raised an eyebrow as the bird tittered, pecking at my hair. "He's never that affectionate with anyone."

"Yes," I grumbled, dipping a bit at the weight on my shoulder. "So I've heard. Could you…" I trailed off, gesturing helplessly at the raven, which was at least a third of my size, perhaps more.

The prince put out an arm, and the raven jumped to land on him instead, where at least his bulk was somewhat better distributed. I ducked with the force of his takeoff. While I liked the raven quite a bit, I'd only carried him around when the statement outweighed the…well, *weight.*

"When did he arrive?" I asked, massaging my arm.

"He's been circling the city," Scion answered shortly as he shifted Quill from his forearm to his shoulder, where the bird fluttered its wings briefly before settling down. "If I do not wish to be recognized, Quill must remain unseen. There are many who may not know my face but would remember the raven."

I wasn't so sure about that—his face, and more so his eyes, were memorable on their own.

"I don't know how you carry him without growing tired," I commented.

Scion looked offended. "I will not dignify that with a response."

The raven made a forlorn sound. *"This is the welcome I get,"* he seemed to say. *"Fine. I'll go, as I'm clearly unwanted."*

I petted the bird's head, and he nipped lightly at my hand. "No, don't go. I didn't mean that."

Scion gave me a very strange look.

THE THIEVES' DEN WAS FAR LIVELIER THAN IT HAD BEEN LAST NIGHT, and I had to force my face into a blank mask so as not to betray my shock when we entered.

Every seat at the bar and the surrounding card tables was full, and the sparring ring was full of action, screaming spectators standing all around shouting jeers and encouragement in equal measure.

Scion and I stepped into the room, and nearly two dozen pairs of eyes turned toward us. For a moment, all movement stopped, and it turned deadly silent. I felt as though every member of the guild had their eyes fixed on me, analyzing my every move, sizing me up like a lamb for slaughter.

Then, all at once, the tension broke.

The thieves barely acknowledged us as conversation resumed, and the misfit army returned to whatever they'd been doing before our arrival: some sparring or else cheering the others on in the fighting area, some seemed to be eating breakfast, and still others were slumped against the wall like zombies, no doubt still exhausted from their night's work.

Scion gripped my elbow and steered me through the center of the room, toward the bar and the card tables at the back where we'd sat with Cross the night before.

"What was that about?" I asked.

"You'll see in a moment," he said through gritted teeth.

I glanced around as we walked, both curious about what I was supposed to be seeing and trying to take in all the faces and commit them to memory. Were any of these on the ships bound for Nevermore? Or, perhaps more pressingly, were any of these faces those Scion had been so concerned might attack me?

I was so lost in thought I hardly noticed when we veered off to the left, parting with the crowd, to avoid something going on in the very center of the room.

I looked up, alerted by Scion tugging on my arm rather than merely steering. "What—"

I broke off. My horror was so absolute that I couldn't even make a coherent sound. I'd not seen carnage like this since the days when King Penvalle haunted the halls of the obsidian palace, and those he took to his bed would come back injured or, worse, never come back at all. I turned slowly to stare at Scion, my mouth agape. "What the fuck did you do?"

Scion's calm expression didn't shift. "Nothing he didn't deserve."

"I thought…"

I tried to imagine what I'd thought. What had I thought Scion meant when he said he *took care* of the incubus?

The scene spread out across the back wall of the thieves' den was clearly what had caused the silence when we entered. Blood dripped down the walls, splattered so thick it was like red paint on the side of a barn in Cheapside. It all stemmed from a violent effigy nailed to the wall.

The incubus had reverted to its natural face—some sort of gray, leathery creature—but I didn't have to think twice to know it was him.

Scion had not merely killed him; he'd destroyed him. He'd physically severed every limb, finger, toe, and other body part and systematically placed them back in order, nailed against the wall of the guild den like a warning to anyone who might think to commit the same offense.

• • •

THE WEAPONS RACK, WHICH LAST NIGHT HAD BEEN FULL, WAS NOW empty. Every sword and dagger was poking out of the wall, holding the puzzle of bleeding skin and bones in place. I nearly gagged when I noticed that there was no sword holding the incubus's cock to the wall and was afraid to ask what Scion had done with it.

I stared at the mangled figure before me, my heart pounding with dread and terror. My mouth moved without making any sound.

"Calm down, rebel," Scion whispered, guiding me away from the small crowd surrounding Kaius's mangled body. "This was necessary. Believe me."

The crowd was not nearly as large as I thought it should have been, and I found it all the more eerie that the majority of the room was simply ignoring the situation.

Granted, had I not done that too? Had I not also stood by while King Penvalle lay in the blood of servants I knew?

"But why?" I hissed, too incensed to bother arguing about how I still did not fully trust him. "What could possibly necessitate this sort of reaction?"

His fingers tightened on my arm. "Someone was bound to get bold enough to attack, but now the others will think twice about it. There will be less likelihood of contracts on your head or knives in your back."

"This was still barbaric."

"You would not complain so much if Bael did this."

I reeled back. "That's because Bael wouldn't do this."

He gave me a condescending look. "You are impossibly naive. Bael is in a cage at present because even I am not sure I can control him and would prefer never to find out. He'd do this and worse—you simply ignore it because you like him better than me. At least be consistent with your morality, rebel. It is difficult to believe you are truly against violence when I have seen you bash in more than one skull, and you are more than halfway in love with a male who has ripped out more hearts than currently beat in this room."

My mouth fell open, my heart pounding, but I recovered myself quickly. "I still do not see why you care?" I hissed. "They wouldn't get the crown. It's not a hunting night."

"This was also not only about you." His eyes narrowed, and he lowered his voice. "Kaius was helping Cross locate and destroy shipments of a drug that induces lust. If there is any question at all that he took some instead…that it still exists in the city or was used on you, then he needed to die as an example. We cannot let anyone get ideas."

I shook my head, shivering slightly with disgust. "He was an incubus. Was this not simply his…nature?"

"Probably, but we take no risks. Furthermore, there are any number of reasons someone might still want to kill you. To throw the country into chaos. To challenge me while I'm escorting you. To test your power…I could go on." He took a step closer, his terrifying gaze piercing, dark, and immovable. "As of right now, you are the crown. Attacking you is attacking the kingdom, and it's an insult to me as I have forbidden it."

I shivered, the magnitude of his words falling over me. "So this is about you, then? Your ego?"

"No, rebel. It's about the kingdom. Everything I do is to protect the kingdom. Remember that."

27

LONNIE

THE CUTTHROAT DISTRICT, INBETWIXT

"Sleep alright?" Cross yelled, waving at Scion and me as we made our way across the room.

"Marvelous," I said sarcastically. "It was the most peaceful sleep I've ever had."

Scion shot me a dirty look, but Cross only grinned wider as several people laughed and the crowd parted to let us through.

The guild master sat at one of the rickety card tables beside the bar, which had been mostly empty last night. Now, every chair was occupied. Cross sat facing us, flanked by six or seven of his children, Siobhan on his immediate left and an attractive chest-nut-haired male I didn't know on his right. Siobhan grinned, but the male merely watched us, eyes narrowed.

"I'm so glad to hear that, lass." Cross winked. "But if you change your mind and want a different bed, I'm just down the hall."

Scion made an angry noise in the back of his throat. "Say that again and your children will be orphans for the few minutes they outlive you."

A shudder skittered up my spine. It wasn't so much what he'd said as the calm tone with which he said it. He had no doubt in his mind he could take on every one of these thieves at once and win.

The chestnut-haired male to Cross's right began to rise out of his seat, no doubt to defend his guild master, but Cross stopped him with a look. "No, Arson," Cross said, putting a hand out as if to hold back the male beside him. "I've tested the prince's patience enough. My apologies to the queen."

I shook my head. It seemed to me that Scion might be the one who needed to apologize—after all, Kaius's blood looked like it was going to become a permanent part of the decor—but Cross didn't seem to mind one bit. In fact, he made no mention of the situation at all as we sat down opposite him, though it was impossible that he wouldn't have noticed.

Maybe I was overestimating how much Cross cared about his children or else underestimating the relevance of the drug Scion mentioned. Cross was, after all, the head of a violent criminal group. Being close friends with Scion likely meant he was at least willing to engage in torture when needed.

"Breakfast?" Cross offered brightly. "You must be hungry."

I was about to decline when my stomach betrayed me, growling loudly for all to hear. I nodded. "If you don't mind."

"Not at all. We can plot with full stomachs."

"As long as we get this started," Scion grumbled. "I'd rather not waste any more time than we have to."

Cross shook his head. "I have never forgotten how impatient you are, yet it always astounds me all over again. Smell a rose, will you?"

Scion's scowl deepened. "You could show me the most beautiful fucking rose on the continent, and I would still tell you I have more important things to do than waste my time on flowers."

I caught Siobhan's eye across the table, and she smiled, rolling her eyes as if to say, "Males." I shook my head in response and glanced down, swallowing a laugh.

Then, in the oddest way, a wave of grief hit me.

My sister would have laughed at something like that—something so innocuous and foolish. Since her death, I'd had no friends. No female companionship beyond the occasional moment with Iola or Enid. No glances to convey more than silence.

It felt wrong—too soon—to share even a laugh. And worse, with a *fairy* woman. Like betraying Rosey.

I folded my hands in my lap and did not look up again, letting the conversation wash over and around me as we waited for breakfast to arrive, glancing up only when Cross made introductions. To my immense relief, he did not bother to introduce all two dozen of the thieves milling around the den, focusing only on the three seated at the table with us.

"You've already met Siobhan." Cross gestured to the female, who gave a little wave. It might have been friendly had she not been spinning a dagger between her fingers only moments before, which she tossed into the air and caught again, never missing a beat. "Siobhan is an expert safecracker. There's no lock in the city she can't open."

I nodded in response and gave a weak smile. I might have asked if she could teach me to do that, but now, with my sister on my mind, even the thought of friendship was too raw.

"This is Arson." Cross gestured to the large, chestnut-haired male on his right.

I raised an eyebrow. Upon a second glance, I thought Arson might be half-Fae at most. His ears were pointed, but his face, while handsome, led me to believe he might be part human.

It was a difficult distinction to make—since Fae and humans were not so different from one another in broad strokes, yet while I might not be able to explain that ineffable "something," I could certainly see it. Perhaps it came down to symmetry—overall perfection, as the Fae did not get sick as we did, age as we did, or show exhaustion or blemishes on their faces. Perhaps I would ask Bael, when I saw him again, what the Fae perceived to be the difference—if there was something that they thought to be ugly within their own species.

"Hello," I said shortly.

Arson merely glared, clearly not liking that we were here. I felt Scion shift beside me.

Cross did not seem at all perturbed by whatever was upsetting his son. "Arson is a talented swordsmith."

"Is that necessary?" Scion sneered.

"Hear out the plan first, Sci," Cross said lightly, even as Arson shifted as if he were going to stand and show Scion just how necessary he was. "You can't be in every room at once."

Scion looked like he wanted to argue but said nothing. I let out a breath I hadn't realized I'd been holding. For a moment, I'd thought I was about to have to watch Scion torture this thief, and in that moment, I realized I agreed with him. The best swordsmith in the world probably wouldn't be necessary.

"And last," Cross said as if there had been no interruption, "this is Vander."

A thin, pale male at the end of the table merely nodded at me. He was pale in every way, with hair so blond it was white and eyes that held the milky hue of blindness. Still, he faced me as if he could see, and his eyes seemed to stare straight into me. I shuddered. "What do you do?"

"Plan," Vander replied in a soft voice that did nothing to appease my anxiety.

Thankfully, I was saved from responding as, in that moment, the food arrived, providing a welcome distraction. A teenage boy, dressed in the same all-black clothing the thieves seemed to favor, approached, balancing a teetering tray of plates on one shoulder.

Without conscious thought, I pushed my chair back and stood to assist him, grabbing the edge of the tray before it could go crashing to the ground. "Here, let me help you."

The boy's eyes widened, and he shrunk back. "No!"

Ignoring his protest, I swiped the largest plate and placed it on the table, the hot edges burning my thumbs.

Scion caught my eye. "What the fuck are you doing? Sit down."

I froze, realizing everyone was staring at me.

I swallowed thickly, knowing my only choices were to pretend I'd intended this all along or to admit that I was still so accustomed to serving it was like a well-worked muscle. I might despise serving the Fae, but I would still feel more comfortable, safer, standing against the wall with a tray than sitting at Scion's side. There was no logic in it, but I'd grown comfortable with the hand I'd been dealt. Learned to move within only the confines of my cage.

"I'm saving your breakfast from landing on the floor," I replied, forcing a bravado I didn't feel into my voice. "Perhaps try saying 'thank you,' my lord. I only meant to save this poor boy the honor of being asked to lick wine from your boots."

The thieves laughed as I took my seat again, clearly not understanding the reference, but Scion didn't move. His gaze remained fixed on me, his food sitting untouched in front of him.

I reached for my fork, slowly beginning to eat as the tension in the air grew thicker between us. The thieves resumed their conversation, not watching us, but I felt as if I could barely breathe.

Finally, the prince leaned over, his breath hot on my ear. "You seem to ruminate on that moment often, rebel. Should I take that to mean you wish you had complied with my request?"

I stiffened and did not look at him, staring straight ahead as I continued to pick at my eggs. "Only because it is proof of your true abhorrent personality, my lord."

I felt him smile. "I think you're a liar, rebel. You want to get on your knees for me, but you like to hide behind this notion that I might force you. Pretend all you like, but we both know that when you come to my bed, you'll not only be begging me to fuck you, you'll say 'thank you, lord,' when I'm done."

I spluttered, dropping my fork with a loud clang that made everyone look up. "Sorry," I mumbled. "It slipped."

My face burned, and I refused to reply or look at him throughout the entire rest of the meal. I had to assume that at least Siobhan and Cross, who were seated nearest to us, could hear the whispered conversation, but neither commented. Maybe this was more common than I realized among the Fae, or maybe they just didn't want to upset Scion—there had to be some perks to royalty, I supposed.

Despite my desperate desire to run, we still had a heist to plan, and I was glued to my chair for at least another hour.

"No one has seen Dullahan in the city," Arson said shortly once his plate was cleared. "Which in effect means he isn't here."

Scion nodded. "I'd expected as much."

I looked up at him, surprised. "You did?"

"My brother wouldn't just come quietly, rebel. Even if he was the one to ask for the meeting, he'll still want to ensure it happens in the last way you might expect."

I stiffened, something about that phrase rankled, and I couldn't quite name it. "So what are we going to do?"

"We're getting to that, lass." Cross leaned toward me, his elbows on the table. "Vander here might've seen someone who worked as a lookout while out an' about last night."

I glanced over at Vander again, taking in his blind eyes, and decided not to ask how he'd *seen* them. "How do you know they worked for Dullahan?"

"All the rebels dress the same," he answered. "You seen them? They have these long cloaks, like—"

"I've seen them," I cut him off sharply.

Immediately, the image of my sister's face peeking out from beneath the hood of her long cloak flashed through my mind. Of all the cloaked figures running into the camp, like nightmares come to seek waking vengeance. I hadn't realized that was something they wore all the time—it hadn't even occurred to me to consider it. If it had, I no doubt would have had a much easier time locating someone to question about Dullahan in the capital on the several occasions that I'd tried.

"Why would they want to identify themselves?" I asked. "If everyone knows the cloaks are the uniform of the rebellion."

Siobhan shrugged. "Not everyone does know, but for those who do, it's not usually much of a deterrent." She threw a sideways glance at Scion. "There are many sympathizers who are not necessarily part of the army."

"I'm well aware," Scion ground out. "As long as none of those sympathizers sit at this table, then we shouldn't have a problem."

"Where did you see the rebel?" I asked, covering the uncomfortable silence that followed his statement.

Vander ducked his head slightly as he replied. "The Side Saddle. He was there all night, as far as I saw."

Siobhan guffawed. "And you were as well, were you?"

"On business," Vander snapped, his too-quiet voice rising. "All the patrons there carry far too much gold and don't watch it carefully."

Arson laughed, smiling for the first time since we'd been sitting here. "I wouldn't either with some nymph's cunt in my—"

"Alright," Cross cut them off, his brow furrowing in vague annoyance. The way he looked at the others, one really would think they were his children.

I stared around at the group, marveling at the dynamic. This was a different sort of family than the Everlasts—at least from what I'd seen of them. The Everlast siblings might hold this sort of easy banter with each other in private, I didn't know, but Cross's family seemed far more open, no matter who joined them for dinner.

"The Side Saddle is the den of the pleasure guild," Cross explained. "It's everything you might expect from that description, the only unique thing being that the madam is quite difficult to get one over on."

It sounded like he spoke from experience.

"We suggest going there this evening to try and smoke out the rat," Arson said bluntly, looking at Scion this time.

"And what if he's not there this evening?" Scion asked.

"All the better," Siobhan replied, grinning. She leaned over, speaking directly to me now. "The madam of the guild is called Phillipa Blacktongue. She keeps a close watch on all her charges and has very extensive records of everyone who passes through her establishment. If we could get her book, we could undoubtedly track down the location of the lookout, but it's not that simple. We've tried to get a look at her books before, but she keeps them in an enchanted safe on the second floor of the Side Saddle."

"I thought you could break any safe," I replied.

She didn't seem offended. "It's not the safe that's the problem. It's her. She watches that thing like a hawk, especially on busy nights, and she'd recognize any of us the moment we walked in the door."

"So what do you want us to do?"

Cross grinned, his twinkling gaze full of a mischief that reminded me painfully of Bael. "Blacktongue has an office on the first floor for entertaining important guests."

"Important like royalty," Scion asked, his tone resigned.

"Exactly," Siobhan answered. "We don't need a large diversion or even a complex one. Just keep Phillipa Blacktongue in her office for ten minutes, fifteen if you can."

"We'll do it," I said at the same time as Scion said, "I don't fucking think so."

I glanced at him. "What's wrong? It's a ten-minute conversation."

Cross clapped his hands together. "Wonderful! We'll let you work out the particulars and meet back here in a few hours." He looked me over. "You'll need to wear something else. Perhaps Siobhan can lend you something."

I barely heard him, all my attention focused on Scion. I twisted my hands in my skirt, feeling intuitively that the other shoe was about to drop. "Why should that be difficult? Talk to her for ten minutes?"

The prince grimaced, his heated gaze landing hard on me. "Because there's not likely to be much talking involved."

28

LONNIE

THE CUTTHROAT DISTRICT, INBETWIXT

"What do you mean exactly by 'no talking'?" I asked several hours later.

It had taken quite a while to come back around to the topic of Phillipa Blacktongue—partly because Scion was clearly avoiding me and partly because he and Cross had spent several hours behind closed doors in some sort of private meeting that I was not invited to. I supposed I should have been grateful that it had taken so long for me to be shut out of a conversation—it was far better than what I'd been used to before—but instead, I was bitter as I used that time to take a real bath. So bitter I couldn't even enjoy the feeling of washing the grime from my skin.

"I mean," Scion said flatly as we walked through the city square that afternoon, "that Phillipa Blacktongue doesn't take on clients unless there is a very good reason."

I looked sideways at him shrewdly. "How do you know?"

He rolled his eyes. "I know nearly every important player in the city, rebel, whether or not I like or socialize with them. I also make it a point to be aware of potential enemies. Blacktongue is a succubus, and like you may have noticed earlier, I do not particularly care for their kind."

I shuddered. He certainly did not.

"So?" I asked. "I'm sure she's capable of a normal conversation."

"Capable, certainly, but whether she'll be willing is another matter. She does not bill her time merely to gossip."

Embarrassment stained my cheeks. No matter what he claimed, he certainly seemed to know a lot about it. "Then what will we do?"

He grimaced. "Well, seeing as you have committed us to yet another errand without consulting me, I suppose we will have to improvise."

I raised an eyebrow. I was not sure I liked the sound of that, but I had no better suggestion, so I kept my mouth shut.

WE'D VENTURED INTO THE CITY SO THAT SCION COULD MAKE GOOD on his promise to find me something new to wear, but I had to admit, it was more overwhelming than I might have anticipated. A battle of inner afflictions rather than those that lurked outside the city walls.

The Cutthroat marketplace was lively and bustling, even more so than the streets we'd walked yesterday. There were rows of booths selling potions, herbs, weapons, sweet-smelling pastries, and smoked meats. One vendor had nothing but cloth-bound books, while another sold strings of glittering gemstones on long, leather cords. I saw many stalls selling clothing yet nothing that caught my eye.

"They seem to have more free humans here than in the capital."

Scion followed my gaze to where a human man was standing behind a booth selling colorful hats. "I suppose. Cutthroat has long been a haven for misfits who don't mind signing over their freedom to the guilds in exchange for protection, but be careful, rebel. Not everyone is friendly."

I laughed. "Because everyone in the capital is so kind to humans."

Scion shrugged. "Many agree with you and choose to come here, but the laws are equally harsh to ours in different ways. I suggest you stay close, unless you wish to grow more intimately familiar with what those ways are."

"I wasn't planning to wander. Didn't I promise I would cooperate?"

"Just ensuring you remember that. I know how you like to act as if your word means nothing, if only because you are not bound to the truth as we are."

My brow furrowed. That shouldn't have stung, but it did—perhaps because it was true. I'd always been proud of being a liar. It was a good trait to have among humans in Elsewhere. Now, though, among Fae, I found myself gravitating to the truth far more often.

"I believe there is more clothing over there," I said stiffly, making a beeline for another row of stalls.

Walking past a stall where a High Fae vendor was showing off reems of colorful fabric, I reached out to touch the edge of a bit of silk, then pulled my hand back as if burned. Guilt stabbed at my middle, painful and impossible to either expel or explain.

Until moving into the obsidian tower, I'd never worn anything new. All my clothing had been old dresses, made over time and time again to fit as I grew, or else bought secondhand or adopted from other servants when they left the palace or died. Shopping for new clothing in a market square was a completely foreign concept, and so, too, was choosing something I might truly want.

"What's wrong?" Scion asked.

"Nothing," I lied as we passed a small band of minstrels playing a lively tune for a twirling nymph with a tambourine.

I wasn't sure what I would have said to him anyway. He didn't care—he was merely asking out of habit, I supposed, or concern for optics.

Even if I could have explained, I wouldn't have wanted to. I was being stupid. It was only fabric.

Scion glanced from me to the blue-green silk. "If you don't like that, there are others. Don't you typically wear warmer colors?"

I frowned. I supposed I did, though not for any particular reason, and it was especially odd that he would notice. "No, it's not that…" I struggled for an excuse. "That's merely fabric. I don't have time to have something made in a day. I need clothing immediately."

That wasn't it either, though. Liking something—liking anything—was an entirely new idea for me. I'd only recently gotten used to the idea that I might get food every day. That I might not be attacked or beaten or tortured. I was still barely able to process that the male asking what color of silk I preferred was not going to slit my throat. *Liking* something was an extreme luxury.

Scion nodded as if that made sense. "Perhaps an indoor shop?" he asked, glancing around uncomfortably.

He'd left Quill at the thieves' den and looked *almost* normal among the other city dwellers, but still, we were attracting glances.

"Yes," I agreed, though I was less concerned about the shoppers watching us and more desired to limit my choices. "A single shop would be easier."

"We should have shadow walked back to the capital and had Aine help you," he grumbled.

"Would that not have defeated the purpose of your infernal mission, my lord? What if we run into Ambrose Dullahan here in the market?"

He looked taken aback, then frowned. "Yes. You are correct, of course."

I was sorely tempted to point out that even he didn't seem to think it was likely that we would run into the rebel leader at any given moment of the day, thus making it pointless to stay in the capital indefinitely, but as I'd sworn to cooperate, I let it go.

In the center of the square sat a small, brick-built tailor's shop, its walls decorated with gaudy pastel hues.

Statuesque mannequins stood in the window, adorned with more color and silk than I'd ever had any desire to see, much less wear. It seemed that the fashion in Inbetwixt leaned toward bright, contrasting colors and bold, printed silks. The simplest thing I saw in the shop window was a sapphire-blue tailcoat with an emerald-green belt, intricately patterned with gold and silver embroidery.

I grimaced, yet the lure of a quieter environment proved too hard to pass up.

I pushed the door open, and a bell rang somewhere in the shop, and a tiny woman in a yellow-and-orange apron came bustling out to greet us. Her wide, toothy grin stretched from one ear to the other as she chattered away in a language I recognized as the old tongue but didn't understand.

I shifted my weight from one foot to the other and nervously glanced over at Scion. This had probably been a mistake. "I don't understand her."

"She wants to know what you're looking for," he said. "And what happened to your dress."

I looked down at my gown, which was getting increasingly less lovely by the hour. "Er, I don't know what I want, and tell her anything you like about the dress. I'd like to see someone's face if they knew you kidnapped me."

He rolled his eyes and spoke rapidly back and forth with the woman for several minutes before she ran off into the back of the shop at top speed.

I shifted where I stood, glancing back and forth between the prince and the door where the tailor had disappeared. "Wait, what just happened?"

"You are quite hindered by not speaking the old language," he said, unbothered.

"They don't speak it in Aftermath," I snapped. "What did you say?"

"She asked what size you wear, what you'd be doing, and who was paying…that was most of it."

I narrowed my eyes. "And what did you say?"

"That she has eyes and a tape measure, that I would pay, and that I wasn't sure what you would be doing, but I have no doubt it will infuriate me."

"Right," I said awkwardly, my cheeks heating slightly for no reason I could explain.

I took a few steps back and leaned against the long fabric-cutting counter, facing the prince. Behind him, the sunny square was as bustling as ever, but in here, it was almost too quiet.

"It has been some time since I was in Cutthroat, but I believe the city has grown since I was last here," Scion said blandly.

"Is that unusual?"

"Unfortunately, it is," he said, pushing his blue-black hair out of his eyes and taking a seat on the bench under the window. "Most of the villages are shrinking as the population shifts and grows smaller each year."

I raised an eyebrow. Was this his idea of casual conversation? "How can a population dwindle if you are immortal?"

Leaning forward with his elbows on his knees, he stared up at me. "We are immortal, not invincible, and Fae need magic to thrive. The magic has been failing for centuries. Now, some Fae are born with no powers at all. I'm not sure what that makes them—something else entirely, I suppose. A new subspecies."

I chewed on the inside of my cheek, considering this. It was the kind of thing I had never thought much about—servants didn't worry over evolution or population growth or politics. Those were questions for, well, queens. "It's a luxury I have never known to think so deeply about things that do not affect me directly."

He shot me a quizzical look. "I don't understand."

"You wouldn't," I replied. "You haven't spent every day of your life in fear or poverty or pain. To you, it is a burden to consider the fate of the country and of people you will never know, and it is a noble burden, but at the same time, it is a luxury to carry that burden."

"You make it sound that to be born and raised royal is some kind of blessing."

"Isn't it? Would you have preferred my circumstances?"

I hadn't expected him to give me a real answer, but he surprised me by considering the question. "No," he said after a moment. "But I still believe you are underestimating the difficulty of running a kingdom."

I let out a sarcastic laugh. "As far as I can tell, it's no hardship at all."

He evidently did not perceive my sarcasm. "That is because you are running nothing, making no decisions, and have no responsibilities."

"Aside from staying alive," I snapped.

His face twisted into a sneer. "Which you can barely manage, even with a truly baffling amount of assistance and coddling."

We glared at each other, and for a moment, I forgot there was anyone else here. The tailor in the back may as well have been in another province, the people in the square nonexistent. I'd almost had time to marvel at the fact that we were having a civil conversation that did not revolve around my death or any imminent crisis, yet now unfulfilled tension seemed to crackle in the air like a tangible presence.

"Did you have a point to make, Prince Scion?" I said slowly. "Or were you merely looking to make mine for me? For someone who claims to have so many responsibilities, you certainly have the luxury to spend a lot of time obsessing over what I'm doing."

He'd stood up, and I realized I had no idea when it happened, but now he was standing only inches away. His jaw had gone so tight his next words sounded physically painful. "I am merely trying to say that not everything about royalty is a privilege.

Some things are horrific, painful, and violent, and there's no one else to take the burden of them."

I raised a skeptical eyebrow. I'd lived at the court of Everlast long enough to see plenty of horrific, painful, and violent things. I was sorely tempted to list some for him and force him to pass judgment, but I had to admit I was curious:

What did Prince Scion, the queen's executioner, think was horrific?

What did the prince whose talents lay in causing pain so extreme it drove Fae to madness and humans to death think was painful?

What did the male who could clear a battlefield by threat of his presence alone think was violent?

"Like what?"

29
LONNIE
THE CUTTHROAT DISTRICT, INBETWIXT

"I assume my grandmother knew the rebellion was coming," Scion began, shifting to lean against the counter.

I held my breath and rocked back on my heels to put a fraction more space between us. I had no idea what to expect out of this and no reason to think it would be a pleasant conversation, but somehow, he'd captivated my attention with only a few words.

"Grandmother Celia was the best seer born since the Oracle of Isles End, but she didn't always share her knowledge with us."

"Why not?" I asked.

He smiled bitterly. "Knowing the future will inevitably change it, but not always in the way one expects. She was very precise about when and with whom she shared her prophecies—it was maddening."

I raised my eyebrows. In the years I worked in the palace, I'd only seen Queen Celia once, as she almost never left her chambers. It was odd to hear her spoken about thus by someone who not only knew her personally but found her "maddening." Like if someone told me that the ancient Queen Aisling, who we swore by, actually feared the dark and had terrible table manners.

"So if she knew about the rebellion, why wouldn't she try to stop it?" I asked.

"I'm getting to that." He grimaced. "Just over two decades ago, the volcano that is the source of all magic erupted for the first time since the age of Queen Aisling. There was no warning, even for the seers, and within a single day, the city of Nightshade was destroyed."

"I know," I said uncomfortably. "Everyone knows what happened in Aftermath."

"Aftermath" was what they called Nightshade after it had been destroyed by the eruption of the Source. At first, everyone had spoken of "the aftermath of the catastrophe in Nightshade," but after two decades, now the area was simply known as Aftermath. I always squirmed to hear this story as I was intimately connected to it in a way that others were not. I'd been born in the burning city on the same day as the disaster.

If my discomfort showed on my face, Scion didn't seem to notice. He stared straight through me as he continued his story as if I hadn't spoken. "When the Source erupted, the city was effectively crushed. A third of the population died in the initial explosion, and another third died in the days that followed, some from injuries, others from lack of resources or infighting. By the time that soldiers and healers from Overcast arrived to help, there was only a fraction of the people left."

"Why from Overcast?" I asked too fast. "Why not here?"

"I don't know how you can have lived your entire life on this continent and know so little."

I flushed and looked down. "Bael mentioned some history," I said, somewhat defensively. "I am not totally ignorant."

His face split into a wide grin. "Oh, then you're doubly fucked. Never take Bael's advice on anything but wine, horses, or women."

He seemed to realize what he'd said because he closed his mouth a bit too fast, but I was too focused on his face to focus much on what he was saying. The contrast between his stoic scowl and when he smiled—actually smiled—was staggering. Like striking a match in pitch-darkness. My heartbeat picked up a fraction, and I chewed on the inside of my lip, willing my breathing to even out.

"Er." Scion cleared his throat, looking back at his hands. "To answer your question…Inbetwixt and Nevermore have their own armies and governing families. Inbetwixt would strongly prefer to succeed from the kingdom, but as you saw earlier, it would be impossible. Nevermore has considered leaving in the past but ultimately stayed. They are not a culture that relishes war."

"And Overcast?"

"Overcast has never had their own army nor a culture much separate than ours. Their lord and lady are distant cousins of my family."

Not quite so distant from what Thalia said, but I didn't think it was worth interrupting him to ask about. I remembered what he'd said to Thalia when she was explaining how they did things in Overcast, about how they didn't fight wars. "So Overcast is your northern outpost," I said shrewdly. "To keep everyone else in line."

He glanced sideways at me. "I suppose so. Of course, at one time, every city was its own individual entity. When the continent first united under Queen Aisling, Nightshade was the capital, so one cannot claim this was entirely by design."

"Perhaps not by design but intervention."

He nodded, conceding the point. "We keep forces stationed in Overcast at all times, so those soldiers were the closest when the Source erupted. Only by the time they arrived to help, it was too late to do much more than collect the dead."

I sighed, knowing there was far more to this story. We'd begun with his desire to explain how difficult ruling could be, and if this horrible history was merely the background, I wasn't sure I wanted to get to the end, yet I couldn't help but demand to know more. "Then what?"

"Relatively quickly after the disaster," Scion continued, "the survivors again dwindled down. Some left, moving into the valleys below the mountains, and survived. Some tried to stay and were forever changed by the Wilde magic, becoming afflicted."

I shivered bodily at that. "I know."

"Knowing it is one thing, but seeing it is indescribable," he replied. "Had you ever seen one before the other day?"

I opened my mouth to tell him I had seen the afflicted—many times, in fact—and then closed it again. I shook my head.

Scion didn't notice my indecision as his eyes were fixed on some point off in the distance, his expression haunted. "One afflicted is horrible enough, but many are unlike anything you can imagine. They're Fae…or they used to be, but they no longer know that. Some are mad and barely more than beasts; some are like dark phantoms wafting through the streets. Some are simply noise, just endless, never-ending noise."

He rapped his hands on the counter, as if wishing for something to do with them. Indeed, this was the kind of conversation perhaps better had over drinks. Perhaps never. "My father went to Aftermath with the first legion from the capital and immediately returned to report back to my grandmother. I recall him saying that the situation was too hostile and we should further decimate the area."

My eyes widened, this time with confusion rather than awe. "I don't understand."

He turned fully to face me, and our knees knocked together. "Which part?"

I didn't bother to move away, instead leaning forward against the bar, too caught up in the story to care how close we were sitting. "What did your father mean, 'further decimate the area'?"

Scion pushed his hair out of his eyes, looking wary. "That is a complicated answer, rebel."

I wrinkled my nose. Did he realize he kept calling me that or that it no longer made sense? He'd seemed to realize I was not part of the rebel forces…so what was he trying to say?

"I will try to keep up," I said darkly.

He scowled. "This is a tangent that bears more than a simple explanation, but let us simply say that my father viewed the afflicted to be a threat so great that he advised my grandmother to destroy the entire province to remove them."

I gaped. "How could you possibly destroy an entire province at once?"

"Do you know what Bael's primary ability is?"

Again, I wondered if I should lie and for some reason decided against it. "Yes."

"That's how," he said flatly. "They were quite certain he could do it, but most believed it was too dangerous to consider. Even now, his control is tenuous, but then, it was nonexistent."

"Of course it was." My tone came out defensive. "He was what? Twelve?"

Scion didn't react. "That is strange to you, perhaps, but not to us. Power far supersedes age or seniority in most matters. Bael at nine would have been more important to the family than his mother is now, and so forth."

"So you would let Elfwyn walk onto a battlefield tomorrow?"

He grimaced. "Elfwyn is not my child, and, thanks to you, I am not the king, so it would not be my decision."

That sounded like a deflection to me, but I let it go. "Bael didn't go, I take it?"

"No. It was determined that the cost of destroying the afflicted was likely to be every other living thing in the region and perhaps the Source itself. Grandmother Celia was not willing to take that risk."

"To save the people?" I asked, hoping for an answer I did not think was coming.

"No, to save the Source. If the fires had been put out or buried beyond retrieval, no one was sure what might happen to the Fae as a whole."

"Hmmm," I said, noncommittal.

He did not seem to realize this was also my history he was discussing. That in a way, they'd decided to spare me without knowing it.

"Grandmother ignored my father's suggestion, but she agreed that the threat of the afflicted was strong. She feared the Wilde magic would spread to the rest of the continent, so—" His expression turned grave. "—she began sending prisoners from every province to assist in cleaning up the area."

I stared at him for a beat. "Cleaning up the area?"

"The magic, once absorbed, wouldn't spread, so she sent it more hosts to feed on…" He sighed. "And then sent more soldiers to remove those hosts."

I gaped at him, my mind working double time to try and follow what he was trying to explain. It was made all the harder because he kept using flat, nondescript wording, almost like it was something he'd been taught to say…a technical truth.

"So…she created the afflicted," I clarified. "Or more afflicted, I suppose, by sending prisoners to Aftermath to be fed on by the Wilde magic, and then she sent your army after them to destroy the very monsters that she herself created."

He nodded. "Yes."

"How can you sit there simply explaining that as if it's not mass murder."

"It *is* mass murder," he snapped, the anger I'd come to know from him finally seeping back into his tone. "But that is precisely my point. Some of the burdens of royalty are so horrific that there is no simple answer. There is no right choice, and one must choose which might save more people or have the better outcome in the long run, knowing that one might be wrong, or even if they are right, thousands will still die."

I sat in stunned silence.

He was right—I would give him that much.

That was, in fact, one of the most horrific, painful, and violent things I'd ever had the misfortune to know.

"But Queen Celia was a seer," I argued. "She had to know which the best choice was."

"She likely did, and so she chose to kill thousands to save millions, knowing it would start a rebellion that led to her family losing their throne for the first time in seven thousand years. Knowing her grandson would abandon the family and her favorite son, my father, would die in battle. Knowing her second son would go madder than he already was and ultimately be beaten to death with his own crown by some human servant." He gave me a pointed look. "And likely, there's more. She likely knew more outcomes that we can't even conceive of yet."

I swallowed thickly. I understood what he was saying, but I still couldn't stomach it. "I could never do that—send people to die. I wouldn't."

"That's what queens do. Do you still think it sounds so simple and wonderful?"

Now I saw the trap he'd walked me into, but I refused to concede. "I still wouldn't do it. I'd think of something else or… take care of it alone."

He laughed. Laughing because there was no possible way in his mind that I could ever take on anything of that magnitude on my own—and maybe he was right…right now…but hypothetically? If it were a matter of the lives of millions?

"Stop," I hissed, balling my hands into fists. "There is no humor in this."

He shook his head. "I'm laughing because you are not the first I've heard say something to that effect, but I cannot say that I recommend you try it."

A tiny voice screeched a greeting, and Scion and I both jumped, and I whirled around to see a huge pile of fabric teetering toward us on tiny legs. I rushed forward to help and lifted what had to be several pounds of clothing off the top, slamming them down on the counter. My eyes widened. Thankfully, the colors were not quite so garish as I'd feared, but there were still more garments here than I could recall ever seeing in one place. Tunics, dresses, trousers, shoes, all in shades of pinks, reds, and purples. There were leather trousers, velvet coats, silk gowns, and—my cheeks heated—quite a few sheer lace ribbons peeking out from between everything else that could only belong to some truly scandalous underthings.

I reached out and picked up a dark wine-purple coat with a corseted back and oversized hood, running one thumb over a heavy silver button. I was not precisely sure what I would have liked to wear if given the choice, but this might be close.

Turning my back slightly so as not to offend the tailor, I widened my eyes at Scion. "This is lovely, but surely, I cannot be expected to try all of it? We will be here all afternoon."

He looked slightly bemused. "No, of course not."

My shoulders slumped in relief.

"We're taking all of it."

"I think I must have misheard you," I blurted out. But I hadn't misheard him; it was only that it seemed entirely impossible. So extravagant that I was almost suspicious. "I can't take all this."

Scion waved me off, ignoring my alarm. "You wanted clothing. Is this not sufficient?"

I laughed. "Sufficient? You cannot pretend not to know what this is worth. What do you expect in exchange?"

His eyes narrowed slightly, and now he turned his back toward the tailor as well so she could not even read our lips as we spoke. Of course, she probably had no idea what we were saying, but that hardly seemed to matter.

"Just take the clothing, rebel. If you want to pay me a favor in return, you can refrain from arguing about it. I'd buy you all the clothes in the city for a single fucking day's reprieve from this."

I reeled back, surprised by the sudden aggression in his voice. Then, somehow, I heard myself agree. "Alright."

He let out a sigh of what could only be relief and looked over his shoulder at me as he moved toward the tailor to discuss the cost. "Think of it as education."

"In what?" I asked, despite myself. My heart had sped up, and my breathing sounded slightly uneven.

"Humility." His eyes flashed with humor. "I will admit, not everything about being born into royalty is quite so awful."

No, perhaps it was not.

30
LONNIE
THE CUTTHROAT DISTRICT, INBETWIXT

The Side Saddle turned out to be far less intimidating from the outside than I'd imagined. A tall building at the end of a busy street with a tattered purple-and-red awning—it looked like any other tavern.

Scion and I approached slowly, which had the dual purpose of looking as if we were in no hurry and making it easier to walk in my new, high-heeled boots. Along with the boots, I wore a deep raspberry blouse that laced up the sides like a corset and a pair of black leather trousers. My long hair still covered most of my nearly bare shoulders, but every time the wind shifted, I would have to reposition it so as not to feel too exposed. My heeled boots were tall enough to reach over my knees, but they were hard to walk in, as I was not used to the height.

I gazed around at the group as we approached, and heat crawled up my neck. There was something very different about knowing where we were going in theory than when we were here in truth. It was too late to turn back now.

"Don't eat the food," Scion bent to whisper in my ear as we drew closer.

On his shoulder, his raven, Quill, made a squawking sound. *"You should know better, stupid human child,"* it seemed to say. *"We should not even be having this conversation."*

I looked up at the raven as I replied, "I know."

"Do you?" Scion replied. "This entire place is meant to make Fae spend their coins and fuck anything in sight. It's a relatively strong enchantment, even for the High Fae. I don't know what it would do to you."

"I wouldn't risk it, anyway."

He nodded, and again, Quill made a soft cooing sound, as if to say, *"As long as we understand each other."*

"Don't speak to anyone unless they speak to you first," Scion grumbled the closer we got to the front doors. "And perhaps not even then."

"I know," I snapped. "I did manage to survive a decade working in your palace."

"That will never cease to amaze me."

My lip curled up in a sneer. "So you're saying you would have killed me if we'd met in the palace?"

He shook his head. "No."

I blinked, surprised. "So, what, then?"

He didn't answer, and eventually, I stopped expecting him to.

I felt the weight of several sets of eyes on me, and unease crept up my neck.

"Wait!" I hissed, tugging on Scion's arm.

He glanced down at me. "What?"

"That is a *brothel*," I hissed.

"Well spotted." He smirked. "Have you only just remembered your name and age as well?"

"No, this isn't funny." I rolled my eyes and began searching around for somewhere to speak unheard. "Come here."

Spotting an alcove between the houses on our right. I wrapped my fingers around his and tugged him with me into the semi-darkness. To my surprise, he allowed himself to be led.

There was a barely three-foot space between the two houses, not quite an alley like where we'd arrived, but surely large enough for us to stand in. Quill took flight, landing on the roof above us, while I leaned against the stone wall of one of the houses and tried to look casual. I squinted up at Scion as he loomed over me, his face nearly impossible to see clearly in the dark. "I can't go in there."

He looked more than a little annoyed. "And why is that?"

"It's a brothel full of Fae. They'll all *see* me," I emphasized "see," trying to make him understand what I meant.

He evidently did not, looking at me as if I were some raving lunatic. "Of course they'll see you. That's the fucking point."

"No," I moaned. "You don't understand. The Fae always *see* me —it's like some sort of magnet. I can't go in there."

He ran his hand through his hair. "You have certainly turned up to enough events with Fae before now where this wasn't a problem."

"I—I don't know why," I stumbled over my words. "You're right, it hasn't been as bad lately, but I do not wish to test it in *there*."

"Convenient that this would become a problem now, but not over the last few weeks…"

My frustration rose—more at myself for anything for not having thought of this while we were planning. "You're saying you don't believe me?"

He paused, considering, and then frowned, his expression turning darker and more jaded than I'd seen in days. "No, I believe you." He sounded like he wanted to laugh. "There is certainly something about you that's…unusual. I'm just wondering what dampened the scent before now."

"Scent?" I asked, slightly disgusted.

"Unimportant right now. You have no idea why it would be better or worse? Whom it affects or…" He broke off, seeming as frustrated as I felt.

"If there was anything I could do to stop it, I would," I said almost defensively. "It's always been like this. Almost my entire life, Fae were—"

"Drawn to you," he finished.

"I suppose. I wonder why it doesn't affect you," I wondered out loud. "Do you think you've managed to hate me so much that you're immune? I didn't know that was possible."

He froze, eyes widening slightly, and coughed before he was able to speak. "Unimportant right now. Do you trust me?"

"No," I blurted out reflexively.

He laughed hollowly, shaking his head again. "Fine. Do you at least trust that I won't hurt you?"

"Yes." The corners of my mouth turned up. "I'm sure you'd want to draw it out more. This alley would make for a terrible torture room."

"Good. Then don't scream."

I had no time to ask what he meant by that before he took a step forward, closing the rest of the distance between us. For one wild second, as he loomed over me, pressing my back harder into the wall, I thought he was going to kiss me. Instead, he ducked his head and pressed his mouth to the place where my neck met my shoulder.

He ran his tongue up my throat to my ear, tasting my skin and sending tingles all over my body. My pulse quickened, and heat descended over me, pulsing in the depths of my core and making me wish to press my legs together. His earlier words ran through my mind: *"You'll not only beg me to fuck you, you'll say thank you, lord, when I'm done."*

No—*fuck*, I should not go there. He was only trying to get under my skin, and I couldn't let him.

"Wh—what are you doing?" I gasped as he moved to the other side, laving his tongue over my other collarbone.

"You smell like magic, rebel. It's…unusual."

"So what, will this mute it?" I asked a bit breathlessly.

"Maybe." He pulled back, and his expression was carefully neutral. "I'm not sure that's possible, but this may help. It should be a sort of deterrent."

"What should I say if anyone approaches me?"

He looked down at me, his silver eyes meeting mine with an intensity that stole my breath for a moment. "Tell them that you're mine."

THE FIRST THING I REALIZED UPON ENTERING THE SIDE SADDLE WAS that it was far larger inside than it had appeared from the street.

The second was that the atmosphere made the fairy orgies at the obsidian palace look tame by comparison.

The front room was packed nearly to bursting with patrons, drinking, dancing, and chatting with the numerous scantily dressed men and women who stood on tables or lay on couches around the perimeter of the room. Toward the back of the room stood a well-stocked bar and a lively four-piece band in the corner, led by a well-endowed faun playing a lute.

My eyes fell on a woman lying on a nearby table. Broken dishware and food littered the floor, evidence of what had been going on not all that long ago. Now, her dress was unlaced to her stomach, breasts bare for the whole room to see. Her skirt was miraculously still in place, though from the movements beneath it and the way she was moaning, it appeared that someone was hidden underneath the fabric, making her writhe and whimper for the audience of men and women at the bar.

"I'm guessing she ate the food?" I asked, trying to keep my tone light.

Scion threw the woman a disinterested glance. "No. She's simply working. Anyone who ate the food is already upstairs."

"Ah, of course." I looked down, trying to banish the curiosity swirling in the back of my mind. "You certainly seem well-informed."

"I don't need to pay for sex, rebel."

"Right. I suppose, being a prince, you could have anyone you wanted."

He laughed bitterly. "Not anyone. Now, focus."

I swallowed thickly but did as instructed, letting him drag me through the crowd, past the bar, and toward the bottom of the long staircase. On the bottom landing stood a curvaceous brunette woman in a gossamer sheer red dress and ample amounts of golden jewelry. Her long, spiral curls were piled on top of her head in a sort of cascade that I immediately envied as the sort of hairstyle I would want, had I any skill in that department. Her large eyes were painted with kohl liner to appear even larger, and she had bright red paint on her lips to match her dress.

To the woman's immediate left stood a very large male, whom I assumed had to be her guard. He was large, even by Fae standards, with a stature reminiscent of Prince Gwydion. That, however, was where the similarities ended. While all Fae were attractive, this male had a face that one might call "unusual." His features were hard, like he'd been hit in the nose one too many times and not healed quite right. His hair was long and dark and pulled back into a ponytail at the nape of his skull, and he had a long scar running over the bridge of his nose.

"Evening," the woman said nervously as we approached. "Going up?"

"No," Scion replied stiffly. "We're here to see Phillipa Blacktongue."

The woman looked us over once again, and sure enough, her eyes flicked from Scion's face to the enormous raven on his shoulder. I saw a flicker of indecision in her eyes, which I interpreted as she wasn't positive about who we were but was afraid of making a terrible error by even asking.

This, more than anything so far, proved Scion's original assertion that, out of context, he was unlikely to be recognized. I supposed that was reasonable—I wouldn't expect the Everlasts to travel alone into strange brothels without guards, and I guessed if you had never seen any of them up close…it made sense, yet still, could she not see the crest on his shoulder?

"Sorry, love," the woman said finally. "Miss Blacktongue doesn't take visitors."

"Don't embarrass yourself, Slúagh." Scion looked down his nose at her. "Go get your mistress before I become annoyed and find her myself."

I opened my mouth to simply tell her who we were rather than forcing her to guess, but before I could, the guard at the woman's side stepped forward, baring his teeth. "No admittance."

My heartbeat sped up—I'd known this might happen, and yet I still wasn't prepared for it when the guard screamed a high-pitched, soul-crushing scream I did not think could have come out of a male that large.

His eyes bulged, and he dropped the knife I'd only just noticed he was holding, letting it slide down the steps to the floor at my feet. Then, his body began to twitch as his screams turned into sobs and gasps for breath, his body crumpling on the landing.

Scion barely moved beside me, seeming not to even see the man writhing in pain before us. He looked up at the woman. "Would you care for another demonstration?"

"No, my lord," she said quickly, clearly getting it now. She tried to do something in the way of a curtsy and only managed to trip. "Yes, um…I'll just go get her."

She turned and sprinted up the stairs, moving rather impressively fast, given the length and cut of her dress. I could sympathize with that. Mortality was a strong motivator, and I'd ruined many gowns while trying to stay alive.

I looked down at the male on the floor, who was no longer twitching but had not moved from where he'd landed. "Is it fair to simply torture people without warning?"

Scion's lip curled. "Do not tell me you are starting to grow fond of the Fae. I thought you had vowed to hate us with your last gasping breath."

"I—no." I could not recall saying that specifically and narrowed my eyes. "I simply see a difference between you and these unsuspecting bystanders. If you don't, that's further proof of my point."

His lips turned into a thin line. "That male—" He prodded the guard with his foot. "—is in charge of watching the female so she doesn't escape. Would you consider him to be a person worthy of your sympathy? Is there no nuance to the situation?"

I grimaced and turned away. "Perhaps."

He dropped it, and we did our best to ignore the guard while we waited, the same as we ignored every eye that bored into the backs of our heads and the whispers that swirled around us.

Ten minutes passed, and then another ten. The longer we stood, the more nervous I became, and the more the shadows on the ground seemed to swirl as Scion grew more and more annoyed.

I glanced around the room, hoping to alleviate my boredom, and immediately regretted it.

Everywhere I looked, there was nothing but fairy debauchery. The room had grown slightly fuller in the time we'd been there, and the band in the corner kicked up, playing some lively tinkling tune. I thanked the gods it wasn't the hypnotic music that sometimes played in the capital, as I was already having a hard enough time focusing with Scion's fingers curled so high on my thigh and the sounds of pleasure rising all around us.

The woman who'd been on the table when we arrived had since finished her show and now danced on the bar with two other members of the pleasure guild—a man and a woman—each of them in various states of undress. In the shadows by the stairs, bodies writhed together, just barely out of sight, and at a table to our left, a male knelt on the floor, keenly servicing the diners.

"Is she coming down?" I asked breathlessly.

"Most certainly," Scion muttered. "This is likely an attempt to establish dominance."

I glanced sideways at him. "Over you or me?"

"Both." He smiled, showing all his teeth in a way that sent a shiver down my spine. "A pointless attempt, obviously."

I wasn't so sure about that, at least for me. I would not have called myself dominant. Willful, perhaps, inflexible, but not naturally authoritative. "As long as she gets here soon. I'm sure Siobhan and the others are growing anxious."

That, and the atmosphere of this room, was beginning to get to me.

Scion straightened up from where he'd been leaning against the wall by the stairs. He turned his head to mutter something to the enormous bird on his shoulder, who took flight, fluttering over everyone's heads and down some dark back hallway.

"Where did he go?"

"Out," Scion said shortly. "He'll go sit on the roof. This room is too confined for him as it is, and we're about to go somewhere far smaller."

My mouth fell open. Scion grabbed my hand and began to tug me through the crowd again. My anxiety spiked higher as I practically jogged to keep up with his long strides. "Where are you going?"

He glanced back at me, and my chest squeezed, my breath catching at the shocking grin he wore. Mischievous and excited rather than the usual rage—it sent a flush over my entire body.

"Fuck this. I don't wait. If Phillipa Blacktongue wants to find us, we'll be in her office."

31
LONNIE

THE CUTTHROAT DISTRICT, INBETWIXT

I'd seen enough public sex as of late that I'd undoubtedly learned a thing or two.

I wobbled in my boots, chasing Scion down a dark hallway toward what I assumed was Phillipa Blacktongue's office.

The hall was full of couples gyrating to the slightly muffled music. Their dancing looked like sex, and in some cases, it absolutely was. Some groups were of three or four, their hands and mouths everywhere, making it hard to tell where one partner ended and another began. The scent and sound of pleasure were overpowering, making it impossible to focus on anything else, but I had to think about where I stepped, or else I would trip and break my neck on my new boots.

I snorted. If I slipped in this hallway, there was a good chance my hand might land somewhere—or on something—it shouldn't.

My breath heaving, I was more than relieved when we came to a halt at the end of the long hall in front of an innocuous wooden door on the right-hand side. I tested the knob, only to find that it was locked.

"I can't say I'm surprised," I called over the sounds of the hall.

Scion sighed. "I'd hoped to avoid this."

He didn't explain further before grabbing my waist and stepping purposefully forward, as if he intended to walk directly into the closed door.

I let out a yelp of surprise, which was lost in the shadows.

This time, the darkness only lasted a moment. My head swam, as if I'd plunged underwater for slightly too long, and I sucked in a gasping breath, my eyes opening again on a small, warmly lit room office with a chaise lounge on one end and a mahogany desk on the other. The walls were painted a dark burgundy, and there were shelves of books all around the walls.

My stomach churned, but thankfully, not nearly as bad as the last time. Perhaps because I was growing used to the travel, or perhaps because we'd only gone a few feet, but this did not seem nearly so bad. In fact, the only thing that I found disorienting was that rather than coming out directly on the other side of the door as if we'd walked through it, we now stood on the other side of the room facing the door. *How did that work…*

"What if she can't find us now?" I asked.

Scion crossed the room and threw himself down on the green-and-copper-patterned chaise, spreading his arms over the back. His smile was smug. "She will."

I moved slowly about the room, running my fingers over the books along the shelves. Many seemed to be unusual volumes from other provinces: *The Fall of Nightshade Vol. I-IV*, *The Diary of Laertes the Unlucky*, *Druidic Teachings*, and *The Accords of Underneath.* Nothing in particular would have led me to believe I was standing in the office of the madam of the pleasure guild.

"Do you know Phillipa?" I asked.

"I know of her," Scion replied. "We've never met. We would not get along."

"Why?"

He paused. "The pleasure guild is mostly made up of succubi, who are dominant by nature. I will submit for no one."

I bit the inside of my lip, a spark of awareness traveling through me like a flame. "Yet, you knew where the office was."

He paused. "I sent Quill down this hall first. He went out the back door, which we would have encountered had we continued."

I looked up, startled, from the title I'd been perusing, *The Black Scroll: Waking Dreams*. "Can you talk to him, then?"

"In a sense."

I wondered now if every time I'd thought the bird was speaking to me, it actually was, or if I was losing my mind. "How? How does he talk to you? Can you hear him, or is it a feeling…"

I probably sounded like I was losing my mind. Gods, perhaps I was losing my mind.

"Why?" Scion asked, suddenly sitting up.

"Nothing," I said too fast. "It's not important."

Flushing with an embarrassment I couldn't quite explain, I made my way over to the desk and inspected it, opening the drawers and peering inside. Rude? Certainly. But then, so was barging into the woman's office, so I supposed we were well past the point of no return. "I don't see anything all that interesting."

"What were you expecting?"

My flush deepened. In truth, I supposed I'd been expecting something more appropriate for a madam. A bed, maybe. Lacy underthings…ropes and whips and other things of that nature. It wasn't that I was innocent, far from it, but I'd never been inside a brothel; I could only guess what was going on upstairs that might be different than in the hallways.

I crouched low, bending to open the final drawer. "I don't know…I suppose—"

I broke off as I yanked the drawer open and a cloud of dust exploded in my face. Instinctively, my eyes slammed shut, but still, whatever it was coated me, penetrating my mouth and nose, burrowing deep into my pores. Everything tasted sweet, like burnt honey, and then the room was spinning.

For a split second, panic gripped me. Something was wrong. Desperately, acutely, *wrong*.

My vision narrowed to a point, the edges turning dark and everything around me going slightly fuzzy. My skin suddenly felt too hot, too alive, like I was humming, aware of every single goosebump, and all of them were buzzing with energy. My own heartbeat turned deafening, and my pulse quickened, thrumming low in my belly.

"Rebel?"

I looked up, wanting to say…something. What was it?

I lost track of my thoughts. Scion was in front of me, bending low to meet my gaze. He sounded upset, and I couldn't fathom why. I felt wonderful—amazing—far better than any drink of wine or notes of fairy fiddles. A thousand times better and more potent than when Kaius had tried to glamour me.

"What is this?" Scion said from seemingly very far away.

He ran his fingers over my cheek, and I leaned closer, moaning at the feel of his skin on mine.

I blinked up at him, a bit dazed. All I could focus on was the feel of his hand on my arm and the lovely buzzy hum in my head. I'd forgotten what he was talking about before he was halfway finished with his sentence. I opened my mouth to ask, but what came out instead was "Your eyes are like the moon."

He jerked back, his expression becoming one of abject horror. "Oh, fuck."

I giggled, having no idea why he was so upset. His too-handsome face swum before me, and I couldn't tell if it was him or me who was moving. I reached out to steady myself, and my hands landed on his chest.

"No, don't," he said, trying to inch away from me. "I don't know how it works."

"You're so angry." I laughed.

"By fucking Aisling."

I laughed again. "Yes, fucking Aisling. She started it, right? It's her fault you're so angry."

He moved back again, running both hands through his hair. The small amount of dust he'd wiped off my face sparkled on his fingers, turning his hair iridescent. "Stay over there. I'm just going to go…" He trailed off.

I struggled to my feet, the dust shaking from my hair and clothes in an enormous shimmering plume. My eyes widened, and I marveled at how lovely it looked in the air for the split second before I stumbled through it.

"Wait." I reached for the prince's arm, only just managing to grab him before I toppled to the ground again.

Seemingly on instinct, he caught me before I fell, then swore loudly. "Fuck! No, don't touch me."

"But why?" I laughed, delighted by how free I felt. I couldn't remember any problems I'd ever had. There was nothing to fear in the world, no pain, no secrets, only the wonderful floating feeling in my head and the heat building all over my body.

I reached out and tried to press my shimmering fingers to Scion's sharp cheekbone.

"What are you doing," he practically groaned, tearing my fingers away.

"But—" I began, but before I could finish my thought, my gaze caught on his too-perfect mouth, and I lost my train of thought. I wanted to taste his lips, wanted them all over me, wanted—

My chest heaved, and my gaze flicked down to his mouth. "You need to be less serious."

I pressed my lips to his.

For a split second, Scion didn't move.

Every muscle in his body tightened, as if he'd been turned to stone by my touch.

Some vague awareness pulled at the back of my mind, as if a voice called to me through the shimmering haze in my head. I blinked and shook my head, trying to clear whatever was making it so hard to think of anything but the heat racing over my skin.

"I think—"

Finally, as if he could not hold his breath any longer, Scion inhaled sharply through his nose. The dust on my skin swirled between us, and I watched his eyes dilate, black nearly eclipsing silver.

His large hand shot out and curled around the back of my head, tugging me closer in a strong, possessive grip. Control finally slipping, his lips crashed against mine once more, this time with far greater intensity that sent tremors quaking through my body. I moaned, opening my mouth to him and pressing my entire body closer, closer, seeking the heat of his skin like a plant stretching toward the sun. His tongue thrust between my lips, flooding my senses with the taste of burnt honey, taking control with a fierce dominance that made my teeth ache and my pulse throb deep in my core.

He gently pulled at my bottom lip with his teeth, and in an instant, I'd lost what was left of my awareness, forgetting completely where we were, why we were doing this. Nothing mattered except finding the release my body desperately craved.

Scion moved the hand in my hair down the back of my neck until he could circle my throat. He dug his fingers into my skin and pulled my head back, forcibly breaking our kiss. "On the desk, rebel."

A shiver of pure excitement ran through me. Of ecstasy. Anticipation.

I retreated backward until my ass hit the edge of the desk and hopped up, spreading my knees so he could stand between them. He prowled toward me, gaze assessing, judging, owning me even as his pupils were blown so wide he was almost unrecognizable with jet-black eyes, only barely rimmed with silver.

Standing between my legs, I could feel the thick outline of his cock pressing into my center, and it was an effort not to let a whimper escape. My pulse throbbed lower with every tiny movement, every brush of skin.

"This wasn't exactly what I had in mind," he drawled, looking down at me on the desk.

"No?"

"No."

He grabbed a handful of my hair and yanked. Pain shot down my spine, and I gasped, need flooding my core. I slid off the desk, and he spun me around, pressing my cheek flat into the wood.

I whimpered, but not from pain, and arched my back to grind my ass against him.

He leaned over only long enough to let his face fall against my neck, inhaling deeply, like a drowning man taking his first breath. Straightening again, he cupped me between my legs. "All the times you've worn skirts…it would have been so easy to already have you wrapped around my cock, but now I have to get you out of these fucking leather trousers."

He ground harder into me as if to accentuate his point, and I moaned, my clit throbbing so intensely I was sure I could fall apart from this alone.

I pressed my ass harder into his cock and felt him twitch behind me. "You don't like them?"

"You could wear rags and look just as tempting, rebel."

A gasp erupted from me, surprised by this admission, even as he undid the button of my trousers with one hand. His fingers dove beneath the waistband.

"Take them off," I practically begged, suddenly not caring how weak I sounded. I felt weak. Desperate.

He let go of my hair, and in the same moment, the closure on my pants ripped as he tore them down my body. Buttons flew, pinging off the floor, the bookshelves, but I barely noticed or cared when his fingers found my entrance. "Fuck."

"Good, rebel. I want to hear you when you finally surrender."

I knew I should probably be alarmed by that, but I wasn't. I couldn't remember why I would be when all I could hear was the sound of his belt coming undone. When all I could feel was his fingers stroking slowly, leisurely over my clit. "Oh gods."

"No gods, Rebel. Say my name when I fuck you."

I pushed myself up on my palms on the desk, arching my back, tiny sparks of pleasure shooting all over my body, stemming from where his fingers still teased at me. My heart pounded too fast—out of control—as wetness pooled in my core. "My lord."

His hand came down hard on my ass, a sharp pain that was as much pleasure as punishment. A violent snarl erupted from his chest. "What's my fucking name?"

He leaned down, running his tongue over my neck, and I writhed, practically crying with the need racking my body as he positioned himself at my entrance. His teeth scraped against my skin, and I gasped. "Scion."

Then, in the split second before he slammed into me, he bit down hard on my neck. I felt the skin break, and I screamed, the pain becoming pleasure in my hazy, unfocused mind.

Scion froze.

My entire body shook, and I glanced over my shoulder, my eyes still blurry, head still hazy. I didn't understand why he wasn't moving—why he wasn't filling me, fucking me, destroying me.

My gaze locked with his, and my confusion only grew as silver eyes stared back at me, wide and horrified, my own scarlet blood dripping down his chin.

32

SCION

THE CUTTHROAT DISTRICT, INBETWIXT

"Come back," Lonnie moaned. "Please?"

Shut up, shut up, shut the fuck up.

It was already hard enough to think with so much dust in the air and the feel of her skin fresh in my mind, her blood in my mouth; I didn't need her lying on the desk begging to be fucked as well—and yet, of course, she was. This was clearly the gods punishing me. Just the latest in a long string of trials, like some fucking myth of eternal suffering.

Gancanagh's Dust.

The most fucked-up of all arcane substances.

Fuck! I should have realized what it was the moment the dust touched Lonnie's skin, but I'd never seen it at its full strength before. I knew something was wrong, but I didn't realize precisely what until I'd breathed it in and it was too late. I was merely a bystander in my own body.

Why her blood had stopped it, I had no idea. I wasn't sure if I was grateful or horrified. Grateful, I supposed, because Gancanagh's Dust didn't just cause insatiable lust. With the amount in that drawer, it seemed likely that we would have literally fucked to death. Still, I couldn't exactly say I was thrilled, given that a bite like that could mean nothing good.

I glanced at Lonnie, who was now lying on the floor, gazing up at the ceiling. Fuck, she was probably as trapped in her own head as I'd been, and I had no idea what to do with her. If I touched her again, would it get fucking worse?

I'd have to risk it—fuck the consequences, this mission, anyone who got in my way.

Holding my breath as I shook more dust out of my hair, I waited a beat for it to fall. The dust didn't react to skin, only when it was ingested—fuck, I'd have to tell Cross. His team had missed some on those ships and, possibly, had been missing the drug's presence in the city for quite some time. This must be what Phillipa Blacktongue mixed into all the food and drink in her miserable den of sin, the evil cunt.

I practically quaked with rage. There had been whispers for years that even the Fae should think twice before eating the food or drinking too much, but it was hard to pinpoint the cause.

Well, if nothing else, now I knew where to direct my ire at missing out on finding information about Ambrose. Unfortunately, I wouldn't be able to do anything to her tonight, but that would only give me longer to think of a punishment vile enough to match the offense.

Smiling slightly at that dark thought, I took a step toward Lonnie where she still lay on the floor. "Let's go, rebel. Stand up."

She made some sort of unintelligible noise, somewhere between a whine and a moan. Good fucking gods, this was going to be the end of me.

I reached for her, trying my best to touch only her clothing and not her skin. I noticed, with a wince, that the buttons on her pants were still undone, and half were missing, though mercifully, she'd pulled them back on so that at least nothing was showing. The only real evidence that anything had gone on, aside from her bruised lips and glazed-over expression, was the brutal bite mark on her shoulder. *Fuck.*

I pinched the skin between my eyes, keeping them closed as I asked, "Does that hurt?"

"Hmmm?" she hummed.

No, probably not, then.

For Fae, something like that would heal almost instantly. For her…well, I had no idea.

"I'm sorry," I said, the words feeling foreign on my tongue. "I'll look at it later, after you've washed the dust off."

Of course, I couldn't fix it, not really, but at least perhaps it could be bandaged once the Gancanagh's Dust finally wore off. The idea of covering it made me oddly, irrationally angry, but I shook it off.

"Well, isn't that precious," a high, trilled voice spoke from the doorway. "Only one might ask themselves why such a sweet scene is playing out in such an inappropriate location?"

I stiffened. The timing could not have been worse, except, I supposed, if she'd walked in while I'd had Lonnie bent over the desk and—

No! I shook myself. I would not think about that. I was to act as though this had never happened.

I spun slowly, my face turning to stone before I faced the newcomer. "One might also ask themselves why there is an entire drawer of Gancanagh's Dust in this office when the substance has been outlawed for some two thousand years."

The tall, middle-aged Fae woman stood on the threshold and smiled at me in a way that I recognized as a peace offering. I remained unmoved.

To the human eye, Phillipa Blacktongue and I might have appeared the same age, but we were not. It was clear to me from the slight pale hue of her hair and the upturn in her eyes that she had a few hundred years on me, at least. By Fae standards, she was plain to look at, with unremarkable pale hair and a heart-shaped face. But then, I knew it wasn't her appearance that most were interested in.

"It is not often I am honored by royalty, Your Highness," she said. "You'll have to forgive my lateness."

I would do no such fucking thing. "If I were advising a smarter woman than you, I might suggest not reminding me about how long you forced us to wait."

She let out a tinkling laugh that made the hair on the back of my neck stand on end. "Unavoidable, I assure you. Now, what can I do for you, my lord?"

I racked my brain, trying to recall the story we'd invented. There was little reason to visit a brothel aside from the obvious, and I'd been horrified at the idea of either feigning interest in Phillipa or offering up Lonnie as some sort of pet. I'd intended to ask her something innocuous about guild politics, but now, all that came out was "How do I fix her?"

Phillipa looked at Lonnie, who still lay on the floor. "Oh dear… well, I daresay you can't."

I took a step toward her that may have been slightly too aggressive had I cared to control my behavior. "Think harder," I growled, my fists clenched. "You do not want to know what happened to the incubus that I suspected may have even touched this shit."

She laughed. "I am not afraid of pain, my lord."

My lip curled. "No? Do you understand what happens to the mind of an immortal when it has experienced so much pain that it ceases to believe that the body still lives? The body may never die, but the mind will. It will rot and cease to exist, and what then? What happens to you if you cannot even return to the Source, as your body holds you hostage here, unmoving, unthinking, for all of eternity."

The only sign that she'd heard me was the slight widening of her eyes. Phillipa was clearly used to being in charge; she'd let the fucking queen of Elsewhere stand unattended on her steps for nearly thirty minutes. It was no wonder Cross's children had had difficulty with her. But that ended here and now.

"That might be…interesting to try once," she said finally, clearly flustered.

I laughed. "I was not finished. We so rarely send anyone to Fort Warfare anymore I sometimes forget it is an option at my disposal, but I think in this case…it's warranted."

This time, she blanched, her face going slack. "Yes, of course. I see," she stammered. "It will wear off eventually, but in the interim…" She looked at a loss. "There's nothing to be done."

"Then why am I not mindless?" I demanded. "I was also affected."

She looked me over, confused. "I can honestly say I don't know. Gancanagh's Dust affects everyone equally. Mated couples are often spared, but I've never seen someone be affected only to shake it off."

My heart began to beat faster as a stone dropped into my stomach.

I wasn't foolish enough to ignore every possible sign…the bite, the prophecy, the fact that my magic didn't work on her. Usually, that would mean a mating bond, but there was one critical problem: mates always, always, had comparable power levels, or the more powerful partner would kill the other. That was half the reason that blood sharing had become so taboo and why Bael had nearly drained Lonnie by sheer accident. Especially powerful Fae always formed bonded groups to share the burden of strength. None of my family could ever find true happiness, but if we could, we would never have been able to bond anyone as weak as a human without killing them.

Maybe it was just the dust, I told myself. I was out of my mind, and she did have my blood in her system…maybe that's all it was.

"Where did all this come from?" I demanded of the madam, wanting to get all the information I could out of her before she lost her mind at Fort Warfare.

"We produce it here," she said, sounding slightly proud.

I was going to be ill. They produced it and then drugged patrons and possibly now were smuggling this shit out of the city in the hulls of standard trading vessels.

On the floor, Lonnie moaned, and every hair on my body stood on end. I couldn't wait here and interrogate Phillipa Blacktongue. Not now. The problem was how to make sure she didn't leave this room until I could send someone back to retrieve her.

Stepping around the desk, I gave the madam a cold look. "Come here."

Her back straightened, and when she walked, it was with clear discomfort, like she did not like taking orders. Months ago, I might have enjoyed this—breaking someone like Phillipa Blacktongue—but now, all I could think about was the whimpering woman on the floor and how this was not at all what I'd meant when I said I wanted her surrender.

I picked Lonnie up, cradling her in my arms, and immediately, a barrage of emotions flooded me. This could not work—I couldn't touch her like this, or she'd ruin me all over again. I put her back down, but at least this time, she stayed on her feet.

Phillipa had watched us the entire time without a word, and now, I smiled at her, pleased, finally, that I'd thought of a punishment to fit the offense. "Get on the floor and lick all that dust off the carpet."

She widened her eyes at me, and for a moment, it looked like she was considering it, not because I was demanding but because she thought we were going to stay here and watch. "All of it, Your Highness?"

"All of it. Now."

I waited just long enough to make sure she was complying before I turned my back, ushering Lonnie toward the door. The key Blacktongue had used was still in the lock, and I snatched it, locking the door behind us just as the madam began to scream.

She might not need to go to Fort Warfare after all. A day or so alone in the room with no one to alleviate her mind-numbing lust would drive the effects of the dust from pleasant to hostile. She'd be madder than my uncle Penvalle when she emerged, if she managed to survive at all without tearing herself to sheds.

I LICKED MY LIPS AS LONNIE AND I STEPPED OUT OF THE OFFICE INTO the hall. I could still taste her blood there, and I was sure it was still visible on my face from the looks I was getting. It wouldn't matter if I hadn't made sure everyone knew who we were—who she was.

Lonnie might not realize it, but she'd become equally recognizable when put in the right framing. Without a crown and out of the capital, most might not realize who she was, but the two of us together? We were about to be fighting an information war as much as a physical one.

This morning, the most important thing in my life was getting the information that would lead us back to Ambrose. Now, everything had narrowed to a point around the limp human woman hanging off my arm. I hardly gave a fuck that I'd only bought Cross five minutes.

The afflicted could destroy the continent.

My brother could have the damned castle.

Let the world burn.

The bar had grown too crowded, the upstairs brothel leaking downstairs into the main floor of what should have been advertisement only, and the scent of sex and noise of pleasure was making it no easier to focus. Still, I shook my head, forcing some reason back into my mind, and dragged Lonnie toward the nearest door.

"Scion?"

The sound of my own name startled me, and I looked down to find her staring up at me through wide, unfocused eyes. "What?"

"Carry me. These boots hurt."

I pressed the heels of my hands into my eyes. "I can't. You must walk on your own."

"Why?" She grinned.

"Because I don't want to touch you too much like this."

"But isn't that what you love to do? You and Bael both, all you princes just love to drag me around."

By the fucking Source. I didn't want to be reminded of all the ways I was acting similarly to Bael. Bael, who had been fucking intolerable ever since she arrived. Bael, who was clearly halfway in love with her.

Bael, who was going to murder me with his bare hands when he finally found out about this.

"WHERE ARE YOU?" SHE ASKED INTO THE DARKNESS.

"I'll be over here."

Two hours later, I'd managed to get Lonnie back to Cross's house and dunk her in a bath, which was about as graceful as it sounded, before forcing her into bed. She now sat, hair still dripping, in the middle of the bed, staring at me as if expecting some further entertainment. I swallowed a groan. I could not recall working this hard on anything, ever, in my life. Even being in the army, battles weren't as difficult as keeping one inebriated human woman from inadvertently dying or sprinkling sex dust on some unsuspecting stranger and causing additional pandemonium.

She was chaos incarnate, a wildfire hidden in a matchstick.

I shifted on the small wooden chair in the corner of the room, kicking my feet up on the trunk beneath the window.

"That looks uncomfortable," she said. "How will you sleep?"

"I've slept like this before," I growled. "I'll be fine."

She moved to kneeling on the edge of the bed, the undergarments she'd elected to sleep in leaving absolutely nothing to the imagination. "There's plenty of room for you here."

I snorted a laugh. The irony of this almost hurt. "No. Not tonight, there isn't."

"Why not?"

I desperately wished to know her true name in that moment, if only to give it more emphasis when I told her to shut the fuck up. "Do not tempt me. Now, go to sleep."

This had absolutely nothing to do with chivalry and everything to do with the fact that I wasn't sure I could control myself if I climbed into that bed with her. I now had the persistent pull of her blood pounding in the back of my mind, combined with the residual tremors of the Gancanagh's Dust. If I moved a single inch from this chair, it would be over, and that would spell disaster for more than just me.

She frowned and glared at me, her expression turning frosty. "Oh, my mistake," she said louder. "Of course your lordship wouldn't want to sleep here with the likes of me—you might never get the smell out."

I groaned. What was she talking about now? "Go to sleep."

"Maybe we should switch? Would it not make more sense for me to sleep on the floor?"

I ran a hand through my hair, exasperated. She'd clearly taken offense to something—or perhaps not. Perhaps it was just some new facet of the hell that was this evening. "Stop saying things like that."

"Why? Isn't that what you've been saying for weeks? Years, really? That you are better than me in every conceivable way, and I'm barely more than an animal in your eyes."

"I didn't say that," I snapped.

"What does 'Slúagh' mean to you?"

I glanced away, an odd discomfort washing over me. "Stop."

She scrambled onto her knees, the mattress creaking a bit as she knelt on the edge facing me. "Of course, my lord." She made a mock bow and nearly tipped off the bed. "Sorry, my lord."

"Stop," I growled again. "You'll hurt yourself."

She bowed again. "Yes, of course, my lord. Anything your lordship desires. Shall I lick your boots, sir?"

My eyes flashed, and I had to bite back a sharp response. "You're not funny."

"On the contrary, I'm very funny," she said, sliding off the bed onto the floor. She grinned as she knelt before me. "I'm the funniest one in this room, in fact."

"You are the most tiresome one in this room."

She leaned forward. "Forgive me, my prince. Did you want me to lick something else?"

My control wavering, I shot a hand out and gripped her hair. Her mouth opened in a silent "oh," and I had to hold back a groan. Fuck me, she clearly liked pain. "As I recall, the moment our positions were reversed, you were more than happy to make your own demands, my queen."

She gasped as our gazes locked. I pulled slightly, forcing her to come up higher on her knees. Shit, I had no excuse for this, yet the air in the room seemed to thicken around us. Her tongue darted out to wet her lips, and my eyes traced the movement.

"And yet," she breathed, "you have yet to pay any measure of fealty."

By the fucking gods.

This was too hard. Too much. I had never claimed to be a decent male…but somehow, my mouth moved without conscious thought as I unwound my hand from her hair. "You're drunk, rebel."

She smiled, struggling to her feet. "So? I wasn't when I made the request."

I groaned audibly, no longer caring to hide how much this was affecting me. "Ask me again in the morning if you still want it. I suspect you won't. You'll hate yourself and me in the morning for this, but you'd hate me more if I didn't tell you to simply go to bed."

She frowned, looking more sad than angry. "Why should you care?"

I waited several minutes to answer, returning to my chair in the corner so that by the time I did, I was almost certain she'd fallen asleep at last. "Because I would rather my future wife not hate me."

33
LONNIE
THE CUTTHROAT DISTRICT, INBETWIXT

A weak stream of sunlight shone through the spotted window, casting long rays over the faded reddish carpet. Shelves upon shelves of books lined the walls, stretching further back than I could see, filling the room with the scent of aged parchment. Before me, tiny glittering specs of dust drifted lazily through the air, swirling and dancing in the sun.

I lay on the floor, my spine cushioned only by the well-worn carpet, and turned the pages of some ancient tome propped on my lap. My own hands looked almost foreign—unfamiliar—long-fingered and pale.

"Find anything, little monster?"

I looked up and was surprised to see Bael sitting on the armchair before me. He had a book of his own open in front of him, resting on my ankles, which were propped in his lap. I thought, perhaps, his hair looked longer than the last time we'd spoken…maybe?

"Not yet," I heard myself say. "But I've barely scratched the surface. The handwriting here is hard to decipher."

"This is fucking pointless," another familiar voice said behind me. "At what point do we accept that there's nothing here?"

I tilted my neck back, looking up at the bottom of Scion's sharp jaw, set as usual in a tight scowl. My head was cradled in his lap, and despite his obvious annoyance, he absentmindedly played with my hair with one hand, holding his book out to the side with the other.

"Well, of course you would think that," Bael said, grinning over at Scion. "Forgive us if we don't take your opinion too seriously."

"Meaning what?"

"Meaning," I said lightly, "that you're biased, my lord."

He rolled his eyes. "Stop calling me that."

My grin was wide enough to rival Bael's. "Never, my lord."

"Try this one."

I looked up as a third male strode toward us out of the stacks, holding a large, leather-bound book. He smiled briefly at me as we made eye contact before glancing down and slamming the book on the table. "There you are," he said.

"Here I am," I replied, smiling. "You've made us wait an awfully long time, you know."

He looked confused for a moment. "Actually, I don't know. Isn't that strange?"

The dream changed.

Pale moonlight cast a long shadow over the floor of my room in Inbetwixt, and it was only by its glow that I could make out a figure in the corner.

My eyes connected with the stranger's through the holes in his mask, and I gasped. I sat up, throwing off my quilt, my heart pounding wildly out of control. "What are you doing here?"

"I don't know." His tone said he was smiling behind the mask. "Even I could never have foreseen meeting this way."

I WOKE SLOWLY, UNWILLING TO LEAVE THE WARMTH AND SAFETY OF my cocoon. I snuggled deeper into the heat of my bed and sighed.

As with all my dreams lately, the world of sleep lingered just a bit too long after awareness dawned so that for several moments, I had to parse out what was real and what was imagined. If I didn't know better, I would say my dreams felt more like memories as of late…perhaps they had for some time.

Only that couldn't be. I could hardly imagine a reality such as the one conjured in my subconscious. Perhaps I was reading too much into things. Becoming too influenced by all the talk of seers and of my sister's journals so that I was starting to see signs where there was nothing at all.

A noise from somewhere in the room, like a throat clearing, penetrated my thoughts, and I frowned. Confusion pulled me from the safe space between sleeping and waking, where everything was warm and soft and bright behind dark eyelids.

My eyes popped open.

Disoriented, the contented feeling in my stomach left me in a woosh, to be replaced with dread. The remnants of the dream fell away, replaced by images of last night.

Very real images.

I sat up, pressing a hand to my forehead, and the room spun slightly, where… I let out a strangled gasp as everything came flooding back in a rush: opening the drawer and wondering for a split second if I'd made a mistake before everything was eclipsed in total euphoria. Suddenly having that wonderful feeling of elation, of being too hot, too big for my own body. Like nothing was wrong or ever could be wrong again. Like I was everything, knew everything, and needed to share it.

Why couldn't I have simply forgotten?

"Are you alright, rebel?" Scion's voice spoke from the other side of the room.

I turned to look at him, and another wave of shame hit me all over again. Shame at what I'd said, at how I'd infected him with whatever had been in that drawer, at what we'd done…

He sat in the same chair he'd been in hours ago, cramped and uncomfortable, clearly too tall for the small wooden frame. I doubted he'd slept at all last night.

I couldn't find the words to answer his question. Indeed, I wasn't sure I wanted to speak to him at all. I had no desire to hear whatever scathing things he no doubt thought of me right now.

Throwing my quilt off, I practically fell over myself to reach the ground. My bare feet hit the floor ungracefully, and my head spun. I pitched forward and had to catch myself on one hand before my nose slammed into the carpet.

Immediately, I heard the chair in the corner creak and saw the outline of heavy boots in front of me. There was a long moment of silence. "Do you need assistance?"

"No," I said, staring blankly at the wall with unseeing, horrified eyes. "I'm fine here. Simply leave me."

"Right." He sounded more than a little uncomfortable. "I'm sorry…"

I looked up sharply. I wasn't sure why he was apologizing when I was the one who had caused this and brought it all on him as well. "I wish I could enjoy your first-ever apology, but I'm not sure it's warranted."

"You're not angry?"

"No, although I would quite like to be left alone to die of shame if you wouldn't mind."

I shifted, kicking my legs out straight on the floor. They were bare. *Wonderful.*

I closed my eyes, willing myself not to picture everything last night and failing miserably. It was too fresh in my mind, as if I'd been a passenger in my own head, unable to control my body, but now with full awareness after the fact. I could recall every kiss, every touch, every filthy word, feel the heat on my skin and the fingers bruising my throat.

And worse, if not for the overwhelming embarrassment of the entire situation, I would have liked it.

I did like it.

I groaned. "Please just get out? I cannot stand you staring at me."

Of course, Scion didn't move. "Gancanagh's Dust."

"Excuse me?

"Gancanagh's Dust," he repeated, dropping his high-born dialect a bit to more closely match mine so it sounded more like "Gan-can-na" rather than "Gon-con-nah."

I smiled in spite of myself at his brutally bad attempt at a northern commoner accent. "What is that?"

"One of the most vile substances my kind has ever come up with. You've probably heard of it before…fairy dust?"

I blinked at him blankly. Of course I'd heard of fairy dust in passing, but I still didn't understand what he was trying to say. "Bewitched sand?"

"No." He shook his head. "It's not really dust at all. It's the skin of marrows and blood of succubi combined with ground-up moondust leaves."

Suddenly, my skin felt like it was crawling, and I desperately needed to take another bath. "That's horrific."

"Yes, and it makes one wonder how the mixture was discovered since moondust leaves are so poisonous. It was once used often, mostly to drag unwitting humans away from their homes to be pets and prisoners. I assume it was not hard to convince them, as the dust causes insatiable lust that, once ignited, is impossible to control."

My face burned. He certainly didn't have to tell me that—I knew all too well what he meant. "Why would anyone think of that?"

He laughed without humor. "Haven't you noticed? We Fae are obsessed with love. We don't understand it in quite the same way that you mortals do, but we can see it. We want it. All of our best inventions are born of trying to force love upon those who will never willingly stay with us."

My heartbeat picked up, and for a moment, I almost forgot to be embarrassed—forgot why we were having this conversation at all.

But it only lasted a moment before I had to look away again. *Gods, why?*

Scion bent down, crouching so he was nearly eye level with me. Nearly, because even on the floor, his stature was so much larger than mine it was hard to be exactly nose to nose. I tilted my chin up to make up the difference.

"This is all to say," he said, "that no one could have resisted that. It doesn't have to matter."

Why was the only time he'd ever been nice when I wanted to wallow in self-pity?

"You resisted it," I pointed out mulishly.

"Only by a hair." He barked a real laugh that was half humor, half bitterness. "I will be honest, I have no idea why that was. I don't even want to speculate."

My fingers flew involuntarily to the throbbing bite mark on my neck. It hurt a little, but not nearly as much as I would have expected. I touched it, and a tiny shiver ran down my spine.

"Instinct," Bael's voice screamed in my head.

I tore my hand away. "Yes, best not to speculate, and I think it would also be best to pretend this never occurred."

"Alright."

I let out a dejected sigh. "Now, can you *please* leave me alone."

He was quiet for a moment, watching me, his eyes tracing searing paths over my skin. It was more than long enough for me to sink deeper into self-loathing. Oh my gods, how was I ever going to—

"You know," he said, interrupting my thoughts, "if I had been gifted with sight, I might have reframed my assertion yesterday."

"Which one?" I asked in spite of myself. The dirt under my fingernails had become highly fascinating as I traced my fingers over the pattern on the carpet.

"I might not have said that the next time you came to my bed, you would beg…it was, in fact, a desk."

I bristled and looked up at him, sudden rage sparking in my chest. "You fucking prick. What happened to 'I couldn't have controlled it'?"

He smirked and straightened up, looming over me. "There you go, rebel. There's that rage that should undoubtedly have gotten you killed long before now."

I stood as well, fully aware that I was taking his bait and unable to leave it. "Should have gotten me killed?"

"Undoubtedly," he replied blandly. "I often wonder how you have survived as long as you have with all your limbs intact when you are unable to tolerate even the most minor insult."

"So you would have killed me if we'd met palace," I said angrily, recalling his earlier refusal to answer my question.

"No." He looked down at me, dark heat swirling in his gaze. "You want to know what I would have done if I found you first?"

My breath caught—I wasn't sure who or what he meant when he said "first," but it didn't seem worth questioning. Not when my anger and…other things…bubbled so close to the surface. "Yes."

"It would have been such a waste to kill you when instead, I could have had you on your knees, begging to submit to me. I would have kept you imprisoned for far longer than a year, chained to my bed, where I could taste your pretty cunt anytime I wanted. I'd destroy you, and every time you swore you hated me, I would have fucked your insolent, lying little mouth and made you beg for more."

"Oh…" My mouth fell open, and words failed me.

He grabbed my chin with two fingers, forcing me to hold his unflinching gaze. "Don't be embarrassed about last night, rebel. Don't pretend it didn't happen. And when you decide you want more, I would be more than willing to pay fealty to my queen… all you have to do is ask."

34

LONNIE

THE CUTTHROAT DISTRICT, INBETWIXT

It was nearly midday by the time we finally made it down to the thieves' den to speak with Cross and his children. Scion reminded me in a flat, uninterested tone I could swear he was putting on simply to try to make the situation less uncomfortable of how long Phillipa Blacktongue had stood in the office with us last night. Only five minutes at most, so our expectations were not high that Siobhan had managed to get anything out of her safe that might lead back to Ambrose Dullahan.

For my part, I prayed they'd found something for more reasons than simply wanting to catch the rebel leader. I had less to worry about when it came to the rebellion than the Everlasts, as I didn't particularly care who ran the country. Of course, I cared about the afflicted, but I was willing to bet that Scion would have demanded to find his brother, regardless of whether the afflicted had moved south. His concern was for the crown, which was something I would do well to remember as well.

Mostly, I prayed that they'd found something so that perhaps I could still ask this Dullahan about Rosey. So that perhaps he would know how to break the curse, as Bael had suggested.

Because perhaps he would be able to tell me even more about my future…everything.

When finally we stepped inside the thieves' den, we were immediately met with the sound of steel on steel. Blades flashed through the air, and voices rang off the walls as pairs of fighters danced across the floor, sparring with an intensity that I could have sworn implied they were actually trying to kill one another.

Quill's talons dug into my shoulder, and he flapped his wings nervously. I batted at him with one hand. "Ow, stop that. You're too heavy as it is."

He pecked my hand as if to say, *"Be grateful I tolerate you at all, small human."*

"Be grateful I tolerate *you*," I replied.

Scion gave me an odd look as we edged around the perimeter of the room to avoid being beheaded by one of the spinning swords. "Are you speaking to him?"

I flushed. "I know it's foolish. Do not mock me."

His gaze traveled from me to his bird, and he shook his head. "Unbelievable."

Cross stood on top of a table at the far end of the room, surveying the fighters, his arms folded over his chest. He held up a hand to stop us as we approached. I came to an immediate halt several feet away from the table, and Scion stopped, albeit more reluctantly, beside me.

"I saw that!" Cross screamed at the top of his voice. "Do not think you can sneak chivalry past me, lass."

A pretty, dark-haired girl in a set of tight, black training leathers dropped her sword on the dusty stone floor with an echoing clang and stomped toward us. Her hair was pulled back in a tight bun, displaying small pointed ears, but she had a smattering of pale freckles across her nose. *Half-Fae.*

Ignoring me and Scion completely, she scowled up at Cross. "Oh, so I was supposed to stab him?"

The same teenage boy who had served our breakfast yesterday tore after her, sheathing his own sword as he ran. I raised an eyebrow when the blade glinted in the light from the warm overhead lamp. That was no blunted training sword but a real blade.

"Get over yourself," the boy scoffed with all the cocky arrogance of youth. "You couldn't have stabbed me if you wanted to."

"Oh, I wanted to," the girl sniped back. "I simply know better than to strike before I know I'll land the kill."

The boy grinned in a self-satisfied way that was a bit lopsided now but would undoubtedly break hearts in a few years. "Which is just another way to say you're scared."

"Enough!" Cross pinched the bridge of his nose, closing his eyes with deep exasperation. "Dodger, your right flank is wide open—you'll be lucky if you don't bleed out before you turn eighteen. Twist, the next time you fumble an easy hit, you're out. I'd rather you fucking kill him than waste my time with pointless drills."

The boy—Dodger, I gathered—hung his head, seeming appropriately chastised. "Yes, Father."

The girl said nothing, merely turning on her heel with an expression that looked as if she was plotting murder. If I were taking bets, I'd say her next hit would land, should she choose to take it.

Cross grunted some sort of noise of approval and waved them off before jumping off the table to stand in front of us. "Apologies," he said jovially, his stern tone melting away in an instant. "You know how it can be."

"Actually, I don't." I gave him a weak smile. "I don't think I've spoken more than two words to a teenager since I was one myself."

"I can't say I recommend it. Those two will be worth their weight in gold in a few years, maybe better than Siobhan and Arson, but that's only if they don't die first."

"What are they doing?"

"Just training exercises. Why?" Cross asked, lip curling up in a smile. "Are you interested? I could use a court spy."

"She's not interested," Scion snapped. "And don't you fucking dare send a spy anywhere near me unless they're a gift. I've been meaning to let Bael kill Mordant, anyway, so we'll need a replacement."

Cross laughed. "Noted."

We followed Cross's lead, taking seats across from him at one of the rickety card tables. "So, how did it go with Phillipa?"

I blushed, but Scion cut in, giving such a limited explanation of what had transpired I would almost swear he lied. "We've found your problem, though," he concluded. "She had a whole drawer of Gancanagh in her office."

"I might've suspected that," Cross replied. "But we haven't been able to get in there until now. Seems everyone got what they wanted."

I grimaced. I did not feel precisely triumphant. "Was Siobhan able to get into the safe?"

Cross grinned. "Of course."

My jaw dropped. "She was?"

I realized then that I hadn't really believed that she would—I so rarely expected anything to work out well that when it did, it didn't feel real. Like I'd somehow cheated the gods simply by avoiding catastrophe.

"Didn't I tell you she's the best," Cross replied smugly.

"Well, where is she?" Scion asked.

"Sleeping, but it's no matter. I have the documents."

"Well, don't leave us in fucking suspense," Scion grumbled.

Cross seemed to be a showman who enjoyed drawing out a reveal simply for the drama of it, whereas Scion was about to tear his own flesh from the bone if he was forced to wait another second. I could not imagine how these two had ever become friends, though I supposed I should be grateful that they were.

Reaching into the inside pocket of his black leather vest, Cross pulled out a stack of parchment tied together with a knot of red string.

I looked at it skeptically. "I was picturing a book."

"This is what a book looks like after the cover has been torn off and left to burn on the hearth of the leader of the assassin's guild," Cross said happily.

"Why…" I began before breaking off. Never mind, I was not sure I wanted to know what he was up to.

"Did you find anything in there?"

"Not yet, lass. We'd be looking for an outsider. Someone not from Inbetwixt, certainly. A big bloke, from what Vander said. Tan, tattoos on his head, green eyes."

Scion looked up sharply. "You never mentioned that was the description."

"Why? Does that mean something to you?"

"Perhaps." He sounded unsure. "My brother—Dullahan, that is—he travels with one of his men more than the others, and he fits that description."

"You got a name?" Cross asked.

"Riven," Scion replied shortly. "He's from a village in Wanderlust, no family name that I know of, no magic."

I looked sideways at Scion. "You know quite a bit, then."

"I've been tracking my brother for years, rebel," he replied, glancing down at the papers.

"Can I look?" I asked, even as I was already pulling half the stack toward me across the table.

I flicked through the papers absently, scanning names without thought. There were so many that were so obviously fake—*Jack InIrons, Jenny Greenteeth, Gwyn ap Nudd*, and so forth—that I had to wonder if Phillipa Blacktongue was running quite as tight a ship as she believed she was. Every so often, though, I would come across something that seemed real. *Fionn Stormbow. Bard Inbetwixt, Osin Highwater. Rhiannon Skyeborne.*

I was so focused on my thoughts that for a moment, I thought I was hallucinating.

I blinked and looked again, an odd buzzing noise starting low in my ears.

I wasn't hallucinating at all—there it was, at the bottom of the third page: "Rhiannon Skyeborne," followed by some numbers that could only be the date, time, and price of whatever had transpired.

I pulled the page out with a swift flourish that nearly tore the edge and stared at it more closely, as if the ink might disappear, then quickly scanned the other pages to make sure there were no other entries.

"What is it, rebel?" Scion asked.

I stiffened, eyes narrowing, and watched his reaction carefully as I held out the page for him to see. Would I recognize genuine shock? Had I played enough fairy games to avoid falling into a web of verbal trickery?

For a moment, it felt as if I were looking at two different versions of him. Like a window through time—Scion sat here, now, watching me with benign concern, and he was also standing with his uncle on the other side of a run-down alley in Cheapside, ordering my mother to be dragged out of the house where we'd been hiding. Which was real? Could it possibly be both versions? Could I reconcile with that?

"You must understand that this doesn't mean your mother was here," Scion said, his voice echoing back at me all through the long, narrow tunnel out of the guild den: *"here, here, here…"*

"And why is that?" I asked venomously. "Perhaps because you killed her?"

I heard his sharp intake of breath and knew without having to look that he'd clenched his jaw, his nostrils flaring. "That's, at best, an exaggeration if not an outright lie. I didn't kill your mother."

"But you know what I'm referring to?"

"Yes…" he ground out.

I picked up speed, nearly jogging now to stay ahead of him.

I hadn't been able to sit at that table for another moment with the buzzing growing louder in my head, my skin too tight, my panic rising.

Logically, I understood that my mother wasn't—couldn't be—here. That even if she were in the city, it was preposterous to think she would have visited the Side Saddle at all, let alone at the same time as some unknown rebel sympathizer. Logically, someone else had signed her name for me to see later. Someone who, I could only guess, learned the name from Rosey. So on top of being a cruel trick or some strange attempt at a joke, this was just another layer to the endless mystery.

I knew all that. But logic had no place next to the fresh wave of bitterness that had suddenly crashed over me and now lapped at the insides of my mind, begging to be allowed to flow freely.

"Where are you going?" Scion demanded as I dashed up the stone steps at the end of the long tunnel.

"I need fresh air."

I flung the door open on the storage room in the basement of the tavern and wove my way through all the barrels and crates toward the second flight of stairs. The tavern, which I now realized was little more than a front for the guild, was nearly empty, and no one noticed as I sped through the bar and out the front door into the sunshine of the busy street beyond.

I inhaled several deep breaths through my nose, crossing my arms tightly over my chest as if I could physically keep the painful memories out.

"I didn't kill your mother," Scion said again from somewhere behind me. "You have many reasons to be angry, but at least blame me for things I've actually done."

I whirled around, daggers in my eyes. "But you remember? You came to our house that day."

He nodded slowly, mouth practically disappearing his lips were so tightly pressed together. "I didn't want to. I didn't care at all about your mother; I didn't know who any of you were. I remember listening to her screaming and wondering what ill fortune had befallen her that we'd been sent after you at all."

"Is that supposed to make it better? Should I feel comforted by the fact that you didn't care about us and you still destroyed my family?"

He ran a hand through his hair. We'd never discussed this—not really—but like everything else, it would have to be talked about eventually. All of it would, I realized—and not only with Scion but Bael as well.

"You have to understand," he said, "that when Grandmother was alive, we did everything by her word. We never questioned an order, no matter how odd it might have seemed at the time. Even now…" He broke off. "Well, let us simply say the family still follows her orders, even from within the Source."

I raised an eyebrow, thinking of her orders to send prisoners to Aftermath to be turned into afflicted. Had they never once questioned that? They'd never advised Queen Celia otherwise? "But you had to wonder what might have happened when she was no longer there to give orders."

He shook his head. "Not in such a direct way as you seem to imagine. Grandmother Celia was over one thousand years old, and she'd ruled for centuries. My father had been the Prince of Ravens for some five hundred years, while Penvalle got quietly madder and more twisted in the background, never once thinking he might be king. It was not until the last three decades or so that things became less stable."

I frowned, relaxing my crossed arms. One had to wonder what caused that shift—if anything. If perhaps it had not just been the natural cycle of things. "So your grandmother demanded my mother killed? Why?"

"Again, not killed, merely taken," he said vehemently. "If the queen wanted your mother killed, it would have been far easier for me to do it right there in the street. I would've preferred that to dragging her, screaming, all the way back to Aftermath."

I reeled back. "That's where you went?"

He nodded, and my heart began to pound.

I hadn't known for sure what happened to her, and I couldn't imagine that Scion would have answered me if I'd asked up until recently—very recently. Something seemed to have changed with him, and it could not just be that he seemed to be at least somewhat attracted to me. No one changed this much this quickly over sex alone, which meant this was probably some new trap I had not yet worked out.

Before I could put any of that into words, a horrifying idea occurred to me, driving all else from my mind. "She wasn't turned into an afflicted?"

Scion grimaced. "Not that I'm aware of."

That was not a no. Oh gods…what if she'd been one of the ones in the woods? Or was still there now? What if her body had decomposed, but she'd turned into endless, static noise like all the other angry, afflicted spirits?

"Take a breath, rebel," Scion said, putting his hands gently on my shoulders.

"Do not be nice to me," I snapped. "I do not have the time nor the energy to sort out what game you are trying to play."

"Fine." His lip curled, but he did not remove his hands. "I'll spit on your face later if you like."

I choked on a laugh, if only because it was such a shockingly out-of-character thing to say—and worse, he had to be completely serious.

At the very least, it snapped me out of the spiral that threatened to consume me and brought me back to the moment. "Do you know why she was taken? What did your grandmother want?"

He thought for a moment, eyes darting up as if he were searching for a memory. "She'd had a dream about the fall of Nightshade. A nightmare, I believe it was."

I could have groaned. I was so sick of thinking about prophecies and dreams and seers. It was like some large puzzle, slightly out of focus, where everyone had a piece except me. "And what did she see?"

"After that nightmare, she sent us to find women born on the day that Nightshade fell. Your mother had just recently escaped from the palace, and I was sent to retrieve her."

My heartbeat sped up, the wheels in my mind turning. I remembered less than I would have liked about the days, even hours, leading up to our leaving the place. It was slipping away with time, leaving only the most poignant moments behind, but I would have given almost anything to know exactly what caused us to leave. "You were sent to find us, you mean."

"No." His eyes narrowed. "Just your mother. I was told to find the escaped servant woman with the red hair who was born on the day of the fall. I went to find her…I didn't know she had children."

My heart beat, if possible, even faster. "But my mother wasn't born on the day that Nightshade fell." I widened my eyes, urging him to realize the impossibility of that. "She would have been far too old, and in any case, she wasn't born in Elsewhere at all. She was a changeling child from the human lands."

"Then—" His eyes widened, and I watched as realization dawned on his face, followed almost immediately by horror and,

I was fairly sure, embarrassment. "I didn't realize, but I take it *you* were born on the day of the eruption."

I let out a frustrated breath, nodding. "Yes, but not only me, my lord. My sister as well, so we may never know who you were meant to take."

A cold numbness washed over me. Somehow, the knowledge that this had been an error all along made it worse. Now, rather than feeling relief or closure, I felt only guilt. Renewed anger. What would have been different if it was me instead? What had happened in Aftermath?

I shook my head, my red curls bouncing wildly. I could not let myself descend too far into despair, or I would never surface. Since we'd been in Inbetwixt, and perhaps slightly before, I'd not thought much about all the horrid things that I usually spent so often ruminating on in the quiet hours of solitude spent within the castle. The reason was clear enough: I'd had company. Something to do. The hunt and talking with Bael had been distraction enough, but then the attack, and now constantly fighting with Scion in between plotting. It was…if not pleasant, then at least different. I hated to admit that I was feeling more myself these days, as that would mean admitting that I might not despise the company of the Everlasts as much as I'd thought—as much as I wanted to.

I uncrumpled the paper in my hand and stared at it again, this time with all the clarity brought on by pain. "What I don't understand is why my mother? Why would anyone choose to sign her name? Was taunting me really so important?"

Scion frowned but did not protest my change of subject. "May I see?"

I handed him the paper he'd already looked over and watched carefully again as his eyes darted back and forth, reading. "I don't see any handwriting that looks the same. They are all different, so they—"

"What?" I asked eagerly as he broke off, his eyes widening. "Did you see something?"

The prince made a furious sound in the back of his throat, so abrupt I jumped back in alarm. "That fucking traitorous prick."

"Who?" I demanded.

The prince's smile turned feral, slow and dangerous, and a shiver of anticipation skittered over me. He crumpled the paper in his fist, looking down at me with an almost manic gleam in his eyes. "We need to pay another visit to the lord and lady."

35
LONNIE

THE CUTTHROAT DISTRICT, INBETWIXT

We blew back into the home of the Lord and Lady of Inbetwixt with no warning.

The house was silent when we appeared, and Scion was like a whirlwind of shadowed rage, storming down corridors and into empty rooms in search of someone to unleash his anger on.

I, mercifully, did not vomit upon traveling through the shadows and found myself able to keep up with him as long as I jogged. I barely paid a lick of attention to where we were going until we burst into a chamber on the second floor and several lights flared on.

"By the damned Source, who—my lord!" The Lord of Inbetwixt's yells went from enraged to confused to frightened so fast it was almost comical.

I shielded my eyes from the sudden light as I skidded into the room and saw that we'd clearly burst in on Lord Bard and Lady Acacia in bed. It was a large, grand primary bedroom, with a rumpled four-poster bed and two very confused-looking Fae, rising and reaching for dressing gowns.

Scion marched inside, ignoring any semblance of propriety. He grabbed the lord by the collar of his off-white nightshirt and lifted him clean off the bed. "Do you realize you continue to hold this position only because I allow it, Bard?"

"Ye-yes, my lord," the other male stammered.

"Then knowing that, and that I am already not particularly fond of you, why the fuck would you flaunt your feeble attempts at rebellion in my face?"

"I—I what? No!"

Scion threw Lord Bard down on the bed again, and he bounced off, sliding sadly to the floor. I gaped, wondering why he did not bother to fight back. Surely he must have some magic?

But then, perhaps this was how it was for the Everlasts overall. They'd ruled this long because even among their own kind, there was no competition.

Strangely, seeing this High Fae lord reduced to a blubbering mess made me feel much better about my own attempts at survival. I hadn't done all that terribly for a human if this was the standard set by the High Fae.

Scion reached into his pocket and whipped out the papers that Cross and Siobhan had retrieved from the Side Saddle. He pointed sharply at it, jabbing his finger so hard I was sure the lord could not make out an inch of the parchment. "Is this not your name?"

"Yes, lord."

"Then, were you not meeting with a rebel associate two nights ago? Perhaps to discuss the sunken ship you seemed so overly concerned with when last we spoke."

I glanced sideways at Scion, willing everything to fall into place for me as it evidently had for him. My heartbeat sped up. "What was on the ship?"

"Gancanagh's Dust," he spat to the room at large. "Cross told me. That's why they sunk the ship, which I'm sure you knew."

The lord and lady glanced at each other. Lady Acacia stepped forward, and despite her frail appearance—made worse by her night clothes—her voice did not shake as it did the other day. "Of course we know. We have been more than clear in every communication with the capital that the guilds are out of control, yet we have received no aid to stop them. Clearly, you, or whoever is holding this grudge within your house, is looking to squeeze us until we beg to leave the city of our own accord and can be replaced with a more sympathetic ruling family."

"No amount of bitterness justifies the production of that poison," Scion barked back at her. "What are you even planning to do with it?"

Lady Acacia laughed. "Not us. We don't care—it's the pleasure guild making it, and now it seems Blacktongue has found yet another stream of revenue by selling her excess to the highest bidder. I suppose that's the rebellion, now." She waved a hand as if to say she didn't care. "I only know that our standard trading ships became the means of delivery. What could we say? We can't very well shut down trade altogether, can we? We're responsible for feeding an entire city, just as you are supposed to be responsible for assisting us."

I glanced between her and Scion, unsure who was right here—or if perhaps it was a bit of both. My head spun a bit. This felt like one of those problems of royalty we'd discussed in the market square—where there was no good answer, and no matter what happened, someone would be hurt.

Perhaps many someones.

"Why would you meet with the rebellion, though?" I asked bluntly. "If you both have no desire to get involved further."

"I didn't," Lord Bard said quickly, his entire body still trembling. "I swear it."

Scion reeled back. That had evidently startled him, and he looked from the paper to Lord Bard, to me, and back again. Finally, he said to the lord, "This is your name, though?"

"Yes."

"Could it not be another case of a random name written down to confuse us?" I asked, lowering my voice slightly. It was pointless, as everyone could hear my heart beating well enough, and a whisper was more than audible, but it felt like the principle mattered. "Aisling only knows why, but it's not as if he's lying, and you said yourself my mother cannot have been there…so someone was clearly scribbling false names."

"Perhaps," Scion said slowly, his tone implying all on its own that he did not believe that one bit.

We stood in uncomfortable silence for a fraction of a second, the tension hanging thick in the room.

"Oh!" I exclaimed, the obvious solution hitting me all at once. "Where is your son?"

From the way Lady Acacia's lips turned into a thin line, I knew I was both correct and that she'd already put this together but had been in no hurry to help us.

I did not know the name of the son we'd seen in the drawing room the other day, but he fit the first description Cross had given, if not the second. It was Rosey's other dream. The meeting in the tavern. The male from Wanderlust and the fair-handed youth discussing the ships.

Moreover, the feeling of contempt that had wafted off him when he saw me was enough to tell me quite clearly that the younger Bard Inbetwixt had some preconceived notions about me—and they likely were not flattering.

Now, I wondered if perhaps it was not so much me he had a problem with but my face. Or, more accurately, my sister, who had shared my same face up until the day she died.

THE YOUNGER BARD INBETWIXT GLARED UP AT SCION WITH AN entirely too-familiar venomous expression. Familiar, because it was exactly the sort of hatred I'd seen in the mirror most every day of my life. The same disgust I'd shown when looking at the High Fae—until recently, that was.

Now, I feared to even know what my face might look like when I stared up at the Fae—and, most especially, the Fae princes. I found myself unable to accept the possibility that maybe, just maybe, my feelings were slowly changing.

It might have begun some time ago—perhaps when Bael first pulled me from the dungeon and killed that guard. Perhaps when he first kissed me or saved my life with his blood. Perhaps when the whole family began using my name or sharing spontaneous truths.

Scion was right: I had to reckon with my sense of morality.

I had liked what he'd done to the incubus, enjoyed fighting with him, wanted…other things.

I was in a between space. A shadow realm, neither respect, nor disgust, nor love, nor hatred. An acceptance that was not quite as begrudging as it had once been.

Bard Inbetwixt suffered no such confusion. He was clearly filled with burning hatred, if not for the Fae, then for royalty. The only question remained: why?

I watched as Bard Inbetwixt twisted his silver ring on his finger, his eyes narrowed. His jaw clenched and unclenched as he tried to find the words to express his displeasure.

"Let me warn you that you do not want to waste any more of my time than you already have," Scion said angrily. "Now, why were you meeting with the rebels at the Side Saddle?"

The lord and lady's son looked down at his shoes, unable to withstand Scion's furious gaze. "Why the fuck should I tell you anything? You'll kill me either way."

I clenched my fingers into fists. "Because if you don't, it will be far more fucking painful for you and your entire family."

Scion's silver eyes widened with shock, and for a moment, his eyebrows twitched up towards his hairline before he calmed his expression. "Precisely. I have no qualms about causing pain, but I do hate to be wasteful. I won't let you die until you tell me what I want to know, so you may as well make it easier on yourself."

If a human said that, I might have thought they were bluffing or exaggerating, but not Scion. He meant it. This male would die, but whether he would die easily or brutally like Kaius was still up for debate.

Bard shuddered, unable to hold in his fear. "It was my first meeting," he said bitterly.

"With who?" Scion demanded.

"Any of them. The rebellion is buying…shit from Phillipa Blacktongue." He struggled, trying to avoid the truth and stuttering. I was sure pain was tearing down his throat.

"We know about the Gancanagh's Dust," Scion snapped. "Why were you there?"

Bard looked surprised, but fortunately for us, the fact that we already knew the worst of it seemed to embolden him. He smiled meanly and spoke faster. "They want to get the dust out of the city and put it on ships like before, but this time, they need a new route." He licked his lips, looking eager, almost like he was excited to be involved in this even moments before he'd die for it. "They're looking to move it down to Underneath without crossing the Hedge."

Scion looked over at me, but not as if he was accusing, more like he wanted my opinion.

I had none to give. "Why would they do that?"

"I dunno," Bard said. "But I did my part. The rebellion is coming, and there's nothing you can do about it now, Slúagh cunt. I only wish the both of you would've burned down with the rest of your cursed court and that godsforsaken castle. Next ti—"

He stopped midsentence, eyes widened in shock, as Scion's fist made a sickening thump against his jaw.

A spray of crimson droplets dotted my face as Bard stumbled backward and slumped against the wall behind him.

Neither Scion nor I moved, the shock of it freezing us both in place.

"No magic?" I asked after a moment.

It was a foolish question and far too simple in the moment, yet it was all I could think to say.

Scion looked just as shocked as I felt, and perhaps that was why he answered a bit too honestly, "I didn't think of it."

My lips parted, a tremble passing through me. I had to wonder how often—if ever—that had ever happened to him. That he'd reached for physical violence over magical combat. From the look on his face, I was willing to bet almost never.

"I wish I could say that was illuminating, but now I have more questions than we entered with," I said before I could let myself wander too far down the path of questions.

Scion grunted in agreement. "Of all the wild and incomprehensible things my brother has ever done, I think I find this the hardest to believe. I might go so far as to say I don't believe it, except that the evidence is all there."

"Ambrose—er, Dullahan wouldn't use the dust?"

Scion looked uncertain and a bit lost. "I cannot say, but I would not have believed so. Not after knowing what it did to Penvalle, but can we really ever know anyone?"

My eyes widened. "What did it do to King Penvalle?"

"You have a way of making me blurt out things I did not mean to tell you."

Him and me both.

He swallowed thickly. "Over time, the dust turns lust to aggression, obsession to madness. Penvalle was something of an addict."

My stomach turned over, remembering the gruesome scene at last year's hunts. "So would the end goal of buying something like this in large amounts be to cause people to riot or slaughter each other?"

Scion's face was blank, impassive, like a mask. "That is certainly one possibility, but one must assume that there would be simpler and faster ways to cause violence. Harnessing the afflicted, for example, would be far more efficient."

Unless the rebellion was not truly able to harness the afflicted, I thought nervously. *Unless we were chasing after Dullahan for entirely the wrong reason.*

"So, if not for the violence, then why would they want it? And in Underneath of all places."

Scion stared at me with slightly haunted eyes, and I had the strongest urge to reach out and touch his face. "I don't know, rebel, and that is what worries me."

36
LONNIE
THE CUTTHROAT DISTRICT, INBETWIXT

That evening was torture…and *not*.

We'd be returning to the capital in the morning, regardless of any further investigation on the pleasure guild or signs of Ambrose Dullahan. To no one's surprise, Scion seemed to believe that meant we should spend the night trying harder to force the arrival of the rebel leader. The thieves, however, had something else in mind.

I might have guessed that the guild threw even wilder parties than the royal court, what with the fact that they had a bar on every floor, but I would not have been able to picture the sheer revelry until I saw it for myself.

I stood near the wall of the guild den, nursing the same drink I'd had for the last hour and watching the thieves who danced and twirled in a coordinated line, made all the more different from the royal court by the bright, contrasting clothing of Inbetwixt. There was no black training leather in the room tonight, and neither was there any tinkling fairy music, no bewitched wine, or writhing mass of too-beautiful naked bodies.

Somehow, the feeling of camaraderie when the fiddlers played a well-known shanty and voices rose in unison had its own kind of magic, affecting even me.

"What do you think of Cutthroat?"

I looked up and smiled, stepping over slightly to make room for Siobhan to stand beside me. Her eyes were bright, her hair sweaty on her brow from dancing, and she panted shallow breaths as she leaned in to hear my reply.

"Of Cutthroat or of the guild?"

"Both!"

She had to yell to be heard over the sound of raucous music, dancing feet, and cheering.

"It's different," I yelled back.

"How so?"

I was not sure how to put it into words. I could not say that the guild was exactly kind—they were clearly violent and rough in their own way, and Kaius had certainly been unpleasant, but they seemed to have a much more relaxed attitude toward many things. Humans, for one. There were quite a few human and half-Fae in the crowd, being treated no differently than the others, and since I'd been here, I'd not found nearly as much reason to hate the High Fae as I typically did.

"Royal parties are different. I'm mostly not allowed to go, for one thing."

"That's bullshit." Her expression turned hostile on my behalf.

"The dancing is different…" I said. "And there's more sex."

She laughed, and as if on cue—it may have been; I was not precisely sure who was listening to us—the fiddles picked up, playing a faster tune. Someone near the back of the room started banging on a drum, while others clapped, urging those in the center of the room into some sort of synchronized spinning dance I didn't know.

Siobhan passed her drink smoothly to Vander, who appeared out of nowhere behind her, and grabbed both my hands, dragging me into the middle of the room. She spun in a wild circle, her skirt flying behind her like a twirling halo and forcing the group of dancers to give us a wide berth.

"Different dancing does not mean better," she laughed and let go of one of my hands, guiding me into one of the lines of dancers. "And as far as the sex, I'd say you can take your pick, but I don't think you'd get very far."

"Why not?" I asked too loud.

She didn't answer for a moment, nodding her head in time with the beat of the drum, the heel of her boot stomping against the floor as everyone around us clapped in unison. When the beat changed, she grabbed my arm confidently and linked it with the dancer on her left.

"Because," Siobhan said when she finally swung back around to me. "Everyone can see these."

She reached out to point at the mark on my neck, and I almost slapped her hand away, but she stopped short of actually touching me. My reaction seemed to amuse her because her grin turned into another bout of cackling laughter. "You should see your face."

She grabbed my arm and linked it with hers and the person beside us on either side, swaying to a rhythm that only she seemed to know.

I allowed myself to be dragged around the dance floor, surely missing half the steps but not caring as my mind raced.

"It's nothing, anyway," I said when I swung back around to Siobhan again.

She sobered slightly. "I hope you're not serious. That's one of the most blatant claimings I've ever seen. Not that you see all that many. With magic so low, most Fae marry now rather than mate."

My stomach lurched unpleasantly.

"Maybe normally that's how it is, but these don't mean what you think they do. One was a mistake. If I should have any mark, it wouldn't be this..."

I trailed off, unsure what to say—or if I should say anything at all. It didn't feel exactly right to say they were nothing, but I couldn't claim they meant whatever she thought they did.

"Oh, so you have two, then? Interesting."

I flushed. "No! It's not like that either."

"Calm down. Even if it was, that's fine unless one species practices monogamy." She looked like she was trying to remember something just out of reach. "I can never remember who the monogamists are. Dwarves...dragons...most druids. Anything that starts with a *D*, apparently."

"Er, no. Nothing that starts with a *D*."

"Then you're fine. Go wild." Siobhan clapped and linked her arm with mine, moving us back into position for another verse. "But I still think you'd be hard-pressed to find anyone here willing to get nailed to a wall just for a chance to fuck you. I'm not sure even royal cunt is worth that."

I burst into laughter, throwing my head back. The rhythm changed again into a steady clap-and-tap pattern, and she lifted her face to me and threw a bright smile in my direction, holding out her hand for mine. I grabbed it without hesitation and followed along, clapping just as loudly.

We spun through the night, and I was amazed to find that I wasn't filled with regret or sorrow. There was nothing familiar about this place—nothing to make me feel guilty for finally smiling since Rosey passed away.

It was all too easy to forget everything back at the capital while swinging around and around with Siobhan and Vander and even miserable Arson.

Finally, I stepped away from the dance floor, panting, sweat beading on my brow. My smile was so wide it hurt my face, and I pressed my hand to my chest to catch my breath.

Then, I shivered as I felt a pair of eyes burning into me.

When I lifted my gaze, I found Scion's intense silver stare across the room. He was in midconversation with Cross, yet it seemed like his attention solely lay on me—too focused to be coincidental.

For a moment, I forgot about everything that had come before this night—the pain, the loss—and focused on nothing but the present moment.

A sudden jolt of adrenaline shot through my veins, and I felt a flutter deep in my stomach. My heart raced as a spark of anticipation ignited in me.

The mark on my neck seemed to pulse. Not pain exactly, but awareness. *That's one of the most blatant claimings I've ever seen.*

I should not like that. Should not be interested in what it meant…especially since it would not, could not, mean anything.

But as our eyes met across the room, all I could think was that all I needed to do was ask.

37

SCION

THE CUTTHROAT DISTRICT, INBETWIXT

"Are you listening, mate?"

I looked sideways at Cross and blinked a few times before taking a sip of the drink in my hand. No, I wasn't listening, and the bastard fucking knew it. "Fuck off."

We were sitting on the bar rather than at it, as Cross liked to watch his whole flock at all times, and I had no desire to join in with this…mess.

Cross wore an expression of wild delight as his gaze roved over the room. I hadn't been present at such a raucous gathering since my early days in the military, yet I still found it too boisterous for my taste. Cross, however, seemed to thrive on the frenzy.

It seemed that Lonnie did as well.

My eyes found her among the dancers, knowing exactly where she would be. If only by accident, I'd memorized the pattern of this stomping sea shanty so that every time I looked up, I found her immediately, skipping in a circle with the safecracker.

"Is she safe with Siobhan?" I asked abruptly.

Cross scoffed. "Safer than she would be with you."

Truer words were never spoken.

My friend turned away from watching the room and focused on me. "I was going to say congratulations this morning, but you both ran off so quickly."

I narrowed my eyes. "I don't know what you're talking about."

He nodded at the dance floor. "She's not being all that subtle with that mark. I should've known she was your mate when you were acting like a fucking lunatic." He grinned. "I'm happy for you."

His words stirred something in my chest, and a strange combination of feelings rushed over me. Dread, mainly, as well as a mix of exhilaration and alarm.

Had I not uttered a similar sentence to Bael just days ago? He was practically unhinged when I saw him last, and I'd most certainly accused him of lunacy over this same damn woman.

Only now, my muscles tensed, and it was as if my chest swelled with a strange, primal urge to give her even more marks to show off. The thought kept slamming at the back of my mind, trying to force its way out of my mouth.

I gritted my teeth and forced myself to utter the correct words—the ones I knew I needed to say but felt too close to a lie to be entirely comfortable. "This is…not what it appears," I struggled to say. "She's not my mate."

When I could say the words with no pain in my throat, I realized there was a trace of regret. Disappointment.

That was fucking unacceptable.

Cross looked over at me, confused. "You've got a screw loose, mate. Did ol' Daddy Belvedere fail to explain mating bonds to you, because it's a bit late, but I suppose I could—"

I sent a shock of pain through his mind—not enough to truly damage him, but enough that he toppled backward off the bar, spilling his drink everywhere. I smiled.

That was what I should have done to the Lord of Inbetwixt's stupid fucking son. Outside of a boxing match, I'd never once punched someone when I could have more easily used magic. I had no idea what came over me.

I found Lonnie in the crowd again. She'd stopped dancing, and this time, she seemed to feel my gaze. She looked up and met my eyes across the room. My vision narrowed in on a point, my heartbeat speeding up. Her wild curls of red hair were aflame around her face, her skin radiating like the sun with a brilliant glow. She was breathtakingly beautiful and dangerously tempting.

Cross climbed back up, scowling. "What the fuck was that for? That ale was expensive, I tell you."

"You stole it."

"Yeah, course. But it was expensive before I took it." He looked incensed. "Don't take out your issues on my merchandise."

I ignored him.

If I had any issue currently, it was that tomorrow we'd have to return to the capital. Not only had we not made the progress I'd wanted, but now I'd have to find some way of explaining to Bael that I'd marked his mate. I wasn't—

My thoughts stuttered to a halt, whatever I'd been thinking before fleeing my mind.

Lonnie had returned to the dance floor, her hair flying out around her like flames, her smile a bit too bright as Arson lifted her off her feet. He twirled Lonnie effortlessly in time with the music. I clenched my fists, feeling my heart twist as an unfamiliar surge of jealousy flooded my veins.

No. Absolutely fucking not.

Before I realized I was moving, I found myself standing beside them, catching her waist as Arson dropped her back down to the floor. She jolted in surprise, and when she looked up at me, I saw my reflection in her wide eyes.

"Are you going to dance with me?" she asked.

The word "dance" left her lips, and I instinctively flinched. My disdain for court dancing was well documented, so it wasn't surprising that the idea of doing some unrefined line-dance filled me with dread.

But she'd said, "with me," and I knew before I opened my mouth, there was no chance of denying her.

"You're ruining me," I said.

"What?" she yelled over the music.

I shook my head, saying nothing as she grabbed my hand and pulled me into her wild dance.

It was the third night of sharing a bed, but the first one where it felt like torture. Like a test and a punishment all at once, designed especially to ruin me.

Maybe she'd already ruined me, then, if this was too much to handle. Maybe I was well and truly destroyed because I was finding it hard to remember exactly what I disliked so much about her in the first place or why being with her would be so terrible.

Why should we be enemies when we would make such better lovers? Why fight when together we could rule?

Part of me wanted to ask her that—tell her—simply throw everything else aside and throw her down on the bed the moment she walked back into the room, but another far-too-rational part remembered all the reasons why that was the worst idea I'd possibly ever had.

I could probably write this off as a fleeting interest, spurred on by the blood and Ambrose's influence. If he'd never mentioned marrying her, I never would have thought of it.

Yet, I argued with myself, I forbade anyone from harming her before I'd ever spoken to my brother. I'd spoken to him in the first place because I was conflicted about the upcoming hunt. Then, too, Lonnie had always been...attractive...beautiful, even. Not only for a human but generally.

Even when Bael was dragging her around, pale and trembling in that bright blue gown, during the feast before the first hunt. Even when she was drenched in blood and lying in the dirt on the forest floor. Even while dirty and starving after the dungeon...

I frowned, my chest aching slightly.

I'd never let myself feel guilty about that—not really. It was not about her; it was for the kingdom. Everything, always, for the kingdom, and if I admitted that I might be sorry...that I might have done something different if given the chance, then how many other things would follow? How many other decisions would look wrong in that light? Ruling was not supposed to be easy or pleasant, and people were often hurt for the greater good. To be worthy was to know that.

The door swung open again, and all other thoughts fled my mind. Lonnie stepped back into the room, and my eyes widened, my fists clenching under the quilt where she wouldn't see.

Fuck me.

She walked toward me in a nightgown that left far less to the imagination than her underwear had. My eyes immediately flew to the mark on her neck, and my pulse raced, all blood rushing from my head to my cock. I closed my eyes, simultaneously horrified and entranced.

I expected her to come toward me, but instead, she hovered by the door, seeming poised to say something. I sat up. "What is it, rebel."

Her eyes narrowed, turning warmer, more determined. "I hate you."

I reeled back, slightly confused. That wasn't precisely new information, though I had to admit she had seemed to be getting over her dislike in the last few days.

My lip curled, almost out of habit. "Alright. Is there anything else?"

"I just want to make sure you know that. I despise you, and nothing will change that."

I wanted to say I hated her in return, but I didn't. *Not really.*

She'd asked me once point-blank if I did, and I wasn't even able to answer in the affirmative. I was beginning to hate our situation…things she was causing, doing, the way she made me feel. I hated everything about that, but not her. *Never her.*

"Fine," I snapped. "Has time run out on your cooperation?"

Fuck, if she'd taken that promise too literally… Images of tying her to the bed overnight flashed in my mind, most of them not entirely utilitarian.

She took a step forward into the ray of moonlight from the window, and as she got closer, I realized the sound of her breathing had turned husky, her heartbeat suddenly a drum in my ears. My nostrils flared, the scent of honey filling the air.

Oh. *Oh, fuck.*

"Rebel," I said against my better judgment. "I suggest you not test me right now. Say what you mean."

She sucked in a breath and ran her tongue over her perfect lips, and even that small pause was too much—so long I felt like I might spontaneously combust from the anticipation.

"I mean," she said, "I'm swearing that I hate you, and I believe you told me what would happen the next time I did that. So are you going to fuck my insolent little mouth now, or are you the liar?"

38
SCION

THE CUTTHROAT DISTRICT, INBETWIXT

"Come here," I told her, my voice sounding a bit raspier than I was accustomed to.

Lonnie climbed onto my lap, facing me, her knees on either side of my hips. She ran delicate fingers up my chest, even as I bit back a groan at the realization that she'd worn nothing under that too-sheer nightgown, clearly planning for this. It was only the trousers that I'd left on out of respect for sharing the too-small bed that prevented me from thrusting up into her, even as my cock swelled and she ground her ass down over me in slow, rhythmic torture.

"Not like that," I said sharply, lifting her by the hips until she hovered just over me.

She tilted her head to the side. "Then where do you want me, my lord?"

For fuck's sake.

I knew she said that as an insult of sorts—she only did it to mock or when she was angry—but damn if it didn't make my cock throb just thinking of all the things I would do to her while she begged her lord for mercy.

She'd mentioned letting me fuck her mouth, but probably only because I'd said it first.

I'd said a lot of things I wanted to do to her.

Most of all, I wanted her screaming and wet and ready first. To ruin her, like she was ruining me without even trying.

Fingers still digging into her ass and hips, I shifted her forward while I moved lower on the bed until her hands crashed into the headboard, her knees on either side of my head.

Her expression went from confident and laughing to shocked. She gasped and looked down, color rising in her cheeks, and I took some satisfaction in the idea that I'd managed to surprise her. "Take off your nightgown. I want to see you."

She raised the scrap of fabric over her head, even as she asked, "What are you doing?"

I had to tear my gaze away from her perfect breasts, all her curves, and smooth, soft skin. I raised an eyebrow and pressed one cheek to the inside of her thigh, feeling her shake with anticipation and nerves. "What does it look like I'm doing? Were you not the one who stood in front of three hundred fairies and suggested that I lick your cunt?"

"I was not being literal," she gasped.

Bullshit. She might have meant that to be hyperbolic, but the invitation had since been restated. I pressed a kiss to the inside of the other thigh, warming her up, moving slowly. "Have you ever done this before, rebel?"

She trembled, and I knew she'd felt the words skating over her most sensitive skin. "No."

"Never?" I pressed another kiss to her thigh, higher this time. "At all, or merely in this position."

Her face was flaming. "Never. I—"

She broke off, making a high-pitched mewling sound when I finally brushed a kiss against her clit, letting my breath linger there before moving back again.

"Ne-Never," she panted.

"Isn't that a tragedy."

I gripped her ass, pulling her down hard against my mouth, and she squealed, trying to squirm out of my hold. I caused the shadows to rise around us, binding her to the headboard. It was not so much because I couldn't hold her here as because I hadn't been able to get the image of binding her this way out of my mind for days.

"Fucking prick," she shrieked as the shadows snaked around her, skating over her skin.

"Good, rebel. Tell me how much you hate me."

She cried out in frustration, but I only went back to focusing on making her cry for other reasons.

I sucked her clit into my mouth, rolling my tongue over it, under, massaging small circles with the tip.

Her knees began to shake, and I stopped, instead dragging long licks over her center until that became too much, then licking inside her, fucking her with my tongue. Every time she began to shake, started to clench around me, I'd move. Torturing her. Making her cry and whine.

After a while, she seemed to forget to maintain her embarrassment, grinding against my face and chasing her release.

I reached up, toying with her bare nipples, rolling them between my thumb and forefinger. Without a thought, I pinched hard—too hard—and only realized what I was doing when she moaned even louder.

She liked pain—and gods, that made this so much harder because now, she was perfect for me. Except that I hadn't ever been able to use pain against her.

"Please," she begged.

Her pleas echoed those in my head. I'd never wanted anything more than I wanted to lift her onto my cock and feel her orgasm tear through her. I wanted to sink my teeth into her, possess her. She looked down at me, eyes glazed, and suddenly, I knew I couldn't look up at her face while she came. Couldn't look at her at all.

I pulled my face back. "Turn around."

She didn't seem to mind, completely unaware of the hurricane thundering through my chest. The shadows let her go, and she turned around, falling forward as I grabbed her hips and buried my face against her, lapping harder at her clit, wanting to drown out any other thoughts. Drown in her.

I ran two fingers over her opening, and she whimpered, pressing back against me, practically begging to be fucked.

I felt her run her fingers over my belt, then lightly over my cock, straining against the fabric of my trousers. "Can I?" she asked. The words came out as almost a purr, burning through me like whisky.

This was not how I typically liked to do things. I'd have had her on her knees, sucking me off while I did something else, if only to prove who was in charge. That was how I typically started with a new partner—if only to set the tone for how it would be. You could never take back power once it had been lost, not really, and maybe that was the problem here. This weak human woman had all the power, and I could never fully take it back.

I grunted in agreement, and she had my belt and my cock free within seconds. She kissed the head, swirling her tongue before wrapping her lips around it. Distantly, I noticed that while she'd never had anyone lick her, she'd clearly done this before—knowing without instruction to use her hands as well as her mouth and when to breathe, how to take me into the back of her throat.

That was a fucking crime. A travesty that no one would have yet worshiped every inch of her.

I moved my fingers faster, sucking her harder as she moved her mouth up and down my length, causing my muscles to clench and heat to pool in my groin. Her knees began to shake again, and this time, I didn't let up, wanting to feel her clench around my fingers, taste her coming all over my tongue.

I curled my fingers inside her, and I felt her clench around me, trembling, all her screams lost as I choked her with my cock, thrusting up until I hit the back of her throat.

I didn't bother to hold back as I might have if I'd planned to honor her request, thrusting harder into her throat and squeezing my eyes shut, spilling into her mouth, light bursting behind my eyes. I nearly groaned again when I felt her swallow. Fucking amazing.

She released me and panted, her breath coming too hard and fast. I could feel her chest rising and falling and almost wished I'd watched her face, her perfect tits, when she came.

But no—I was sure, without knowing how I knew, that seeing that would have destroyed whatever tenuous hold I had on reality. The reality where I still didn't get to keep this woman—not really. Where she would never be mine, and I was never going to be happy.

Then she finally slid off me and turned around in the bed. I rose and didn't look at her as I strode, naked, across the room to go find a towel. "Tell me again how much you hate me."

"I—" Behind me, she coughed hard, her words getting caught in her throat. "As much as you hate me, I'm sure."

39
LONNIE
THE CUTTHROAT DISTRICT, INBETWIXT

The castle made it difficult to find your way around if you were not wanted or didn't belong there. When I'd worked below floors, I had no difficulty navigating the corridors, but as soon as I'd moved upstairs, where the Fae neither liked me nor appreciated my presence, the castle suddenly became a maze of dead ends and twisting corridors. Maybe it had finally accepted my presence here. Maybe its masters had.

Skidding to a halt in front of a familiar door, I gasped for breath. The air was sharp and ashen in my lungs, and I coughed, leaning against the wood for support.

The air in the room was no better. Stale, the power palpable. Magnetic. It surrounded me like a prison of oppressive energy, and a chill permeated my body like death itself had descended.

The darkness was so complete that it took a long moment for my eyes to adjust to my surroundings, yet I knew exactly what I would find there: the bedchamber was taken up almost entirely by an enormous bronze cage, which housed most of the furniture one would expect to find in a standard bedchamber. The last time I'd been in here—the only time—

I'd noted that the bed was chained to the bars, making me question what could possibly necessitate such a thing.

An enormous shape leapt off the bed and prowled toward me, coming to a halt on the opposite side of the bars. The air seemed to quiver, quaking with the force of the energy in the room as a pair of golden, catlike eyes glowed at me out of the darkness.

"There you are," I said. "Didn't you know I've been hunting for you?"

I SAT UP WITH A START, PANTING, AS IF I REALLY COULD NOT breathe. My heart thundered in my chest, and my entire body quivered, making me feel as if I were shaking the entire mattress. I opened and clenched my fists, trying to expel a terror that would not subside.

"What's wrong?" Scion's sleepy voice asked.

My chest clenched. "Nightmare."

He said nothing, not even opening his eyes. How then did he realize I was awake, much less upset?

I tried to lie back down and could not stop trembling, could not calm my breathing no matter what I told myself. Just because Rosey's dreams might have been prophecies, that did not mean mine were…mine never had been before.

The castle was fine. Bael was fine, or he would be here. This was anxiety over tomorrow and would be proven false the moment we returned.

Scion put out a large, muscled arm and threw it over me, saying nothing as he pulled me back into his chest. I froze.

He was asleep—or mostly asleep. Not thinking. Just like I hadn't been thinking earlier…

I made no move to shift away from him. Did not try to wriggle out of his hold and hated myself just a bit for sinking into the warmth.

"I hate—" I tried to whisper.

And just as they had earlier, a pain like nothing I'd felt before, like burning flames, licked up my throat, making my eyes water. I pressed my lips together, holding in a sob that had nothing to do with the pain.

PART THREE
Smoke and Shadows

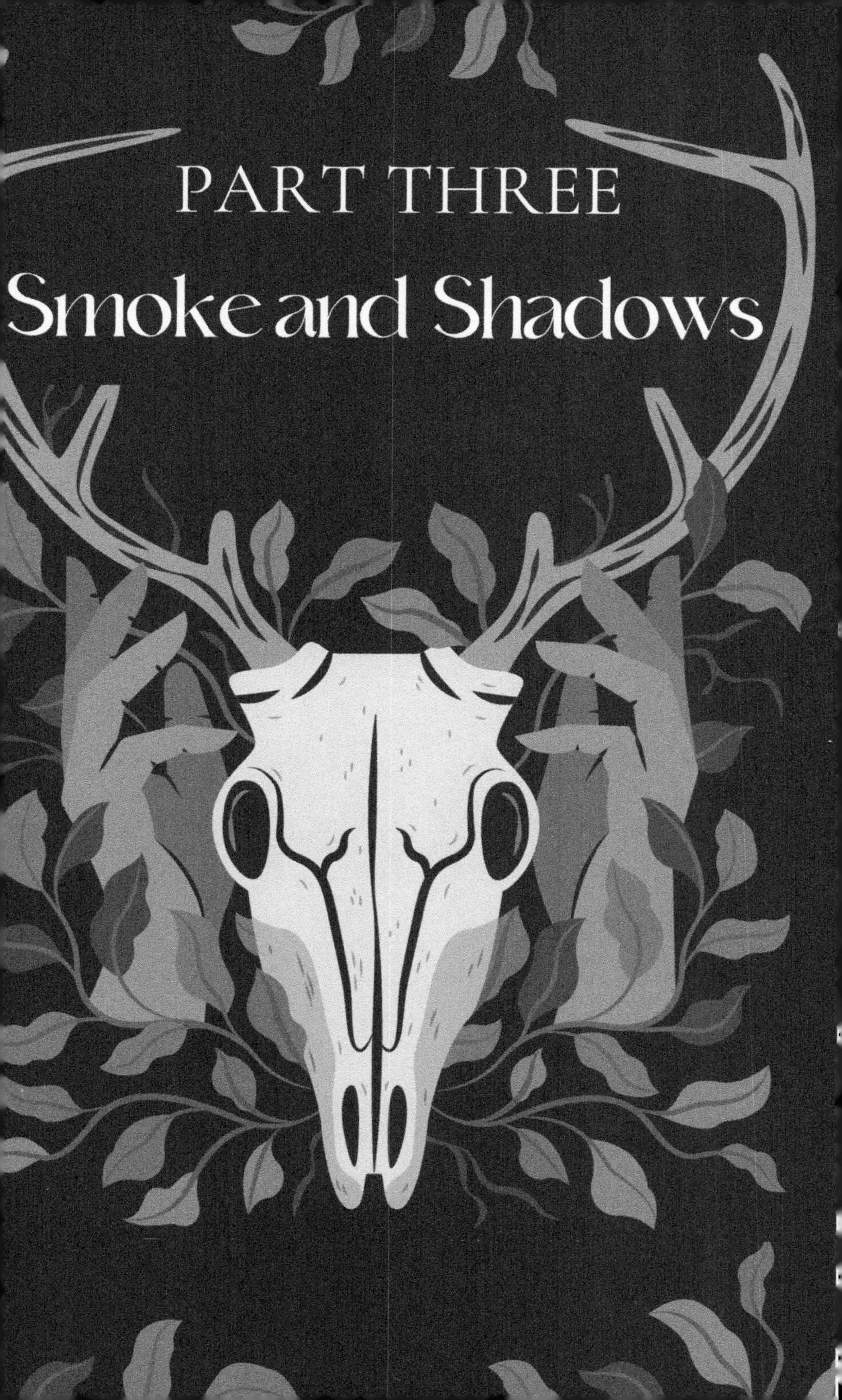

40
LONNIE
THE CUTTHROAT DISTRICT, INBETWIXT

The following morning, Scion's mood was as dark as Quill's feathers.

"You must realize that Bael is likely unconscious," the prince groused as we stood outside the Crossroads tavern, preparing to return to the capital. "I have not a shred of doubt that if my cousin were aware you were gone, he'd already be here."

"So say you," I muttered. "I can't say I know anything of the sort, actually, given that I don't know what's wrong with him."

I heard myself and immediately knew I was lying.

I *did* believe Scion that Bael would be here with me if he could. More, I could feel it, deep in a part of myself I wasn't even aware I could feel anything until all too recently. But wasn't that even more reason to go back and see him?

"That was your choice. I would have told you." Scion grumbled.

I still believed I'd got the better end of the deal by negotiating to return and choosing to hear whatever secrets Bael had from the male himself.

It didn't matter now, anyway. I'd done my part. I'd cooperated, and now I needed to leave.

We'd already bid farewell to Cross and his children, but Scion still seemed reluctant to leave. "You are quite positive I cannot make you understand that Bael will not talk to you? You do not need to go rushing back when we could still be useful here."

I put a hand up to shield my eyes from the setting sun peeking over the tops of the buildings, making it slightly difficult to make direct eye contact. "Perhaps if we'd found anything, but I do not see any point in waiting around for nothing."

That, and honestly, I was not sure I could handle the tension. With the last lead turned cold, there was little to do but wait for something else to happen, and in the meantime, Scion and I were stuck in close quarters.

He could never convince me *that* was a good idea.

Most especially not now, with the added complication of the bite mark still red and raw on my throat. No, any more time spent alone was a terrible idea. *A terrible idea, indeed.*

WE APPEARED ON THE OUTSKIRTS OF THE CAPITAL CITY EMPTY-handed, with little to show for the last three days than wasted time and an additional layer of tension cast upon our acquaintance.

My knees nearly buckled, but I managed to stay on my feet as I blinked furiously, clearing the shadows from my gaze.

Scion had dropped us at least half a mile away from the palace gates, in the middle of the dirt road that led to the outer village of Cheapside. I squinted at the hazy dark sky of the horizon, which was the near total opposite of the sunny street in Inbetwixt. We were just far enough away that the tall towers of the obsidian castle were not yet visible over the crest of the sloping hill. "Feeling like a stroll?"

Scion scowled at me. "Sarcasm is barely better than lying, you know."

I scoffed. "I would bet everything I own that if you could use it, sarcasm would be your native tongue."

"Everything you own…meaning the clothing on your back?" he said dryly, looking me up and down.

I flushed. "But truly, why land so far away from the castle?"

"It wasn't intentional. I got distracted," he replied, nostrils flaring slightly.

Interesting. "How does it work? Traveling through the shadows."

Scion thought about it for a moment as we started up the road. While he was silent, I looked around at the painfully familiar surroundings: the woods on one side of the path, the rolling fields on the other. The muddy boot prints, seemingly permanently etched in dirt. The air smelled sour, as if some cart of garbage had recently overturned nearby, and there was smoke in the air—no doubt coming from the chimneys in the village, burning early in the season to combat the unseasonable chill.

It had been quite some time since I'd walked this road, though the view was familiar as prior to the night that everything changed, I'd often walked this way to run errands or meet Caliban in the stretch of trees behind the small, thatched houses.

It seemed now like someone else's life.

"I cannot say," Scion said finally. "But I would wager it is similar to if one were to fold a map and walk within the crease."

"That is entirely unhelpful."

He huffed out an annoyed breath. "To travel through the shadows, you must not think about it. You have to simply try to fall between the worlds."

"But this time, you overshot it, I take it?" I grinned. "What distracted you?"

He paused for another long moment before answering. "I was thinking that—"

He broke off, and as I looked up at the road ahead, there was no need to ask why. Indeed, I forgot what we'd been discussing entirely as the tops of the castle towers came into view on the horizon.

Far in the distance, enormous orange and red flames engulfed the tower, licking up the sides and sending plumes of thick gray smoke into the air. The sky, already gray, was growing darker by the second—a dull slate fading into black.

Alarm rang through me, and the ground seemed to tremble, shock tilting everything on its edge. Even as I watched, a tremendous slab of stone broke off from the top of the nearest tower, shaking precariously for a moment, before sliding out of sight and crashing to the ground below. A dull roaring filled my ears, and my mouth fell open in a silent exclamation.

From where we stood on the road, the entire castle and the sweeping grounds surrounding it would soon be visible, though it was still not close enough to hear the impact of the stone on the ground or the roar of the flames. The scent of acrid, sour smoke wafted to us, seeming magnified tenfold now that I could see the source in front of me.

My muscles seized up, my body warring with itself as I simultaneously wanted to run toward and away from the disaster ahead.

Scion swore loudly and took off sprinting several yards in the time it took me to blink. "Stay there," he said, not looking at me.

"Wait!" I found my voice again. "Take me with you!"

"No!" His answer was sharp and final. Like he hadn't even wanted to waste time with a second syllable.

I dashed after him, knowing there was absolutely no scenario in which I might actually catch up. The painful irony that would be running toward the danger of the burning castle rather than away from it was almost unbearable. This was how I died, surely: not in the hunts or by the hands of the Fae, but through sheer, stubborn stupidity. If my poor mother could see me now.

"Let me help!" I yelled.

Scion shimmered midstride and turned semitranslucent, giving me the strangest impression that I could see through him to the castle beyond. Then he stopped and became solid again, glaring silver daggers at me. "I do not have time to argue with you or to indulge your maladroit tendencies."

"Why do you care?" I heard myself snap.

Shit.

Immediately, I was sure I'd said the wrong thing, which was only confirmed when Scion's eyebrows pulled low in a scowl. "I most especially do not have time for your self-loathing."

I made a rough noise of frustration in my throat. "That's not what I meant."

I could have kicked myself. For once, I hadn't been trying to antagonize him.

Yet the question lingered. Why should he care if I injured myself? Why did it matter to him at all what I did—surely one bite, or even last night, could not be that strong of a motivator when he'd hated the air I breathed for months. Even so, he was right in the sense that there was no time to argue.

I had no words—nor, indeed, the time—to explain every thought racing through my mind, all jumbled together and confused. I hadn't told Scion about my dream involving the fire—why would I tell him about any of my dreams? Now, though, I desperately wished I'd explained it. Wished I'd had the conversation about Rosey's journals with him, if only to give it more context. If only I'd explained why I was so adamant about seeing Bael. "If you don't take me with you, I will only make my way there myself."

A muscle in the prince's jaw twitched, and storm clouds rolled over his eyes. He stalked toward me, looking for the first time in several days as if he would have liked nothing more than to choke the life out of me. "You are the most infuriating creature."

A spark of genuine fear lit inside me like cold fire, and it was all I could do not to flinch when at last he reached for my arm and dragged me into the darkness once more.

My stomach lurched, far more so than it had barely ten minutes prior, and it was several long moments before I could open my eyes. As soon as I did, I had to blink several times, not sure if I was seeing correctly. "Why did you bring us to the stables?"

The Everlast stables stood behind the castle, on the opposite side from the garden that hid the entrance to the servants' quarters. I recognized them immediately—or rather, I recognized the emblem of the house crest emblazoned on the saddles hung along the wall to my right and inferred from there.

The stables were enormous, dimly lit, and smelled of smoke and manure. They housed easily fifty horses at any one time, perhaps more, and were attended by some two dozen or so squires and stable hands.

Scion and I stood in the center aisle, rows of stalls facing us on either side, reminding me uncontrollably of the dungeon. The unnerving sounds of terrified animals, stomping and snorting, filled my ears, and in the distance, I could hear the shouts of men over the blazing fire.

"I told you," Scion said shortly. "I don't have fucking time for this. Where is the crown?"

I recoiled, sure I must have heard him incorrectly. "The what?"

"The crown, Lonnie. The only fucking crown I daresay you've ever seen, no less owned! You do not have it, so where is it?"

"You are worried about finding the crown? Not your family?"

My stomach twisted into a knot. Some part of me had started to think maybe he was not quite as abhorrent as I'd believed, but this was unforgivable. They were not even my family, and I could not claim to be any great supporter of the Everlasts, but even I would have saved nearly any of them over the *crown.*

"My family are no doubt halfway to Overcast by now. That is where they would go in a catastrophe, and if there is one thing they are good at, it's caring for nothing but their own preservation."

I met his eyes, squinting to see him in the low light. That might be true, but I could find no comfort in it until I know for certain that Bael was not locked in a cage while the castle burned around him. "I need to find Bael."

"No, you don't. Bael can take care of himself far better than you can."

"You don't know that."

"No, you don't know what the fuck you're talking about. You need to stay here, and I need to get the damned crown back."

"Why?" I practically yelled.

"Without that crown, there is no way to break the curse. There is no monarchy, period. It's not only some bit of jewelry. The mere act of owning it matters."

Any other time, I might have bothered to marvel that it was the first time he'd mentioned their curse to me in so many words. Perhaps he was under too much pressure to realize that he'd said it. Regardless, the thought flew from my mind only a moment later.

Shadows rose out of nowhere, just like they had on that first day in Inbetwixt. The dark, translucent ropes snaked around my arms and torso, binding me so tight I could hardly breathe. I felt my arms yanked behind my back, and then I was flying backward against the rough wooden wall.

Bile rose in my throat, sending the revolting taste of this morning's breakfast back up to brush the back of my throat. "Get off!"

He merely took a step back, barring his teeth. "Stay here. I'll come back for you when it's safe."

Electricity seemed to travel through my body, different somehow than the heat that always licked up my skin whenever I got this angry. "Like you came back the last time you locked me up, you mean?"

His serious gaze flashed like a strike of lightning, burning, charring me from the inside out. "I will never apologize for protecting you, even if you hate me for it."

"Don't you mean protecting the kingdom?"

He stepped away, holding me trapped in that look as he faded into nothing. "Don't delude yourself, rebel. You know I can only ever say exactly what I mean."

41
LONNIE
THE CITY OF EVERLAST

I didn't allow myself to wallow in pity or self-loathing.

As soon as Scion disappeared, I frantically tried to pull at the shadowy ropes binding my wrists, ignoring how it squeezed tighter into my skin with each desperate twist and yank.

My fingers merely passed though the cords like vapor, only for them to solidify again within seconds. I let out a sound, somewhere between a scream and a gasp. Sweat beaded on the back of my neck and around my hairline, the exertion and the heat in the air already starting to take its toll.

He'd run his twisted shadows through and around the door to one of the horse's stalls, giving me barely a foot of space to move. Perhaps if I could only break the wood?

Panting, I tried again, dropping all my weight until I was hanging by my arms.

The wood creaked, but did not budge.

I paused again, gasping for another breath. Through my efforts, my hands felt less constricted, but the rope around my waist and torso seemed to have been pulled even tighter to the point that I had to stop for fear that I would suffocate.

I screamed in frustration.

When I got out of here—and I would, it would not be like last time—I would kill Scion. No matter how long it took, I'd end him. Perhaps by blade, or better, by feeding him to the serpent in Inbetwixt.

I took a deep breath through my nose, willing myself to calm down, but only succeeded in raising my pulse higher. If only I could walk through the shadows, then it would not matter that he'd bound me, I'd simply take the damn ropes with me.

Realization hit me like a physical blow…could I do that? Could I have done that all along? *Aisling*, if so…no, best not to dwell on all the things I couldn't change now, especially not when I was not yet sure it would work.

I had no worldly idea what made up the minute differences in power that the Everlasts seemed to view as if to have different gifts nearly made you different species. Who was to say where shadow walking fell within that spectrum?

Who was to say what might happen… a tiny, traitorous voice spoke in the back of my mind. The voice sounded strongly like a hissing snake, and then, like my mother, urging me to never reveal my secrets, never use any magic. Of course, she was right —I knew that, I'd see what could happen… but at this point, what was one more disaster if it meant achieving a greater-good?

Gods, Scion's mentality was beginning to rub off on me if I now thought ends justified means.

Pushing that horrible thought aside, I focused instead on the task at hand. There was no point worrying about it if I couldn't achieve shadow walking in the first place.

Like folding a map. Like walking in between two shadows.

I shut my eyes, trying to conjure a mental image of the obsidian castle; of the long, winding halls, the gleaming black crystal and never-ending maze of locked doors.

I certainly did not want my first attempt at shadow walking to succeed, only to land in the middle of a battle, or the blazing tower.

I inhaled deeply and visualized the kitchens. I clenched my teeth, feeling the muscles in my jaw twitch with tension. I could feel beads of sweat gathering on my forehead as I took a single, measured step forward, as far as I could go with the ropes holding taut.

I knew before I opened my eyes that it hadn't worked.

I willed myself to open my eyes, a deep-seated dread filling my heart. I had expected the sensation of free-falling and the pressure of nausea in my stomach, yet nothing. The floor remained beneath me, unmoving. There was no darkness, no spinning whirlwind.

I can do this. It cannot possibly be that hard.

I tried again, this time imagining falling into darkness. Tumbling down a long slide, arms flailing, untethered and unattached.

But again, when I opened my eyes, nothing had happened.

Nothing.

I stepped in the other direction, as far as the ropes would let me go. I moved faster, more abruptly, jumped, went backwards.

Nothing. Nothing. *Nothing.*

My hope crumbled like ash in my hands. Burned away like the flames licking up the burning castle.

There was nothing to be done. Again, I would be trapped, helpless, unable to do anything to protect myself or anyone else I cared about. Again, I would have to face that whatever I might like to think to the contrary, the Fae would always best me, always be stronger. I'd tried to protect myself with ignorance, and in reality, I'd crippled myself. I might have once had the spark of a weapon, but I had no idea how to use it. I'd never learned to protect myself and now there was nothing I could do.

I would have laughed, but I couldn't find the energy, bleak despair washing over my mind. Like slow moving shadows.

My arms ached, and the muscles in my shoulders burned from all the pulling, and my mind felt more exhausted even than my body. I closed my eyes and sank to sit on the dusty floor, leaning sideways against the rough, wooden stall door. The air felt thick, or perhaps that was the lump in my throat, the buzzing in my ears drowning out every other sound.

Then, all at once, I jolted, realizing I was still leaning, leaning too far with no door to fall against. My stomach lurched as I felt myself tip sideways, the darkness swallowing me, until it was no longer possible to tell if my eyes were open or closed.

I screamed. Or, I thought I did.

Then all at once, I toppled onto flat, familiar, stone.

42
LONNIE
THE OBSIDIAN PALACE, THE CITY OF EVERLAST

My senses returned slowly, one by one.

First came sound. Muffled screaming and pounding footsteps, combined with the blood rushing through my ears. Every noise felt too loud, rattling my bones and making my teeth clench painfully together.

Then, sensation, as I registered the meaning of pain at all and understood that I'd landed too hard, my knees biting into the floor, and my arms still bound behind my back.

Scent and taste—the odor of overpowering smoke and ash was hot and acrid in my nose. I gagged and could taste the metallic bite of sulfuric acid on my tongue, the bile rising into my throat.

And finally, my sight came back to me, my eyes cracking open, as slowly and painfully as a newborn foal.

I pushed to my feet, wobbling on my baby legs, wondering now if I had indeed been reborn. Changed. Remade in the shadows and by the magic, and birthed on the other side as something that could not yet fend for itself.

Dizzy, I blinked again and looked down. The shadow ropes, it seemed, had not made the journey with me.

I would repay Scion for that, and for so many other things—assuming I could find him in this burning mess.

I was both surprised and not that I stood in the tiny room I'd once shared with my sister. It looked impossibly smaller now than it ever had when we'd lived here. Indeed, the ceiling was so low that my head almost brushed the rafters, and I was hardly tall to begin with. There were only two small cots and a tiny table where there had once sat a pitcher and washing basin. The small window was now completely covered—or perhaps the sky outside was so dark it only appeared to be.

If I'd had time to feel grief, I might have wallowed in memories of the room, but I was distracted entirely by the oppressive feel of the air and, more so, the sounds of pounding feet coming from above,

I'd thought that the fire was stemming from the tower, but now my instinct was that it originated much lower. With luck, it would not yet have consumed the bottom floor or, worse, have started here.

Dashing for the door, I threw it open and skidded out into the hall. Instantly, I reeled back. The heels of my boots skid against the stone, but it was too late—I slammed directly into a woman walking past in the direction of the kitchen. "Ah!"

Startled, she jumped back with a gasp, and her arms flew up in the air in reflex, windmilling before she only just managed to stay on her feet.

"Ooph—I'm sorry!" I exclaimed.

My inadvertent victim's milk-tea hair had fallen in front of her face, and she brushed it aside, taking a moment before looking up at me with a disgruntled scowl that turned into an expression of awe. "My lady!"

"Iola!" I said at almost exactly the same time, mirroring her shocked expression.

"What are you doing here?" Iola cried. "Not that I'm not glad to see you. I am, but not now. Any other time would have been better, really. You understand?"

I smiled despite myself. "Yes, I'm glad to see you too, bad timing notwithstanding."

Iola had been my maid for barely a few weeks, but she'd still been kinder to me in that short time than anyone else had. It was especially appreciated, as barely anyone else had so much as spoken to me during many of those long days, and when they did, it was in the form of threats. The last time I'd seen Iola, she'd been poisoned during a ball and healed by Prince Gwydion.

Her eyes widened, and she looked from me to the room behind me and back again, shaking her head. "How did you get down here? And in that room, no less?"

"Never mind that," I said quickly. "What are you still doing in the castle? You need to leave."

Now that I thought about it, was it possible the servants did not know about the fire? It seemed impossible, but perhaps…

No. I breathed a sigh of relief, answering my own question before I had to ask.

The long, thin corridor, which ended with the kitchens on one end and the largest of the servants' dormitories on the other, was almost entirely deserted. On a normal day, it would have been packed with servants and their families, almost like a small village within the castle, but now Iola and I were two of only a few stragglers left, all moving toward the exit.

Footsteps pounded overhead, as if there were still quite a few people on the floor above, but that was another question entirely.

"I was leaving just now," Iola said vehemently. "I was sleeping when it began."

"When did this begin?" I asked, even as I steered Iola back in the direction of the exit. "And where? What happened?"

She grimaced but began to walk alongside me. Immediately, the problem—and the reason she was still here—became apparent without her having to say anything: her breathing was labored, her movements slow and sluggish, despite her clear efforts otherwise. My eyes widened in alarm.

"It was so fast," she said between breaths. "Of course, I did not see the attack last year when…"

"I killed Penvalle," I finished for her, wanting to save her lungs the effort.

"Yes, that, but I believe it was much the same."

"Did any afflicted attack the castle?"

Her eyes widened even further. "No! At least, I do not believe so."

If she didn't believe so, then there hadn't been any. The afflicted were certainly not difficult to miss. That was both comforting and horrifying simultaneously, in that it now seemed doubtless that anyone but me could be at fault for the last attack. Surely, if this was the rebels come to seize the castle as Scion had feared, they would bring their ultimate weapon—if indeed they had it. Surely, if Ambrose Dullahan could call the wretched creatures that had chased Bael and me nearly to ground, he would do so again.

Of course, I'd known this. Suspected, but to hear it all but confirmed put a stone in my chest.

"What were the rebels after?" I asked, ignoring the roiling in my stomach.

Iola shook her head and glanced up at the ceiling. I followed her gaze, and we both listened to the sound of pounding footsteps, like hundreds of running men and women in steel boots. The palace soldiers didn't wear steel armor; it was all made of other materials: bone, leather, obsidian. Even the humans didn't wear any metal out of respect for the Fae commanders.

"I don't know," Iola said. "I thought they wanted to find *you*, only everyone knows you'd left with Prince Scion and Lord Bael."

"Just Scion," I corrected her.

She looked confused. "But you were all gone."

I didn't waste time explaining where Bael was, immediately filling in for myself that no one realized Bael was still in the castle. In truth, it didn't matter that he was if he couldn't help them.

They'd been ambushed at exactly the right time, when Bael was unable to help and Scion was away from the capital. Most of the royals left in the castle had passive magic—like Gwydion's healing and Lady Raewyn's sight. Who did that leave to defend them?

"Perhaps the rest of the Everlasts were the target," I said dully. "Or the castle itself."

I was surprised to find I cared. Perhaps not for all of them, but I did not precisely wish to see Lord Gwydion killed, nor Lady

Thalia or Lady Aine. Princess Elfwyn was only nine years old… surely no one would storm the castle to murder a child, fairy or not.

I shook my head, shocked at the direction of my own thoughts.

What was I thinking? Of course the rebellion would not care that Elfwyn was a child. They would kill all the Everlasts, if given the chance, and view little Elfwyn as an easier target due to her age, not someone to be spared. Until recently, I would have agreed with that. Cheered for her death like anyone else. When had that changed?

Iola did not respond, and when I looked, she was clutching a stitch on her side, her walking slowed to barely more than a shuffle. Anxiety rose in my throat.

It was quite a large castle, and I'd already deduced that the fire likely started one floor above us, somewhere near the entrance hall or the throne room. If it had already spread all the way up to one of the towers, that was certainly alarming, but Iola and I were separated from the worst of it by several tons of obsidian and long expanses of winding corridors. We were not yet in so much danger that we needed to sprint for safety, but the air was growing quite warm, the smell wafting in from grates and cracks between bricks getting stronger the longer we delayed.

"Are you well?" I asked. "What's happened?"

"Nothing, my lady," she said between breaths. "It's been this way since…well, you know."

I recoiled. "I thought Lord Gwydion healed you."

"Well, I am still alive," she said, somewhat dispassionately.

I furrowed my brow. That didn't seem right, especially for an Everlast. Given the way the others' magic seemed to work… I slowed my walk to stay in step with Iola, even as my skin crawled and every one of my muscles screamed at me to move faster. I could have danced in place for all the pent-up energy coursing through me. "May I at least help you?"

She began to protest and gave up, slinging an arm over my shoulder, which did speed things up a bit.

My mind reeled as we made our way toward the door, with me half supporting, half dragging Iola along. "You never did discover what caused the poisoning?"

She shook her head, and I wondered if words were becoming more difficult. "I was already ill that evening." She gave a weak smile. "Sometimes I believe things just happen as they are meant to, and perhaps I was not meant to survive."

"Iola, that's not—" Shock made the words die in my throat. "By the Source!"

She looked at me, alarmed, then to the door ahead of us, seeming to fear that I'd seen something blocking our path. "What is it?"

I did not stop walking, though I wanted to sink to the floor. "You were ill. Iola, oh my gods—" My voice broke. "This is my fault. I'm so, *so* sorry."

There was no way to say you were sorry for nearly killing someone. For making their life a daily hell. What could I possibly do now?

Her eyes widened in mingled alarm and confusion. "I don't understand. You didn't poison me?"

"I told you to drink moondust tea. I didn't know it was poisonous."

It had just come together in my mind, spurred on by seeing Iola. Scion had mentioned it the other day, when we were discussing how that horrible lust drug was made. Moondust trees were poisonous.

I reeled, waves of shock crashing over me.

Not only had I poisoned my friend by accident, but this meant that certainly Rosey had lied about her tea. Why, though? Why would she need to visit those trees so often? It certainly couldn't have been just to hide the journals for me to find.

Unless it wasn't. Unless the journals were left for someone else and never meant for me at all.

By the Source!

Iola made a noise of surprise that brought me back to myself.

"How can I ever make this up to you?"

Her expression carried more shock than anger, and finally, it broke into an incredulous laugh that turned into a cough. "Is it crazy to say I'm a bit relieved?"

"Yes!" I almost yelled.

"I was afraid there was some murderous plot at work, but a mistake at least puts that to rest. I do not want you to be more unsafe in the castle than you already are."

"Don't think about me," I snapped, almost angry—not with her so much as myself. "I nearly killed you."

"You also saved me, or so I hear."

"Yes, and look how well that turned out for both of us." I scowled. "I do wonder if perhaps there is more to Prince Gwydion than the background player he pretends to be. Do you not find it odd that the house of Everlast would produce a mere healer, and he would not even succeed at that?"

Iola furrowed her brow. "I'm not sure, my lady. I don't know much about the royal powers."

I considered that and was surprised to realize that at this point, I did—know a lot about their magic, that was. When placed beside his parents and his siblings, Gwydion did not fit.

If I made it out of this damned castle alive, I would add Gwydion to my ever-lengthening list of people to investigate.

His name could go right below that of my sister, who, the more I learned, was starting to seem less and less like an innocent victim.

Scion was correct: could we truly ever know anyone?

43
LONNIE
THE OBSIDIAN PALACE, THE CITY OF EVERLAST

Iola and I made it into the empty kitchens and through the door that led to the vast gardens that wrapped around the side of the castle. The sounds of distant shouting and roaring flames only confirmed my thought that the attack was centralized to the front and middle of the castle, where the throne room stood.

I extricated myself from under Iola's arm and stepped back. Guilt still racked me, and I wished desperately that I could go with her.

"Where will you go?" I asked.

"Go?"

We stared at each other awkwardly, and I realized that maybe not all servants had the same experience that I had. Maybe she would not have taken this opportunity to run, as I undoubtedly would have in her place—as Enid had, without a second thought. Maybe things were different in Overcast, or Thalia was a pleasant mistress.

"Will you not leave?" I asked finally, not wanting to waste much more time than I already had.

"And go where?" she asked. "I don't have anywhere to go."

I shook my head. That was a familiar feeling. I wished there was something I could do for her…anything.

I shrugged out of my expensive new coat and began to yank off the boots as well. I debated giving her my blouse too, but I could not stomach running around the castle in merely my underthings.

"Here." I shoved the coat into her outstretched arms. "Trade boots with me. These are new—they'll last you much longer. It's not much, but it should help."

I supposed I really did own nothing more than the clothes on my back, and even those I was now giving away. It was worth it, though, especially as I could never make up for my mistake that had stolen her health.

Her eyes widened. "I can't."

"You can. There's no way to know if the castle will even still stand tomorrow. Don't wait around to serve masters who may not return."

And would not wait for you, I added silently.

I thanked the Source that I hadn't worn the high-heeled boots today and that Iola didn't put up much more of an argument about switching shoes. Hers were too small on me, but it didn't matter. If she didn't want to wear mine, she could sell them and buy others, and I was used to uncomfortable clothing.

"I'll give them back when I see you again," she insisted.

I wanted to say that, of course, I would be along shortly. That of course I would see her again, but it was entirely too close to a lie, and for some reason, I didn't want to give her the false hope in case I did not come back. So I merely said, "I hope so. Now, go before this corridor crumbles on both of us."

That was not likely—not yet, at least, but still she smiled and turned away.

I turned as well, dashing back toward the door to the greater castle beyond.

"Lonnie!" Iola screamed after me, her ruined voice cracking at the end.

I looked back, slowing but not stopping to speak to her. "What is it?"

"You'll have to go to Nevermore for the next hunt. I could meet you, perhaps…"

"No," I said. "Do not limit yourself like that."

She wasn't listening. "Then I'll wait for you. Only tell me where…I don't have any family. I don't have anywhere else to go."

Her expression was desperate, pleading, and I died a small death hearing her speak the word that I so often thought to myself. No family. No friends. Nowhere to go unless she was kept here as a servant.

I didn't have anyone either—not really—not anyone except the Everlasts, and most of the time, I was barely convinced that I had them.

"Don't go to Nevermore." I inhaled sharply through my nose. I might not come back for her, but I could at least try. "I won't be traveling there, no matter what happens today."

"What about the hunts?"

"Fuck the hunts," I said and was surprised to hear I meant it. "There is nothing about allowing oneself to be beaten and stalked like prey that proves worthiness to rule."

Iola laughed nervously. "Where, then?"

"Go wait in the stables." I laughed bitterly. "I have a feeling that the battle will be kept away from there. If I don't come back for you by tomorrow, make your way to Aftermath."

"Aftermath?" she said, alarmed. "Isn't there nothing left of that city?"

I smiled grimly. "I would not say *nothing*."

44
LONNIE
THE OBSIDIAN PALACE, THE CITY OF EVERLAST

As soon as I stepped out into the corridor beyond the kitchens, my breath caught in my throat, my lungs screaming for air. It was so much warmer, more stifling, than it was only a door away.

I coughed and covered my mouth, blinking soot from my streaming eyes. The smoke filling the air blinded me, choking me, urging me to turn back.

There was a stairwell to the upper floors on the right, which seemed to be the source of all the smoke. That was a small relief.

The fire was spreading, evidently faster than I'd realized, and while this corridor might not yet be engulfed, I did not have long to find Bael before even shadow walking would not save us.

I turned left, running down the corridor, praying that, as in my dream, breathing would become easier the closer I got to Bael's room.

If I'd had any hope in the world that I could shadow walk again without wasting precious moments exhausting myself trying to work out how I'd managed it, I might have attempted that, but it was hard enough to walk normally, let alone through spinning darkness.

Thankfully, Bael's room wasn't far—something I hadn't known in all the years I'd spent haunting these halls and hardly would have expected, given his status. Now, it was the only thing that made me put one foot in front of the other.

It's not much further, I chanted to myself. *Only another few paces.*

I put out a hand and felt for the sharp corner of the corridor and turned, thundering down a second hallway.

We would not die here.

Bael's door swam into view far, far ahead of me, and my lungs strained harder to reach it. *Just a bit further. Only a few more steps.*

My foot caught against something lying across the floor, and I stumbled, lurching forward with enough force to send me sprawling. The jolt was so sudden it felt as if I'd swallowed my tongue. As if my breath had been knocked out of me. I remained on my knees for a quick moment, the warmth of the stone floor unnatural against my skin as I fought to regain my composure. I supposed I should be grateful that I hadn't broken my nose.

After several long seconds, I looked back, scowling at whatever had caused me to fall.

My heart dropped.

I should have been accustomed to the sight of corpses by now; it wasn't the first time I'd run across one, and the gods knew it wouldn't be the last.

In the first hunt, there had been all those who had fallen to their peril over the cliff. More recently, there were the bloated, half-eaten victims of my serpent friend and the servants who had not escaped the tremors caused by the coming of the afflicted. There was the guard in the dungeon, the fate of the incubus, the unavoidable reality of death that hung over the city at every moment.

Yet nothing, not even the tragedy of my sister's passing, could have prepared me for the sight before me. It was almost too much.

Some things should remain unseen.

They'd been devoured, I realized once my mind had grasped the full extent of the terror. Flesh hung from exposed skeletons; scraps of skin still clung to bones that seemed to have been gnawed on. Still more bones lay scattered among an enormous pool of blood. Whoever this once was had been torn to pieces. *Mauled.*

The gruesome sight made me recoil in horror, retching.

This was not the work of the fire, nor surely of any rebel soldiers…but I couldn't think of anything…couldn't imagine…

It was only then that I realized the door to Bael's room stood open. The bodies that had stolen my attention lay on the threshold, propping the door wide, the darkness within making it impossible to see. Not that it mattered, but in my dream, the door stood closed before I'd reached it, venturing into unknown darkness.

A deafening roar, like some enormous beast, shattered the silence of the hall.

The walls quivered, the shadows of the corridor seeming to flicker. Instinctively, I scrambled to my feet, ignoring the pain in my knees, the strain in my lungs, and took a few stumbling steps back, away from the open door.

The ground seemed to shake in a small tremor, and I trembled, awed, as my eyes met a huge pair of glowing, catlike, golden eyes only seconds before an enormous shape leapt out of the darkness and fixed its gaze more firmly on me.

My mouth fell open, my knees beginning to tremble uncontrollably.

The creature that stared at me looked a bit like an enormous mountain lion—if that lion had been sculpted from memory by an artist who had only their childhood nightmares as reference.

The face and body were unmistakably feline and covered in a familiar reddish-gold fur. The paws, however, were black, as if dipped in shadow, with long, almost talon-like claws that I'd guess were longer than my entire hand. The beast overall was larger than any lion I'd ever seen in the wild mountains near the Source—perhaps three times the size of a wolf and far more muscular. The teeth were too sharp, the eyes too intelligent, almost humorous. Mocking.

Smoke rose and swirled near the floor as the enormous feline-looking beast prowled toward me on soft paws, too quiet to match its gigantic size. I blinked a few times and realized the smoke had nothing to do with the disaster going on in the castle.

My heart started to pound harder, faster, out of control. My fear took over, my eyes darting to the mauled bodies on the ground. I let out a tiny whimper.

Run, a voice in the back of my mind whispered. *Run, run!*

But just as quickly, another thought answered the first, as if I was arguing with myself:

The mountain lions of Aftermath never gave up their prey. They hunted them for days on end, stalking, watching, waiting, until finally they struck. You should never run from cats, as they viewed it as a game and would turn the hunt into your ultimate torture.

You should never run from monsters.

I gasped and was unable to keep the tremble out of my voice as I whispered, "Bael?"

45
LONNIE
THE OBSIDIAN PALACE, THE CITY OF EVERLAST

The monster had no reaction.

He didn't blink, didn't even twitch, to show any sort of recognition at the sound of my voice, at his name.

"Bael?" I asked again, my voice trembling.

I was sure I was right. Somehow, this creature was Bael. Or perhaps Bael was the creature?

Even without the cage, now half-visible in the room across from me, the eyes were too much of a giveaway, even magnified to the size of my fist. They looked identical to the gaze I'd come to know on the prince—yellow and too intense, almost predatory. I didn't have to understand exactly what was happening to know that this…transformation…was what caused Bael's disappearances. The only question was, did he recognize me?

My heart thumped in my chest as the enormous cat sauntered toward me, stalking me like I was about to become dessert. Could it even be called a cat anymore when it likely weighed the same as a small horse? Lion, then. Beast. *Monster.*

The beast moved closer, forcing me to walk backward down the hall. It—he—didn't seem bothered by the thickening air nor by the heat that grew stronger the further we moved, but sweat broke out on my brow. I sucked in shallow breaths, coughing, my entire body screaming in terror. What would I do if and when he attacked?

My heart raced with terror, and I felt my muscles tighten. I attempted to scream, but my throat was tight, and only a whimper escaped. "Bael!" I tried again, a scratchy, desperate cry. "Can you understand me?"

The creature's gaze burned into mine, and it let out another ferocious growl. Its eyes were pools of liquid fire, and its maw was filled with rows of razor-sharp teeth that seemed to glisten in the dim light.

The low growl rumbled down the hallway, reverberating off the walls. Then, finally, the beast launched itself into a full sprint. It ran headlong toward me, leaping into the air.

I finally managed to let out a true scream of terror, knowing it was the last sound I'd ever make.

The gigantic cat stretched its body long, flying over my head, shadows trailing in its wake. It landed too quietly on the floor behind me, and I whipped my head around, heart pounding out of control.

A very human scream joined the chaos of the hallway. My mind numb with shock, it took a beat to understand what I was seeing. To gather that a tall, cloaked figure now lay pinned to the ground under paws nearly as large as a grown man's chest. The figure let out another long scream, and I caught a glimpse of his face before Bael swiped at it with one enormous claw.

He was a stranger—a rebel, I supposed—and carrying a large sword that now clattered uselessly to the ground beside him. He let out a final bloodcurdling yell that sent shivers down my spine, then gurgled, going quiet.

Bael's powerful jaws snapped shut around the man's throat, tearing through skin and sinew. A sickening crunch reverberated around the hall. I watched in horror, my stomach turning as blood splashed against the stone and the coppery smell filled my nostrils.

I was wrong to think that meant it was over.

For several more long minutes, as the heat of the hall only worsened and the air grew thicker, I kept wondering when it might end. It didn't.

I backed away, my stomach churning in revulsion. I hadn't realized a single body held so much blood. There were always more bones to crunch, more blood, more ways to utterly destroy the rebel who had only thought to raise his sword behind my back.

Sweat streamed down my face, having nothing to do with the exertion, and I wiped it away, coughing. The beast that was Bael finally turned to look at me, perhaps startled by the sound. There was crimson coating its fur, skin caught in its long claws. It stared at me again, with a slightly more humanlike expression on its animal face.

I only had the slightest second to wonder how I was going to force him to leave with me before, with a cracking of joints, his body shifted, morphing before my eyes back into the prince.

Shit.

I realized I hadn't been entirely convinced until I saw the transformation that it was Bael I was looking at—not really. Now, there was no doubt, and I still couldn't wrap my mind around it.

I took an instinctive step back, even as Bael moved forward. He stalked toward me, just as predatory and dangerous as he had been moments before, but now in an entirely different way. "Hello, little monster."

My pulse thrummed, electricity buzzing all through me. The strange combination of fear and adrenaline turned in on itself, confusing my nerves, making horror feel like excitement. "All you have to say is 'hello'?"

"What should I say, instead?" he asked, voice smooth and sensual, as if he hadn't just devoured half a man in a single sitting. "I'm not sure if I should scold you or thank you."

"Why do either?" I breathed, each word difficult to find.

"I should complain that you would put yourself in danger this way, little monster." His lip turned up at the corner. "But I cannot recall ever having a better wake-up call than this one, so I may let it go."

I spluttered, searching for the right words.

I'd never seen Bael's fully naked body before, which I now realized had been a blessing in disguise. Every part of him was just as perfect as his too-beautiful face. He had some sort of white tattoo, almost like scars drawn into a design, on the right side of his chest, curving under his arm and out of sight onto his back. Far more noticeable, though, was how the prince was dripping in blood. It coated his skin, running over the ridges of every muscle like water and making his curls stick to his forehead. It completely banished anything about him that was angelic—too perfect—instead making him look wild and untouchable.

Now that I knew what I was missing, it would be nearly impossible to keep from murdering the entire house of Everlast through lack of willpower.

"I—" I opened my mouth but could find no words. "How could you not tell me this?"

He laughed, low and sensuous, and the sound seemed to wrap around me, hitting me everywhere all at once and making my pulse pound far too low in my belly. "How could I keep a secret from you? I don't know, little monster, perhaps the same way you do."

"This is a bit more extreme than my secret," I hissed.

Probably. Possibly. It was hard to know without laying everything bare and comparing.

Bael seemed to have the same thought because he said, "Is it? I wouldn't know."

I pushed sweaty hair out of my eyes, and my voice cracked slightly. We should leave now, yet I couldn't force my feet to go. "I still would have liked to know why I couldn't see or speak to you for *days*. I think I deserve an explanation."

"You do? How deliciously ironic." He reached me, and one bloody hand came up to cup my cheek. "Why would I owe you anything?"

I froze, knowing what he wanted to hear, what truth he wanted to wrench from me, and suddenly, I was too tired to fight it anymore.

Like Iola, I didn't want to have to continue to say I had no one and belonged nowhere. Both my mother and my sister died alone with only the strength of their secrets to protect them, and I refused to follow them.

"Because I'm your mate."

His eyes locked with mine, and then I suddenly could not hold back any longer. The desire to feel his lips on my skin and his hands in my hair overcame me in a rush. Yet still, I wasn't sure who leaned in first when our lips met in a bruising kiss.

His strong hands grasped my waist, pulling my body against his. His fingertips left a trail of heat along my sides, leaving behind stains of vivid red on my lilac blouse. I gasped, losing myself in the moment, savoring every delicious second.

It would have been all too easy to ignore anything going on around us. To forget where we were standing or the revolting mess that used to be a person that lay all over the floor. To forget all about the fire raging upstairs, and the attack, and what had caused us to be standing in this hallway in the first place.

To let ourselves burn down with the castle, if only to prolong the moment.

It would have been easy, but we couldn't do that.

"Wait," I murmured against his mouth. "We need to leave."

He made a noise, suspiciously like an actual growl, and finally seemed to realize the state of things. The stifling air of the hallway and the identity of the male he'd just slaughtered. Eyes widening, he stepped over the bones on the floor to drag me backward into his chamber.

I shot a furtive look at the bodies in the doorway. "What happened?"

Bael looked down at them, unconcerned. "I don't know."

I thought they must be guards who'd probably come to find him when the rebels first attacked or else stray rebels like the other male. Still, I'd have preferred fact to speculation. "How can that be?"

"Do you want to stand here and discuss my memory, little monster, or can we perhaps delve into details later?"

"Fine," I agreed. "But it's only…why didn't you attack me?"

His gaze bored into mine, fierce determination combined with something else. Something stronger, harder to name. "How many times must I say it? It's impossible for me to hurt you even if I wanted to. I can't. I'd sooner tear my own heart out than yours."

My heart fluttered, and this time, I finally believed him.

46
LONNIE

THE GROUNDS OF THE OBSIDIAN PALACE

The obsidian palace typically had four towers, all rising far above the rest of the capital and over the tree line like enormous swords standing straight up on their hilts. Now, there were only two.

In the time it had taken for me to find Bael, the rebellion had well and truly infiltrated the castle. The boots I'd heard upstairs must have been the last of them because as Bael and I appeared outside by the stables and stared out at the burning castle, all we could do was gape with horror.

No one was there to see us when we shimmered into existence in the shadows between the barn and forest tree line. Scion seemed to have made a good choice in putting me in the stables to begin with, as from here, Bael and I were mostly invisible, but we could see *everything*.

Cloaked figures poured over the grass of the sloping lawn like living shadows, looking almost like afflicted. The flames had risen higher, licking up the sides of the remaining towers, eating away at the ivy and bursting out of windows and doors. Some people were still visible on the walls, either looking for a way out or making some vain attempt at defense.

For the first time, I realized just how many rebels were in the castle. How many servants and courtiers must have fled already or were lying dead somewhere inside. How little the kitchen corridor was really affected by the disaster in the upper floors and what hell it must be in the two remaining towers—if anyone was still alive to see it.

"You're alive!" Iola threw her arms around me the moment that Bael and I stepped into the stables, only to grimace and step back. "And bloody…are you quite alright?"

"Barely," I muttered. "Has his lordship returned?"

Iola looked at Bael with wide eyes, which I supposed was reasonable, given that he was still covered in blood and looked a bit like some wild god risen from the depths of the woods. She shook herself slightly and turned back to me. "Who?"

I felt my chest squeeze slightly, even as I continued to wrestle with my anger. "Prince Scion. Is he back?"

She shook her head. "Should he be?"

My pulse sped up, and I turned to Bael, who was watching me with an odd combination of worry and interest. He reached out and ran a thumb over the bite mark on my neck. "Seems like I've missed all the fun, little monster."

I shivered when his thumb grazed my skin. "I would not quite say that?"

"What would you say, then?"

I bit my lip. I didn't know, but surely he couldn't want an explanation. Not now? "Never mind that now. I expected to return to find your cousin irate that I'd managed to escape. He should have been back long before me."

Unless he wasn't planning on coming back. Unless he was held up. Unless…

"Escape?" Bael looked entirely too amused for the seriousness of the moment. "Oh, little monster. You've been withholding such entertaining secrets. I'm hurt, frankly, and possibly a bit proud."

"Do not patronize me," I snapped.

Bael frowned, dropping his tone to something a bit more serious. "Scion is nearly invincible. He's hardly going to be brought down by a few rebels."

"That's more or less what he said about you, yet if I hadn't arrived, where would you be now?"

Bael's frown deepened.

I could not believe I had never seen it before now, but the Everlasts had an obvious weakness. One which Thalia had alluded to and, no doubt, Ambrose Dullahan, being one of them, would know about. "You all think you are all powerful, but you are not. You rely far too heavily on magic and the strongest among you. This attack was made possible because no one was able to defend the castle without you or Scion. If the rebellion knew about that, who is to say they don't know more and don't have other plans."

I wanted to mention the dealings with Gancanagh's Dust and the possible ties between the rebellion and Underneath, but as there was no clear connection, it was too long of a story to waste time on.

"You win, little monster," Bael said, even as one of his eyes rolled up into his head, spinning as though he were searching for something out of reach. "I'll go get him. Where—fuck!"

"What?" I gasped, fear pounding through me.

Bael's expression had gone hard, and a sudden cold seemed to fall over him, all traces of a smile vanishing. Anger radiated off him in waves, and he practically shook as he replied, "You're right. I need to go up to the tower."

Which one? I wanted to ask. I hadn't thought to look if any of the others had caught fire, though I assumed we'd see soon enough.

"Take me with you," I demanded, tilting my chin up defiantly to meet his gaze. "I will not be dropped on the lawn to watch or some other absurd and insulting thing."

"I can't risk your safety, little monster."

"Do you realize how absurd this is? I will only follow you."

"Don't." He reached for me and gripped the back of my hair, pulling me in so our foreheads touched, our lips only a hair's width apart. His eyes flashed with anger—possession. "You are still far too breakable."

"So you are telling me I have to wait here," my voice cracked. "No. I won't."

"No, I'm telling you to run." He looked behind me to Iola. "Ready two horses. You're leaving. Now."

47
LONNIE
THE OBSIDIAN PALACE GROUNDS

For the second time, I watched a prince of Everlast disappear and screamed with frustration.

The horses stomped nervously, and Iola jumped. "Are you alright?"

"No," I snapped. "I will be back shortly."

"No!" she said, nearly as loudly as I'd screamed. "You heard Lord Bael. You can't."

Cold…something licked up my fingers, that same feeling I'd had earlier in the barn. Not the same as the flames, but no less angry. "I am tired of being left behind."

I clenched my jaw—furious, afraid, so many other things I couldn't name. I wasn't sure what I even intended to do now or where I needed to go. Before, I'd had a clear plan, but now, I simply could not stand by and do nothing.

"Wait here," I told Iola.

I didn't wait for a response. This time, I didn't shadow walk, instead striding out of the doors and onto the dark lawn.

The burning castle was the only thing illuminating the darkening sky. Night had truly fallen now, and embers flew into the air like will-o-whisps or twinkling cinder-stars. I might have been beautiful if it were not so horrifying. If it did not remind me so very much of the flames in Aftermath, the fires in the pits of the Source, and the flames that flickered inside me, begging to be set free.

With no clear idea of what I intended to do, I took off running toward the castle. My feet pounded a violent, familiar rhythm against the well-worn path, and for a moment, it was only me in the darkness, the sound of the roaring fire and the beating of my heart.

I slammed into something hard and unexpected and bounced off.

Light danced behind my eyes, and my breath left me in a woosh as my spine slammed into the hard ground. My lungs spasmed, and I gasped, struggling to breathe. Nothing hurt, aside from my lungs as they worked to even out my breathing, but the shock of the impact had been all too overwhelming.

My eyes shot open, and I blinked up at the shadow of a stranger looming over me. My blood ran cold as I realized that I'd just run headlong into a trap.

"Dullahan," I breathed.

It was and wasn't a question, and the moment I spoke, I knew for a fact that I was telling the truth. My heart raced with mingled fear and something like excitement. I'd been looking for Ambrose Dullahan for months now, for so many reasons I would have to start a list of all the things I needed to ask him.

The male stepped toward me, the same dark cloak and stolen mask as I'd come to recognize making him look almost unreal in the hazy air. He cocked his head before reaching up to push the mask off his face. "Since we are being direct, what name are you going by now, Elowyn?"

48
LONNIE
THE OBSIDIAN PALACE GROUNDS

My mind stuttered to a halt, and it was a moment before I could speak.

Ambrose Dullahan looked every bit the Fae royal, with an arrogantly handsome face, high cheekbones, and straight jaw. His complexion was fair, while his eyes were so dark and fathomless that the dark sky looked gray in comparison. His hair was the same moonlit silver of his brother's eyes and shaved on one side to reveal a long scar that ran the length of his skull.

While he was not quite as angelically beautiful as Bael or as intensely seductive as Scion, there was something in the way he carried himself that radiated power.

He had the sort of power that made soldiers march and kings kneel.

The power that started rebellions.

The power that inspired women to run into battle with his name on their lips.

I scrambled to my feet as words returned to me. "How the fuck do you know my name?"

He stepped forward, and my knees shook, wanting to buckle all over again. "I always thought you would grow up to be interesting. I wish you'd managed to be polite as well, but alas, polite and interesting so often contradict each other."

"I will be far more impolite if you don't answer my question."

"You know my name. Is it not only fair?"

I bared my teeth at him. If I had not already known that this male was truly a prince of Elsewhere, that answer alone would have made me believe it. He spoke in a way that was opaque at best, answering nothing, nearly threatening, while staring at me in a way that left me unsure if he meant to kill me or fuck me right here on the lawn while the castle burned behind us.

I closed my eyes, willing myself not to panic. *It may not matter,* I reminded myself. If he didn't have the power to control me… There was some faint glimmer, I supposed. A tiny hope that even knowing my name, he could not use it.

I didn't believe that one bit, but I was happy to tell myself the lie.

"Well?" I asked, willing my voice to sound even. "You wanted to see me, and after this display, I hope there is a good reason."

The rebel leader laughed, and the sound seemed to wrap around me. "I am very pleased to finally see you. As for the reason, I suppose that depends what you mean by 'good.'"

Another nonanswer. An Everlast answer, which we hardly had time for. "I've played far and away enough fairy games this year. If you do not intend to speak plainly, say nothing at all."

"I'd hoped to have this conversation under more pleasant circumstances."

"Then perhaps you should not have attacked the castle."

"Do you care? After how we met, I would have thought you'd hold no love for my family."

He'd fit so much into so few words—the fact that he'd been in the dungeon with me, his acknowledgment of his family, his opinions on my feelings. "Do not pretend you know me. And of course I care—you are burning the home of hundreds, not only your half dozen family members. You're murdering people."

He cocked his head at me. "Some deaths are necessary or even justified, don't you think?"

"I—" My mind finally wrapped around what he was saying. "Did you kill your family?"

My heart beat in my ears, too loud, too fast. *Which ones? When?*

I could do without, perhaps, Lysander or Raewyn. He was more than welcome to take Mordant right along with them, though he was not technically family, but Scion? Bael? I'd strangle him with my bare hands.

That, in itself, was an alarming realization.

Ambrose pressed his lips together, watching me intently, as if he knew exactly what was running through my mind. "I have killed some of them, yes. So have you. What does that say about us, do you think?"

I wanted to scream. "Which ones?"

Again, he sidestepped my question, seeming almost to take pleasure in it. "Would you believe that my mother was pleased to see me? She wanted to leave. I suppose being silent in this castle for so long makes my life look like a pleasant alternative."

I could feel my hands shaking, tingling. Part of me feared the possibility of the afflicted, and another part could not, would not, find the will to care. "And the others?"

"That's up to you, I believe. No one will be shadow walking out of the tower as injured as they are, and I do not believe even Bael can take five others with him at once...if he manages to fight his way through every rebel in the corridor to reach them, that is."

I quickly assessed. Five? That was probably Gwydion, Thalia, and Aine...who else, I wasn't sure.

I made a noise I hardly recognized—nearly animalistic—and took in a sharp breath through my nose. Clenching my fists at my sides, I tried desperately to hold in my rage. There was no time for this, and he had to know that. Or else, he was hoping to stall me so long that the fire engulfed the hall, turning my nightmare into a reality.

Even now, Scion might be looking for the crown to no avail. Bael might have run out of power. They might be fighting off waves of rebels while the fire raged around them.

"Either tell me what you want or attack now. We do not have time for pleasantries or games."

His expression twisted into annoyance for the first time. "I told you. I wish to offer you a bargain."

Told me in my dream, he must mean. So, he knew. How odd.

My eyes flashed. "And I told you, I would rather die."

"I'm afraid I can't accept that, Elowyn," he said, looking almost apologetic. "You must know by now that a bargain is little more than manners. When the Fae see something they want, they take it. Bargains are an empty courtesy. Like knocking on the door before you invade a home to rob it."

The way he kept using my name was starting to sound intentional. Like a threat. Like if I didn't agree, I might no longer get a choice.

I frowned. He had a point, of course. "Then why ask at all?"

"It's polite."

I set my jaw. "What are you looking to steal, then? Is this only about the crown?"

He leaned in, and his cloak gaped open, and two things caught my eye—likely both were intentional.

First, he had a sword in his belt. I was no expert in weaponry, but from what little I could see of the blade sticking out of its sheath, even I could tell that it was no amateur bit of steel but a silver, Source-forged blade covered in runes, worth more than the homes of even the wealthiest Fae families in the capital. That was a sword for killing Fae.

Second, he had the obsidian crown.

My eyes narrowed on it. It looked so much smaller tied to his belt just above the sword than it felt on my head. I remembered what Scion had said about the mere act of owning it—possessing it—and hoped that was only superstitious nonsense.

Ambrose looked down at the obsidian crown. "In a sense, yes, it is about that, but no…not entirely. This is part of the greater plan, and as you can see, I already have it."

I furrowed my brow, confused. "If I doubted before that you are related to this family, I would know it for certain now."

He barked a laugh, which seemed out of place, his ominous words still hanging in the air. "And why is that."

"All of you have a way of saying so much and yet nothing at all."

He tipped his head toward me as if in agreement. "Hear this, then: your family was tied to mine long before you ever came to this castle in more ways than you can probably imagine. There were more threads pulling not only you but your entire bloodline here than you could possibly realize. But I see them, as I was there."

My heartbeat sped up. Did he know, then? Was this the conversation—the answers that I'd been searching for, both consciously and unconsciously—for months? Longer, really. My entire life.

"Tell me," I demanded.

I couldn't keep the longing from my face, and Dullahan—Ambrose, that was—smirked at me. Like he knew he'd hit his target.

"I was sent by my grandmother some thirty years ago now to search for the person who might end our curse. The curse of Queen Aisling plagued the Everlast bloodline for generations, but the catalyst that forced Queen Celia's hand to truly search for a cure began some thirty years ago or so."

I bit the inside of my cheek, remembering what Scion had said. Ambrose left the family without warning just over thirty years ago, prior to the eruption at the Source. He reappeared in the northern city of Nightshade, but it was not for several years that the fall of Nightshade caused Ambrose to join and ultimately lead the rebel army against his own family. "But what happened thirty years ago?"

"Have you ever spoken at length with Raewyn?"

I coughed, surprised. "No. Of course not."

I wanted to add that it was all too strange to me that I was speaking at length to *him*. Sometimes, I still found it difficult to speak to Bael—I was hardly about to walk up to his mother, the last remaining child of Queen Celia, and strike up a conversation. Whenever I'd been in the same room with her, she'd seemed to view me as little more than a barnyard animal.

"Raewyn has three children, but only one was born of her true mate. Some thirty years ago, we realized the danger that would come to the family if Raewyn's willpower were to be tested and went to search for a cure in the form of a worthy head for the crown."

I gaped. "Bael's parents are true mates?" I clarified.

He nodded. "And it was that near catastrophe, the almost union of Raewyn and Gancanagh, that set so much else in motion."

I jerked back. That was a familiar name. Did Bael know? He must—that would be far too much of a secret to keep from him if others in the family were aware. "But what does that have to do with me? I was not to be born for another decade, on the day that the Source erupted."

The male smiled at me, taking a step closer. "Not so fast, Elowyn. You must also know you do not get secrets without giving something in return."

"Have I not already given something? Has the city not paid whatever price you could possibly want? You are destroying the castle, killing people—your rebels are ransacking everything as we speak."

"Do you consider this castle yours to give? Interesting, but no, that's not sufficient." He grinned. "I will tell you anything you like if you simply come with me."

I laughed, and it came out high and musical, a bit too Fae for my liking. "I do not believe there is any price you could pay that would make me want to do that."

He shrugged. "Your sister joined me quite willingly."

I went still. Every part of me seemed to freeze, like those words had put a stopper on my anger, reminding me of every other unpleasant feeling—grief, loneliness, terror. I forgot to be angry and shook, my mind reeling back to images I wished never to relive yet I could not banish entirely. "And it is because of you that she died." My voice quavered. "It's your fault that I no longer have any family."

He fixed me with an impassive stare. "That is…not entirely true."

Moments stretched. Seconds. Minutes—I was not sure. A humming began in the back of my mind, a buzzing, rising ever louder, like a swarm of angry moths. "Why?"

I could have been asking anything. Why did Rosey join him? Why did he want me to go with him? Why did he think this attack was justified? "Why" to so many other things. So, I was not sure which question he was answering when he said:

"Because complacency breeds the worst in all of us, and my family have become used to their misery. They have forgotten that it can always be worse, and it's only through great suffering that they'll be compelled to end the curse on this country.

"And because I've spent over thirty years searching for a worthy successor, and I've come to believe that there isn't one. There is no one person born worthy. The new heir will be created, forged of Source fire like any other weapon, and I will be the villain who burns cities to the ground until I can pull a single worthy hero from the ashes."

49
BAEL

THE OBSIDIAN PALACE, THE CITY OF EVERLAST

If I was going to die, this was how I wanted to do it: in the middle of a battle with the delicious scent of blood and death in the air.

I stood in the entrance hall, the flames leaping out of the open throne-room doors barely registering as wave upon wave of rebel soldiers came toward me. Just like during the hunt, cloaked figures appeared out of thin air, their black hoods blending together as they moved. The only things visible were the gleam from their silver swords and a few glimpses of faces.

The noise was deafening, the chaos overwhelming.

It was intoxicating.

I wanted to laugh as another rebel fell to dust, and I barely made the effort to bite it back. I had hidden that part of myself for so long, and now it was leaking out in bursts.

Granted, of all the times for violence, this might be the best one —when the castle burned around me, and the only souls there to witness it were the rebels who would soon fall at my feet.

I fought my way across the entrance hall and down the stairs with little effort. Though I would have liked to stay longer—play longer—this castle was coming down, and my family may go with it if I didn't reach them soon.

I blinked several times and sucked the mortality from another rebel, only to turn and simply snap the neck of a second. *Exhilarating.* The monster in my mind was currently satisfied. Sleeping. Yet, I knew he would not remain so for long.

I knew it had been days since my last memory. It was always that way, yet I only had strange, hazy flashes of everything that might have happened since the afflicted attacked in Inbetwixt. I could have sworn that my little monster never left. That she'd been there in the cage beside me right up until the moment when I awoke to find her there.

Her scent differed from before. Stronger, and it had nothing to do with Scion biting her, though I'd been more than aware of that the moment I smelled her. She'd gotten stronger—no longer quite so breakable and all the more enticing for it.

If not for the fire, I wouldn't have been able to keep myself from taking her right there. Completing the bond while I was still not entirely in my right mind. In a way, I was almost glad that my home was burning, if only because now we might live. Another part of me wished I'd ignored it and claimed her anyway, damn the consequences.

I dashed up a flight of stairs and hit a wall of flames. No matter—I only reappeared several floors above.

The higher I went, there were fewer rebels to catch, Scion clearly having been here first. Still, I grinned as I drained two more on my way down another corridor.

Finally, reaching the top of the final standing tower, I took a brief second to catch my breath. The sound of steel made me jerk my head up again and narrow my eyes.

What the fuck?

Scion had his back pressed against the wall, eyes darting back and forth, as a group of rebels steadily advanced toward him. The only thing between him and imminent danger was the end of his long sword, which shone bright silver in the low light.

When I'd looked for him back when we stood outside the barn, he was facing a much larger group and had not yet been cornered, but it was the sword itself that had panicked me. Scion was not a good swordsman—it was almost a family joke. The soldier was the worst with a blade because he'd never had to use one. Why my cousin would pick this moment to practice swordplay when he could have cleared the entire castle faster even than me was beyond comprehension.

I darted forward to help, reaching out a hand to wither the soldiers closet to my cousin.

Surprised, Scion looked up at me, and his right side was left completely unguarded. In that split second, a rebel soldier behind him made their move. I watched in horror as the soldier's Source-forged blade caught Scion across the face.

The blade hewed diagonally into his cheek, biting deep. Blood spattered onto the wall, and I felt a sudden chill run through me.

I growled, surging forward to help, dropping more soldiers in my path, even as Scion pressed a hand to his bleeding face.

"What the fuck are you doing?" I bellowed.

He didn't even ask how I'd come to be here—either taking it for granted that I'd found my way out of the cage or forgetting altogether with everything else happening.

He shook his head, blood spraying between his fingers. His visible eye looked more angry than wounded, which gave me slight hope this was nothing more than a flesh wound. "I'm going to fucking kill Ambrose. I'll slaughter him for this."

That was an unusually specific threat. "Why wouldn't you just clear the hall?"

He extended a hand to me, and I realized the problem a split second before I saw it. A flame danced in his hand, just like the one I'd been able to make before I'd spent several days in the cage.

"I don't know what Ambrose did," Scion barked. "But he… fucked with something. I can't use any of my magic, just this fucking fire."

It was an effort not to gape at him. Laugh. Something.

My cousin was not stupid generally, but he was certainly putting in a great deal of effort to seem so. His denial was so strong he'd seemed to have entirely discounted the laws of our world—misunderstood even the most basic of principles.

My immediate assumption when we encountered my little monster in the woods over a year ago now was that she was special. She'd resisted Scion's illusion, which hardly ever meant anything other than a bond. But then she'd bitten me, and I was immediately interested in her. I'd held her back from running after the rebels as long as I could without being noticed. I thought even then that she might be mine, or perhaps both of ours.

Scion, however, had taken the same set of facts and assumed she was part of the rebellion. He'd twisted himself into knots, justifying clear signs with absurd causation, believing only the worst possible option, the strangest scenario. Perhaps he didn't want a mate? It was hard to argue with that in our family, where to find your mate was always a death sentence or further misery. Perhaps he simply didn't believe she was anything other than human. This, though, was truly absurd.

To be sharing her magic, he must have given her blood at some point. He must be able to feel her power. The same damned thing had happened to me when Lonnie was attacked on our grounds, and suddenly, there was hardly anything I could do but watch.

How, then, could he possibly still believe this had anything to do with Ambrose?

Maybe if he only had it spelled out for him.

"You fed Lonnie your blood, and I saw the bite on her neck. That's—" I broke off, seeing the expression on his face. He looked…ill. Like he was in greater pain than a moment ago when his face was slashed. "What's wrong?"

"I'm sorry," he said shortly.

My eyes widened. Scion did not apologize. Ever. I might have been pleased if only I knew what the fuck he was apologizing for. "Why?"

It was his turn to look confused. "I didn't mean to mark her like that. It was…there was Gancanagh's Dust—" He broke off and gestured toward us vaguely. "This will only confuse things further."

I laughed incredulously. "You self-loathing bastard. I didn't know it was possible to be this oblivious."

He narrowed his eyes at me, looking almost angry now. "She's your mate."

"Yes, she is," I said evenly. "And apparently, I am cursed to share her with the thickest, least self-aware male on this continent. If we were not related, I might start to question the strength of your bloodline for such blatant stupidity."

His pained expression turned quickly to anger, twisting and pulling at the edges of the gash across his cheek. "I am not the one refusing to see the truth. She's not my mate. I would know by now if she were, I'm sure of it, but I don't feel…" He waved his hand at me. "Whatever you're supposed to feel."

"Sci…" I said, running my hand through blood-encrusted hair.

I was fairly certain he simply didn't know what it felt like to find one's mate, but that would be impossible to explain. He wouldn't believe me until he was smacked in the face with it. Fuck, he'd probably kill us all by accident just to prove she wasn't his.

"Don't you see now what's meant to happen?" Scion hissed. "Sooner or later, you will realize that you cannot break this curse, and then you'll ask me to marry her to keep her safe for you, and I will because I can't say no to either of you. But no, she's not my mate. She's yours. So, until you're ready to ask me to take her from you, please keep her as far away from me as possible and try not to kill us."

Knowing we didn't have time for this if we were going to get the family out before I found Lonnie, I merely nodded at him and darted into the tower.

THE REBELS—ALL FUCKING ONE HUNDRED OF THEM—HAD CLEARLY been dispatched to guard my brother and sister, as well as Thalia and, oddly, Elfwyn.

The small group sat on the floor near the foot of Scion's four-poster bed. It was clear why none of them had shadow walked out of here. They all had burns, cuts, and other wounds all over their bodies. All except Gwydion, who looked more or less healthy except for a singe on his hair. They all seemed to be coming back into consciousness, some faster than others. I darted over, bending to peer into my sister's dazed eyes. "Are you alright?"

Aine scowled at me, which I took as a good sign. "I shall live if that's what you're asking," she said, her voice shaking slightly as she pushed to her feet. "But no, I am not fucking alright."

"What happened? Why the fuck didn't you fight back?"

She scowled at me. Aine hadn't used her powers in ten years or so as far as I knew, but to save the castle? My sister would have…I was almost sure of it.

"I couldn't. They did…something. They had this powder. At first, I thought it was an accelerant to the fire, but then, I may as well have been human for how weak I was."

Scion and I exchanged glances. I'd never heard of anything like that.

"We'll discuss it later," he said roughly. "We need to get out of here before the castle comes down around us."

I looked around, noticing but not commenting on the fact that clearly none of them had the crown. It wasn't hard to guess who had it now.

Scion's comment about the castle was more right than even he might have imagined.

We landed again on the lawn, and my cousin glanced over at me. His exhaustion was clear, having just dragged Gwydion, Elfywn, and Thalia out of the castle in addition to himself. Scion could shadow walk through almost any circumstance, but even he was struggling to recover.

Now, though, he seemed to become alert again. "Where is she?"

I didn't have to ask who he meant; his panic at not immediately seeing her was telling enough.

At the very least, I could tell in that moment that I no longer had to worry about Scion attacking Lonnie. He might not have accepted it, might not be entirely aware of it, but she owned him too.

If I knew him at all, he probably thought she was going to destroy us, but I didn't think so. We were monsters long before she arrived. Fragmented, fucked-up shells of what we were supposed to be. If morphing into something other than that was destruction, I was happy to see the *aftermath*.

"I told her she should run," I told him. "She's likely—" I didn't finish my sentence.

The ground trembled, and a roar erupted from the castle as stones flew everywhere in an explosion of fire. The tower where we'd been only moments before crumbled, falling to the earth in a billow of smoke, and the walls of what was left of the castle collapsed in on themselves.

I could only stare until, a split second later, an anguished, horrified scream tore through the night.

An all-too-familiar scream that had me running before I knew what I was doing.

50
LONNIE
THE OBSIDIAN PALACE GROUNDS

I will be the villain who burns cities to the ground until I can pull a single worthy hero from the ashes.

I let out a harsh laugh. "That sounds like exactly the kind of twisted nonsense a fairy might say."

Ambrose Dullahan raised an eyebrow and leaned toward me slightly. "Your self-loathing is highly disturbing, Elowyn."

I tensed, not liking that implication one bit.

I took two steps back. "Well, go burn down something else. No matter what you offer, I will not go with you."

His lip curled. "Not even to see your mother?"

I gaped at him, the words ringing in my ears. Too much—impossible to comprehend, let alone answer in a single moment. "What do you mean?" I said finally. "Is she alive?"

He was about to answer when behind him, all that was left of my world shattered in a single moment.

I watched in horror as the vibrant orange flames consumed the castle, inch by inch. The last tower groaned and creaked before it gradually started to collapse into a pile of smoldering rubble. The earth below shook as it tumbled from its peak, sending ripples of smoke and debris in all directions, caving in on itself until nothing remained but dust. The fire spread quickly, consuming everything in its way. Sparks from the burning embers flew high into the sky and descended like fireflies back to the ground, igniting more buildings in its wake until the entire landscape was engulfed in an inferno.

I felt my heart pounding and tears streaming down my face, my throat constricted before a deep guttural scream erupted from within me. *Primal.* It was a scream of long-suppressed pain and anguish, as I'd not let out since the day my sister died.

Ambrose Dullahan stepped forward, seemingly unconcerned by the blaze that surrounded us. I glared at him through tear-streaked eyes. "What have you done?"

He shrugged nonchalantly. "It was inevitable this would happen one way or another."

What was inevitable. The deaths? The destruction? Did that mean he got to decide when, like he seemed to have done with Rosey?

My breath caught in my throat. I forgot to care what might happen if I gave in to the constant gnawing at the back of my mind and felt my hands tremble, cold fire licking down my arms.

I quaked, pent-up power and rage melding into one, surging until it physically hurt to hold it in. Until I could not keep it inside for fear I might combust.

This time, when I opened my mouth, it was a roar that left me. A lion's roar, a roar like fire, like pain.

As I stood frozen, the ground beneath my feet began to rumble and shake violently. The trees swayed wildly, their roots ripped from the earth.

A low rumble shook the ground, followed by a loud crack. The dark chasm that appeared seemed to reach down into eternity, and flames lashed out from it, illuminating the night sky with an orange glow. Thick smoke rolled out, blanketing the area in darkness.

The familiar acrid scent of sulfur reached me, but this time, I welcomed it. Called for it.

The fog became smoke, became twisted ropes of shadow, then took shape into the riders. The afflicted. Into every twisted, ugly, pain-filled face I'd ever made or could possibly imagine.

I screamed and screamed, expecting the afflicted to be called to swallow me, but instead, only more seemed to steam from within the earth.

Gentle hands clamped around mine, and I yelped, trying to jerk away.

Through streaming eyes, I saw Bael's wickedly sharp features illuminated by the flickering flames. He reached out toward me again with both hands. "Stop that, little monster. Come back to me."

I let out a choked sob and glanced around. Behind him, Scion and, strangely, Ambrose Dullahan had made a wide circle of magic, pushing the afflicted back from the rest of the family in the center. Scion's gaze met mine for a moment across the lawn, and I was caught in the intensity of it.

Distantly, I knew that this was what my mother had been afraid of. This was what the serpent had been talking about. This was how the sky turned black. And this must have been how Aisling felt. She didn't ask the gods to open the Source to curse the king.

No, she turned the sky black herself, screaming her pain and inflicting it on the world.

I looked back up at Bael, my body now trembling with exhaustion. "I don't know how to stop."

Now that whatever this was had been unleashed, it was too much, too overwhelming, and I couldn't fit it back inside my body.

Horribly, shamefully, I wanted it to.

51
LONNIE
SOMEWHERE NEAR THE COAST

We shadow walked to one town, then another and another. By the fourth or fifth jump, I lost track of where we'd landed, my head lolling against Bael's shoulder.

I was somewhat aware that we were traveling in such an odd, jerking manner because not everyone among us could travel for long distances, and their injuries were only slowing down the process. Iola, Elfwyn, and Thalia—who was more severely hurt than Aine or Gwydion—could not shadow walk at all.

No one said a word to me after what I'd done in the wake of the fire except Bael and Iola. Even Scion seemed distant. Angry, perhaps. Though, if I didn't know better, I might say he was afraid. Certainly, the others were afraid of me.

I was afraid of me.

THE SCENT OF ROTTING FISH, RAIN, AND MOIST EARTH ASSAULTED MY senses, filling my nose and driving out anything that might have come before.

We'd landed in yet another swampy fishing village, somewhere along the coast. It was the kind of way-station town that I'd pictured before seeing Cutthroat. Dank, dilapidated, and nearly abandoned. The outskirts of the town were surrounded by a wall, though it hardly mattered as the gates were open, and no guards stood outside.

Any other time, I likely would've found the odor offensive, but now, when where we'd been was so, so much worse, I would gladly plunge my head into a barrel full of rotting fish. I'd smell this for the rest of my life if it meant never again breathing in the sulfuric smoke of Aftermath.

"May we finally stop?" I asked.

No one answered me, but almost in response, Aine said, "I am so hungry I think I may know what starvation feels like."

I pressed my lips together and caught Iola's eye over Aine's head, smiling slightly for the first time since we'd left the capital.

"Fine," Scion barked. "We'll stop here."

No one bothered us or even looked up when we walked up the muddy road and through the gate into the tiny village square. I was somewhat surprised not to draw more attention. Eight was a large number to arrive in such a small village unannounced but a terrifyingly small number to have escaped a castle that held hundreds. I supposed if anyone realized that royals stood in the street, the reaction might have been different, but glancing around, it wasn't hard to see why no one would recognize us.

Iola looked the least damaged, while Bael was by far the worst: shirtless, still covered in dried blood, and wearing an expression that warned of violence. I practically shivered to look at him—

whatever smiling, joking prince I'd known was gone, replaced entirely by the beast now dominant in his energy.

Scion walked beside him, looking hardly any better. The gash on his face appeared as if it would scar, given that it had been made by a Source-forged weapon and hadn't yet healed. Oddly enough, the wound didn't detract from his appearance and only added to his dangerous aura. The only thing that made him look less lethal was the fact he was carrying Princess Elfwyn.

As if she could read my mind, the child opened her enormous silver eyes, unblinking and eerie. The last time I'd encountered Elfwyn, she'd tried to kill me. Now, she seemed as lost and innocent as any other child who had just lost their mother.

Although, I reminded myself, *Mairead may not be dead. She had possibly left with the rebellion. What little there was left.*

Thalia and Aine walked on the far side of the group, their heads together, whispering so low I couldn't hear them. Both had burns on their hands and arms. Thalia's long, blonde hair was so burnt I suspected it would no longer brush her shoulders when she finally untangled her braid and saw what was salvageable.

My eyes flicked over everyone once more, comparing. Considering. I wondered distantly what I must look like. Not that it mattered, but had I truly been changed, or was that simply my mind lying to me as usual?

We walked down the main road—the only road, I noticed—passing a few shabby wooden houses on the right and a blacksmith on the left. A yowling screech pierced the night, and a door opened and slammed again, bringing with it the sounds of voices wafting toward us on the breeze.

"Shall we find an inn?" I asked dully.

What I really wanted to say was "Now what?" or perhaps to merely scream, but I could not find the energy. Perhaps after I'd had something to eat. Washed the gore from my skin. Slept. Anything.

"I don't know that we can," Thalia said, acknowledging me for the first time. "Being recognized could only lead to further trouble."

I glared at her, already finding myself baring my teeth, preparing for an argument, but Scion beat me to it. "Next time, I shall try to remember to land somewhere more remote," he snapped.

No one replied, and the silence was almost physically painful as we walked for another few minutes. I glanced over at Bael, hoping to communicate with my eyes that any plan would be better than none. It didn't matter.

"We need to rest," Bael said as if reading my mind. "We'll take the inn. I doubt there are enough villagers to cause a real risk."

"But—" Thalia began.

"I can bewitch all those inside," Elfwyn said, her tiny voice an octave higher than anyone else's.

"Is that wise?" I asked Bael.

He didn't grin or shrug or make any of his usual jokes, merely staring straight ahead as he answered. "She's capable of it."

I wasn't sure how to say what I meant to ask. "Yes, but should she be allowed?"

He looked over at me now, eyes flashing with pent-up aggression that I knew had nothing to do with me or the conversation we were having. "No one else has the energy to bewitch a fly, little monster. If Elfwyn can't do it, we'll just kill whoever is there. It's worth letting her try."

There, I realized, was the real answer to why we'd landed in this small village and every small village before now: fewer people meant fewer witnesses. Fewer bodies to clean up. Less blood on our stained hands.

THE VILLAGE INN WAS LITTLE MORE THAN A HOUSE, WITH A FEW extra rooms upstairs and a tiny, lightly stocked kitchen. There were seven people inside when our bedraggled group traipsed through the door. Elfwyn removed five, sending them back to their homes with a mere suggestion. The other two were now lying quietly in the wine cellar.

I was growing numb to violence. To killing. I wished I could blame that entirely on the Everlasts, but in truth, was it not I who had picked up a crown to beat in the skull of a king? Was I not the one who just unleashed a hoard of afflicted on the world?

It was something I would need to consider, but not tonight. Not when I had so much else swirling around my much-abused mind.

An hour later, we'd eaten all there was in the small kitchen and sat in the main room of the inn, in only slightly better spirits.

Though everyone was tired, filthy, and clearly needed rest, no one seemed to want to go upstairs. At least, not immediately. It was as if sleeping, bathing, doing anything would put a finality on the night that upset the Fae more even than me.

"Well, the good news is there are beds," Aine said as she stomped up the cellar stairs. "The bad news is even if the water worked, I would not set foot in that bathing room to save my immortal soul."

I raised an eyebrow. "I do not believe it is that bad. Your standards are simply too high."

A ghost of a smirk played across her lips. "Go see for yourself. If you are willing to wash here, I will pay you—" She broke off, coughing, and frowned.

I turned away as I walked up the stairs, already knowing what must have happened. She'd likely been about to offer me something she no longer owned, as whatever it was had been burned up with the flames. As soon as she'd begun the lie, the pain would have been excruciating.

As it turned out, Aine was not wrong about the bathing room. It was little more than a hole in the floor in the cellar, and though I did find a wooden tub that I suspected might have once been used for laundry, there was no other option as far as washing. By Aisling, and I'd thought the showers in the servants' quarters to be revolting. Now, I would have taken a lukewarm shower with goat milk soap any day if it meant I could get this blood off.

I returned to the main room of the tavern, grimacing. "She's right."

"Ha!" Aine said with a bravado that did not reach her eyes.

"There's got to be a stream or something around here," I said a bit desperately. "They cannot simply not bathe in this town."

"I don't know about that, little monster," Bael replied. "There was quite a smell when we arrived."

No. I refused to accept it. I could not sit in the blood and guts and ash for another moment.

"Well, I'm going to find a stream or…something."

No one moved. Finally, Bael, looking a bit bemused, said, "Fine. I'll take you."

"Don't look so disappointed," I grumbled.

"Oh, I'm not. I am simply trying to avoid another town burning to the ground."

"What—"

But my question was drowned in the sound of a slamming door, and I jumped, realizing that without my even noticing, Scion had disappeared upstairs.

52
LONNIE
THE WAYWOODS

The gods must have had quite the sense of humor because it seemed that no matter what I did, I couldn't stay out of these damned woods.

Much like how I couldn't keep from drawing attention to myself any more than I could keep from drawing breath.

We walked for what felt like quite a while before the sound of the water rushing led Bael and me through the trees to the bank of the small stream. I dragged my feet through fallen leaves, hating to admit to myself that I was scanning the area for any sign of Scion's black armor or perhaps Quill, swooping between the trees.

Why, I had no idea. He didn't say he was coming with us, yet I felt…strange…leaving the dark prince behind.

"You'll be glad of the distance soon, I'm sure," Bael said mysteriously.

"What is that supposed to mean?"

"Only that I doubt you want an audience."

I wanted to ask, "To what?" but I was fairly sure I already knew what he had in mind. So, instead, I tossed him a smirk and asked, "Like you, you mean?"

"I'm not an audience member, little monster. I'm a participant."

"You are not afraid of me, then?" I asked.

The question was mocking, but there was real vulnerability behind it, and I thought Bael must have known that because there was no humor in his voice when he replied. "Never. The only thing that scares me is the thought of you getting hurt."

I COULD FEEL YELLOW EYES ON ME FROM THE VERY SECOND THAT I stripped off my filthy clothing, leaving it in a pile on the bank, but I pretended to ignore it. Pretended that Bael's gaze didn't heat my skin, despite the chilly water, and that I was not aware of every splash and movement as he drew closer.

I waded in up to my waist, goosebumps rising on my arms, my nipples pebbling, before I finally worked up the nerve to dunk my entire body under the surface.

I gasped, coming up quickly—the water was icy, far too cold for swimming, and it felt only marginally warmer once I was entirely submerged, and I could not decide if it was preferable to linger under the water or above it.

Could there be a giant serpent beneath the water or some terrible, carnivorous leeches within the silt at the bottom? Possibly.

Probably, even, but I didn't care.

There was nothing I needed more than to be clean. Clean of the soot and ash. Of the stray cinders that had burned into my hair and stung my skin. Of the blood splattering my face and coating my hands.

I was considering wading back out again when I heard a splash behind me, and suddenly, the cold water suddenly felt far warmer, the radiating heat of Bael's skin and the pounding of my adrenaline warming me all over. I turned this time, no longer willing to play coy unless we were moving to dry land. My breath caught in my throat.

Bael moved toward me, slow, prowling. Those dangerous predatory eyes watched me hungrily, letting me know without words there would be no room for escape once this started. No going back.

He stood in front of me for a moment before dipping to submerge entirely in the water. When he came back up, pink rivulets ran down his golden skin, making his bright blonde curls turn to dark ochre spirals. I had the oddest desire to lean forward and lick one of the pink trails from his cheekbone, his neck, lower…

"I wish I could say I'd missed you these last few days, little monster, but I don't remember you not being there."

My chest squeezed slightly. "Oh. That's no matter."

"To be clear," he said, stepping closer. "Lately, I dream of little but you, so I do believe it got a bit jumbled. I could have sworn you were there."

My breath caught, my pulse racing all the faster. At least I was not alone in my dreams, then. "I wanted to come back…I asked. I tried, but—"

"It's alright." He chuckled and ran one thumb over the bite on my neck. "I daresay there will be many more occasions when Scion needs you more than I do. Not that you would not always be wanted."

A shiver traveled over me when he touched the still-tender spot on my throat. "That was an accident. There was this drug, and—"

He cut me off, pressing his lips to the same spot on my neck in a kiss that seared me to the core. "Don't overthink everything, little monster. Some things are merely instinct."

I shivered. "How can you be so calm about this?"

I wanted to say, *"How can you be so calm about this when I am losing my mind?"* but I did not.

"Truthfully, I'm not sure. I'd like to assume that's a good sign because if I try to think too hard about most anyone else touching you…" His eyes flashed dangerously, and he did not have to elaborate. The bodies on the floor of the hallway sprung, unbidden, to my mind.

"Most anyone?" I asked.

He pressed his forehead to mine. "Most. Speaking in absolutes is for mortals and demi-Fae, little monster. Who knows what might happen tomorrow."

He pressed another kiss to my neck. "If I am jealous of anything, it's that I haven't gotten a chance to give you one of these myself."

"Then do it," I said, sounding entirely unlike myself.

"Not right now. I want to wait."

"Why?"

"Because." His lip curled, and he gave me an almost devilish smirk. "It has been long enough since we shared blood that I do not believe I could use your magic anymore."

"Do not try!" I exclaimed, panicked.

He laughed. "No…I don't think I'll be trying that again for quite some time. At least not until you've mastered it."

I wanted to ask another question about that but didn't get the chance as he moved his lips to mine, kissing me first gently, then harder as I snaked my arms around his neck. I was all too aware that we were both entirely nude, and while either one of us had been before, never both at once.

He swept his tongue between my lips, owning and consuming, before reaching down to grip the backs of my thighs and lift me into the air. A waterfall poured around us as I wrapped my legs around his waist, held high above the surface of the stream.

His hard cock throbbed between us, pressing against my center, making me writhe for more friction—more pressure. He moved his mouth to cover my breast, sucking one nipple into his mouth and pulling hard enough that I felt it deep in my core.

"What are we doing?" I gasped—more rhetorical than anything else.

He let my nipple go with a grin, giving it a small lick before he moved his eyes back up to mine. "I told you, I can't make fire right now."

It took a moment for his implication to sink in, but when it did, my eyes widened. "Is that how that works?"

"I don't know, but I know there must be a way."

Understanding dawned on me—he knew there was a way because of what Ambrose told me. Bael's parents were mates, and no one died. Equally, or possibly more importantly, his father's name was Gancanagh. Like the dust.

I should have asked more about why he knew that. I knew I should have, but I couldn't bring myself to stop and ask questions. Not now.

I ground against him, twining my arms around his neck as if I could fuse myself to him. "What are you waiting for, then?"

He slammed his mouth back down on mine, kissing me hard enough to bruise. I felt his cock twitch again, hard and ready, and ground shamelessly against him as he devoured my mouth, our tongues and teeth misaligning in our frenzy to get closer.

Then, abruptly, he pulled back. His eyes were wild—almost glowing in the darkness. No trace of the male left there, no humanity—only that barely contained beast in its human skin, shaking the bars of its bone prison.

"Run," he growled at me.

"What?" I murmured, my hands still twined around his neck.

He pushed me roughly back, and I splashed against the cold water, only just managing to catch myself before I fell. A terrible, growling, roaring sound came from within him, and this time, I knew I wasn't imagining it. His eyes truly did flash with…something.

"Run."

I stumbled out of the water, splashing up on the shore, and glanced around for my clothing for the briefest moment before realizing it was a lost cause.

Bael wouldn't hurt me. I knew that. Yet, a spark of true fear shot through me. My heart raced, and my hands trembled as I sprinted over the grassy bank and toward the trees.

The darkness seemed to press in around me, and the trees loomed taller, the space between them shrinking to near-nothing.

I glanced back, sure that Bael was already behind me, and the tiniest hint of excitement skittered up my spine.

The cool air nipped at my skin, my damp hair, and felt strange and freeing on my naked body. A prickling awareness traveled over me, lingering in my core. I could never outrun him…so what would happen when I was caught?

I ran faster, faster, my breath heaving as I leapt over roots and around low-slung bushes. Branches whipped out at me, and my vision blurred.

I looked back again. He was gaining on me.

Awareness and anticipation heated my center, and then, suddenly, he was there.

A loud shriek escaped my lungs as a heavy body came crashing down on me, too warm, the scent of smoke and mulled wine surrounding me.

My breath left me in a woosh as Bael pressed me down into the ground, grinding his hips into my ass, forcing my face against the dirt.

I whimpered, the pain bringing wetness to my core.

He flipped me over onto my back, and I looked up at his hungry, jewel-bright eyes. His fingers wrapped around my throat, hard enough to cut off the moans I would no doubt have let out at the brutality of it.

I already knew before we'd even gotten started that sex alone wasn't going to be enough. This was too much, too overwhelming, and still my teeth ached, my chest felt too full. I needed more, now, something just out of reach.

My knees fell open, and he rubbed the tip of his cock against my bare center, teasing, taunting, making me writhe with the need to impale myself on him.

"Didn't I promise I would always catch you, little monster?"

I whimpered, unable to find the words to reply.

He dug his fingers hard into my hips, my ass, lifting me enough to push inside me just slightly—enough to tease and stretch. To make me whimper, needing more. The press was too thick, too much, and I moaned, rolling my hips.

I moved my hands to his hair, gripping hard—too hard, to the point that any normal man would have been screaming—and shifted my hips forward, helping to impale myself on his length.

I nearly screamed as he filled me, and for a moment, I couldn't move, the combination of pain and pleasure brutal. Dizzying.

His fingers stayed wrapped around my throat as he plunged into me, over and over, punishing, possessing. I bucked my hips, wanting him deeper, and dragged my nails down his chest, fascinated when I saw I'd drawn blood.

"Scream loud for me, little monster. Scream so loud that the forest knows you're mine."

I whimpered, then cried out, my muscles spasming, shuddering, the heat and pressure building in my belly.

He reached between us, pinching my clit roughly, too hard, and I screamed—whether from pain or ecstasy, I wasn't entirely sure.

I pressed my own arm into my mouth to keep from waking the entire Waywoods and felt the muscles of my core clench around him just as he yanked himself free, covering my stomach with his release.

I blinked a few times, dazed, and stared up at the canopy of trees overhead as I willed my knees to stop trembling. It took far too long, and finally, a long time later, I registered the sting in my arm. My eyes widened at the sight of it, and I raised the wound to show Bael.

He shrugged. "Instinct."

I shook my head. That was not what worried me. The wound on my arm was perfectly done, like an animal bite.

My teeth should not be that sharp.

53
LONNIE
THE INN, COASTAL SWAMP TOWN

I woke the following morning cocooned in Bael's arms. The inn was indeed revolting, but I'd slept better than I had in a long while.

Not wanting to wake him, I tiptoed out of bed and moved toward the door on quiet feet. It was early yet, and I doubted anyone would be awake.

I was wrong.

I opened the door and immediately walked into Scion on the landing. I jerked back, and he and I danced around each other, suddenly awkward. I flushed slightly, remembering the other night and how abruptly things seemed to have shifted back to… if not normal, then certainly not the way they'd been in Inbetwixt.

"Good morning, my lord," I muttered.

"Don't fucking call me that," he snapped.

I raised an eyebrow. I couldn't recall him ever specifically telling me not to say it before—though, to be fair, I was only doing so out of habit…or mocking. "Why not?"

We stood in the dimly lit stairwell, and though he was a few steps below me, we were about the same height, able to make eye contact for once. It was…overwhelming.

He looked like he was about to reply, but then he shook his head, retreating down a few more stairs. I deflated, entirely too disappointed.

"So, do you now hate me again?" I asked. "Should I worry about assassination attempts? Or are you afraid of me like everyone else?"

He looked back up sharply. "I'm not fucking afraid of you."

"So you hate me, then, or am I still not worth even enough for that."

He clenched his jaw, refusing to answer. That sparked my interest—he'd always answered questions like this before, even direct ones. I took a few steps closer.

"Don't," he said sharply. His expression was conflicted—haunted. Like an addict who has grown to hate their vice but still cannot turn away.

"Don't what?"

My heart was thundering, and I wasn't sure why. We were on the edge of…something, and I only wanted to know what. I took another step closer.

His hand whipped out too fast and gripped my throat, right over the spot where he'd bitten me. A spark of excitement, of arousal, shot through me, and I didn't resist when he backed me up against the wall of the stairs. "Don't look at me like that. Don't get so fucking close that I can smell you. I don't want to think about you or hear your voice. Just stay the fuck away from me."

I glanced up, meeting his too-intense gaze. "You are the one who cannot seem to stop yourself from capturing me, my lord."

His eyes met mine for half a second, hungry, filled with a violent intensity, and then he crashed his mouth down on mine. His hands tangled in my hair as he kissed me almost angrily, like it was the last thing he ever wanted to do.

I could taste the desperation on his lips, the longing and need coming from him in waves as his body pressed against mine.

I whimpered against his mouth and opened for him, biting down hard on his lip, and he moved against me. He responded in equal measure, and pain sparked on the tip of my tongue, but I reveled in it, moving my hands to grab onto his shirt, clinging for dear life.

The kiss seemed to last an eternity until abruptly, he pulled away. His breathing was uneven and ragged as mine as he pushed away from me slightly.

I panted. "I'm not sure what I did to make you so angry, but—"

"You nearly died."

I had nothing to say before he turned and fled down the stairs, disappearing out of sight.

Sometime later, I made a second attempt at descending the stairs to the main room of the inn.

Now, I was dressed, and most everyone else was awake. It was both my growling stomach and the need to move on that pulled me from my room.

Stepping off the bottom stair, I immediately made my way over to Iola. "How did you sleep?"

She looked up at me from where she was stirring something resembling porridge over the fire. "Fine. The beds here are larger than in the servants' quarters."

I smiled weakly. That they were, and yet I hadn't thought about it. Was it a good thing or a shame that I was starting to lose some of my bitterness and comparisons to my old life? "I'm sure we will find you a better bed eventually," I said. "Though, not immediately."

"Where are we going?" Iola asked. "Aftermath?"

Several others looked up at that. Thalia and Aine sat by the fire, with Gwydion slightly apart from them. Elfwyn had not yet come downstairs, which was good, I supposed, as she was too young to be considered in the discussion. Bael moved to stand behind me, while Scion did not move from his position near the wall.

"Aftermath," Aine scoffed. "Should we not make our way to Nevermore?"

"Or at the very least to Overcast," Thalia said. "Raewyn and Auberon are there, as well as my parents."

Admittedly, speaking to Raewyn was on my list of priorities, but not yet. Not immediately.

I'd told Bael about not only my trip with Scion but the conversation with Ambrose Dullahan last night, and while I didn't want to share my opinion with the others, he was in agreement that no matter what we did, we'd likely be running into the web he'd cast for us.

Cross had said it best: we couldn't outmaneuver a seer when he was always ten steps ahead, one to the side, and somehow came out behind us.

Scion and I had already learned that, chasing him all the way through Inbetwixt, when now that I thought about it, I had met him under the cover of darkness. In my dream.

So, since we could not possibly chase him down, the only thing to do was behave as we would normally—whatever passed for normal in the entirely abnormal situation.

"I am not going to Nevermore. There is no point now since Ambrose took the crown, anyway."

"He can't do that," Gwydion snapped.

"Evidently, he can," Scion said quietly, with no inflection behind it.

I looked up at him and found that he was not meeting my gaze. Or, for that matter, anyone's. The formerly haughty, too-perfect prince seemed to have been shaken, and the mark across his face was like a badge of his shifting identity.

I couldn't help but recall the dream I'd had, where there was a scar on Scion's face. It was a far different scenario than we found ourselves in now, and the cut had looked long healed.

I had never been a patient person, but I supposed all I could do now was wait and see.

"You are all welcome to do whatever you like," I said. "But I am going home to Aftermath."

The silence that followed was thick, palpable.

"Why?" Scion asked finally—not judging, merely…curious.

I sucked in a breath. "I believe there is someone I may need to see or at least look for…" I paused. "Among other things."

Other things, like get a better understanding of whatever powers I'd never been allowed to learn about. Like, see my birthplace and that of the rebellion. But most of all, if my mother still lived, I needed to find her.

My mother had lied every day of her life; including, it seemed, about her death—and I needed to know why before anything else.

Before chasing the crown, or worrying about any rebel trade with Underneath. Before worrying overlong about what magic I might have unleashed on the continent, and what that might mean in the future.

"What do you mean 'home?'" Thalia asked. "There's nothing in Aftermath. It's a barren, toxic hell."

My lips tipped up in a smile. "I would not say that."

Bael reached out and ran a finger gently over the back of my neck. I leaned back against him, falling into the warmth of his chest, then looked up, my eyes finding Scion's almost involuntarily. He glared back, as if he could not look away.

I had a feeling that, no matter where I went, both would follow. And, of course, Ambrose Dullahan would likely be right behind us.

Three Everlast princes.

One to each side, and one not too far behind—or perhaps ahead—always following, waiting, watching, in my dreams.

ALSO BY KATE KING

WILDE FAE

Lords of the Hunt

Lady of the Nightmares

The Last Heir of Elsewhere ~ March 2024

Kingdom of the Monsters ~ Summer 2024

WILDE THIEVES

The House of Doublecross ~ Coming Soon

THE GENTLEMEN

Red Handed

Thieves Honor

Damned Souls

The Gentlemen Omnibus

THE BLISSFUL OMEGAVERSE

Pack Origin

Pack Bound

Pack Bliss

The Blissful Omegaverse Omnibus

STANDALONES:

By Any Other Name: A Deliciously Dark Romeo and Juliet Retelling

COMING SOON!

Wilde Fae Book Three:
THE LAST HEIR OF ELSEWHERE

Coming March 2024

AND

Daddy Cross, Siobhan, Twist and Dodger, Vander, Arson, Phillipa Blacktongue, and more will return in…

Wilde Thieves Book One:
THE HOUSE OF DOUBLECROSS

THE WORLD OF WILDE FAE

THE WORLD OF WILDE FAE

YOUR GUIDE TO EVERYTHING YOU NEED TO REMEMBER FROM BOOK ONE!

1. Book One Recap
2. The Extended Everlast Family Tree
3. The Calendar
4. Pronunciation
5. Map of Elsewhere
6. Glossary of Characters
7. Glossary of Places
8. Glossary of Terms, Items and Creatures

BOOK ONE RECAP:

Lonnie Skyeborne is a human kitchen maid living in the capital of Everlast with her identical twin sister, Rosey. Unlike her sister, the Fae have always taken a particular interest in Lonnie, making her an outcast among the other servants. The twins are orphans, however, they still follow their mother's lessons: always lie, never make bargains, and never get noticed by the Fae.

In Elsewhere, the monarch proves their worthiness for the crown through a series of "Hunts." The monarch is "the hunted," and anyone who wishes to take the crown becomes a hunter. On hunting day, the monarch enters the arena. They must then either cross the finish line or survive until morning to keep their crown. If they die, the person who killed them becomes the new king or queen.

When the previous matriarch of the Fae royal family, the Everlasts, dies and her son Penvalle is crowned as king, the hunting season begins, however no Everlast has lost a hunt in over seven thousand years.

On hunting day, Lonnie meets two of the Fae princes, Scion and Bael. The princes realize that she is unaffected by their illusions, and Lonnie finds herself the unwilling recipient of their attention. Later, rebels attack the capital, and Rosey is revealed to be among them. Rosey is killed while trying to assassinate King Penvalle, and in a fit of rage, Lonnie kills the king before escaping into the woods. As it is a hunting day, she unwittingly becomes the mortal queen of the Fae.

Prince Scion throws Lonnie in the dungeon, believing she is also a rebel, and acts as king himself. He shows his cousins, Bael and Aine, a prophecy written by their grandmother before her death that says Scion will be the last Everlast king.

One year later, Prince Bael finds Lonnie in the dungeon and offers to help her win the next Wilde Hunt if she helps him obtain the crown (over Scion). Lonnie has no choice but to agree, and Bael heals her by giving her his blood. Bael wants to seal their bargain with a name oath, but Lonnie will not reveal her true name to him. They seal it, instead, with a kiss.

Lonnie narrowly survives her first hunting event with Bael's help and moves into the palace. Despite her title as queen, she is met with hostility from the Fae. Scion threatens her constantly, and the rest of the family refuses to acknowledge or help her.

Lonnie becomes obsessed with finding Ambrose Dullahan. She sneaks into the village to investigate what her sister was doing prior to her death and goes searching for her journals. Meanwhile, she begins having erotic dreams about Prince Bael and (occasionally) Prince Scion and grows closer to Bael while training for upcoming hunts.

Meanwhile, the rebel forces are growing stronger in the north, and Scion demands that Bael stay away from Lonnie. Bael disappears, and no one will tell Lonnie where he went.

At a ball, Lonnie dances with Prince Scion and feels a strong sexual tension between them despite the fact that he swears he intends to kill her. Lonnie's friend and servant, Iola, is mysteriously poisoned but saved by Bael's brother, Prince Gwydion, in exchange for learning Lonnie's real name.

One afternoon, Lonnie is attacked on the grounds and nearly killed by rebels. She consciously attempts to use the power she has alluded to several times, and nothing happens. Scion and Bael come to rescue her, and Scion is shocked at how worried he is for her safety. He kills all but one of the attackers and tells the survivor to spread the word across the kingdom that Lonnie belongs to the Everlasts. No one is allowed to hunt her.

Bael takes Lonnie back to the castle and once again feeds her his blood. He tells her a story about Aisling, the first queen of Elsewhere, and her three mates. The story ends with an explanation of a curse on the kingdom and the Everlast family:

"As long as the crown is not returned to a worthy wearer, the obsidian kingdom will know everlasting misery. If ever any member of the royal house should experience a moment of true happiness, all those who share Everlast blood will wither and die."

The night before the second hunt, rebels attack the castle and break into Lonnie's room. Meanwhile, Lonnie has snuck out to the village to look for Dullahan and her sister's missing journals. She runs across the royals and their court throwing an orgy in the woods. Bael sees Lonnie and tells her to leave, as she isn't safe, but ultimately gives up trying to stay away from her. Bael stops short of them having sex and tells her to leave. Prince Scion witnesses this encounter and is jealous.

Lonnie leaves, only to find her sister's journals in the palace garden. She returns to her room and finds that it has been ransacked in her absence, and there is a note from the rebel leader, Ambrose Dullahan, requesting that she meet him to speak during the second hunt.

Lonnie feels she cannot go to Bael (her closest ally) for help after their encounter at the party, so she returns to her old servants' quarters and sleeps there. Bael learns of the attack and is terrified that Lonnie has been hurt. He finds her and reveals that by feeding her his blood for the last few weeks, he has been sharing his powers with her, and that wouldn't be possible if she were entirely human. He also reveals that he believes they are fated mates, but they cannot be together because of the curse on the Everlast family. Finally, he demands to know the truth of who she is, insisting that he knows she's been lying to him as he can feel her powers through their bond.

In the Epilogue, Prince Scion ventures down to the dungeon, where he speaks to Lonnie's former cell neighbor. This is revealed to be Ambrose Dullahan, the leader of the rebels and Scion's estranged brother. Scion agrees to Let Ambrose go in exchange for his help interpreting Queen Celia's prophecy.

The Everlast Family Tree

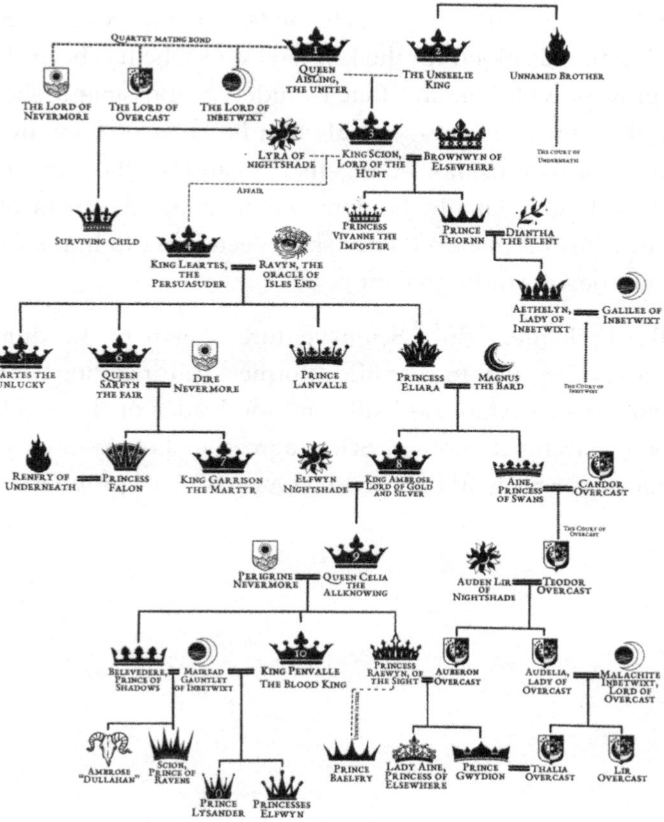

Quartet Mating Bond

1 Queen Aisling, the Uniter

2 The Unseelie King

Unnamed Brother

The Lord of Nevermore

The Lord of Overcast

The Lord of Inbetwixt

The Court of Underneath

Lyra of Nightshade

3 King Scion, Lord of the Hunt

Brownwyn of Elsewhere

Affair

Surviving Child

Princess Vivanne the Imposter

Prince Thornn

Diantha the Silent

4 King Leartes, the Persuasuder

Ravyn, the Oracle of Isles End

Aethelyn, Lady of Inbetwixt

Galilee of Inbetwixt

The Court of Inbetwixt

5 Leartes the Unlucky

6 Queen Sarfyn the Fair

Dire Nevermore

Prince Lanvalle

Princess Eliara

Magnus the Bard

Renfry of Underneath

Princess Falon

7 King Garrison the Martyr

Elfwyn Nightshade

8 King Ambrose, Lord of Gold and Silver

Aine, Princess of Swans

Candor Overcast

The Court of Overcast

Perigrine Nevermore

9 Queen Celia the Allknowing

Auden Lir of Nightshade

Teodor Overcast

Belevedere, Prince of Shadows

Mairead Gauntlet of Inbetwixt

10 King Penvalle The Blood King

Princess Raewyn, of the Sight

Auberon Overcast

Audelia, Lady of Overcast

Malachite Inbetwixt, Lord of Overcast

Ambrose "Dullahan"

Scion, Prince of Ravens

Prince Lysander

Princesses Elfwyn

Prince Baelfry

Lady Aine, Princess of Elsewhere

Prince Gwydion

Thalia Overcast

Lir Overcast

CALENDAR

- January — Danú (Da-new)
- February — Imbolc (Im-blk)
- March — Ostara (Ow-staa-ruh)
- April — Walpurgis (Wal-pur-gus)
- May — Beltane (Bel-tayn)
- June — Litha (Lee-tha)
- July —Annwn (A-noon)
- August — Lammas (la-muz)
- September — Mabon (Mah-bon)
- October — Samhain (Sow-wen)
- November — Bálor (Baw-lor)
- December — Yule (Yule)

PRONUNCIATION

- "Acacia" —Uh-kay-sha
- "Aine" — An-ya
- "Aisling" — Ash-lin
- "Ambrose" — Am-broz
- "Auberon" — O-ba-ron
- "Baelfry" or "Bael" — Bale-free or Bale
- "Beira" — Bay-ruh
- "Belvedere" — Bell-ve-dear
- "Caliban" — Cala-ban
- "Celia" — See-lee-uh
- "Ciara" — Keer-ah
- "Dullahan" — Doo-luh-han
- "Elfwyn" — Elf-win
- "Elowyn" — El-lo-win

- "Gancanagh" — Gan-can-ah
- "Gwydion" — Gwid-ee-in
- "Iola" — Eye-oh-luh
- "Kaius" — Kai-us
- "Lysander" — Lie-san-der
- "Mairead" — Muh-raid
- "Mordant" — Mor-dnt
- "Penvalle" — Pen-vail
- "Raewyn" — Ray-win
- "Rhiannon" — Ree-ann-in
- "Roisin" — Row-sheen
- "Scion" — Sigh-on
- "Siobhan" — Sh-von
- "Slúagh" — Slew-uh
- "Thalia" — Ta-lee-uh

AFTERMATH
THE SOURCE
THE WAYWOODS
FORT WARFARE
THE HEDGE
UNDERNEATH

OVERCAST
THE
UNDERTOW
NEVERMORE
ERLAST

GLOSSARY OF CHARACTERS

If you need an instant character index, here it is! This information is as of the end of *Lords of the Hunt*, so there are many spoilers in here for that book, but none for *Lady of the Nightmares*. I hope this is helpful!

PRIMARY CHARACTERS AS OF *LORDS OF THE HUNT*:

LONNIE SKYEBORNE:

At the start of *Lords of the Hunt*, Lonnie is a twenty-year-old kitchen maid, but by the end of book one, she is twenty-one and the first human queen of Elsewhere. She has no known powers and is not a particularly adept fighter, however, she is unusually good at surviving deadly circumstances and alludes several times to having powers that have not yet been revealed. Due to drinking Prince Bael's blood in *Lords of the Hunt*, she was temporarily able to use his powers.

Lonnie has curly red hair, brown eyes, and a scar on her ear where the tip appears to have been torn off. She is extremely mistrustful and fearful of Fae, who killed her mother and sister.

Her mother taught her to avoid Fae at all costs, but the Fae have always been extremely interested in her. During *Lords of the Hunt,* this is not fully understood but seems to be attributed to giving off a magical scent or aura. Bael and Scion note that she "tastes like magic." She seems to have some immunity to the Everlast's powers but insists that the immunity doesn't extend to all Fae.

Lonnie may be the fated mate of Prince Bael, but that has yet to be confirmed. He believes that she is. Lonnie has also expressed sexual attraction to Prince Scion, although she does not like him.

By the end of *Lords of the Hunt,* Lonnie has been revealed as an unreliable narrator as she lies often to protect herself from the Fae. As Bael says, Lonnie lies so often that she herself isn't sure what the truth is anymore.

SCION, THE PRINCE OF RAVENS (SIGH-ON):

"The Prince of Ravens" is the kindest name given to Prince Scion, the heir apparent of the Everlast family. He is also sometimes called the Prince of Nightmares, the Queen's Executioner, or the God of Pain.

A former soldier in the queen's army, Scion spent his adolescence and adulthood fighting rebels in Aftermath. Scion's magical ability is illusion, which he primarily uses to inflict crippling pain on opponents in combat. He also creates shadowlike visual illusions. Like a bomb, the prince can clear entire battlefields on his own, so often his presence is enough of a threat to end a conflict. Scion hates the northern rebels due to his experiences fighting them and reacts harshly to any mention of them.

Scion is described as handsome and dangerous, with black hair and magnetic silver eyes. He is second in line to the throne after Penvalle. His father was Celia's first son, Belvedere, who is dead. His mother is Mairead, who is now married to Penvalle. He often expresses that he dislikes everyone, including his family, but this is shown to be mostly untrue in practice. He views lifting the curse on his family as his responsibility and believes he is destined to be the last Everlast king. He has two half siblings through Mairead and Penvalle (Elfwyn, 9, and Lysander, 15) and one significantly older brother through Mairead and Belvedere (Ambrose).

PRINCE BAEL (PRONOUNCED "BALE" NOT "BAY-EL"):

Bael is the youngest of the adult children in the Everlast family. He is described as angelic-looking but slightly unnerving. He has blond hair, yellow catlike eyes, and unusually sharp teeth. During *Lords of the Hunt*, he tells Lonnie he was twelve during the fall of Nightshade, making him about thirty-three years old.

Bael is as powerful or possibly more powerful than Scion but is not in the running to be king because his powers are chaotic and potentially dangerous. While it is not clear by the end of book one exactly what the full extent of Bael's magical abilities are, he is seen to have some powers relating to conjuring smoke as well as making objects turn to ash. It is mentioned that he has "bad nights," and he has a cage in his bedroom.

Publicly, Bael's parents are Princess Raewyn and Lord Auberon, but it is an open secret that he has a different father than his two older siblings (Aine and Gwydion).

Bael wants Lonnie to win the Wilde Hunts and give him the crown but says that he does not personally want to be king. His best friend is Scion, and he believes Lonnie to be his mate.

LADY AINE (AN-YA):

Raewyn's daughter, Bael and Gwydion's sister. Aine is thin and willowy, very tan, with curly honey-colored hair. She is a cynic with unclear motives. She is good friends with Scion and her brother Bael. Her mother wants her to marry her cousin, Scion. She is a princess like her brothers but is never called Princess Aine. She mentions to Lonnie once that she hates her title. Her magical talent is unknown.

PRINCE AMBROSE EVERLAST/AMBROSE DULLAHAN:

"Dullahan" is a major player in the rebellion against the Everlast family and the person responsible for Rosey attempting to kill King Penvalle. It was revealed at the end of *Lords of the Hunt* that Dullahan is actually Ambrose Everlast, Scion's brother. His parents are Belvedere and Mairead, and he is a seer like his grandmother Queen Celia. Since the death of Queen Celia, Ambrose is now the strongest seer alive. Ambrose had a letter sent to Lonnie asking her to meet him during the second hunt and then was released from prison by his brother, Scion, later that same night. He is the visual opposite of his brother, possessing black eyes and silver hair.

CALIBAN:

Lonnie's former lover, Caliban, is a guard at the palace. While Caliban and Lonnie did not have any great affection for each other, he did help her stay alive in the dungeon. He is often used by Scion to do errands he does not want to take credit for (like bringing Lonnie food). The last time we saw Caliban, Scion had him stationed in the dungeon, guarding Ambrose.

PRINCESS ELFWYN (ELF-WIN):

Penvalle and Mairead's daughter. She's nine with black hair and silver eyes and has similar powers to her half brother Scion, whom she idolizes. Elfwyn tried to kill Lonnie in *Lords of the*

Hunt because she thought Scion would be proud of her. She has no personal ill will toward Lonnie.

ENID:

Lonnie's former nemesis turned sometimes ally. Enid is a maid in the kitchens who is only out for herself and her own survival. She doesn't dislike Lonnie but wouldn't lay down her life for her either.

PRINCE GWYDION (GWID-EE-IN, RHYMES WITH GIDEON):

Bael's older brother, Gwydion, is a healer with an excellent court reputation. He is large and muscular, very tan, with curly dark blond hair. He is everyone's friend, and even the servants say he's not that bad. He is betrothed to Thalia. During *Lords of the Hunt*, Gwydion showed his cunning side by forcing Lonnie into an alliance in exchange for healing her friend Iola, who had been poisoned.

IOLA:

Lonnie's former maid and friend Iola was poisoned at a ball but is recovering due to Lonnie's bargain with Gwydion.

PRINCE LYSANDER (LY-SAN-DER):

Penvalle and Mairead's son. He's fifteen, and his powers have not yet emerged. Lysander hates Lonnie for killing his father.

MAIREAD GAUNTLET (MUH-RAID):

Scion, Lysander, and Elfwyn's mother, Penvalle's wife. She has the power of illusion but doesn't use it. She has not spoken much in years. She is originally from Inbetwixt (for more on this, see the glossary entry on Inbetwixt). Mairead has technically held the position of princess (through marriage) and queen consort, but she is not treated as such.

MORDANT:

The Everlasts' stuffy and prejudicial head of staff.

KING PENVALLE (PEN-VAIL):

Celia's only living son at the time of her death, Penvalle is murdered by Lonnie early on in *Lords of the Hunt*. Prior to his death, Penvalle was cruel and barely sane and considered to be dangerous even by other Fae. His magical ability was mind control.

He was married (not mated) to his brother's former wife, Mairead, and father to Lysander and Elfwyn. Prior to his death in *Lords of the Hunt*, it was mentioned that Penvalle and Scion looked very similar.

PRINCESS RAEWYN (RAY-WIN):

Queen Celia's daughter. Raewyn married the lesser lord Auberon Overcast and has three children: Gwydion, Aine, and Bael. Raewyn's greatest ambition is for one of her children to take the throne so she can rule by proxy. She is a seer like her mother but far less powerful. She is very accurate, but her visions are random and infrequent.

ROSEY SKYEBORNE:

Lonnie's mild-mannered identical twin sister. Although Lonnie and Rosey look the same, Rosey does not attract attention from the Fae in the same way as her sister. She is much less rebellious and cynical as a result. She writes daily in journals and seems to have no secrets until she suddenly is seen to be part of the rebellion against the Everlasts. In the month or so prior to her death, Rosey was very sick and drinking tea from a tree that only bloomed at night.

THALIA OVERCAST (TA-LEE-UH):

Gwydion's fiancée. She was originally brought to the royal court as a bride for Scion (they are both illusionists) but is now betrothed to Prince Gwydion. This situation has not been explained as of the end of book one. Thalia is described as pale and unusually beautiful, even for a fairy, but always looks like she was recently crying.

Thalia is technically a cousin of the Everlasts several times over. She is a first cousin of Gwydion (her mother is his father's sister). She is also a second cousin through Queen Celia, who was her great-aunt.

MENTIONED OFF PAGE OR DEAD AS OF *LORDS OF THE HUNT*:

QUEEN AISLING THE UNITER:

The long-dead historical queen of the Fae who first united all the provinces into the country of Elsewhere. She had three mates, but her story ended tragically when her family was murdered and she was violated by the Unseelie king. She cursed the king, leading to the curse on the Everlast family.

PRINCE BELVEDERE:

Scion's father, Mairead's former partner, Penvalle's brother. He was the heir to the throne before he was killed in the war with the rebels.

QUEEN CELIA THE GREAT:

The longest-reigning Everlast queen, who has just died as of the beginning of *Lords of the Hunt*. She was a very powerful seer who left letters for some members of her family with instructions after her death. Only Scion's letter has been revealed so far.

RHIANNON SKYEBORNE:

Lonnie and Rosey's mother. Seen only in flashbacks in *Lords of the Hunt,* Rhiannon was a changeling child stolen from the human realm and brought to Elsewhere to serve the Fae. She was stolen as a child (not an infant) and lived in the North of Elsewhere (Nightshade). Eventually, she became the mother to Lonnie and Rosey. She spent her entire life training her daughters to hate the Fae, likely due to her own upbringing and early memories of being stolen.

She was taken away by Fae soldiers for punishment due to some unknown transgression and never seen again. Prince Scion was part of the group that captured Rhiannon.

A/N: In LOTH, Rhiannon is seen speaking a language that Scion does not understand. This language is English. Being a changeling, Rhiannon speaks English, while her daughters do not.

THE KING OF UNDERNEATH/UNSEELIE KING:

The monarch of the separate realm below the border.

THE KING CONSORT:

Queen Celia's late husband and father/grandfather to all the Everlasts, who died before the events of book one. Though it is not relevant to the events of *Lords of the Hunt*, his name was Peregrine, and he was from the province of Nevermore. For more on this, see the glossary entry on Nevermore.

GLOSSARY OF PLACES

ELSEWHERE:

The country where the story takes place. It is located "beyond the veil," somewhere in the North Atlantic Ocean.

EVERLAST CITY (INTERCHANGABLY "THE CITY OF EVERLAST" OR "THE CAPITAL"):

Not to be confused with the Everlast family, this is the capital city of Elsewhere. It is named after the royal family. It is mostly populated by wealthy Fae (some noble, some not) and free humans. There is a large class divide between even the poorest Fae and the wealthiest human.

The capital city is extremely small compared to other cities in Elsewhere in terms of both size and population. In technical terms, it is more of a vassal township than a city, being only a tenth the size of Inbetwixt. It is bordered by the Waywoods on one side and farmland on the other.

The most important (and only) landmark is the obsidian palace. The palace is over seven thousand years old and built by the former Unseelie King of Underneath. The palace is the southernmost structure in Everlast, and there is nothing but untamed wilderness between the palace and the Hedge.

NEVERMORE:

The richest and most insular of the four provinces, Nevermore sits on an island slightly separated from the rest of Elsewhere. They speak in a different dialect than the mainland (Referred to by the characters as "the old tongue") and are governed by a council rather than a single governor. Nevermore might govern themselves if not for their friendly relations with the Everlast family and prosperous trade with Inbetwixt. Queen Celia's late husband, the king consort Peregrine Nevermore, was integral in making sure that Nevermore did not succeed from the rest of the kingdom. The royal-appointed governor now acts as an ambassador. Their climate is temperate to cold, and most of the island is covered in mountains. The Fae of Nevermore live peacefully alongside some species of noncombative Unseelie, such as dwarves and sirens. Since the fall of Nightshade, Nevermore now has the highest population of druids and witches (human magic users). Fae with particular magical talents in Nevermore tend to possess mental abilities like mind-control and clairvoyance.

INBETWIXT:

Inbetwixt is a trading port that grew into a city of travelers with a violent reputation for being unwelcome toward outsiders.

They have the largest and most diverse population of non-noble Fae, Unseelie, free humans, and hybrid monsters. Their climate is warm and often rainy. They are bordered on all sides by the Source Mountains, the Waywoods, the Wanderlust, and the

Undertow, making it easy for Inbetwixt to control access to the city. Every road in and out is guarded, and tolls are high.

The governing noble family of Inbetwixt has been loosely at odds with the Everlast family for the last century. Lady Mairead Everlast was born Mairead Gauntlet in Inbetwixt. She was not a noble but the daughter of a wealthy merchant who met Crown Prince Belvedere while he was traveling with the queen's army. Mairead was a talented illusionist and came with a large dowry, and therefore, her non-noble blood was completely ignored by Queen Celia and King Consort Peregrine, who favored Prince Belvedere above their other children. This incident enraged the Lord of Inbetwixt and his family, and they are still bitter about it.

OVERCAST:

Overcast is a small but relatively prosperous northern seaside province known primarily for its political neutrality and lack of army. Their governing noble family is heavily enmeshed with the Everlasts, as they are all not-so-distant cousins. Their governor is Thalia's mother (Lord Auberon's sister), but it will likely soon pass to Thalia's brother.

Overcast sits in the shadow of the Source Mountains, directly downwind of Aftermath. In the years since the disaster that destroyed Nevermore, they have had increasingly erratic weather and are now struggling to deal with the toxic clouds rolling in from their neighbors to the northwest. There are only two ways into Overcast: through the Wanderlust or across the Undertow. It is far easier to cross the Undertow, especially in the twenty years since the fall of Nightshade. Thalia marrying into the Everlast family is intended to ensure that Overcast is not overlooked and cut off from the rest of the country, as they need their own expanded water access unhindered by Inbetwixt. The population of Overcast is almost entirely Fae, and there are no free humans in their city.

AFTERMATH:

Previously called Nightshade, the mountain province of Aftermath sits at the northernmost part of Everlast. A third of the population died in the initial volcanic eruption, with another third dying in the following weeks from injury, starvation, and effects of the Wilde magic. Survivors quickly fled to the valleys on the opposite side of the mountain, closer to the Waywoods, and most eventually left entirely. Aftermath is considered mostly uninhabitable, with a climate similar to Underneath.

After the disaster, Queen Celia began sending prisoners and slaves to Aftermath to assist in rehabilitating the area. This punishment was viewed by many as cruel and unusual and led to the beginning of the organized rebellion.

NIGHTSHADE (ALSO SEE AFTERMATH):

Nightshade was the fourth province in Elsewhere until the disaster roughly two decades ago that destroyed the land and population. Their city was very large and beautiful, having been built by Queen Aisling as the original capital of Elsewhere, and they were an area of high magic concentration. Despite this, they did not pose much political threat to the Everlasts as most of the population were highly religious academics. The noble court of Nightshade trained spiritual leaders and magical practitioners and sent them out to proselytize to other courts about the way of the Source.

UNDERNEATH:

The home to all hostile Unseelie and monsters, The Underneath is part of the continent of Elsewhere but separated from the kingdom by the Hedge. It is ruled by the Unseelie King. The Hedge is patrolled on the Everlast side at all times to prevent any monsters or Unseelie from crossing over into the capital.

WANDERLUST:

A large marsh between Inbetwixt and Overcast, populated by thousands of Underfae. It is extremely easy to get lost in the marsh and wander forever in the fog or sink into the waters. Crossing it is difficult without an undersea guide.

THE UNDERTOW:

A small sea filled with pirates and traders.

THE WAYWOODS:

A seemingly endless forest that stretches through the middle of the country. No one person has ever explored every part of the Waywoods, and it is said that there are things in there that predate the Everlast family themselves.

FORT WARFARE:

An enchanted prison on an island in no-man's-land on the west side of the continent. It is used most often by the Everlast family, but they do not exclusively control it.

THE HEDGE:

The wall separating Underneath from the capital of Everlast.

MOONGLADE LAKE:

A lake in the capital that is rumored to be enchanted. Queen Celia walked into this lake when she decided to return to the Source.

THE SOURCE:

The volcano that is believed to be the source of all magic. Gods are said to live in the mountains surrounding the Source.

GLOSSARY OF TERMS, ITEMS, AND CREATURES

FAE:

The dominant species, Fae have become the ruling class by numbers alone. They are also called Seelie, to differentiate them from the Unseelie, but this is typically not a necessary conversational distinction to make. All Fae possess some inherent magic and are immortal (though not impervious to death), but only some possess unusual magical abilities. Fewer and fewer Fae are born with special abilities with each generation.

HIGH FAE:

Fae of the noble class. Sometimes interchangeably used to mean Fae with magic, but typically referring to social standing.

"FAIRIES":

Catch-all term for anything non-human, including High Fae, monsters, hybrids, Underfae, etc.

UNSEELIE:

Sentient non-human, non-Fae creatures. The Unseelie are not always malevolent (though they often are). In Nevermore, some of the non-hostile Unseelie, like dwarves and sirens, live alongside the Fae. On the continent, almost all Unseelie are confined to Underneath, although there are some exceptions (like Beira, the palace cook). Some examples are succubi, spriggans, púca, incubi banshees, and shape shifters. The Unseelie are different than monsters, which are abundant everywhere, although some are just as dangerous.

UNDERFAE:

Magical creatures that cannot speak or be reasoned with but are sentient (like pets). Will-o-whisps and all the plant guardians fall into this category.

SLÚAGH:

A rude name for humans. This roughly means "the crowd" or "the army," but the intention is to mean "peasant" or "sword-fodder."

THE WILDE HUNTS:

The competition where the ruler proves their worthiness to keep their crown. There are five hunts, the first taking place on May 1 and the last one taking place on June 21. Every hunt is in a different province in this order: the capital, Inbetwixt, Nevermore, Overcast, Aftermath. Anyone who wishes to challenge the monarch for their crown must kill them on hunting night and take it. If the monarch dies, the hunts end until the following year.

MOONDUST TREES:

Trees that only sprout leaves at night. Their leaves are white and turn to dust in the morning.

THE COMMON TONGUE:

The language spoken most commonly on the continent. It is used by both Fae and humans.

THE OLD TONGUE:

The language spoken most commonly below the Hedge (Underneath) and in Nevermore. This is where the word "Slúagh" originates.

The Everlasts speak old tongue because their grandfather, Peregrine, was from Nevermore. Now, they complain that others don't speak it, when in reality, if they had not been forced to learn, it is likely they would not have bothered.

ABOUT THE AUTHOR

USA Today and International bestselling author Kate King loves sassy heroines, crazy magic, and alpha-hole heroes.

An avid reader and writer from a young age, she has been telling stories her whole life. Ever a fan of the dramatic, she lives in an 18th century church with her husband and two cats, and often writes in cemeteries.

STALK ME!

Visit my website at Katekingauthor.com

Follow me on Instagram and Tiktok @katekingauthor

Join my Facebook reader group "The Kingdom: A reader group for Kate King"

Made in the USA
Monee, IL
26 October 2024